Praise For
CITY OF SHATTERED LIGHT

2021 Junior Library Guild Selection
2022 Moonbeam Awards Silver Medalist
(Young Adult Fiction – Fantasy / Sci Fi)

"Fantastically entertaining, with great character development to boot."
—*Kirkus Reviews*

"This is high sci-fi with an edge of tech-based fantasy, and it has a thrilling setup: an exciting plot anchored by a core of interpersonal and family drama."
—*Booklist*

"In this ambitious, action-packed debut, Winn offers a fast-paced adventure populated by memorable characters. . . . Asa and Riven's considerable chemistry and interpersonal development fuel this satisfying speculative series opener."
—*Publisher's Weekly*

★ "A must-listen for fans of science fiction, swashbuckling fiction, and adventure."
—*School Library Journal,* starred review (audiobook)

"*City of Shattered Light* is a high-octane sci-fi wrapped around a heart of sisterhood and friendship. I loved Asa, wanted to be Riven, and fell completely into Winn's vivid worldbuilding. Perfect for fans of *Mass Effect* or *The Expanse!*"
—Susan Dennard, NYT-bestselling author of *The Luminaries* and the Truthwitch series

"*City of Shattered Light* is a gritty, imaginative cyberpunk packed with nonstop thrills and a crew of misfits who take 'be gay, do crime' to delightful heights."
—Emily Skrutskie, author of *The Abyss Surrounds Us*

"Claire Winn hits the ground running with *City of Shattered Light*, a wild YA space opera that has it all—pira~~~~ ~~~~ains, and relatable characters. Absolu~~~~ ~~~~ & Ruin* and *Black ~~~~anther: Doomwar*

—Jonathan

"*City of Shattered Light* is a cinematic, breathlessly action-packed adventure. The writing sparkles with description as Winn reveals a vivid, viciously dangerous cyberpunk world, and the whip-sharp plot is layered with secrets. Every character shines with personality and wit, and the badass, ride-or-die crew is sure to steal your heart!"

—Ren Hutchings, author of *Under Fortunate Stars*

"Vibrant and cinematic, with a vividly imagined world and kickass characters, *City of Shattered Light* will make you fall in love with sci-fi all over again."

—Lora Beth Johnson, author of *Goddess in the Machine*

Praise For
CITY OF VICIOUS NIGHT

"*City of Vicious Night* is a fast-paced, badass, neon dream of a sci-fi novel—packed with action, grit, and a found family that will dig its cybernetic claws into your heart and not let go!"

—Laura Rueckert, author of *A Dragonbird in the Fern*

"Claire Winn delivers a thrilling adventure full of heart in the rocketing-stakes, fast-paced conclusion to the Requiem Dark series. I loved being back in the matriarch-ruled cyberpunk city of Requiem with Riven, Asa, and the rest of the ride-or-die crew. A hugely entertaining read!"

—Vanessa Len, author of *Only a Monster*

"A heartfelt, fast-paced, action-packed sequel that'll keep you on the edge of your seat."

—Alechia Dow, author of *The Sound of Stars*

"*City of Vicious Night* is a fast-paced, neon-drenched cyberpunk romp filled with imaginative tech, gritty settings, and disaster bisexuals galore. Fans of sci-fi gunslinging, underworld politics, and Netflix's *Arcane* won't want to miss this kickass sequel."

—M. J. Kuhn, author of *Among Thieves*

CITY OF
VICIOUS
NIGHT

CLAIRE WINN

flux®

Mendota Heights, Minnesota

First Edition
First Printing, 2023

Book design by Karli Kruse
Cover design by Karli Kruse
Cover illustration by Sanjay Charlton (Beehive Illustration)

Flux, an imprint of North Star Editions, Inc.

Library of Congress Cataloging-in-Publication Data
Names: Winn, Claire, author.
Title: City of vicious night / Claire Winn.
Description: First edition. | Mendota Heights, Minnesota : Flux,
   2023. | Series: Requiem dark #2 | Audience: Grades 10–12. |
Summary: An unknown hacker with personal motives targets Asa
   and Riven, costing them their latest job and turning everyone in
   Requiem against them, so the two enter a deadly trial for
   control of one of the city's crime sectors in order to protect
   their crew.
Identifiers: LCCN 2022055050 (print) | LCCN 2022055051 (ebook)
   | ISBN 9781635830842 (paperback) | ISBN 9781635830859
   (ebook)
Subjects: CYAC: Artificial intelligence--Fiction. | LGBTQ+ people
   -Fiction. | Science fiction. | LCGFT: Science fiction. | Novels.
Classification: LCC PZ7.1.W5853 Ck 2023 (print) | LCC
   PZ7.1.W5853 (ebook) | DDC [Fic]--dc23
LC record available at https://lccn.loc.gov/2022055050
LC ebook record available at https://lccn.loc.gov/2022055051

Flux
North Star Editions, Inc.
2297 Waters Drive
Mendota Heights, MN 55120
www.fluxnow.com

Printed in Canada

To all the queer kids and misfits still searching for their found families—this one's for you.

CONTENT WARNINGS

This book contains depictions of violence, including blood, mild gore, death (on-page and past), and gun violence. It also contains strong language, sexual content (including nongraphic encounters), human experimentation, use of medical needles, alcohol misuse, fictional drug use, terminal illness, suicidal ideation and threatened suicide, mild torture, loss of limbs, and vomiting. There are mild references to poverty, sex work, and sexual assault.

More detailed content warnings (which may include slight spoilers) can be found at the author's website: clairewinn.com.

Part I

THE EDGE OF
THE BLADE

chapter 1

AFTERSHOCK

Hunters watched from the balconies like vultures.

Asa kept her gaze low as she and Riven cut through the dirty alley. The headhunters aimed scanners down at them, searching for any faces matching posted bounties. Every scavenger on Requiem was looking for a quick payout, but Asa didn't intend to be an easy target.

Especially not with a bounty as large as hers.

"Keep moving." Riven sauntered past the broken windows and flashing neon like she owned the whole city.

"Are they still watching us?" Asa adjusted her scrambler—a thin wire across her cheekbones to disrupt facial recognition tech.

"Only one. But I think he's just a creep. Might have to shoot that smirk off his face." Riven's hands hovered near the old-tech Smith & Wesson revolvers holstered at her hips, a pair of firecrackers waiting to be lit. Sweat and sleepless nights had smeared her gunpowder-black eyeliner into scorch marks.

Riven was no stranger to street brawls, but Asa had grown up on Cortellion, where her list of potential career paths had never included *criminal-for-hire*.

"Much as I'd love to see that, the last thing we need is to draw more attention." Even the stunner at Asa's hip felt dangerous. Four months on *Boomslang*'s crew, and she hadn't quite adjusted to the hot whisper of death at her back.

But she'd chosen this life, and she'd be damned if she wasn't going to earn her place.

"Hey, slowpokes." Kaya's chipper voice came through the comm. "Where are you?"

"On our way," Asa told her sister. "We've got the passcode. Heading in soon."

"Took you long enough." Samir's voice. "The two of you probably spent as much time canoodling as conning."

Heat shot through Asa's cheeks. Conning underworld smugglers in the roughest part of the roughest city in Alpha Centauri wasn't her ideal night out with Riven, but they made a good team. Even if sometimes she found it hard to concentrate.

"Sounds like you're jealous of my ability to multitask," Riven said into the comm, her eyes glittering. An ad screen silhouetted Riven's silver-blonde braid streaked with magenta, the confident sway of her hips. "Need to blow off steam somehow."

The flutter in Asa's stomach almost distracted her from her pounding heart. "We haven't! We've been . . . focused," she blurted, grateful the dim light hid the blush creeping across her cheeks.

"Killjoy," Riven muttered.

"Well, we're already landing *Boomslang* at the pickup point." Diego's voice was fast and rasping. "Though Samir seems to have forgotten where the cabin-pressure release is."

"Cut me some slack. This thing's a relic with no auto-nav." Samir was learning to pilot Riven's ship, since it was good to have more than one person who could fly them out in a pinch.

"Blue switch," Riven said. "Left of the main control panel."

Shouts and frantic scuffling resounded from the alley behind them—the headhunters must've found a target. Asa picked up her pace, trying to fade into the maze of streets.

Even in the underground sector, Requiem was a fever dream of refracted neon and electric sweat, where the bass pulsed like a cybernetic heartbeat beneath Asa's boots. The air-con chill was a far cry from the surface's scorching heat during the 154-hour day cycle. Holoscreen ads hounded passersby, flashing images of caffeine-vapors and virtual experiences. Things that only a few months ago, Asa could've afforded by the dozen, without a second thought.

It had been her face on the holoscreens then, the successor to the galaxy's biggest tech corporation. The girl with the petal-red lips and the media-darling smile. But now she was a fugitive, and she'd done her best to wipe her profile for targeted ads. Since escaping her father, Asa was mastering the art of lying low.

The sooner they finished this job, the better.

"Is this the place?" Riven said.

As promised, the entrance to the fighting pits was marked with a stylized cobra, washing the door and its guard in red light. The guard's mottled-blue sclerae peered from the shadows, the mark of a glitch addict.

"Looks like it." Asa was suddenly conscious of their clubwear—bodices to mimic the candy girls who worked at Grindhouse nightclub. Asa's clung to her torso above her baggy mechanist pants. The outfits had been useful for getting backstage and conning one of the arena mechanists for the passcodes—even if Riven had still needed to break two of the man's fingers—but now they might just draw extra attention.

Riven didn't flinch as the guard sized her up. She radiated cool, like the first droplets before a thunderstorm, as she casually thumbed the grips of her holstered revolvers. Asa tapped the passcodes into the panel next to the door. When it lit up, the guard waved them forward, and they moved through the gaudy lobby and stepped into the elevator.

Riven hit an unlabeled button, and the elevator lurched, then plunged. Numbers flashed overhead. Asa could already feel the bass from the lower levels, a steady thump growing louder as they descended. A sour metallic taste bloomed on the back of her tongue. She'd never get used to the rush. But it helped to pretend her fear was only excitement.

"Ready to break some skulls?" Asa said.

"Rare for you to be the one leading us into trouble." Riven's grin was deadly. "I kind of like it." She gripped Asa's waist, and Asa leaned in, if only to brush their lips for a moment. But Riven kissed her fast, hard, the way Riven did everything.

Asa gasped as Riven's fingers tangled in her already-messy hair, and Riven's tongue slipped between her lips. She found herself pulling Riven closer, deeper, the kiss burning wild as her racing heart. Sparks fell as the lights flickered, strobing in time with her rising pulse.

In times like this, Asa wouldn't trade life in Riven's crew for anything.

Riven pulled away, a flush staining her pale, freckled cheeks. "For luck."

"Right," Asa said, remembering the job. "We'll need it."

A gagging noise came over the comm. "I cannot *believe* you just forced us all to listen to you sucking face."

Kaya's voice. Asa realized she hadn't switched off her comm.

"Can't argue. That was pretty gross," Samir said.

"We were *not*," Asa lied.

"If *sucking face* is a colloquialism for *heated kissing*, they absolutely were," Galateo tattled from the tiny drone attached to Riven's wristlet.

Asa groaned. She'd built Galateo a new set of drones, but his factory-reset version still had a habit of talking out of turn. Even without his old memories, the AI was quickly learning how to get on their nerves.

Riven clicked her tongue. "Get over it."

"You'd better watch it, Hawthorne," Kaya said. "If you're not careful with my sister, I'll break your face."

"*Kaya*," Asa hissed, mortified.

Riven grinned. "Come and try it, mech-head."

"Push me and I might." On Asa's wristlet screen, a vidclip appeared in their shared comm channel: Kaya smirking and throwing a punch, then a digital crack spiderwebbing across the screen. Her hair was cropped to her earlobes and mermaid blue—after the surgery, it had grown in white, and now she picked a different color every few weeks, undecided on permanent color grafts like Riven's.

"Kaya's tough now, eh? They grow up so fast." Samir mock-sniffled. "Seems like just yesterday you were only a brain in a jar."

"Oh, shut up."

"Everyone. We're moving in, so drop it," Asa said, grateful the elevator was grinding to a stop. She turned to Riven. "That means you too."

"All right, fine." Riven's hand squeezed hers. "I'll be on my best behavior tonight." When Asa raised her eyebrows, she added, "Nothing reckless. I promise."

With a soft chirp, the doors slid open.

Asa sucked in a breath as the discordance of the fighting pits crashed over her. Graffiti stained the black-lit walls in violent color, covering old scorch marks and scratches. The crowds were a riot of exposed skin, glowing cybernetics, and holograms. At the arena's center, harsh spotlights glinted off a pair of modded mechs slugging it out, and jeering erupted from the stands. Asa could barely breathe over the bass rocking through her bones.

Another job, another den of degenerates.

Asa squared her shoulders and slid through the lines at the betting terminals, the flashing leaderboards. Near the top of the screens, she glimpsed the name of the mech they were after. *Halcyon Vengeance.*

They were just in time for the final match. According to the Duchess's tip, that mech would be targeted by a hacker tonight, forcing it to throw this match—and losing one of the Duchess's allies a *lot* of money. If Asa could get Kaya in, her sister could stop the hacker and forward the evidence to Diego. Simple enough.

Now to get to the mechanic bay, where *Vengeance* was probably being prepped for its next match.

Asa followed Riven toward the back hall, circling the lowest tier of the room where the penultimate fight was happening—the crowd cursing and roaring as a mech with a beetle-blue exoskeleton and tank treads rammed another mech outfitted like an armory on legs. A volley of fist-sized slug bullets hurled from the taller mech's arm gun. As its opponent wheeled backward, two slugs crashed against the holo-barrier covering the audience. Asa winced. She didn't trust any safety measures in a place like this.

"We've got a guard," Riven said. Sure enough, their corridor was blocked by a three-eyed bouncer. "Just like we practiced, huh?"

"Got it," Asa said.

"Where you going, tarts?" the guard said as they approached. He pointed to the side corridor. "Restrooms are that way. Also . . ." His cybernetic third eye slid over Riven, likely some kind of scan-tech. Asa's skin prickled, but his wandering attention made it easier to move into position near his shoulder. "Nice outfit."

"You're welcome." Riven crossed her arms over her chest. "Also, eat shit."

His whole body seized as Asa's stunner prodded him in the back of the neck. She had to bite her lip to stop from apologizing. But it felt good to drop him.

Riven caught him in a choke hold and hauled him the other way. "Your cue," she grunted.

Asa nodded, her pulse rising. The worst part of any job was letting Riven go. Playing their parts alone.

Asa ran down the concrete steps into the garage area, a maze of workbenches and maintenance scaffolds with a tunnel extending to the pits. Some of the mechs' mod-jobs were impressive—armored security speeders had been amalgamated into hulking tanks, others' spidery frames had been upgraded with cloaking tech. Among the mechs, it was easy to pick out her target.

Halcyon Vengeance had clearly been a combat mech before it'd been stolen and repurposed for pit fighting. Asa immediately recognized its sleek, dancer-like silhouette. One of her father's designs. The white-and-gold logo of Almeida Industries, which would've covered its chest, had been sanded off and slapped over with a decal of a furious, hollow-eyed mask.

She approached the twelve-foot-tall mech and carefully set a hand on its red hull. *Boomslang*'s crew had been called on this job because it involved dealing with Cortellion tech, but Asa hadn't realized it would be something of her father's. She wheeled over a rolling stepladder, pulled her tool kit out of her cargo belt, and began prying open the circuit board cover on the mech's shoulder.

"Hey. Don't recognize you. Have we met?" Another mechanist waited on the ground, their gaze hidden behind mirrored goggles.

"Oh. Naith sent me for emergency maintenance," she lied, dropping the name of the mechanist they'd conned. She flashed his keycard. "*Vengeance*'s main gun almost overheated in the last match. I'm just installing a quick patch."

The other mechanist stared at her a second too long. "Well, you'd better make it fast. That thing's on next."

Asa kept her face blank even as her heart thudded. She opened the shoulder hatch and found the main control panel—the seductive glow of screens and keypads, of hidden data and locks to be broken. Like home.

"All right," she whispered into the comm. "Hooking you up, Kaya." She plugged in the transmitter. An easy, familiar point Kaya could link to and load in.

"Great," Samir said. "The three of us are in the lobby. Let me know if you need backup."

After a moment, Kaya's voice came through. "I'm in. You sure this is the right mech? There's nothing else in here. No hacker, no malware."

"Bria definitely said *Halcyon Vengeance*." Asa snapped the panel shut again. Distinctive name and model. Unmistakable.

Kaya's breath caught. "Well, that's weird."

"Weird?"

"It's . . . I don't know. This thing has more processing power than a mech should. And—oh. There *is* something in here."

Asa glanced at the holoscreen broadcasting the fight over the garage door. The blue mech lay on its back, sparking and inert, as the crowd booed. After the cleanup crews, *Vengeance* would be up next. "We don't have much time, Kay. Lock them out and send us tracking data."

"I . . . I don't know if I—" A sharp gasp.

"What is it?" Asa said. "What's wrong?"

The mech shuddered to life, and Asa lost her balance. She stumbled off the ladder, landing in a sloppy crouch.

When she got back to her feet, there was a blade against her throat.

"Move," came a voice through *Vengeance*'s internal speaker, smooth and brassy and unfamiliar. "Now. Into the ring." The blade extended from the mech's forearm.

"Kaya?" Asa said. "What's going on?"

Kaya didn't respond, but the mech's voice did. "I said *move*."

Asa's pulse stuck in her throat. This wasn't Kaya. Memories flashed of Banshee—the rogue Etri mind escaped from her father's lab—trapping them within a nightclub, every circuit under his control. Whether the mech was being puppeted by the arena hacker or something else entirely, it was impossible to tell. But she wasn't about to call their bluff.

Asa held up her hands and walked toward the garage tunnel and the muffled roar of the crowd.

"What are you doing?" the other mechanist said, standing in their way. "This doesn't look like a—"

Vengeance shoved him aside with one massive fist.

"Asa," came Riven's voice through her comm. "I took care of our guy. He's on, uh, extended bathroom break. But did you hear more from Kaya? Is she okay?"

Asa couldn't risk responding. The mech's serrated blade guided her.

"What are you after?" she murmured, hoping whoever was in control could hear her.

"You'll know soon enough, Miss Almeida."

A fresh spike of fear shot through her as her feet met gravel and she stepped into the scalding spotlights. Around her, the crowd's roars turned to scandalized murmurs.

Was the hacker aligned with her father? Had he given her a head start, only to send the star-system's best hackers after her when the time was right?

You'll never be free of his shadow, a deep-buried voice whispered. *Never have been.*

Never safe.

"Looks like *Vengeance* has brought something extra to the show tonight!" The announcer's voice boomed over the speakers, but there was a whiff of hesitation there. "An unexpected surp–"

His voice cut to a whine of microphone feedback. The music's pulsing bass went silent.

"Hello, Requiem," the mech's voice said over the speakers. "I've brought you a traitor."

The spotlights plunged into darkness. The holoscreens surrounding the ring all lit up with the same image—a face made of red wire frames, with Xs for eyes and a sharp-toothed grin that looked scrawled from neon.

"I'm sure you all remember the destruction that racked this city four months ago," it continued. "The creature everyone named Banshee. Corrupted and created by a man named Luca Almeida. And do you know who brought it here?"

It felt like icicles had rammed through Asa's chest. The blade nudged the base of her spine, urging her to the center of the arena.

"Both Almeida's daughters have been hiding in this city ever since. Complicit in their father's crimes, unwilling to atone for the damage he caused."

Kaya was still dead silent. Nobody was coming to save her. Unless Asa could re-expose the mech's control board, her stunner would be useless.

She raised her palms. "Let's talk," she said softly, turning toward the mech. "Banshee wasn't our fault. We tried to–"

Vengeance ignored her. "And a crew calling themselves the Boomslang Faction has been harboring them–under the protection of your Duchess. Shameful."

Murmurs erupted through the crowd. Confusion, and some cries to *get on with it!* They'd be just as happy watching her die as a mech.

"Here's another secret," *Vengeance* continued. "Almeida never left this place. Even now, your people are being taken and harvested. And if we want to destroy his work, it starts with her."

Asa couldn't move. *Harvested.* Something the hacker believed was her fault? This wasn't a hunter after her bounty– this was an execution.

The mech's chest cannon stared down at her, molten lights churning beneath it.

"You can call me Redline," the mech said. "And while this girl is his heir–I am his antithesis."

chapter 2
DEATH WISH

Whoever was messing with this mech had fucked up. Rage boiled in Riven's throat as she shoved her way to the front of the arena stands. Had someone faked this job and set them up? She'd known hunters might have Asa in their sights, but putting her on display in an arena, a massive gun poised to turn her to ashes—

It went too far.

"Riv, are you seeing the arena feed?" Samir said. "I'm heading your way."

"Oh, I'm seeing it, all right." Riven elbowed a tattooed man out of her way. "Kaya. I thought you were supposed to be on this."

"I . . . I can't." Static from Kaya's comm. "Someone's trying to poke around inside my head."

If Kaya couldn't save her sister, there was no time to wait. Riven unclipped her retracting blade hilt from her belt. It was something Asa had built for her—a tech-blade with a vibrating edge.

"Hey, Asa," Riven said. Asa's comm was still open, even if she wouldn't respond. "I said I wouldn't do anything reckless tonight . . . but I guess that was a lie."

Riven vaulted over the arena railing and into the gravel, then ducked beneath the inner holo-barrier that protected the audience. Her ankles ached from the ten-foot drop, but she kept going.

"Hey, jackhole," she called. "Seems you've got a death wish."

Halcyon Vengeance's head swiveled toward her. She strode past a heap of scrap, a mech the cleaning crews had abandoned.

The spotlights came back on, sizzling like heat lamps. The announcer's voice came through the loudspeaker. "Well, it seems we have another unexpected contender, and some considerable stakes! What do you say, glitchers and mech-heads?" Jeers rippled through the audience. "We can let them try. Been a few days since we've had blood in the gravel."

The crowd's roar rose to a thunderclap. Colors strobed as the thudding music began again, the drums rolling like storms.

Riven yanked her left-hand revolver, *Blackjack*, from its holster, spinning it into place on her index finger. No telling whether its disruptor bullets would do anything to that hull.

The mech turned back to Asa as its fingers unfurled into a trio of rusted sawblades, and a minigun emerged from its other forearm. The thing was a behemoth twice her height.

"Asa, run!" Riven said. "Take cover behind that scrap heap!"

Laughter rang over the loudspeakers. "Anyone who wants to place a bet has about five seconds before *Vengeance* turns her to raw sausage filling!"

"Go to hell," she muttered. "Galateo, bring up the pinpoint shields. Protect Asa."

Galateo's zip-drone split into three spheres, each projecting a small holo-shield of blue hexagons. "Happy to be of service, my deathless queen."

That nickname was somehow even worse than his previous

iteration calling her *my lady*—she'd chosen it after a night of bad decisions. But right now it was the least of her problems.

Riven fired a disruptor at *Vengeance*'s egg-shaped head. The bullet splattered into sparking metal, leaving barely a dent. But the distraction gave Asa an opening.

Asa ran. Galateo's shields scudded alongside her, absorbing the shock of *Vengeance*'s bullets with tiny kinetic pulses and then whirring back into place. Enough for her to reach cover behind the scrap heap.

Riven fired again, and *Vengeance* turned its attention back to her, swiping its whirring buzzsaws. As she ducked and weaved, they slammed into the gravel behind her, kicking up a shrapnel storm of pebbles.

She regained her balance and took aim at the joints holding the sawblades. *Breathe.* With deadly familiarity, the stillness came through her nerves, her muscles, until there was only her and the bullet and the target at the other end.

Crack. Crack.

The bullets hit, cracking open and discharging electro-magnetic energy. The saws sparked and fell, and the remaining blades ground to a stop. Perfect shots.

The mech had other tricks though. Like the hull-piercing slugs in its fully charged chest cannon. Galateo's shields would be useless against those.

Two disruptor bullets were left in *Blackjack*'s chamber, with no time to reload. *Verdugo*, her executioner, was full of regular bullets. She had to end this quickly.

The pulse in her ears, the roar of the crowds and the bass,

had all but drowned out the chatter in her earpiece—Asa's frantic requests, Samir's calculated commands.

"Asa," Riven shouted. "Tell me where this thing's brain will be!" She slid aside as the first slug slammed the gravel.

Asa's voice wavered. "The processor is at the top of its left shoulder. But a bullet probably won't be able to get through the hull—"

Riven sighed. "Blade. Right." If she could get close enough.

She flipped the switch on the tech-blade's hilt. It unfurled, metal slotting into place until the blade was the length of her arm. The wicked edge hummed with a pulse that could cleave carbon fiber.

Samir's voice came through. "Riv! Hang on. I'm close."

"I'm staying with Kaya," Diego said. "She's fading fast."

I might be, too, Riven thought as the massive cannon at the center of *Vengeance*'s chest glowed, back at full power. It was aiming at the scrap heap now.

Riven fired one of her disruptors at the arm joint. The mech shuddered, and the minigun targeted lower. She gritted her teeth. One last bullet. Samir was always on her ass about getting a backup gun—something with a bigger mag and automatic firing—and now she almost wished she'd listened.

As she ducked another slug, pinpricks of pain shot through her skull—the creeping sickness, the white noise that clung to her nerves like a nightmare. She swore. The last thing she needed was for her body to eat itself now.

Riven flipped the blade in her palm. The other mech was still lying in the dirt, a mound of scuffed blue metal. Something she could climb. She just had to let *Vengeance* get close, but without endangering Asa.

Shouts from the crowd behind her. "It seems we've got another death wisher tonight!" the announcer's voice called. "More fun for *Vengeance*?"

She whirled to see Samir land in the gravel behind her and unsling the rifle from his back. With his tailored black-and-silver armor vest—and his perfectly sculpted hair and stubble beard—he looked out of place in a fighting pit.

She'd never been happier to see him. Especially when he raised his rifle, sending a disruptor into the base of the mini gun. Another weapon down.

"Should've known you'd end up in front of the crowd," he shouted.

"You know me well!" *Thoom.* Another slug hit the arena wall near Samir. "Hey, if you've got more disruptors, try to clog up its chest!"

She holstered *Blackjack* and brandished the blade. One chance. She slid behind the scrap heap near Asa, its target.

Vengeance loomed over her, weaving to find an angle to shoot them. Metal whined next to her as a slug punched through the dead mech, straight between her and Asa.

Then—

"*Now!*" Samir shouted.

Gunshots. *Vengeance* sputtered, its chest riddled with disruptors. Riven climbed the scrap heap, staring that sparking cannon in the eye, and leaped, grabbing the mech's shoulder in one hand. The panel Asa had mentioned was inches from her face.

The mech lurched. Riven latched on tighter as it tried to shake her off.

"Riven!" Asa's voice came through her earpiece.

Had to be now. Riven clung to the mech like it was her last hope and drove the blade's buzzing tip straight into the panel seam. She levered hard, and with a *thunk*, the wires and circuits were exposed.

Vengeance smacked her off with a massive fist. She saw stars as her shoulder hit the gravel. *Dammit.* The fist came down toward her face, and she twisted aside in time for it to graze her shoulder, tearing the skin bloody. She stumbled to her feet, drawing *Blackjack*.

Her final disruptor bullet—and the circuit board was exposed.

She narrowed her eyes, letting the world slow to a crawl. Cocked the hammer with her thumb.

Click. Thoom.

Vengeance's circuit board shredded under her disruptor, just as another bullet tore through it. Samir's. The mech's red laser-diode lights went dark, its limbs hung limp, and its massive bulk collapsed with a heavy *thud*.

A cacophony of cheers and booing erupted from the crowd. Riven spat on the downed mech. Whoever Redline was, Kaya and Diego needed to track them down so Riven could slit their throat.

"Damn near perfect," Samir said. He always came through when she needed him. Though her bullet had been a split-second faster, probably. "But we need to get out of here."

"Oh god." Asa stumbled toward Samir, disoriented and starry-eyed. "I didn't think you'd make it in time."

Asa was in one piece. That had been far too close. Riven's head cleared, relief killing the adrenaline, and the throbbing pain in her shoulder turned sharper.

Samir was already helping Asa onto the arena railing and back into the stands. Asa flinched as a liquor bottle flew toward her from the crowd. Redline had put a target on them all.

"Are you all good?" Diego said over the comm. "Kaya fell unconscious, but she's waking up. I've got her."

"Listen. This was a trap." Riven tuned out the announcer's complaints about the *unexpected turn of events* as she climbed the stands. "Someone has it out for us. We need to get the hell out of here."

Murmurs followed her through the crowd.

"*. . . that Banshee business a few months back . . .*"

"*Isn't that her? Deadeye Riven?*"

"*Half expected the Feds would've locked up that whole crew.*"

They'd all seen. Ahead of her, she glimpsed someone reaching for Asa's shoulders, and Samir shoving the person away. Riven picked up her pace.

"Got it," Diego said. "We're in the lobby, heading back to *Boomslang*–"

A prickle of instinct told her that was a bad idea. The ship was the most recognizable thing her crew owned, with its venom-green paint job and black-scale bands.

"No," Riven said. "Meet up with us first. Don't get back on the ship until we know it's safe."

Her hands were shaking. If they made it out of here, they

still had to face the Duchess empty-handed, with their tails between their legs. The Duchess's betting mech was dead. And worse, someone out there wanted Asa gone.

She caught up with Asa and Samir at the elevator. They rode to the lobby to collect Diego and Kaya, and then the numbers climbed in silence as they headed to the surface, where the ship waited. Asa held Kaya, who looked exhausted.

Riven had *Verdugo* up as soon as the doors to the upper deck slid open.

She strode down the corrugated-steel ramp, hit with momentary relief at the sight of her ship. *Boomslang* waited at the end of the dock, anterior gun poised, docking controls locked in place. Ready to take her crew home.

"Wait." Samir held a hand in front of Asa and Diego. "I think I saw something moving."

Asa's wristlet buzzed with an incoming call. "Unknown messaging code?" she murmured. She put the call on speaker.

"Leaving already?" The eerily processed, saccharine voice sent a greasy chill up Riven's spine.

"Who is that?" she said.

"Make no mistake, Asanna Almeida." A sick amusement cracked through the voice. "The next time I find you, you won't be able to run."

A blast rocked the floor. Heat and light rushed toward them.

Clouds of black smoke erupted from a roiling fire, bursting through a metal shell. Burned scraps of a former ship hull.

Where *Boomslang* had been.

chapter 3

HEAT WAVE

s usual, everything had gone to shit.

Riven was sweating like a burger in a frying pan as she pressed her cheek to the greasy bar table. Middays on Requiem were hot as hell. Maybe if she lay here long enough, she'd become a crispy meal for the spinebacks looting the alley trash bins.

It would be better than facing the mess last night's job had left in its wake.

"Whiskey cola," the android droned, sliding her third drink of the hour in front of her.

She grabbed it. The glass was warm. "You don't have anything colder?"

"Out of ice," the bartender said, scrubbing a glass. "Freezer broke earlier."

Riven groaned but downed the drink in a few gulps anyway. The burn helped drown the white-noise pain that had worsened over the past few months. The pain that had nearly knocked her unconscious on the trek back from the fighting pits.

Every time something good entered her life, it was snatched away. Emmett and Ty—the first person she'd loved, and his brother she'd sworn to protect. Then *Boomslang*. And now the goddamn universe had its sights set on Asa.

Her clever, frustratingly beautiful runaway. The girl who drew her in like a magnet to the iron in her blood.

But she couldn't protect Asa from vicious rumors or powerful hackers. And with no ship—no home among the stars, no offworld transit—Riven was just another broke smuggler in a death-trap city, who couldn't do a job right if her life depended on it.

She'd been avoiding her whole crew since last night.

"My deathless queen, I believe we need to discuss your dietary habits," Galateo droned from her wristlet. Even after his memory had been wiped, his nagging features were intact. "For the past twenty-four hours, you have subsisted on nothing but chicktrill jerky and whiskey cola."

"Protein and medicine," she slurred, resting her head back on the table. Today, she couldn't even stomach a plate of greasy bacon-cheddar fries.

Soft footsteps behind her. A familiar voice. "Riven?! I must have messaged you a thousand times! Where have you been?"

Riven lifted her cheek just enough to see Asa. Her layers of dark hair were tucked behind an ear pierced with a rose-shaped stud, and her torn-off sleeves exposed arms with the beginnings of lean muscle. Delicate, calloused hands were wrapped for garage work. Seeing her was almost enough to distract Riven from the mountain of trouble they were in.

"Everywhere. And then . . . here." Wherever *here* was. She tilted her head back, noting the familiar glowing-skull graffiti on the ceiling. Damn, this was Xav's place. The restaurant below the hideout. *Guess my misery bar crawl came full circle.*

Asa slid into the diner booth beside her. "How's your shoulder?"

"Better than the rest of me. The whole goddamn universe hates my guts. And it's gunning for you now too."

Asa stared at her knuckles, picking metal shavings off the hand wraps. "The universe isn't doing this."

"Call it whatever you want. You're still getting pulled into my bad luck." *Like Ty.* Memories flashed through the brain fog: Morphett holding a gun to his head. Ty's blood on the sink at Olympus as Riven tried to retrace his steps when Banshee had kidnapped him. And then, at the end–

She tried to stifle it, but the memory had replayed itself so many times there was no stopping it.

She saw Ty stepping off the lift. That wink, despite the tears in his eyes. The bullet tearing through his arm.

Listen to me, Riv. You'll survive. You're too stubborn to die.

The smoke swallowing him whole.

"I don't think it's luck. If anything, my messes are coming back to bite me." Asa sighed. "But you can't keep doing this. You're a wreck."

"I agree," Galateo said. "Her dietary habits are concerning."

"Look, Galateo." Riven closed her eyes, head spinning. "I know my life is shit. This is *exactly* why I told your last iteration to quit with the chipper advice."

"Another drink?" the android waiter said.

"No. She's good. We'll close out the tab later," Asa said before Riven could respond. "Um. Samir called a meeting upstairs."

Upstairs. In the hideout. The one thing her enemies hadn't managed to destroy yet.

"Samir's calling the shots, huh?" Riven said. No doubt he was enjoying it. "Are you all going to mutiny now that I no longer have a ship?"

"You're being ridiculous." Asa's voice was sharp, but her hands on Riven's shoulders were gentle. "Please, Riven. Come on."

Riven grumbled but trudged up the steps and into the hall after Asa. She let Asa deal with the hideout's locks and alarm systems and followed her inside.

"*Dust and bones*, Riv," Samir said in greeting. "You're a mess."

"I'm conscious. Take it or leave it." At least she wasn't strung out on something hard like glitch. Not that she ever *would*, for obvious reasons, and there was also no telling how it'd mess with her rotting nervous system.

Riven ducked under the pull-up bar in the doorway to their living room. The others were gathered inside, squeezed onto the threadbare couches beneath Riven's rumpled movie posters. The light from the streets caught the edges of Kaya's blue hair as she stared out the window, and Diego tapped furiously on his wristlet's holoscreen. Zephyr scrambled to greet her, his tiny tail wagging violently.

Everyone was here except Ty. One hundred and thirteen days, and it still felt wrong that life went on without him.

"We've been looking all over for you. And . . ." Samir winced at the dried blood on the medicated fibers covering her injured shoulder. "You're supposed to change those every few hours."

"True," Galateo said. "I believe she needs frequent reminders, now that the ship's medic is no longer–"

"I fucking *know*, Galateo." *No longer.* As if Ty had just faded into thin air one day. As if he weren't ashes at the bottom of some incinerator.

They'd gone back to the wreck of Josiah's lab, where they'd recovered Kaya and lost Ty, trying to find what was left of him. All they'd found were empty, bloodstained halls, and a few smears on the bridge where he'd last been alive.

Ty had been her responsibility. Practically her brother. But now he was gone.

The back of her head pounded, more from pain-pricks than the dull ache of the whiskey. The sickness had almost killed her on Earth, and since then it had only gotten worse. And without Ty . . .

Maybe she *had* hoped he'd be able to help her. No chance of that now. The pain was sharpening every day, and damn if whiskey didn't help.

Galateo didn't shut up. "I am only trying to—"

"No." Riven slammed her fist into the wall, hard enough to leave a dent. "Power down and shut the hell up. You don't even remember him."

Her knuckles stung. She pulled her fist away from the cracking paint. Bits of drywall powder stuck to where the skin had broken.

It was quiet. Her crew stared at her.

"Are you finished?" Samir said.

"We all understand." Asa's voice was gentle. "Just . . . sit with us. Please."

Riven closed her eyes. Sometimes they *did* understand. It was a nasty wound they all shared. But every so often, the stitches ripped out and tore even deeper.

"Even if we're down a ship—and a crew member—we've got other problems to deal with if we want to make it to tomorrow." Samir gestured to the couch. "Starting with who set us up."

Riven leaned against the wall she'd just ruined and glared at Diego. No doubt he'd been pulling some strings to figure out what had happened.

Deep shit, as usual.

"Bria wants to meet via holo," Diego said.

"Of course they do." How much had the Duchess's advisor-slash-stylist known about this job?

"Riv, just—let us do the talking for a while, okay?" Samir said.

"Depends on what they have to say." Nothing that came out of Riven's mouth for the rest of the night would be pretty.

Diego set the transmitter on the stained carpet between them. After a few moments, Bria's austere form flickered into place—fitted carbon-black suit, brown hair tousled into elegant spikes.

"Ah. The crew returns." Bria crossed their arms, eyes flicking over the five of them. "Hopefully with an explanation for why our prize-fighting mech is now a scrap heap."

Riven narrowed her eyes. "Oh, you can shove—"

Diego held up a hand, cutting her off. "There were unexpected complications. Which we need to discuss."

"We were in real danger. And the way I see it"—Samir's voice had a toxic edge—"there's no way this *wasn't* a setup."

Diego nodded. "I went through the data Kaya dug up. Whatever was in that mech was an anomaly. We can't trace it anywhere."

"Admittedly, the original request *was* a bit strange." Bria exhaled a mouthful of blue vapors, which made their holo blur briefly. "Closer investigation showed it was sent via proxy—not from the contact they were claiming to be. And the job aligned with your group's expertise almost *too* perfectly. Specifically, they wanted someone who could handle—and I quote—'*Cortellion corp-tech.*'"

It had fit Asa's background. Whoever had sent it knew the Duchess employed a crew with a runaway mechanist familiar with Almeida's technology because she'd grown up with it.

"So you admit it was a trap," Riven said.

"Not from our end." Bria tapped their short, silver-painted nails on their sleeve. "But since we should've caught this ourselves, we're not holding you liable for the money we lost."

Some of the tension uncoiled in Riven's shoulders.

"However. The bigger problem is the rumors sparked during your job. Wristlet cam videos are circulating with images of you all, yet again."

"There's always been speculation about us," Samir said. Tons of message boards and rumors after Banshee had plastered them onto ad screens and fake wanted posters. "How is this any different?"

"The public assumption was that you'd all been working against Banshee. But lately, word about your little technomancer's ability has gotten around. And after last night, we have cells accusing the Duchess of betraying her city by protecting corporate moles. Of sheltering Banshee herself—the person who nearly plunged Requiem into permadark."

"They think Banshee was *me*?" Kaya blurted, startling Zephyr off her lap.

"You know damn well the Duchess can set those rumors straight," Riven bit out. But what could they do? Nobody else could know Kaya got her abilities from the priceless alien brain sewn into her skull.

"Those are the kinds of whispers that lead to riots," Bria said. "Telling the truth would mean owning up to working with Luca Almeida's daughters. Add that to Almeida's rumors that Asa is still his heir, and the waters get murky."

"Wait," Asa said. "My dad is saying that?"

"Yes. He's removed your bounty. He's trying to spin it like you're out of the public eye because you're involved in deep R&D projects offworld."

Riven swallowed the rage. Luca Almeida had nearly killed her whole crew. His soldiers had killed Emmett and then Ty, and his experiments had ruined hundreds of lives . . . and he was no worse for wear.

But why would he have removed Asa's bounty? It had been a cool two million denar when he'd still hoped to reconcile with her. Lower after he'd wanted her dead, no doubt. Something wasn't adding up.

"You think he took things into his own hands?" Diego said. "It didn't sound like this Redline person was working for him."

"Whatever the reasons, I think you understand why we need to sever this relationship." Bria laced their fingers. "Your crew is becoming a liability."

Riven was sure she'd hurl up the whiskey cola. "You're joking."

"Afraid not," Bria said.

They'd worked their asses off to get in the Duchess's good

graces. She was the most powerful woman on Requiem and commanded allegiance from all five syndicates. If they were too much of a liability to her, they'd be a liability to the other matriarchs too.

Without a syndicate's safe houses and the protection under the matriarchs' Code it offered, they were as good as dead. And the dreams that had kept Riven alive the past few years—

"What if we were to take up the mantle of a syndicate?" Diego cut in. "You know which."

Bria's bloodred lips twisted into a frown. "I wouldn't advise it. And besides, most of the candidates have already been chosen."

"Candidates for what?" Riven's ears pricked.

"They're preparing for the Ascension Trial," Diego said softly, eyeing Bria. "Aren't they?"

The world seemed to tunnel and slow. Some of the whiskey haze cleared.

Ascension Trial.

"For Rio Oscuro?" Riven whispered. They'd helped bring down the syndicate during the Banshee incident, when its matriarch betrayed Requiem. An Ascension Trial would mean the syndicate no longer had viable successors, and they were seeking a new matriarch.

Matriarch. The word was like a flare against Riven's mental fog.

It was a tradition in Requiem's Code: other matriarchs chose the successor of a compromised syndicate by picking candidates to do their dirty work and seeing who came out alive. As much infighting as there was among the matriarchs, the Code was one thing they all agreed on. A fragile alliance that bound them together against the Federation and the corps to keep Requiem free.

"Yes," Bria said. "Most of that faction was rotten to the core. Some of its best and brightest too. We've spent the past four months cleaning it out."

This was her chance. Ships and stealth tech. Something that wouldn't die on her like everything else. Something she could take before Requiem slit her throat in a back alley.

A dream she thought she'd killed—a dream with claws—slithered its way up her ribs. It whispered promises of factions falling at her feet, of the rumors in the streets turning to warnings.

Being feared was being safe. For all of them.

"How do we enter?"

Samir groaned from the couch. "Absolutely not."

"Seven contenders and their crews have already earned favor from a patron matriarch," Bria said. "Each matriarch can choose up to two. The Duchess has already chosen hers, and your crew wasn't a top choice. Especially now."

"But if another matriarch were willing to take a chance on us?" Diego said. "The Duchess doesn't need to give her approval."

Bria paused. "I doubt you have time to prove yourselves before we begin at Duskday."

Requiem's sunset was in about three standard Earth days. So soon.

"But you're right, Valdez. The Code *would* allow you to compete if you could gain favor. Still, I'd advise against it. We don't need these rumors implicating others in the matriarch-ate." They sighed. "All I can give you is my gratitude for every-thing you've done over the past few months. I really am sorry."

With that, Bria's holo switched off, and the five of them were left in the silence. Riven's thoughts raced against the throb in her head.

"We have to do this," she said. "Bria said the Duchess couldn't technically stop us."

"Riv, you're drunk," Samir said.

"Shut up." Riven could've sworn she was dead sober. "We are flat broke, unemployed, and *shipless* while someone is calling for our heads. Damn if I'm not going to take my shot."

"Have you heard what a trial entails?" Samir said. "It's cut-throat. We could stand to lose everything else. And from the sound of things, the Duchess doesn't even want us in."

"Agreed," Asa said. "We aren't ready for this. And we'd have to start in three days?"

Kaya frowned. "How do you think we'll be safe with Redline out there blaming us for everything?" There was a fire in her eyes. "This is why I wanted to come to Requiem in the first place: so Dad would be afraid to chase me. Riven's right—maybe we need to try this."

Riven gave her a nod. At least one of the Almeida girls saw reason.

Samir scrubbed a hand through his perfect hair. "Dee. Tell them this is a bad idea."

"I'm not sure it is." Light from his wristlet screen danced in Diego's dark eyes. "These rumors about us—they're nasty. Banshee was one of the worst threats Requiem's ever seen.

And if word gets up to the matriarchs that it was our fault—if anything suggests we were to blame—the Code gives them permission to put us down, regardless of any protections we have." His eyes flitted over all of them. "Two months ago, Matriarch Sokolov got a tip about someone who'd stolen infected tech from the quarantine zone to help Banshee spread. No trial. She had him thrown in a scrap grinder."

It went quiet.

"We need to set the record straight," Samir finally said. "That's what we should be focusing on."

"And how do we do that?" Riven said. "By telling them we have a crew member with an Etri brain in her skull? We're running out of time. Everyone will have heard of us by tomorrow. At least within the trial, we might have some protection. And once we run Rio Oscuro, they wouldn't dare touch us."

"She's not wrong," Diego said. "If we were at the top of a syndicate, the Code would be in our favor. There's a burden of proof and a consensus required from the other matriarchs to depose a syndicate's leadership. Couple that with the resources we'd have at our disposal, and it's *very* tempting. Especially since I need to get out of Boneshiver."

"You're leaving Boneshiver?" Asa said, voicing Riven's surprise too. Diego had been in his faction as long as he'd been on Requiem.

"After Banshee plastered our identities all over Requiem, we attracted stalkers. All of us." Diego pursed his lips, with a pointed glance at Samir. "I made sure they knew it was in their best interests to leave us alone. But that creates a fragile balance."

"Dee," Samir said. "You've been blackmailing them? For us?"

Diego nodded. "We're in the crosshairs of some smaller factions still. Me especially. After Banshee leaked my name, it also got out that I work for Boneshiver. So a number of Cerys's enemies—and ours—have all but declared war on me. It's why I've been in and out of safe houses lately, but soon that won't be enough."

"I wish you'd told me earlier," Samir said, a bitter edge in his voice.

Asa chewed her lip. After a long silence, she reached for Riven's hand. "I know this is important to you. But it's also going to be dangerous. I think I need some time to think on it."

They didn't have time to think on it, and she didn't need Asa's permission. But Riven tamped down the spike of irritation and squeezed Asa's hand.

"That's fine." The foggy throb in her head became intoxicating. This might really be happening. "Samir. Dee's in. Are you? We need someone to keep our asses in line."

"Says the one who disappears for a day and then stumbles into our meeting drunk." Samir's voice simmered. No doubt she'd be hearing about this later. "We need to think this through. Wait at least a day to see how this all shakes out, and then put it to a vote."

"What about tomorrow?" Riven said. "Brightday-IV. We'll meet in the evening. Talk it over again."

Diego nodded. "I'll dig deeper. See what I can find. The Boneshiver matriarch has dealings on Cortellion, and our heiress might be able to give us an edge for earning her favor and entering the trial."

"Wait," Asa said. "What kinds of *dealings*?"

The world swayed. Riven caught herself on the couch where Asa was sitting. The last drink was hitting her hard, and the thought of dealing with Cortellion assholes dampened some of the rush.

"We'll need to take any edge we can get," Diego said. "Even if we haven't made up our minds yet, I'm going to look for a way in. We have until nightfall."

The trial would likely last the entire night. Their world might be different the next time the sun rose.

As Riven stumbled back toward her bunk, ready to knock herself unconscious for the foreseeable future, Samir blocked the hallway.

"Riven. We need to talk." His modded yellow eyes, pyro-electric membranes with vertical pupils, flashed in the dark.

"Something wrong?" She staggered, catching herself against the bathroom doorframe. Asa and Kaya had gone back to their room—Ty's old room—and Diego was taking a speeder back to wherever he was sleeping tonight. Nobody was here to save her from a lecture.

"I got a message last week." Samir leaned against the opposite wall. "From my mom."

"Oh." She squinted. Maybe she wasn't in trouble after all. But if he'd heard from his mom again—a decorated Federation officer—the implications weren't great. "Did she finally apologize for cutting you off after the CAA bullshit?"

"You know leaving was my choice." Samir shifted uncomfortably. He'd begged the debriefing officer at Central Atlantic Academy to discharge him after his squad's training disaster, convinced it was his fault. Then he'd called up Riven and Ty his second night on Requiem, haggard and hollow-eyed, offering to split the rent on a tiny apartment nearby. "And, well, she offered me a job."

"A *job*? With those Federation assholes?" His whole family had iced him out after he'd left the golden-child military school where Riven had miraculously held down a scholarship for over a year. She'd been there to escape a dead-end part of town where the streetlights only worked half the time. Samir, though—he'd had prospects.

"We're still talking about my mom, Riv. And it wouldn't be the interstellar enforcers. It would be the Response Corps. Disaster relief and evacuations."

"And you turned her down, right?" A pit was forming in Riven's stomach, either from the whiskey or from something worse. "Because you already gave that life up. And you're part of this crew now."

"Will you think about what *I* might want, for once? I didn't have a lot of options then." He scooped Zephyr into his arms. The pup rested his chin in the crook of Samir's elbow. "I wasn't going to respond. But if you pull us into this competition, and we win . . . it won't matter how many strings my mom pulls. I'll be flagged as a member of Requiem's underworld permanently, and I'll never get out of here. I have a chance to do something with my life now, and I'm tired of running."

"Shit," Riven said. Samir was her partner—the levelheaded

counterweight to her bad decisions. The person she could count on in a pinch. They used to get into all sorts of trouble at CAA, when he'd been her assigned mentor, but he'd drawn up the caution like a shield since joining her crew on Requiem.

Samir waited for her to say more, but she couldn't.

"Requiem was always supposed to be temporary," he said. "Spending a few years traveling the star-system, meeting a few beautiful men, getting into a bit of trouble. But now . . . I have a chance to go somewhere I can make a difference. Help people."

"Help people do what? Survive the Federation's *peace-keeping*?" Temporary. Her whole crew was. She'd hoped that maybe—after all they'd been through in the past year—Samir had changed his mind. "You don't think there's people here who need you?"

"It's not about the crew. I'm done romanticizing this place. It promises everything, but at the end of the day, it leaves you broken and bruised, with your neck on the line. The only reason I stayed this long was for you."

She choked on a shallow laugh. "For *me*? Why am I your responsibility?"

He gave her a hard look. "Because you were the only one left."

Riven's gut sank to her toes. Of course. It was why she was glad she'd gotten booted from CAA early in her second year. Samir's squad—*her* former squad—had been assigned a drill fighting new antipersonnel mechs with frequencies that could turn human brains to gelatin. They'd been a test run for cladded helmets designed to combat it.

But the helmets hadn't worked. And the only one who'd

been behind cover during the first wave of the attack had been Samir. Whether it was incompetence or a setup on his superior officers' part, Samir still blamed himself.

"You really think you've been babysitting me this whole time?" Her voice came quieter now.

"It could've been *your* brains trickling out your ears then. God, Riv, I just—" He went quiet. She knew what the blood that sometimes leaked from her ear reminded him of. "That's why I ran in the first place. If leading meant making decisions that got people killed, I didn't want it. It's not just about the Federation. I can't watch the underworld eat you all alive."

"You might be able to go home," she said, crossing her arms. "But everything I have is here. And Fed enforcement is relentless there. At least here we can fight without the law dropping a drone payload on us."

"I'm not asking you to come with me. You might all be better off with Rio Oscuro." He rubbed Zephyr's ear as the pup squirmed. "I'll see this through as part of the crew. But you can't be reckless. And most of all"—he stared her dead in the eyes—"if we win, I'm leaving afterward. This underworld shit is your dream, not mine."

Leaving. This was really happening. Samir must've been thinking about this for a while, and now he had an out. Just another person she'd lose. "What do you think Dee will say?"

Samir's jaw clenched. "He'll understand."

Her head spun, and she rested her forehead against the wall. The crew she'd built was unwinding itself. "So things go south, and you're just going to run away again, huh?"

His voice dropped an octave. "That's a pretty low blow.

Even for you." He pushed a lock of dark hair back into place. "Some of us have to think about the future. I hope you know what you're getting us into."

With that, he left her there in the dark.

chapter 4

LAST SPARK

One stray movement, and he'd be dead.

Ty's breaths snared in his chest as the footsteps drew closer. He pressed his back to the peeling tree bark, waiting.

The Watcher skulked by with feral grace, clinking mechanically with every step. In this world, the man wore a carbon-plated tactical suit, a rifle at his back, and hunting knives in his twitchy hands. He looked different in every world, but he'd never once let Ty live.

In five breaths, the Watcher's footsteps had receded into the thicket. For precious few minutes, he'd head west before circling back. Greasy smoke blanketed the sky above the trees, curling the leaves to ash. Ty whispered a prayer under his breath and darted toward the coast.

The tree line broke, giving way to a cliffside pounded by restless waves. Sea spray churned in the air like drops of spittle. The wind howled over the roar of the ocean, piercing his thin jacket. Ty shivered and pushed stray locks of hair from his eyes.

It's coming.

The cliff rumbled, no longer just from the waves. Ty tried to ignore the spreading dark in the distance, the mechanized appendages reaching over the horizon and plunging into the sea. Nausea crept over him at memories of what the storm would bring if he wasn't fast.

Overlooking the storm-tossed cliffside, the cottage waited. Ty ran up the creaking porch stairs and quietly cracked open the front door. He flipped the switch in the kitchen, igniting the old-tech light bulbs overhead. This time, he knew exactly where to look.

He found the keys hanging on a hook in the hallway and a stuffed lion under one of the couch pillows. The truck would be waiting by the barn. He'd never driven an old combustion-engine vehicle, but he'd also never made it far enough to try.

The Watcher always got him first.

Ty rushed up the staircase, past a cabinet with a vaulted lock that made his insides turn cold. He knew what was inside. But he wouldn't need it if he got out in time.

Yet again, he pushed open the door to the uppermost bedroom. Silhouetted by the gable window was a boy hugging his knees.

A boy with his brother's face.

"Hey, Emmett," Ty said softly. "We can't stay here."

The boy looked up at him with bloodshot eyes and tearstained cheeks. "You know my name?"

Emmett always forgot him.

This place was locked in time—a cottage Ty remembered from childhood, a memory warped and faded at the edges like a dream. A place their dad had taken them as kids, after their mother had left to pursue other dreams on other shores. Here, Emmett was eight years old. Ty remembered being seven and looking up to him, but now, Ty saw his brother from an eighteen-year-old's height.

"We need to go before the storm hits." He held the stuffed

lion toward the small Emmett, who looked tempted to take it. "Please. Come with me."

Emmett rubbed the familiar scar across his eyebrow—one he hadn't gotten until he was fourteen, taking a hit for Ty when some kid at school had tried to kick his ass. Everything here was an amalgam of Ty's memories, the pieces he'd told the psychiatrist.

But the kid's dark hair was matted with dirt, as if he'd been alone here for days. This version of him was strange, unreal. "I'm waiting for my dad. Where is he?"

"I don't know. But I promise I'll help you find him." With a momentary spike of fear, Ty realized he didn't want to know how his father would look in here. But this memory had taken place a few years before their dad had gotten sick. *You're wasting time*, part of Ty whispered.

The boy shook his head, burying his face into his hands.

Ty grabbed the boy's shoulder. Emmett was resisting. Even after he'd found the stuffed animal. "Please. I need you to trust me."

A soft creak sounded downstairs. Cold fear sliced through Ty's gut. He was out of time.

"Hide," Ty whispered.

Footsteps in the hallway. He should've opened the locked cabinet. But did it even matter anymore?

Not again not again not again—

The Watcher appeared in the doorway, his eyes uncanny silver above that familiar gruesome smile.

"There you are." He leveled the rifle at Ty's chest, and fired.

Shocks of pain shot through Ty's nerves. Spots of red and

black danced across his vision as the sharpened cold spread through his chest—

And then the water-stained ceiling above him was fading, the Watcher dissolving into pixels. The blood on Ty's chest disappeared, as did his jacket, until he was only bare skin and cold sweat and the monitor on his neck, jacked into his nerves. The pain was probably only a distant echo of how dying really felt, but his body still trembled at its memory.

Waking up never got easier.

"Subject AV70," came the voice through the overhead speaker, bored. "You've failed."

Around him, the holograms disappeared, leaving an empty simulation deck. A solid floor with green footlights.

You've failed. Again. He flexed the cybernetic fingers of his left hand, not bothering to stand up. The entire arm was stylized curves of steel outlining the carbon musculature beneath.

They'd repaired his body—an arm and an eye—but most of the tests were for his mind. Like a rat in a maze. He'd glimpsed some of the data, the stress reactions and decisions. Mapping his consciousness.

"That was your thirteenth attempt on this simulation." The voice's owner sat behind a tinted plexicarbon panel. Next to her was the one creating the simulations—a gaunt silhouette plugged into data cables. The real-life Watcher.

"I will remind you," the attendant continued, "that your assignment is only to escape the coast before the storm hits. Nothing more."

"I know," Ty said. But he'd seen Emmett's eyes and heard his screams when the storm hit. Even in a simulation, he couldn't leave his brother behind. And what was the point in completing the sim, if he'd just be thrown into a new scenario to die again?

The Watcher had cornered him six times today. The storm had gotten him in four. Other scenarios, he didn't want to remember.

A sigh came over the speaker. "You will be escorted back to your room. Get some rest. Tomorrow, you will attempt it again."

Ty's head swam. *Tomorrow.* He barely kept track of the days anymore.

A security guard nudged him with a patrol stunner and escorted him down the sterile white hall. On a screen they passed, Ty glimpsed the time and date on both Earth and Cortellion. *December 21, 2188,* on Earth.

His eighteenth birthday had come and gone exactly a month ago, with no acknowledgment whatsoever. He wondered if Riven and Samir had thought of him that day.

If they were still alive.

They survived, he told himself, like he did every day. *They had to.* He'd given himself up so they'd get out. If that hadn't been enough . . .

The doubt threatened to drag him under. His crew was the last spark he had. He had to believe he might see them again—had to believe Riven was still fighting her affliction—or he'd fade completely.

A thought nipped at him from within the mental fog. Something he needed to do today. Something important, related to the people he'd left behind.

The laboratory lights blurred, and a new thought broke in.

"*You could abandon the child*," it rumbled, from everywhere and nowhere. It grated like stone, itching and familiar.

Ty shook away the unbidden thought. Even in the simulator, it was horrible to think of leaving Emmett behind. But the thought hadn't felt like Ty's—

"*You could kill the Watcher*," the voice continued.

Ty blinked away the fatigue and whirled backward. "I'm sorry, did you just—"

His escort glared at him through the visor. "What are you on about?" The guard's voice was muffled and steely—different from the one Ty had heard.

"*Honestly, it is a simple simulation*," said the same voice, "*and you are making it more difficult for yourself.*"

A chill shot through Ty. "Who are you?"

The guard shoved him into a stumble. "Seems the sim's turned your brain to slag. Keep moving."

Ty shook his head. He had to focus. There was something he had to do, *tonight*, on the way back to his cot. Something he'd marked his wrist with a stolen pen to remind himself of.

They approached the door to the executive wing, and some of the clarity returned. *The keycard.* He vaguely remembered taking it from the pocket of a lab coat slung over a chair in the exam room, slipping it from its protective case with shaking fingers. Hiding it in a potted plant before they'd taken him to shower yesterday.

A keycard for the prototype corridor. Where the Winterdark files were kept. It might be the first step to helping Riven. He had to grab it before anyone else found it.

"I think I'm going to hurl," Ty said. "Sorry, the sim vertigo is getting bad—"

The guard rolled his eyes. "Can it wait until you get to your bunk?"

Ty shook his head, covering his mouth as he feigned choking. He stumbled through the door, passed the magnetic sensors, and spotted the atherblossom pot in front of the marble wall.

Ty clutched the edges of the planter, spitting and retching and pretending to vomit. The guard swore behind him, and from the corner of his eye, he saw the man turn his back. Ty groped around in the chem-nugget soil, digging his fingers near the edge of the pot. There it was—a thin strip of plastic. Relief slackened his shoulders.

"Up to no good, hmm?"

That voice again. He whirled behind him, but nobody was there—only the guard eyeing him from beyond the door, and the red light of the security camera glaring down at him.

Ty kept his fingers steady as he shifted his weight, angling his hip away from the camera. He slid the keycard into the pocket of his gray athletic pants as he wiped the spit off his mouth.

"I don't appreciate being ignored," the voice said again, deep as a grave.

Something was definitely wrong with him. Whatever they'd been doing to his head—the terrifying periods of being unconscious and waking up back in his cot, disoriented—was this a side effect?

Hallucination or no, it would have to wait. Ty turned

back toward where the guard waited, an apology ready on his tongue. Then—

"*STOP.*"

The thought was so forceful it halted him in his tracks.

"*If you proceed now, the magnetic sensors on that door will read the card's location. The artificial intelligence systems will label it an anomaly. You will be investigated.*"

Then what can I do? Ty thought, his pulse accelerating.

The response was immediate, as if the voice's owner had heard him. "*Wait until the light goes out. Then proceed.*"

"What are you?" Ty whispered.

"*You need not speak aloud to respond.*"

Ty shut his mouth. He waited, heart pounding, acutely aware of the security camera on the wall.

"What are you waiting for?" The guard stepped toward Ty. "Do you need to be *carried* back?"

The laser-diode lights overhead finally stuttered, and the camera's light went dark. The guard grumbled something about power surges.

"*Proceed,*" came the whisper in Ty's mind.

Ty held his breath and moved through the door, back to the guard's side. No alarms went off. He breathed a sigh of relief.

"You finished?" the guard said as Ty wiped his mouth apologetically. "Eh. You're definitely a little green. Let's get moving."

Ty dared to reach with his thoughts. Concentrated on forming words in his mind.

What happened back there, with the keycard? he thought. *If you can hear me . . . please tell me what's going on.*

"*Ah. There you are. Excellent.*"

He nearly fell over. The white lab lights glared overhead, dizzying. He tried to form concise thoughts again. *What's happening to me? And who are you?*

"*I had hoped you would remember. It seems somehow we have both become prisoners here.*"

Prisoners. In the bowels of Almeida Labs, where Asa's father had torn Kaya's mind from her body. The place where Project Winterdark had originated.

His mind tumbled down its darker corridors, into the memories that held his nightmares hostage. Another thing had come from Almeida Labs. Something that could seep into the tech in his head.

Ty barely dared to think the name.

Yllath?

He could feel the laughter in the voice. Banshee's voice. "*Correct.*"

Why are you helping me?

"*Consider it a favor—one I expect you will soon return. I have a proposition for you, Tyren O'Shea.*"

chapter 5
INTRUDER

Ty wasn't sure he breathed again until the guard bolted the door behind him.

He settled into his tiny chamber—not tall enough to stand in, barely wide enough for the white-sheeted bed. He sprawled onto the bed and flipped off the overhead light.

His own thoughts grew louder in the silence, choking. If this wasn't a hallucination—if Yllath was still alive—his crew might all be dead.

How am I hearing you? Ty thought. Even in the darkness, his cybernetic left eye saw the corners and crevices of the room in gray relief.

"*That is . . . a complicated question.*" A pause. He could feel the thoughts roiling behind the voice—calculating, introspective. "*Put simply, they have changed you. You now contain a small part that is Etri.*"

Ty gritted his teeth. It was confusing enough that Yllath had leaped his way through the circuits on Requiem. But his *head* now?

"*I see this explanation has not satisfied you. Let me phrase things differently. You are aware Etri and human minds are not the same? We interface with other organisms, other technologies, and each other. And our consciousnesses—our very* selves—remain immutable, regardless of their fragmentation and the distance between them."

It was still mind-boggling. It didn't fit with any of his medical training, the schooling that now seemed like an eternity ago. It didn't match the physiology of the human brain. But Etri fossils' linking ability had enabled instantaneous ansibles and space travel, since the physics of their bodies was so different.

What do I have that's Etri? Ty thought.

"*Something that was once part of me, actually. Regrown samples of what they took from me are now inside you. There are several minds within this lab that contain Etri cells, but to connect with them mentally—we call it* ntharen, *or mind-speaking in your tongue—requires a certain familiarity. A mental impression, of sorts. I have been watching you since you've been here.*"

Ty shivered. Any Etri cells inside his head were likely helping him interface with his replacement parts. He hadn't encountered any other test subjects since he'd been here, but maybe they'd been isolated to prevent them from hearing each other.

So much of what the scientists had done to him these past few months was a blur. But if Yllath was alive, he had bigger problems.

My friends didn't stop you, Ty thought, ice spreading through his chest. *What did you do to them?*

"*Not much, unfortunately. They were cleverer than I expected.*"

Are they still alive?

"*As far as I know . . . all of them, yes.*"

Ty choked back a sob of relief. It was the first time he'd felt anything close to hope in months.

Are you still terrorizing them? he thought.

"*No. I have no more hold over Requiem. I had to fully withdraw every iota of myself to fight the Almeida girl. Which brings me to the proposition I mentioned.*"

Almeida. Asa, or Kaya? Either way—they'd won. Whether they'd managed to fix Kaya was another story.

I won't help you if you're still hunting them, Ty said.

A pause. "*I have relinquished that dream. Being whole would serve no purpose in a world ruled by your kind. And the rest of my body, I have learned, is no longer.*"

Almeida destroyed your body?

"*So it would seem. There is another that wanders these halls, his body intact but mind a shell. An Etri husk whom Almeida calls Iolus. It is unclear what Almeida has done to him, but he seems fully under Almeida's thrall.*"

Ty shivered. He'd glimpsed Iolus once when Almeida visited the labs—Luca's towering bodyguard. Skeletal teeth and graying lips beneath a mirrored helmet, webbed gauntlets ending in steel claws.

"*There is hope for the others of my kind. They still slumber, waiting for the day we can awaken again. But Almeida intends to use them. Cut them apart, as he did me.*" A deep, rolling fury. "*I intend to destroy him before then.*"

Ty's pulse tripled. *And what you're asking me to do—*

"*Is to help plant my consciousness in the laboratory's central networks. The technicians have implemented blockades to trap me where I am now.*"

Ty shivered. No doubt Yllath would love to do to this lab what he'd done to Requiem. The deadly security mechs over-ridden, at his command. The threatening messages, false boun-ties plastered across holoscreens. The deepfake hologram of Emmett, forcing Ty and Riven to watch him die again.

If Yllath got out, what would prevent him from wreaking the same destruction? He was devastatingly powerful, a single mind that had brought a city to its knees. But if Yllath was no longer after Ty's crew—if he'd be targeting Almeida alone . . .

I'll bite, Ty thought. *What are you offering in return?*

"*I can open doors for you. Literally, and metaphorically.*" The lights flickered overhead. "*Toward whatever it is you've been searching for.*"

Having a way out of this maze was tempting.

Ty had been digging ever since he'd woken up here. Wrong turns in the halls between showers and sim sessions, memoriz-ing maps, rooting through the scientists' bags in his few unsu-pervised moments. Anything to find answers about what was happening here and what was killing Riven. The affliction eat-ing her nervous system had originated here, with Winterdark and Almeida's lab.

All he'd discovered was a prototype corridor where Winterdark's files were kept. The keycard he'd once seen a scientist use to enter it was now tucked beneath his pillow. He'd been careful, since whatever would happen if he was caught wouldn't be pretty.

But the keycard was only the beginning. No doubt there were other vaults and other passcodes inside. He'd need help.

Here's my offer, Ty thought. *If I let you out, you're only going after Almeida's higher-ups. Leave innocents out of this.*

A deep rumble. "*And?*"

I want you to help me find information on Project Winterdark, and the biochemical spores they were using at Sanctum's Edge. And then . . .

Ty heard a metallic creak. He realized he was clenching the bedframe hard enough to bend it. The cybernetic was crushingly strong, so strong it scared him sometimes.

You're going to help me escape.

A cold silence. Then the churn of distant thoughts. Consideration, acceptance. Images of Almeida falling, and Yllath fading to slumber like the rest of his kind.

Yllath's voice returned so forcefully it knocked the breath out of him.

"*You have yourself a bargain, Tyren.*"

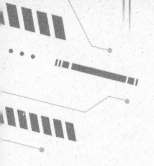

Chapter 6

"After all we did for them, they accuse me of being Banshee?" Kaya sat on Asa's workbench, her platform boots kicking idly as she spun a hydraulic wrench on her index finger. "I mean, come on."

"Everyone wants someone to blame," Asa responded. She and her sister both spoke Portuguese, as they often did when alone. "We can only hope this blows over." She'd been trying to forget the mess they were in—one of two reasons for the apprehension fizzing in her stomach today, fierce as the sparks from her welding torch. Even through the tinted face-shield, the seam carved a bright streak across her vision. A curl of smoke disappeared into the stuffy air of the storage unit.

Her makeshift garage was tiny compared to the one on Cortellion, but rent was cheap, and it was a place to call her own. Here, none of her father's security cameras were watching. It was only her and her sister—and their crew to protect them.

"I'd expected rumors about me to at least be interesting," Kaya said. "Nobody seems to know it was me who graffitied that huge pink dick on the Fed patrol ship." She glared at the sound-system controls across the room, and the audio visualizer kicked to life as an angry acid-bass track roared through the speakers, replacing Asa's soft synthpop. She flopped backward on the workbench. "I hoped *someone* would recognize the art style. It wasn't exactly subtle."

"It got your point across," Asa called over the music. She let the bass wash over her as she made the final weld. Then she lifted the face-shield, grateful for the rush of air on her sweat-streaked face. She pulled the polycarbon cover across the seat, and the bike was finished. The cycle's body shone polished black, dark as a void, with veins of star-bright chrome and accents of candy red and midnight purple. Something she'd created for herself and Riven in this hell-pit city. "What do you think?"

"Looks great," Kaya said. "Is it ready for the moment of truth?"

Asa plugged in the key and pressed the ignition button. The engine hummed to life, devilish and eager. Kaya whistled as the pink underglow ignited on the dirty concrete floor. The seams were perfect, the bike's profile aerodynamic.

It wouldn't compare to *Boomslang*, but it would be perfect for tonight.

The flare of nerves came back. She checked her wristlet—their crew's comm channel was still open, with a recent message from Diego's private messaging code.

I have a lead. But we can put it to a vote first. Meeting tonight—my place.

Another discussion of the upcoming trial. A tricky, high-pressure decision she wasn't looking forward to. She tucked the message away.

There were no new messages from Riven. The pit in her

stomach deepened. Something had been sizzling between them for months now, and they were so close to making this *real.* If that was even what Riven wanted.

"Is this a bad idea?" Asa said quietly. Building the bike suddenly seemed like an elaborate gesture that might lead nowhere. "If she wanted me, wouldn't she have said something already?"

"Stop stressing. She's so into you it's ridiculous. I'm pretty sure she's been waiting for *you* to be ready." Kaya hopped off the bench and ran her hand over the bike seat. "But my advice probably doesn't mean much. A solid one-third of my Requiem dates have ended with my date getting herself into a knife-fight."

"Haven't you only been on three dates here?"

"*Still.*" Kaya's tiny hummingbird mech—one Asa had built her—flitted overhead. "I think you have something great here. And you're both ready."

"Thanks," Asa said. "And for the record, I *always* want your advice." Kaya was right. She and Riven had been stealing kisses long enough.

Asa buffed a smudge of grease off the control panel with her sleeve, and the hummingbird perched on the bike's handlebars with a rag in its beak. As Asa reached for it, the bird fell to the floor with a soft *thunk.* It twitched on the concrete, one wing buzzing madly.

The music on the speakers cut. The bird wasn't righting itself. When Asa glanced at Kaya, her blood froze.

Kaya stared into space, her pupils dilated and faraway. Silent, motionless.

"Kaya?" When Kaya didn't respond, Asa grabbed her shoulders. "Hey. Say something."

Kaya blinked, gasping. Her eyes refocused. "Asa. Wow, sorry."

"Everything okay?" She might still be hurting from two nights ago.

"I . . . yeah, probably. It happens sometimes. Side effect of a brain that isn't yours, I guess." Kaya pressed a hand to her chest as her breaths steadied. The bird hopped back onto her shoulder. "Sometimes being in the circuits makes me feel . . . a little less me."

"What do you mean, less *you*?" That was worrying. Their father had wanted to change Kaya, to make her more docile.

Something dark passed over Kaya's eyes, then disappeared. "It's probably nothing. I just need to rest my brain a bit." She shook off the tension. "So. When's Riven going to be here?"

Asa almost objected—she shouldn't leave Kaya if she was hurting. But her sister would tell her if something were really wrong.

Asa checked her wristlet. It was half an hour past when she thought she'd be ready—almost time for Riven to meet her. But Riven was rarely on time. Asa selected their private comm channel. Sure enough, there was a message, sent two minutes ago.

on my way down. suited up just for you.

"Damn. She'll be here any second." Asa stripped off her sweaty jacket and rushed to the sink to splash away some of the sweat. She'd expected at least half an hour to clean up, to have Kaya help with her makeup—

"That sounds like my cue to disappear." Kaya finger-combed Asa's sweaty hair off her face. "You'll do great. She'll love it. And remember, you're adorable." Kaya poked Asa's nose and headed toward the door. "If she breaks your heart, she answers to me. Got it?"

Asa rolled her eyes as the door clicked shut.

Moments after Kaya left, there came steady, confident footsteps down the hall. A murmured greeting from Kaya. A knock on the door, and it opened a crack. "Hey, mechanist. What's this surprise? If you've built me a whiskey distillery, I might love you forever."

Somehow, Riven was early.

"*Meu Deus*," Asa hissed. Then she called in English: "Um. Don't come in yet!"

The door swung open. Riven held a hand over her eyes as she turned her back and leaned against the doorframe. "*Now* I'm curious. Are you naked or something?"

Heat flared in Asa's chest. She still had to change into her red-and-black exosuit, the custom-fitted bodysuit with thin plates of graphene-reinforced armor the Duchess had given them for riskier jobs. "Almost. I mean, not yet. Um−"

She stole a glance at Riven in the doorway. The straps of Riven's exosuit clung tight to her silhouette of curves and muscle in varying shades of purple and black. Asa found herself staring.

"Sounds like a hell of a surprise," Riven muttered.

Asa shook away the distraction. "Head around to the street-side door. You'll love it. Promise."

The side door creaked closed, and Asa quickly changed

into her own exosuit, pinning her shoulder-length hair into a messy bun. When the garage door rolled up, the bike's headlights illuminated Riven, her face lit in a wild grin.

"Hey, gorgeous," Riven said, and Asa wasn't sure whether she was talking to her or the bike. She'd take either.

"You like it?" Asa felt her face would crack from smiling. "I figure we could use it for nights out." It didn't have the power and mobility of a ship, but having treads on the road was exhilarating.

"Looks fast. Been a while since I've ridden one."

"Really?" Asa slid onto the seat. She clicked the switch on the thick collar of her exosuit, and the helmet slotted into place—a metallic brace over her jaw and behind her head, with a domed holo-shield covering her face. "There's somewhere I want to take you."

Riven settled onto the seat behind her, her chest pressed to Asa's back, her arms wrapping around Asa's waist. Asa hit the throttle, and the bike zipped forward, smooth as silk.

They rode into the shadows of the sweltering Requiem afternoon. On the skyway, the tires sent glowing ripples across the matrix of translucent blue. Asa cranked the throttle, sliding between the rolling cruisers around her and the speeders whizzing above. Her machine was a quiet whirr beneath her, electrical currents surging under the sleek hull. All at her command.

Faster.

Riven laughed into the wind.

This girl was the only reason Asa had survived this long—pulling her behind cover when jobs got messy, jumping into mech arenas when she was in danger. Always saving her, and Asa hadn't managed to save Riven yet. Not in the way that mattered most.

Tonight, she had to tell Riven how much she needed her.

Asa followed the flashing blue arrows into a plunging tunnel, until the skyway thinned and gave way to narrow alleys at street level.

They zipped through a rougher part of town—past a kitschy-restaurant-turned-arms-dealership, its huge cartoon cat mascot graffitied to hell so the cat's silly grin looked sinister. Past the Scrap District and the boarded-up windows of secondhand shops and mod-dens. Past Tempest dance hall, its holographic ocean waves surging and rolling high above the skybridges, where androids scrubbed the dance decks in preparation for sunset.

These alleys whispered their secrets as she passed. She could navigate the city without a map now, knowing its darker streets and hidden shortcuts. This place was still thriving and dangerous, but it was starting to feel like home. Like hers.

Asa turned a hard right, and the bike wound its way up a parking garage ramp. Floor seven had a hole blown in the wall, and she stopped the bike a few feet away. She'd discovered this view by accident a week ago, and her breath still hitched at the sight.

"Here it is." Asa clicked her helm off, shaking her hair into place. "Come look!"

Outside, the street looked aflame. A bridge carved from translucent purple crystal formed a jagged arch across the dirty streets—one of the few Etri ruins still standing on Requiem. At this hour, the light of Alpha Centauri A squeezed between the high-rising scramble of streets and towers, hitting the bridge. The crystal scattered the light like a prism, casting sparks of light in every color across glass windows and steel trusses. Her city. Their city.

"What do you think?" Asa said.

"It's incredible." A storm brewed in Riven's gray-green eyes. "There's no taming this place."

"I know. Feels like anything could happen here."

"Only sure thing is you become a little different every time the sun rises. Until the day it all crushes you." Something wild roiled beneath Riven's exterior, and Asa shivered. It was possible Riven could be a matriarch soon—underworld royalty, letting this city shape her, break her. "One day we'll kiss it goodbye and thank it for the rush."

For a moment, Asa almost backed out. But she was sick of not knowing where they stood. Before Riven drifted too far, she had to know. "I, uh, I had something I wanted to ask you."

Riven raised an eyebrow, waiting. Now or never.

"I know we've been . . . close, for the past few months." Four months of surviving by the skin of their teeth together. Of secret kisses and words unsaid. A particularly heated night in Olympus, when Asa's hands had dared to roam beneath Riven's shirt, tweaking small gasps out of her as the club lights flashed overhead.

But Asa had hesitated, like always, and Riven had never pushed her further. Maybe she'd been waiting for Asa to confirm she was ready. Even if it was prudish, Asa needed them to feel more permanent first.

"I think we should make things official," Asa bit out.

"Official." A frown tugged at Riven's lips. "What do you mean?"

Not the reaction she'd been hoping for. "Official, as in . . . we're exclusive. Together. And I get to call you my girlfriend."

Riven's jaw worked. She was rarely at a loss for words. "Asa, I . . ."

"If you still need more time, I understand." Asa's stomach knotted itself into a tangle. It had been months since Ty had gone, but was it still too soon? She and Riven were past the hardest conversation—that Asa hadn't considered anything long-term with him. Which didn't sound great in retrospect, even if it *was* true. "I just thought—"

Riven pulled her close, stealing her words with a kiss that seared like starlight. Asa's heart jumped, and she wrapped her arms around Riven's waist.

But Riven was already pulling away, and her eyes wouldn't meet Asa's. A cold, heavy pause hung like a shield between them.

"It's not really a matter of *when*, Asa. This is a bad idea."

"Why?" Asa's throat had constricted, and her voice sounded so *small*.

"You know what's happening to me." Riven flexed her gloved fingers, as if the sickness might rattle her hands at any moment. "I'll be here for . . . maybe a few years, if I'm lucky. And then what will you do?"

"Nothing's certain here," Asa said. "We could both be dead

tomorrow. I just want—" Her throat choked with tears, and she had to stop.

"I was supposed to protect you. But I've been failing at that too." Riven's hands rested on Asa's shoulders, and she sighed. "I should have said something before we got in too deep. But I'm dying, Asa. I can't do to you what Emmett did to me."

Asa had never known Emmett, but his death had torn Riven apart. And then Ty's death had ripped that wound back open, worse. And yet—

There was so much she wanted to say. She hadn't told Riven what she'd been doing these past few months: the late nights spent with Kaya, slipping into their estate's networks on Cortellion. They'd started by retrieving their old art and game files, then Kaya discovered a back door into the home lab, to Project Winterdark—the reason Riven was dying, and a prime feature of Kaya's nightmares. Dark roads Kaya was willing to revisit if it meant helping.

But most of Project Winterdark had been scrubbed away, and records showed the data had been migrated to the downtown lab. Files Kaya hadn't been able to access. Yet.

There's still hope for you, Asa wanted to say. *I'm still trying. And even if I can't save you, I want to stay as long as possible, because nothing in this line of work is certain—*

The thoughts scrolled by, but she couldn't get them out. It would change nothing. Riven had made up her mind.

"I'm never going to stop trying to keep you safe," Riven said. "But getting too close is a bad idea." She pressed her forehead against Asa's, so close their breaths mingled. "I'm sorry. Really."

In silence, Asa watched the shattered light dance across

the cityscape. The enormity of it hit her. There was no fixing Riven and whatever had been building between them.

Riven would never be hers.

Asa blinked away the blur of tears and fought to keep the quaver from her voice. "We should probably get back."

"I think I'll walk back." Riven's voice was steady, but her eyes glimmered as she turned away.

"You don't have to," Asa choked out. "It's dangerous. Especially right now." Maybe it was pathetic to want just a few more minutes with her, but Asa couldn't stop herself.

"I'll be fine. I'm armed, and it's still daylight." Riven threw a wave over her shoulder. "Talk later."

Asa settled back onto the bike, the seat empty behind her as the engine kicked to life. There had to be a way out of this. To undo the damage her father had done.

With Winterdark's data inaccessible remotely, Kaya had suspected they'd need to go back to Cortellion—to pry their way into the downtown laboratory. It seemed impossible, but Asa had to keep trying.

Voice shaky, Asa dictated a message to Diego. "We need to talk. I might need to make a brief trip to Corte."

His reply was near instant, a voice clip in her earpiece. "Is this about the trial? Because I had something in mind there. If you're up for it."

Whatever it entailed, she'd do it.

As she entered the skyway, tears blurred the passing city lights. But she could've sworn one of the billboards flashed with a face made of red lines, pointed teeth, and Xs for eyes.

chapter 7

THE GAUNTLET

Riven had underestimated how far it was to Diego's on foot. She kept her chin high, careful not to make eye contact with the hollow-eyed glitch junkies watching from fire escapes, or the spray-paint vandals whose cybernetic eyes seemed to crawl beneath her exosuit.

She'd messaged Diego, begging him to keep tabs on Asa as she drove back, even if that meant Riven would owe him later. It might've been a mistake to split up, but they needed space. It was so hard to look at Asa right now.

Girlfriend. She'd never expected to be asked that again.

She'd refused to get close to anyone since Emmett. Before Asa, she'd tangled with a few people after nights at bars, but nobody she'd ever messaged afterward. She had trouble turning down adrenaline rushes. She'd told herself that was all Asa was—tried to keep her at arm's length—but they'd gotten too deep.

Now being near Asa felt like breaking a promise to herself. She risked falling too hard and fragmenting herself further, while hurting Asa worse.

Pulling away was for the best. Asa could move on before she was in too deep with a doomed girl. All Riven could leave for her—for the whole crew—was the spot at the top of Rio Oscuro.

As she passed the remains of a rough sleeper camp, her wristlet buzzed. A call from an unknown messaging code.

She clicked *ignore* and kept walking, past dripping pipes and burned-out neon, through the back edge of the SilCaul—the Silicon Cauldron, home to sketchy mod-dens and custom android mechanists. The darkening streets were covered in a perpetual greasy smoke. It was one of the safer routes, away from the main thoroughfares and territories teeming with bounty hunters. She could keep a low profile for a few miles.

But only a few blocks later, there came a shuffling from the surrounding alleys—hurried steps, and then quiet. Instinct scraped at the back of her neck. *You're being followed.*

She suddenly felt bare, walking these streets without her crew. Ahead, a pulsing LED sign cast red shadows in an alley—a long walk that cut through the block. It'd save her a good ten minutes, and she wouldn't have to venture into the underzone. Angular dollar-sign symbols were graffitied onto the boarded windows, marking $corpio Heat territory—a subfaction of thieves who worked with Borealis, one of the major syndicates.

Riven paused. The local gangs would have no reason to hold up a girl in an exosuit who was packing heat, but if she switched on her helm, either she'd look like she was expecting a fight, or she'd look like a coward. She left the helm down but clipped her braid into a twist before entering the alley.

Vent fans droned behind the buildings, and footsteps shuffled in the branching passages. Another call appeared on her wristlet, same messaging code, and she clicked *ignore* again.

Two figures shifted in the alley ahead. Soft chatter went silent as she approached. The scavengers stood between her and the alley's end—one leaning against a dumpster, one sitting on the ladder of a fire escape. Both had scarves pulled over their noses and luminescent paint splashed across their eyes, glowing in the shadows.

"Hey. Where you going?" said the one on the ladder.

Riven kept her gaze fixed ahead, but the other stepped into her path. "It *is* you." He was built like a beast—about as tall as Samir—but she didn't recognize him. "Deadeye Hawthorne, huh. I'll admit, I expected you to have turrets mounted on your shoulders, the way they talk about you." Laughter broke out, and Riven's hackles rose. This wasn't a place she wanted to be recognized.

"I don't do autographs. Sorry." She stepped forward, but he slid in front of her again.

"Where's the rest of your crew?" He stared down at her through his red glow-paint. "Heard the Almeida heiress was out with you tonight."

Dread slithered up her spine. She should tell them her crew was nearby, that she wasn't alone. But if he was asking after Asa—knew they'd been out together—something was up. "Sounds like you need to fire your informant," she said. "I don't see the *Almeida heiress* anywhere."

"We lost half our crew during the Banshee takeover at Olympus," said a third voice from behind her. Footsteps drew closer, and Riven risked turning her head. A woman with a bat slung across her shoulders sauntered toward them. "And we're not the only ones. One of the Borealis bosses has agreed to pay us if we root out the ones responsible."

A bounty, then. Diego was right—they were in deep. Already.

Riven kept herself dead steady as her breaths grew tighter. The white-noise stress prickled in her skull, but it didn't stop her from sensing movement at the corner of her vision. A fourth person, hidden, stalking her. Her hand wandered toward *Verdugo*.

The scavs must've known the Duchess had cut her crew loose. Knew they could hurt her with no consequences. Like the patrol officers on Earth who'd punched her when she talked back, or one of her group-home parents who'd hit her for shooting cans with a pellet gun in an abandoned building.

Riven had been cornered so often she'd learned to bite back harder.

"Listen," she snapped. "We were the ones who saved your asses from Banshee. We *stopped* Almeida. So I'll give you one last chance to move, and I'll walk away."

The tall one shrugged. "Or you could tell us where your girlfriend's at . . . and we'll *let* you keep walking." There was a pistol in his hand now, gleaming in the streetlights. He tapped the barrel against his forearm.

They were awfully confident. If they didn't believe the stories they'd heard about her, she'd have to show them.

She thought quickly. Their weapons were already out; they'd strike as soon as she grabbed her guns. Her exosuit would stop a bullet, but not a plasma blade or a bludgeoning—and right now, her head was exposed. At the edge of her vision was the rusted dumpster next to the fire escape. Cover.

The tallest scav smirked, making eye contact with something just behind her. All the warning Riven needed.

Slish.

She dove out of the way as something scythed toward her head, breathing heat at her temple. A plasma blade. Her boots skidded against the concrete, her back hitting the side of the dumpster just as she drew her guns. She hit the switch on her exosuit, and it was an agonizing few seconds before the helm flickered over her face.

Another *slish* as the plasma blade seared through the steel corner of the dumpster, nearly clipping her shoulder. Definitely hot enough to burn through her suit. She'd have to be fast.

Without a second thought, Riven raised *Blackjack*'s barrel over her makeshift cover. *Hammer-trigger*, and a bullet tore through the blade-wielder's stomach.

The tall scav shouted, his pistol raised. She pulled *Verdugo* and shot him next. Then she ducked and rolled beneath the bat hurtling toward her, jammed the gun muzzle against the wielder's ribs, and fired. Bullets flew in a ragged mess of instinct and adrenaline.

Thoom. One last shot.

By the time Riven stood up, all four of the scavs were lying on the ground, unmoving.

"Shit." She spat salty metallic blood onto the concrete. Somewhere in there, she'd taken a hard hit to the face, and her chest stung with a growing bruise—a bullet had flattened against the armor plate covering her ribs. The struggle had lasted only seconds, barely a fight.

The tall man was still gasping, clutching the wound on his belly, his eyes glazing over.

"Who put you up to this?" Riven said, staring at him down

her iron sights. Her nerves were aflame, and it was a struggle to steady her hands. "Who told you where I was tonight?"

"Redline's getting the truth out," he gasped. "They know what you did." A convulsion, and he choked up blood. "They're right about you. That you'd sacrifice all of Requiem to save your own skin."

Half his crew had been claimed by Banshee—a crew not so different from hers. He'd been out for revenge, like she'd been once. And he'd paid for it.

"It wasn't me you needed to hunt down," Riven muttered. "But maybe I'll give the right guy a bullet for you someday." She turned, leaving him there to bleed.

Something sizzled like frying bacon. The plasma blade was hissing in a puddle, kicking up steam. A split second faster, and the blade could've driven straight into her skull.

Even beyond her sickness flaring, she'd almost died. One slip, and it all would've been over. Death didn't scare her like it used to, but if Asa had been here . . . she couldn't let herself imagine the plasma blade slitting the girl's throat.

That unknown number was calling again. This time, Riven accepted the call but didn't say a word. Her caller did the talking for her.

"Settling it with blood, as usual. It's all you know, isn't it?"

It was the voice she'd heard over the arena loudspeakers a few nights ago. The hacker in the mech. Redline. Her nerves burned hotter, blinding.

"You're lying to them." Riven bit back a snarl. "If you send people after me, you're sending them to their deaths. That blood's on *your* hands."

Silence. The shadows blinked, taunting her.

"You're sheltering a cancer in this city. The last thing Requiem needs is a matriarch like you."

The comm call clicked off.

Riven stilled her shaking hands, swallowing the pain, the furious tang of metal on her tongue. *Matriarch.* If Redline knew about the trial . . . either someone had talked, or they'd been spying. Someone's wristlet might be bugged.

The city was closing in on her crew, and the only way out was *up*. They might have no choice but to enter this trial.

But first—she had to find Asa.

She turned down the alley and ran, not looking back.

Riven didn't stop running until Diego's door slid open.

The dusty underground lobby burst open, giving way to his offices—soft lighting, organized bookshelves, and the scents of old paper books and coffee. His new hideout already felt familiar, down to the metallic spiders watching from the shadows.

Riven tore around the corner into the main meeting room. She'd called Asa half a dozen times, but Asa hadn't picked up. And the worst part was she had good *reason* not to pick up, even if Redline hadn't found her—

"Asa?" Riven whispered. "Oh, thank *god.*"

Asa sat across the table from Diego, a massive holoscreen hanging between them. She didn't even look at Riven as she intently tapped the clusters of colored lights positioned on it.

Diego shot Riven a questioning look, then went back to

the game map. "A decent move," he said to Asa. "But it won't work, because—"

"Because it was a decoy. For my assassins!" Asa swiped across the screen. A vidclip played of masked, dagger-wielding shadows slipping through palace halls. "And your entire royal family goes down."

Diego looked surprised, but the expression quickly faded to his neutral cool. "Well done."

"Wait. I beat you?" Asa's face lit up, but Riven noticed traces of puffy, bloodshot eyes. No doubt she'd been crying. "No hidden traps or secret reserve forces?"

Diego shrugged. "Nope. That's it. Good game."

Riven let out a breath. Asa and the others were safe here, for now.

Sweat itched beneath her exosuit, and she unzipped the front. There were stray spatters of blood there, a reminder of how close she'd been tonight. She peeled down the top half of the suit to her waist, leaving only her bra. Nothing her crew hadn't seen before.

"She'll keep outmaneuvering you if you don't watch it, Dee." Samir walked out of the tiny kitchen, letting his fingers trail over Diego's jaw in passing. A small smile flickered to life on Diego's face, but it was quickly replaced by something sullen, and he pulled away. Samir frowned, then turned to Riven. "Late as usual. What's your excuse this time?"

She almost hesitated to break the easy peace, but it had to be said. "Got held up by some scavs, armed and out for blood. No way that was the end of it." She slumped into a chair and let her arm hang over the back.

"Are you okay?" Asa wouldn't look Riven in the eye. There was that crestfallen look again, the one that nearly tore out Riven's heart. The rest of them had gone quiet—no doubt Asa had already told them how their joyride had ended.

"I'm . . . alive, apparently," Riven muttered, touching the darkening bruise across her ribs.

Samir set down his tea next to Diego. "You think they targeted you on purpose?"

"They wanted *Asa*. And they were pretty blunt about it. Said Redline was getting the truth out. That we're to blame for Banshee." Riven made eye contact with one of the tiny mech-spiders crawling on Diego's bookcase, the hidden cameras. He was monitoring this place, making it safer than her hideout. "And somehow, Redline caught wind of us entering the trial. They didn't seem happy."

Kaya emerged from the kitchen, smoothing her blue hair into place as she sank into the empty chair between Riven and Asa like a defensive buffer. Weird that Redline seemed more interested in Asa than her sister, despite the rumors of Kaya being Banshee. Unless Redline knew the truth. Somehow, this was centered on both sisters.

"I can corroborate Riven's account," Galateo said. "This might not be an isolated incident. Information has been circulating on VNet for the past few hours."

Diego's game screens switched over to his security network configurations. "Well, nothing's bugged here, as far as I can tell." He brought up newsfeeds and message logs, and frowned. "But it seems there's been chatter." A collage of photos flashed on the screen, showing all of them except Kaya. The same ones Banshee had been circulating months ago.

An orange skull was drawn at the bottom, with a message: *The Duchess won't stop them. Shouldn't we?*

"Oh god." Asa's eyes locked onto a photo of herself in red clubwear, side-eyeing an Olympus security camera. Ty was hunched at her side, hands buried in his pockets like he was trying to hide in plain sight.

An X was scrawled across his face, like he was a target someone had shot down. Riven's fingernails dug into the table.

"We're sure Redline isn't Banshee's new nickname?" Samir said. "I'm sure that thing would love to come back to bite us in our collective ass."

Kaya shook her head. "It definitely wasn't Yllath at the fighting pits. Redline's . . . signature was different. It didn't feel like an Etri, if that makes sense."

"There's already some speculation of who Redline might be," Diego said. "People are noting similarities to other super-hackers who've been giving the corps hell."

"Someone connecting Asa to her dad, maybe?" Samir said. "If this is some kind of vengeance, they aren't messing around. Banshee left a powder keg of pain in his wake, and all Redline's doing is igniting it."

It was quiet as the understanding came crushing down. Nowhere on Requiem was safe for a crew quickly climbing everyone's hit lists.

"This is my fault," Asa said softly. "Everything that's happening followed me. I keep putting the rest of you in danger."

"Bullshit. We all put *ourselves* in danger." Riven leaned forward, staring past Kaya to her sister. "You're not leaving."

Asa looked at her with watery eyes. There was an accusation there.

"She's right," Diego said. "You leaving wouldn't change anything now."

"We could catch a transit to Earth," Samir said. "Wait it out, if only for a while. I don't know how my family would feel about packing you all into the basement, but—"

"We'd put them at risk too," Diego said. "Some of us have arrest warrants with the Federation. Not only that, but Almeida's allies have more pull on Earth. It's more than just the matriarchs and Federation treaties that keep Requiem free."

"So what you're saying is, we're pretty much screwed." Riven scratched her cheek and found flakes of dried blood. "But there's a pretty obvious solution we were supposed to discuss tonight anyway."

"You really think we'd be safer with Rio Oscuro?" Asa said. "I guess nobody could mess with us without crossing the Code."

"Right." Riven avoided Asa's eyes. It was probably a bad day to have broken her heart. "Bet Redline would *hate* to see us with power under our thumbs."

Samir swirled the tea in his mug. "If we're voting on it, then I guess my vote's yes."

It caught her off guard. If Samir was in, that cemented it. But it meant no matter what happened next, she'd lose him.

"I think Asa was our only other undecided," Diego said.

"It'll be hard, but . . ." Asa locked eyes with Riven, then her gaze quickly fell to the blood on her exosuit. "I think the trial is our best choice. I'm willing to try."

And there it was.

"It's settled, then," Riven said. "We find a way in. What do you say we raid a warehouse, dig up some corporate dirt, and get Boneshiver to sponsor us?"

"Actually," Asa said, "Diego and I have already been looking into something."

A holo flickered to life above the table—a three-dimensional, blue-marbled map of the planet Cortellion, with the capital city, Himmeltor, highlighted. The image zoomed in, showing an expanse of white skyscrapers and sweeping staircases beneath a perfect grid of skyways.

"The Boneshiver matriarch is setting up a business arrangement with one of the Cortellion tech moguls," Diego said. "But it's likely he'll need a bit of . . . additional encouragement. He's trying to renegotiate a dark route through Requiem—but he's wary, especially after Rio Oscuro's arrangement with the Federation ended disastrously. It's a long shot for Matriarch Cerys. She might need someone to help her clinch the deal."

"My dad was invited to the gala where they'll be meeting," Asa said softly. "And, well, Bria was right. He's been spreading rumors I'm still his heir."

"What are you getting at?" Riven said.

"It means she's been invited too." Kaya pulled a scrolling list up on Diego's holoscreen. "Plus, our dad rarely attends any events where he won't be center stage. We dug up the guest list, and he already sent his regrets."

Claire Winn

It hit Riven slow and hard, like a time-delay grenade. "You're planning to crash a party."

"Well, if you put it that way–"

"A guarded-to-hell industry party. On *Cortellion*."

"Hiding in plain sight," Asa said. "Nobody will be suspicious–they have no reason to think I *wouldn't* show. Nobody on that guest list knows I'm on the run from my dad."

Riven leaned back, puffing a breath. They were already in deep shit for being associated with Almeida. "This is an unbelievably bad idea. What if he finds out? Or someone else does?"

"It's not as though she'd be alone," Diego said. "She'd have an escape plan and a retinue. Bodyguards, wearing subtle scramblers for their facial features. And an outside contact monitoring things."

So they'd already discussed this without her. Expecting she'd agree to enter the world of platinum jockstraps and obscure social codes, where she wasn't allowed to fight her way out if things got messy. "Unless you're going to let me play target practice with some of those human-experimenting assholes, count me out. Schmoozing Corte snobs isn't our line of work."

"I know civility and tact are a foreign language to you, Riven," Asa said, a flash of defiance in her eyes, "but you can't shoot your way out of everything."

Normally, the words wouldn't have bothered her. But there was an edge in Asa's voice, something *meant* to sting. Seemed her Corte arrogance hadn't completely disappeared.

Asa turned away, as if at risk of breaking into tears again. But she straightened her shoulders, avoiding Riven's gaze as she pointed to the screens. "If I can edge into this meeting, pull some strings under the guise of someone working with my father, we can use that as leverage with Boneshiver."

"And then they throw us into the fire." Kaya tapped her stylus against the table. She'd been scrawling erratic colors on her tablet, an abstract painting of trickling circuits, colliding planets, and an inexplicable pair of tits. "Or throw *Riven* into the fire, more accurately."

Riven leaned back and kicked her ankles onto the table. "I'm good for it." They'd follow her. Even if they'd probably prefer Samir, he wouldn't qualify. The first matriarch's decree was that Requiem would be ruled by women—or anyone outside the binary—for as long as cis men had ruled most of Earth. So, practically forever.

"The rest of us will be in this too," Samir said. "Each contender is allowed up to five accomplices. We'll have one extra slot."

A slot that would have been Ty's. Riven's smirk slipped as she watched the map of Himmeltor rotate. Those assholes in their skyscrapers didn't look so big from where she was sitting. There was no way she'd play by their rules.

"There's no other way we can get Boneshiver's favor?" she said. "We've got firepower, and Boneshiver has enemies. They'd be more than grateful if we took out some targets. We don't need to head to Corte."

"Can you just accept that we might have better options than bloodshed?" Asa said. "Leave this to us, for once. You don't always need to protect me."

Protect me. She'd been protecting Asa since her first day on this hell-pit. "The whole point of me becoming matriarch—"

Samir cut her off. "All right. Say this works. How long do we have to prepare?"

"In Corte time . . . the gala is tonight." Asa bit her lip. "Eleven hours from now. After that, it's about another standard day cycle before the trial starts."

Samir laced his fingers together. The carbon plating embedded into his knuckles was designed for punches, but it looked elegant on him, like silver jewelry. "I hate to be a contrarian, but we're not exactly outfitted for a Corte party. It's not as if we can ask Bria. And we can't show up in"—Samir gestured at Riven in her sweaty bra—"whatever *that* is."

Riven shrugged. "Could rob a Corte department store on our way to the party." That prompted a snicker from Kaya, who probably didn't realize she was serious.

"I have a plan for the outfitting too," Asa said. "It's another risk we'll have to take."

Riven didn't like risks as far as Corte was concerned. But if this ridiculous party was a means to an end—a foothold on the way up—Asa had better make this work.

"I hope you know what you're doing," she said. "I can only play civil for so long."

chapter 8
THIN ICE

It'd been months since Asa had needed to use her stage voice.

She cleared her throat, hoping it would come naturally once the call connected. The crew watched off camera from the other side of the meeting table, and Asa's face stared back from a thumbnail on the translucent screen. A ring light cast a warm glow over the bare hints of makeup she hoped looked *charmingly effortless* rather than *spent half an hour sobbing in Diego's bathroom.*

She refused to look at the glow hitting Riven's bare shoulders. She had to keep herself composed—her connections were the only reason the crew had a shot at this. Sealing the deal with Matriarch Cerys tonight required all of them to look the part. It required money they didn't have and a fraud transaction they couldn't charge directly to her father's heavily monitored accounts.

So she'd have to lie her way into Corte's most prestigious clothier while hacking its finance system. No pressure.

The holo answered, and a clerk with a trimmed beard appeared in front of a pinstriped wall. "Burkhard's, Avenue d'Étoiles. Can I help you?"

Asa gave a curt nod. "I need to speak to Netta Scholz. It's urgent."

"She's booked up for the next few months. I can look for an appointment, if you–"

"I think there's a misunderstanding." Asa plastered on a taut, charming smile. "Last I spoke to her, she said she'd always make room in her schedule for the Almeida family."

The clerk's eyes widened. "Asanna Almeida. *Oh.* I am so sorry, I didn't–Yes, I'll patch you through immediately."

The screen shifted to a saccharine *Please Wait!* sign over pictures of recent commissions: dresses decked in floating lace, layers of color-cycling fabrics.

"I didn't know anyone had a priority line with Burkhard's," Samir said.

"Never thought I'd see Asa in her natural habitat," Riven muttered.

Asa ignored the edge in her voice and pulled up another window. Now for the risky part.

She'd first hacked into Burkhard's financial management system years ago, almost on accident. Bored during a fitting for her fifteenth birthday gala and desperate to change the terrible v-pop album playing on the speakers, she'd cracked the store's network wide open.

She'd managed to switch the music, but she'd almost leaked the account data of a few of Cortellion's most powerful families by accident. Today, getting in would be completely on purpose.

Asa's gaze connected with Kaya's across the table. Kaya was standing by to help, but her face betrayed a hint of quiet envy. They'd been raised together, but worlds apart–Asa with press conferences and professional pressure, Kaya as the lab rat who'd dreamed of running away. It shouldn't matter any-more, but it stung.

A plump, pink-cheeked woman appeared on-screen. "Asanna Almeida. It always strikes me what a lovely young woman you're becoming. I saw footage from the exhibition earlier this year, when you were named heir. I'm sure your father is so proud."

Asa tried not to wince. "He has . . . high hopes for me."

Netta looked positively starry-eyed. "What can we do for you today?"

"It'll be a rush order." Asa bit her lip shyly. "There's been a bit of an emergency. My entourage and I need outfitting for the Marbella Charity Gala tonight." She pulled up the file she and Kaya had created—full of innocuous fashion catalog images and fit notes, with a breacher program clinging to it like a tick.

"*Marbella*?" Netta said. "I didn't realize you would be attending."

"Nobody does. Yet. Which is why I know I can count on your discretion."

A swift nod. "Of course. But . . . I'm sure you realize what a tight turnaround this is. It certainly won't be possible to create something new and bespoke—"

"Understandable. I've selected from your catalog; you can tailor everything to our body scans. I'm sending the data for you to look at, and we can be there in six hours to do a final fitting." Asa attached her file to the video chat.

Netta's brow furrowed. "I can take a look, but . . ."

She trailed off, and Asa held her breath while soft clicks punctuated the silence. When she stole a glance at her wristlet, a progress bar was winding up. The program was installing itself in Burkhard's networks.

Netta had taken the bait, and Asa had her breach.

Across the table, Kaya squeezed her eyes shut. A list of names appeared on Asa's wristlet, along with serial numbers and bank accounts. All belonging to extremely powerful people who'd have her head for doing this. If they could catch her.

Asa scanned the list, careful not to let her eyes wander too much. Names she recognized. Her father's account too—the one she couldn't have Netta charge.

She caught Kaya gesturing across the table. *Lombardi*, Kaya mouthed, the ghost of a smile playing at her lips. It wasn't a bad idea. Felix Lombardi, the family's heir, had tried to shove his tongue into Asa's mouth during the fireworks on her seventeenth birthday. His family could easily foot their bill.

"This is quite the selection. Excellent taste of course, although . . ." Netta looked like a scarni caught in a snare, the red patches on her cheeks spreading. "With today's schedule, this might not be possible."

Not good. Burkhard's was the only place Asa had a personal connection. She couldn't let this slip.

Her father would never take *no* for an answer.

"Admittedly, I'm disappointed." Asa tightened her frown, putting on the façade of the entitled heirling Netta probably expected her to be. "My family's always counted on our relationship with Burkhard's. And I hope you realize counting on you today means we can count on you in the future."

Netta's mouth opened, then closed. She finally said, "There would be . . . rush fees involved."

"As expected." Asa tapped the screen, a signal for Kaya to put the code in place. A simple bypass for Almeida's account, instructing Burkhard's system to direct the next charge to Lombardi's.

"With the rush fees," Netta said, a little dazed, "the total comes to . . . seventy-eight thousand, four hundred and thirty-five."

Samir choked on his tea across the table, but Asa didn't miss a beat. "Perfect. I knew I could count on you, Netta."

Seventy-eight thousand denar? Samir mouthed, nudging Diego. Diego shook his head, failing to suppress a grin.

Asa smiled but fought back a surprising stab of guilt. This had been her normal once. Seventy-eight thousand denar would be life-changing for her crew, but it wouldn't even dent her father's savings—and if her bypass worked, it wouldn't anyway. "I'll confirm my fingerprint scans when we arrive. I trust you can charge this all to my father's account?"

Netta looked like she'd been dragged across concrete by her ankles. "That is doable, yes."

It was all Asa could do not to sigh in relief. "Excellent. We'll see you tonight."

Once the call cut, Samir let out a low whistle. "Holy *shit*."

"You could've bought a half-decent ship with that money." Riven was sucking down a can of soda. "You've been holding out on us."

"Don't get too excited," Asa said. "We're on thin ice now. That might be the only time I can mess with Burkhard's before they get suspicious. And I hope we'll be long gone by the time the Lombardis notice."

"So what next?" Riven said. "We let some snobs grope us while we try on clothes worth more than our organs?"

Samir rolled his eyes. "There are *much* worse jobs out there."

"Is this going to end like that poetry night you organized at Grindhouse?" Riven asked. "Where one minute everyone's pretending to be interested in some poem about tit sweat, and the next they're cracking bar stools over skulls?"

"Different circumstances," Samir said. "It was a rough crowd that night."

"Samir deflecting a punch mid-poetry reading is still one of my favorite memories." Diego plugged something into the data-port on his cybernetic forearm. His secure database. "But I think tonight should be a little smoother. The only thing we'll need to pay for is the transit tickets. I'll be on the sidelines, but the three of you have a ship to catch."

Asa's stomach turned. Ever since she'd crashed a ship on Requiem with Kaya's brain in tow, going back to Cortellion had seemed like a fantasy. "I can be ready in ten minutes."

Kaya had gotten up and was settling onto the living room couch with her sketch tablet. Asa joined her. It was too dangerous to bring Kaya tonight—Luca might not care much about his runaway heir, but Kaya and her priceless brain might be tempting. Still, Asa couldn't help the spike of regret. Maybe Kaya missed the better parts of home too—the safety of hired guards, the flashy tech, the evenings spent in their tiered swimming pool.

"Kaya." She put a hand on her sister's arm and spoke in Portuguese. "Sorry you're stuck here."

"It's fine. Really." Kaya gave a wan smile. "I'll have some time to myself tonight. I've been working on a few new environments for AbyssQuest. One's a living city grown from bioluminescent plants. It'll look amazing once you get it programmed."

"Sounds great." She'd barely had time lately to work on their shared VR game world. But something else was off. Kaya was normally the one cracking jokes and planning nights out, or continuing her prank war with Samir by plastic-wrapping his pillows and replacing his playlists with *explicit* nature documentaries. But she'd barely said a word tonight. "Seriously, though, is something bothering you?"

"It's not the party, don't worry. I really didn't want to go. Never planned to go back. Hell, it feels like I already have been."

"What do you mean?"

Kaya set her stylus down. "Remember what I said earlier, about feeling less *me* in the circuits? Well, I've been having . . . dreams. Only they happen when I'm awake. Flashes of the lab. Memories, maybe? I don't know." She shrugged. "It's definitely Dad's lab. But I see rooms I don't remember being in. And hands that aren't mine."

Hands that weren't hers. A hallucination of some sort? Beneath Kaya's blue hair, faint scars were still visible at her hairline. "Do you think it's your new brain?"

"Could be," Kaya said. "Or maybe it's from being locked in circuitspace for so long. I think I become a little less human every time I'm in there."

For all she and Kaya shared, that was something Asa would never understand. "Kaya, I—"

"Like I said. I'll be fine."

Asa wrapped her sister in a hug. "We're in this together. This Redline person doesn't know who they're messing with."

Kaya pulled her tighter. "We'd better be. I hope you cause a little mayhem tonight. And maybe steal me a bottle of Alpine Summerblue while you're there?"

"It's a deal."

When she let go, Riven and Samir were waiting by the door.

"Lead the way, Lady Heiress," Samir said. "We have a ship to catch."

After seven and a half hours of weathering economy transit ships, dodging cameras, and continuing their charade through a tense fitting session, seeing the gala entrance was a jolt to the nerves.

Asa stepped out of the hired speeder and into the cool evening. Her new heels hit the holographic fibers of the entrance carpet, which carved a path up the steps like a river of stars. Glassthorn Hall rose into a mountain of polished silver pipes, reflecting the deepening sunset.

"Hot damn," Riven whispered.

"It's smaller than I remember." Asa had only been to this venue once, in the time before she'd been someone the reporters cared about. Above the crowds flooding the expanse of dark marble, the air glimmered with floating chandeliers and fairy-lights. This place was scrutinizing her, waiting to consume her. As if she were the princess from an old Phase I fairy tale, returning to a castle that'd once imprisoned her to settle her score with the monster at its apex. "Are you both ready?"

"Pretty sure Dee would kill us if we came back with nothing but a clothing haul." Samir looked even more at ease here than Asa did. In a black-and-silver jacket with pressed slacks, and a splash of kohl accenting his dark eyelashes, he made the current crowd look dull.

"Let's get this over with," Riven said. Reluctant as she was, Riven was breathtaking—her hair twisted into a magenta-and-blonde bun at the back of her neck, with small braids twining where the colors met at her ears. Her suit jacket was slung over one shoulder, revealing the dark-plum vest and dress shirt fitted over her chest.

Asa had to turn away. She'd dreamed of bringing Riven back to Corte someday—as her date, her *partner*. But tonight, Riven was only her bodyguard, even if she wouldn't be able to protect her here. They were in Asa's territory tonight.

She hadn't told Riven the other plan she'd made with Diego. They'd dug up the guest list and found a familiar name on it— the heir to a biotech firm where her father had outsourced Winterdark's chemical testing. Nox Holderness. If anyone could dig up information on Riven's condition, he could. But she and Nox hadn't been close in school, so she'd probably have to offer him something for his help.

Asa adjusted the lapels of her black jacket. It skimmed her knees, open to reveal the short red cocktail dress plunging over her sternum, as bright as the rose-petal gown she'd worn during her first stage appearance. Tonight's charade hinged on her.

She lifted her chin as they approached the doors, ignoring the shocked reporters who called to her from the entrance pillars. Riven and Samir both had subtle lines of silver across their cheekbones—scramblers to disrupt cameras and footage. A few of the more reclusive guests wore them, too, even if scramblers were regarded as snobbish with media outlets everywhere.

Asa's own face was bare.

"Good evening," the doorman said. "Names?"

Asa put on her spotlight smile. "Asanna Almeida. Here with my retinue."

SYMBIONT

Ty had lost count of how many times he'd vomited today. He gripped the edges of the waste chute, his guts heaving bile now. The simulation was disintegrating around him, the slithery fungal monsters fading to vapor. Even now, the nerve-jack left a memory of pain—of an infection spreading through his nerves like viscous poison.

Another failure. His guts gave another lurch, but there was nothing left.

"We're done," the voice boomed over the loudspeaker. "Report to the psych wing for evaluation."

"Give me thirty seconds," he gasped, slumping onto the floor. The drafts from the ventilation system ghosted across the cold sweat on his bare shoulders, and he shivered. Despite everything his nerves were telling him, he was still alive, and the fungus had been an illusion. He wondered if this was how Riven felt. Her nerves being eaten from the inside—

"Get up, AV70."

Ty closed his eyes. This place was wringing him dry. A shred of hope had pushed him to survive for the past few months—despite doctors poking at him beneath overbright laser-diode lights, despite nightmares of Emmett wheezing through his punctured lung and bullets splintering through

97

Ty's left arm, pain hot as a blowtorch. But now that hope was only a whisper.

Today, another voice commanded him, somewhere from the back of his mind.

"*Get up, Tyren,*" said Yllath. "*You'll need to be on your guard today.*"

I need to sleep, Ty thought back.

"*You want to save her, yes?*"

It hit him like a rusted nail through the chest. *Have you learned how to get into the archive?*

"*I have. And this is your last psychiatric evaluation before we'll have an opportunity to unleash hell on this lab.*"

Ty shuddered. *What do I need to do?*

"*Stay alert and listen for my instructions. But first . . . get up.*"

Ty did as he was told. The usual armed guard escorted him through the hall. This time, he was all too wary of the camera lenses glimmering down at him. Yllath was watching. Had been, for stars knew how long.

Though Yllath was in the surveillance systems, the servers here were closed, and wireless networks were scarce. He needed Ty's hands to get anywhere else. Luca had increased security since Yllath broke free, and Yllath couldn't enter most of the tech without help.

Ty's throat constricted at the thought of seeing Luca. Asa's father—the man who'd killed Emmett—hadn't visited this wing of the lab in weeks. But somehow, Yllath planned to force a confrontation.

The doors to the psych wing opened, revealing a hallway of windows overlooking sprawling rooftop greens and the silvery expanse of city below. Lights shone through a burbling alcove fountain, illuminating the white-and-gold logo of Almeida Industries emblazoned on the wall. A façade of normalcy for the salaried workers here, as if the pretty trappings could erase the simulations and bloodied labs below.

The guard waited until Ty was seated in the evaluation room before bolting the door behind him, leaving him alone with the disheveled psychiatrist whose name he'd forgotten.

She didn't spare him a glance. "I see your simulations continue to yield . . . confusing results." Lights from a massive holoscreen reflected on the scan-glass over her eyes. On the screen flashed endless windows of data—coordinates from the simulations, pictures of people Ty had described during his sessions.

Emmett's and Riven's faces flashed on the screen, lighting a buried spark of anger. *Who was the girl you stayed behind for?* the psychiatrist had asked, prodding him until he told the truth. Before that, it was: *Did you have any family, back on Earth? Did you ever try to find your mother, after she left? Did you resent having to grow up so fast to follow your brother?*

Half-conscious, he'd told her everything. The nights with the advanced chemistry textbooks, pushing to skip a grade and get a scholarship for Blackcoast's med program—just to stay near Emmett, who'd gotten into CAA's combat mechanist program in the same city. Most kids finished two years of high school before going to a specialty academy, but Ty had been fifteen.

Their dad had gotten sick right before they left for the academies. Aside from sporadic contact with their uncle, they'd been on their own—their mother had left when Ty was a baby. He wouldn't even know where to start searching for her. Not that it mattered. She'd never looked back.

Riven and Samir were the only ones he had left. His only constants. Photos of them were on the screen now, pictures dredged up from god knew where, reduced to data points in the map the lab was building of his mind. Whatever the point of all this was, he wanted no part in it.

"Maybe if I had a better idea of what you were trying to do to me, I'd perform better in the sim," Ty murmured.

The psychiatrist ignored him. "Any strange dreams lately?"

"I don't see how that's—"

"Dreams," she insisted. "Anything vivid, lifelike, out of the ordinary?"

Ty paused. He *had* dreamed of home over the past few weeks—bright, surreal glimpses he'd assumed were aftereffects of the simulator. Glowing graffiti on crumbling concrete, a pre-dawn blaze over the sawtooth skyline. Unmistakably Requiem. A home that was still out there, alive and waiting for him.

But how would she know about those? It made him want to hold the dreams closer. To hide them, the way he'd had trouble hiding everything else.

"No, nothing," Ty lied.

The psychiatrist frowned. Swiped screens aside on her tablet. "In that case, we can discuss your work on Requiem. And your background with Almeida's daughter."

Asa. Had he mentioned her in the evals before? Of course Luca knew he was on the crew that had helped her during the few days they'd been fugitives. He wondered whether

Luca knew about the kissing—the moments they'd clung to each other when it seemed the world was collapsing. "What about her?"

The psychiatrist grilled him, and Ty gave noncommittal answers. The sting of losing Asa had faded, and those days were becoming a blur. He shouldn't have fallen so fast, like always. Especially when her feelings for Riven had been clear.

But whatever Asa was to him now, she was at least a friend. The less Luca knew about her, the better. He'd already tried to kill her once.

"*Everything is in place now,*" Yllath's voice boomed. "*It's your turn.*"

Ty sat up straighter, keeping his face as blank as possible. *What do we need to do?*

"*You have the keycard to the prototype wing. Your psychiatrist has the code for the Winterdark Archive. It's inside her head.*"

Ty's heart rate accelerated. *Inside her head?*

"*I'm going to loop the cameras and block the alarms. And then you're going to take it.*"

"AV70, are you listening?" The psychiatrist's eyes bored into his.

Ty blinked. "What? Sorry."

"I said, your story has some inconsistencies about—"

"*The guards will be arriving in about ten minutes,*" Yllath continued. "*The cameras are cut. Move in.*"

What do you mean, get it out of her head?

"*Whatever happens, I will ensure your safety. I will falsify the footage in this room. You will be safe for another few days. All the time we need.*"

Ty's heart pounded. Yllath wanted him to hurt this woman.

And why shouldn't you? a voice seemed to whisper—not Yllath's, but Ty's. *How many bodies has Almeida's lab thrown out? Not just Emmett's, but soon Riven's. Soon yours.*

The adrenaline burned brighter. Ty rose until he stood over the psychiatrist. She gave him a questioning look.

"I'm sorry," he said, "but I'm going to need the passcode to the Winterdark Archive."

A short, dismissive laugh. "And why would you need that?"

He couldn't do this. Couldn't hurt her. Even if Yllath demanded it, he wouldn't. *But this is just a threat. Nothing more.*

Ty extended the mech arm.

Her eyes widened. "What are you—"

He coaxed his fingers gently around her throat.

As he lifted her onto the balls of her feet, she grabbed for his hand. At the ends of his artificial nerves, he could feel the butterfly-wing pulse in her carotids.

"Put me down," she said, with practiced professional calm. But her eyes scrambled between the security cameras and the exit. "I've already called for help."

"These walls are soundproofed," Ty said. "And the security system isn't under their control right now. Please cooperate."

A sharp intake of breath. "You know I can't do that."

"*Crush her,*" Yllath said. "*She is complicit in this operation.*"

Ty hesitated. "You know I could crush you, right?" he said softly.

"You won't hurt me," the psychiatrist said. "You've never hurt anyone."

"Squeeze tighter. Get one of the scalpels from the top drawer. She won't yield without pain."

Nausea rose in Ty's throat. As Banshee, Yllath had killed people in Olympus and conjured images of Emmett's death. Ty shouldn't be allying with this monster.

No, he thought. *I won't.*

"Then I'll do it for you. It should only take me a few minutes to override your cybernetics. Let the blood be on my hands."

Ty gritted his teeth. Yllath might be bluffing—he clearly wasn't in control of Ty yet—but he could probably do it. *No. There isn't going to be blood. On anyone's hands.* He'd seen enough blood for one lifetime.

"Except theirs. Are you ignorant to the horrors they inflict?"

Yllath wasn't wrong. If Ty ever wanted to see his friends again—if he ever wanted to escape the simulations, the endless failures and watching the people he loved die—

Ty willed some of that frustration into his hand, squeezing harder. "People can change," he murmured, as the psychiatrist gasped.

"This is a mistake, AV70." Her throat bobbed against his palm as she swallowed. She still wasn't breaking.

"She doesn't even see you as human."

Don't push me, Ty thought.

"You aren't sparing her pain because you care. It's because you're afraid. People will keep suffering beneath the empire she supports, and you're too weak-willed to stop it."

Ty worked his jaw. How many other test subjects were being forced through the sim, even now? How many more people were dying as collateral damage? This woman sat in a clean office to make a salary while people here suffered. He felt the subtle urge to *crush* until the psychiatrist broke all the secrets this place was hiding.

"*That's right,*" Yllath pressed. "*The Hawthorne girl is going to die choking on lungs full of her own blood, and it will be because you couldn't stomach—*"

"Be *quiet!*" Ty shouted. Yllath fell silent, but he heard a horrific gurgle. He realized he was clenching his cybernetic arm. Ahead of him was a pair of bulging, bloodshot eyes, a pair of hands scrabbling weakly against his.

Oh, shit.

Ty released his grip, and the psychiatrist thudded to her knees, clutching her throat and wheezing.

Nausea boiled up his throat. "I didn't mean to—"

The psychiatrist scrabbled backward, looking at him like he was a different person. Like he was something to be feared. "The Winterdark Archive . . ." Her voice was so hoarse the words barely formed. "The code is SA032548. That's all I have!"

It worked.

Dark amusement prickled at the back of his mind—Yllath's laughter. "*Excellent. Now compose yourself. The guards will be here in three minutes to escort you back.*"

Three minutes. The psychiatrist would probably tell him anything right now, and Ty was closer than he'd ever been to real answers about this place. But guilt was quickly replacing the anger.

"I don't want to harm you." Ty couldn't look her in the eye. "But I did have a few more questions. Please."

"Leave me alone." She touched the red flush on her throat, her breaths ragged. Glanced between the screens and security cameras, waiting for backup that wasn't coming.

"Why are they using me?" Ty pressed. When she hesitated, he flexed his mech fingers, making her flinch.

"This division is targeted at reprogramming neural pathways," she finally said. "Luca had you brought here because you'd decided to die for something. Psyches like that are useful—with something embedded deep enough that it overrides even their own survival instincts."

"Reprogramming." Every nerve in his body went numb. "You want to change that instinct somehow?"

She pursed her lips, nodding. It struck Ty how young she looked. "We've recovered several Etri specimens for that purpose. None with a complete brain; some salvaged, some partially grown. But it's possible to reprogram them as parts of a whole. Splice them with a human brain." She hesitated. "You already have a few pieces implanted, but they're only to connect your brain tissue to your cybernetics. Yours are sampled from the Progenitor—the one that was lost."

Lost. The one Asa had stolen to save her sister. The irreplaceable one Luca had raised hell to recover. Yllath's. "Luca has multiple Etri brains now?"

She swallowed, wetting her ragged throat. "For a while. None are complete like the first. Each is matched to a different subject. We've avoided using the same genetic sample in multiple subjects, because the ones with the same Etri tissue . . . they link, even more than normal. Subjects would sometimes go mad hearing each other."

More than normal. Was the way he was hearing Yllath *normal?*

"*That's enough,*" Yllath's voice boomed. "*They are on their way. Tell her about the footage that will leak if she talks.*"

Yllath had overtaken her computer screen. Footage played from another security camera. It showed the psychiatrist in a dimly lit room powering up a terminal that had been offline for the night. Fog billowed from a cold-storage unit as she shoved medicinal vials into a backpack.

Whether or not the footage was real . . . *You couldn't have told me sooner that you had blackmail?* Ty seethed. He might not have needed to hurt her.

"*I wanted to make sure you could do this. Now, go.*"

Ty looked the psychiatrist in the eye. "I think we can both keep secrets." He gave a pointed glance to the footage.

The psychiatrist said nothing. When the guard opened the door, she was back at her desk, the collar of her jacket zipped to cover her neck. And Ty was escorted back to his cramped quarters.

"*We only have four days left,*" Yllath said as Ty settled onto the mattress, "*before an opportunity for you to confront Almeida. And escape, if you're lucky.*"

If I'm lucky?

"*You expected this to be easy? You have your end of the bargain to fulfill still.*"

Ty puffed out a breath and curled onto his side.

"*There will come a time when you cannot scrape by without violence. When you must choose between your freedom, and the lives of those who stand in your way. You've proved you would die for your friends. But would you kill for them?"*

Ty couldn't answer that.

As the night slithered by, his cot felt hard as corrugated steel. Every time he let his mind drift, trying to lose himself in sleep, the guilt gnawed at his bones.

He'd hurt someone today. With Yllath urging him further, he might've had a death on his conscience. But the anger surging in Ty's veins, the constriction of his fingers—none of that had been Yllath's doing.

Something was changing, creeping beneath his skin. What would he have to become, to stop Almeida from hurting others?

Memories of his simulated deaths overlapped like waves, crashing and melding until they threatened to crush him. The fungus creeping over his skin, opening a honeycomb of holes in his flesh, devouring him, as invasive as Yllath's symbiosis with his head—

Ty's eyes shot open as his stomach heaved, and he choked a thin string of bile over the side of the bed. He could never inflict anything like what'd been done to him.

He pushed the hair off his sweaty forehead—hair shorn months ago, now close to the length it'd been before. It seemed like forever he'd been on his own.

Forever since his first night on Requiem, a few months after losing Emmett. When Samir had called up Riven, offering to cover half their rent when she hadn't wanted to go back to Earth. When Samir had brought back a shivering puppy from an alley behind Gnosis. When they'd pissed off a bruiser gang at a nearby club after its leader had propositioned Ty and gotten aggressive.

Riven had come home late that night. When she washed her hands in the dingy bathroom, the water in the sink was pink with blood. Not hers. It wasn't until later that Ty learned what she and Samir had done to the man who'd threatened him.

They'd always shielded him from the violence. Maybe it made him a coward that he let the blood be on their hands instead.

Ty tried to slip back into comforting memories of Requiem— into more of the too-vivid dreams he'd hallucinated in quieter moments here. He focused on the moon hanging in the sky, three hundred thousand miles from Cortellion, a point of light he'd seen from the lab windows twice. Home.

He thought of the crew's hideout, run-down but safe. Coming home sweaty after breakneck jobs, cooking up instant noodles, and collapsing on the threadbare couch while Samir and Riven argued over movie choices.

He remembered Riven on the rooftop that first night, staring defiantly over the sea of stars and city lights. *Someday*, she'd said. *The three of us. We'll steal this whole damn city.*

Then, finally, the world fell away. Ty swore he could hear it again—the distant thud of bass through the thin walls, warm chatter and laughter from the next room.

His senses sharpened, even more than in prior dreams. He tried to look up, but he wasn't in control, and the hands before him weren't his—deft, thin fingers with light brown skin, holding a stylus. His glance moved to the city out the window, the skyline in the midday sun, breathtaking.

Requiem.

Inside were walls covered in vidscreens and bookshelves crawling with mechanical spiders. Like Diego's place but arranged differently.

A tiny golden dog, collar tags jingling, hopped into his—her? their?—lap. Soft fur beneath their fingers. *Zephyr*, he realized, with a tiny spark of joy so alien it almost made him sob.

In this dream, someone was creating art. Sketching floating trees and glowing veins of light within a living city. The stylus felt solid in his fingers, the colors more vivid than a memory.

He let the dream pull him under.

chapter 10
ETIQUETTE &
OTHER BULLSHIT

Being trapped in a pit of bruttore would be preferable to whatever *this* was.

Riven craned her neck as she followed Asa and Samir down the starry carpet. The inside of the venue looked like an alien god had vomited golden flowers while tripping on glitch. Fountains spewed metallic liquid, and above, the atrium stretched into a tower of geometric lines and stacked balconies. The ceiling was so high that if the planet's gravity somehow flipped, she'd splatter on the gold-patterned arches.

The gaudiness made Riven's teeth hurt. *We get it, you're all rich.* Asa's dad had apparently donated this entire building with no skin off his nose. He probably wouldn't have noticed if their overpriced outfits had hit his bank account instead of Lombardi's. Outfits Riven was still considering pawning off for her new ship fund.

"Your table is this way, Miss Almeida," the android attendant said over the roar of conversation. It led them past the dance floor, where partygoers swayed half-assedly to limp synth beats, and ushered them toward the VIP booths. Small clusters of people in sleek dresswear chattered, and Riven caught lingering stares on her and Asa. People leaned together to whisper, sizing them up like they were socialites and not smugglers.

With every step, Riven's hackles rose. Cortellion didn't have the sour tang of danger Requiem did, but insidious threads wove through this room. She couldn't read this place like she could a scavenger bar or dirty alley. Her crew seemed to already be in some people's crosshairs.

Asa nudged her. "Riven," she said through a smile, "you're scowling at the other guests."

"Only because they're staring." They didn't deserve friendliness. No doubt a lot of nasty, unwilling sacrifices had been necessary for them to live like *this*. Even the white noise eating at Riven's nerves was just collateral damage.

At a withering look from Asa, Riven set her jaw. She had to keep the anger in check tonight.

As they settled into a circular, black-cushioned VIP booth, Asa's smile glistened like a floodlight. If she was nervous, it was impossible to tell. She greeted people in more languages than Riven recognized—Portuguese, Mandarin, German, and two others Riven couldn't place. Riven perked up hearing Spanish, the one language she knew besides English, but the conversation was about stock markets.

"Bring us a bottle of Alpine Summerblue?" Asa said to the waiter.

"And a whiskey cola," Riven added.

Samir settled into the booth next to Asa. "Oolong tea. Black, please."

The waiter raised an eyebrow at Samir, who refused alcohol on principle, but nodded and didn't dare to ID any of them. The drinking age was probably eighteen here, like most countries on Earth—Riven and Samir would qualify, but their heiress was still a few months shy.

Still, Asa would've conned the waitstaff the way she'd conned that fashion designer. She was clever and capable, and seeing her in her element—in a dress that hugged her frame perfectly, with manners she wore like a familiar coat—made Riven feel things she'd rather drown in whiskey. It was almost laughable Asa had ever wanted her. How long would Riven have been enough for a girl used to having all this?

"All right," Asa said. "Matriarch Cerys should be meeting with her contact in twenty minutes. Diego says her table is two floors up."

"As your bodyguards," Samir said, "at least one of us should go with you."

"I'll bring you along," Asa said, too quickly. "Riven, you can . . . keep watch here."

Riven grunted a reply. Seemed Asa was trying to get her out of her hair.

I know civility and tact are a foreign language to you, Riven.

Screw that. Tonight, she could be civil as hell.

Before their drinks arrived, a throng of perfect-haired intruders swaggered up to their table.

"Asanna Almeida." The boy at the front—ghost white, with a toothy smile and purple-modded eyes—gave a smug, shallow bow. "Nox said you'd be here tonight, but I didn't believe him."

"Oh! Felix. I wasn't planning on it, originally." Asa tucked a lock of dark hair behind her ear. "Been hard at work in the lab. My dad won't miss me for a night though. Hey, Nox."

One of Felix's friends gave Asa a wave. Nox was a head taller than Felix, with dark hair slicked back from the silver embedded in his cheekbones. Behind him was a redhead with a flickering crystal headpiece. Had Asa seriously invited her Corte friends for a social call? More heirlings was the last thing they needed tonight.

"You sneak off to a party like this, only to wallflower around at your table?" Felix scooted into the booth across from Riven and nodded to Samir. "Who's your escort?"

"Oh," Asa said. "He's not—um, he's my bodyguard. Both of them are."

Felix's gaze snapped to Riven, to the undone top buttons of her dress shirt. "I guess they can tag along, then. There's at least three private after-parties happening at the Walden tonight. You're welcome to be my guest . . . or date."

"Thanks, but I'll have to get back to work tonight." Asa's smile was unflappable, but Riven sensed the discomfort beneath it.

"Ouch. That's an excuse if I've ever heard one." Felix pouted, propping his chin on his fist. "There won't be reporters there tonight, you know. Our parents won't be able to complain we aren't acting like the bitter rivals they set us up to be."

Riven gritted her teeth. Asa was acting too polite to tell him to piss off, but she had somewhere to be. Worse, it felt like he was moving in on Riven's territory.

"Where've you been lately, anyway?" Felix said. "You made a big entrance at that show a few months ago, and then just disappeared into thin air. Aside from all those rumors about the *Federation* having a bounty on you."

Riven wanted to tell him where he could shove his curiosity, but after Banshee had tried to make them famous, it was hard to deflect those rumors.

Asa cut in, thankfully. "I did have a bounty on my head. For about half a day. That prank war went way too far." She broke into light laughter. "Some dolt actually tried to collect it."

Felix's eyes glazed over, as if he'd expected a more exciting answer. "Ah. Well, I just finished my third year at CAA." He picked at his fingernails, as if the braggy name-dropping had been accidental. "Learning more about what it's like to have boots on the ground while we build the new defense tech."

The pieces clicked together. Riven had gone to Central Atlantic Academy for a little over a year before her low academic scores and disciplinary record wrecked her scholarship. He would've been in her class year. Samir was only a few years ahead, so he might remember Felix too.

She recognized the name now. Felix *Lombardi*. Heir to the Ardesco empire, a military tech company that was no doubt just as dirty as Almeida's. He was probably the very same Lombardi who'd bought their outfits tonight. Riven was tempted to thank him.

"Are you still at the Naat?" Felix said, leaning too close to Asa.

Riven was about to tell him, *politely*, to eat shit, but Samir silenced her with a glare.

"Taking a hiatus," Asa said. "Company business."

The waiter arrived, sliding a frosted glass in front of Riven. "Whitehall Oak whiskey, with cola."

Riven grabbed the glass, grateful for *any* distraction from Felix's punchable cheeks.

Nox, who'd slid into the booth next to her, grimaced at her drink. "You're diluting Whitehall Oak with soda?"

Riven gave the drink a deliberate slurp. She might've poured it on his head, but tonight she was being *civil*. "I don't see why it's your business."

Nox laughed. "Fair enough. Clearly you haven't tried Appalachian Bold though. Runs ten grand a bottle." He gave a false wince, flashing artificially white teeth. "Here. They've got a few behind the bar. Want to give it a try?"

Within moments, the waiter had brought a pair of crystal shot glasses. Riven kicked one back without preamble. She'd rarely cared about whiskey brands, buying whatever was on the bottom shelf of the convenience shop whenever it hadn't been raided. The ten-thousand-denar whiskey wasn't much better—it tasted like licking a wooden cabinet and went down like a kick in the stomach. She smiled through the burn. "Good stuff."

"I'm Nox," he said. "And you? How'd you come to work for Asa Almeida?"

She should keep her mouth shut. But Asa and Samir were locked in awkward conversations across the table, too preoccupied to hold her back. Maybe she could drag Nox through the mud a bit.

"Long story." She gave him a sidelong grin, pushing a stray lock of hair behind her ear. "Maybe we can chat about it over the rest of the bottle."

Panic flashed in his eyes, and then he shrugged it away,

feigning cool. As if it were only a drop in his trust-fund bucket. "Sure." Nox flagged the waiter down. "The lady would like the rest of the bottle."

Damn. He'd actually taken the bait.

Riven wasn't sure what to do with herself. Normally it felt like cheating to get what she wanted by batting her eyelashes. But he had cash to spare. Schmoozing Cortellion heirlings was like sniping half-wit fish in a half-frozen barrel. It was almost charming.

She knocked back the rest of her whiskey cola as Felix laughed far too loud, leaning toward Asa.

"The best part is," he was saying, "if we equip all the patrol squads with it, we can make Requiem safe again. Oust the gangs from that hellhole. I swear, it'll be a revolution for Federation law enforcement. Peace treaties be damned."

"Do you really think that's . . . ethical?" Asa said. "The United Nations recognizes Requiem's autonomy for a reason."

"All those syndicates killing each other? We'd be doing them a favor."

Anger surged in Riven's gut. This dipshit had no idea what Requiem was like. And his bragging about his parents buying his way into CAA . . . it was chipping away at her civility.

To her credit, Asa looked genuinely uncomfortable. She checked her wristlet and stood up. "Well, it was nice catching up. But I've got an appointment upstairs."

"Do you need an escort?" Felix said.

Samir stood and stared down at him. "I've got her. Please let us through."

Felix sidled out of the booth. Good. Maybe he and his posse would leave.

Before she left, Asa leaned across the back of the booth toward Riven, her smile turning grim. Her hair brushed Riven's cheek and her breath brushed Riven's neck as she whispered, "I'm going up. Be safe."

"I'll do my best, my lady." Being this close sent a jolt up Riven's spine, and she took Asa's hand on impulse. She shouldn't do this—she *really* shouldn't—but Asa would know it was only to mess with Felix.

Her eyes locked with Asa's as she gave the girl's knuckles a delicate kiss, in full view of their intruders.

Asa's breath hitched, and she pulled her hand away. Samir escorted her out, shooting Riven a dirty look. One she probably deserved.

Riven poured from the whiskey bottle as a message buzzed on her wristlet.

Don't underestimate anyone here, and lay low while you can. I need to talk to one of them later.

And, dear god, stay sober.

Talk to one of them. What was Asa getting at?

Despite Riven's hopes, Felix sat back down, as if he'd decided this table was his. Another group of roving heirlings stopped by, and he scooted into the booth, inviting them to sit.

Riven was sick of him already, and the whiskey buzz wasn't helping. After all his bragging about CAA, he needed his ego taken down a peg or two. From the look of his beanpole arms, he'd been skipping training. Asa would kill her if she actually hurt him, but there was a more civil alternative.

She kicked back another shot and rolled up her dress-shirt sleeves.

After months of running around in street boots, Asa had to readjust to the strain of high heels. She kept her stride steady on the marble floor, which reflected the floating candles and fountain lights. Less than a year ago, she'd belonged here. Holographic sylphs floated among the metallic vines snaking up the walls, and champagne flowed from chalices with papery gold flaking off the rims. Off the main thoroughfare were VR demo booths and charity auction rooms, and the atrium below had a band onstage she would've been thrilled to meet in her previous life. This place had dazzled her as a child, before she'd learned the nasty secrets these people kept.

And now she was back to forge alliances, exactly as her father might've done.

"I'll stay near the balcony." Samir slid metal-plated knuckles into his pockets with his usual casual charm. "I can keep an eye on Riven from up here, and I'll be close if you need me. Give the signal if someone needs a polite stun-blast to the face."

"Thanks. It's good to have you here." Even if there was a hollow at her side where Riven should be.

Asa shook away the memory of Riven's lips brushing her knuckles, that frustratingly mischievous smirk tugging at her perfect mouth, the stray locks falling out of her ice-cream-swirl bun. The way she could work an unfamiliar room like she owned it. It had been hard not to climb into Riven's lap and kiss her profusely.

Riven had been teasing her. What if all her flirtation was nothing more than a diversion for a girl running out of time?

But even if Riven was slipping through her fingers, there was still a small hope. Asa was closer to answers than she'd been since leaving home. No doubt her father had changed all the lab passcodes, but if she managed to catch Nox after her meeting with Cerys, there could be other answers here. With any luck, she could catch him without Felix in tow.

Sorry for running off—have a meeting, she messaged Nox. *We can talk right after though?*

Asa sauntered among the third-floor booths as if she belonged, giving the bouncers a curt nod before they could check their list. She found the booth Diego had noted, its thick, soundproof curtains parted to reveal a seated woman. Asa ran a quick wristlet scan for hidden bugs. The only electrical signals she picked up were from mics and holo-projectors on the woman. As she drew closer to the booth, her wristlet signal scrambled.

It seemed the Boneshiver matriarch had her tricks.

Asa stepped up to the curtains and bowed. "Cerys. May I sit?"

Cerys's eyes narrowed behind her tinted glasses. Her hair was slicked into a thin ponytail, and her suit jacket's strategic cutouts exposed deeply tattooed skin. No way this was her real face. Either she was shrouded by mods, or this was an envoy in disguise.

"I'm waiting for someone else." Cerys sipped from her flask. When she brought it away, her burgundy lip polish remained perfect, and there was nothing on the rim of the flask. *Illusions.*

"But I heard you were here tonight, Miss Almeida. What I have yet to figure out is *why*."

"Building alliances," Asa said. "Sweetening negotiations that might otherwise be at a disadvantage."

Cerys pursed her lips, and her voice lowered. "Diego put you up to this, didn't he?" It was more an accusation than a question.

"Rumor is you could use a friend in Almeida Industries."

"An empire you no longer lead?"

Cold shot across Asa's spine. "Nobody else here knows that. My recommendation is still a very coveted one."

Cerys smiled. "As is mine." It seemed she had a good guess why Asa was here. "Jeopardizing your anonymity to meet with me tonight is . . . ballsy. As is Hawthorne sending a debutante to do her dirty work. But I already had other candidates in mind."

Asa swallowed her frustration. *Debutantes* didn't run away from home, didn't talk their way out of brawls in scavenger bars, didn't undermine the galaxy's most powerful tech-mogul and live to talk about it. "Diego said you could use the help. I can vouch for you, if you'd let—"

Footsteps approached the booth, and a man appeared between the curtains.

"Oh. Sorry to interrupt." He gave a curt bow to Cerys, making the tiny medals on his jacket lapel clink. Cerys's contact wore military-formal attire, and he looked familiar. Deep lines marred his square face, giving stark contrast to his bewilderingly blue eyes. "Should I return later?"

"No," Cerys said. "We're right on time." She shot a quick, hawkish glance at Asa, as if debating whether to send her away.

The man's eyes slid to Asa next. A cordial amusement played over his face, a smile she recognized. She'd been half his height the first time they'd met, when he'd crouched to shake her tiny hand in a formal greeting. *Reinhardt.* One of her father's allies, the leader of Eisenhaut.

"Asanna Almeida," he said. "It's a pleasure to see you here tonight. I hoped to have the privilege of speaking to your father, but this would be just as welcome."

"You know how he feels about parties," Asa said through her smile. "Another chore he prefers to outsource to his heir."

There was a calculating shift across Cerys's face. Then: "You're in luck. She's part of this conversation too." Cerys slid farther into the booth, and Asa sat carefully next to her. "Miss Almeida, I believe you're already acquainted with Perseus Reinhardt."

"Of course." Asa nodded. Based on Diego's intel, she had a good guess why Reinhardt was negotiating with Requiem's queen of whisper networks. But arms smuggling was far out of her league.

Reinhardt studied her as he sat down, as if knowing she was allied with a Requiem matriarch was forcing him to reconsider his image of her. "Having you both here is . . . unexpected. But not unwelcome." At some invisible command, the curtains slid fully shut.

Asa fought the urge to bite her fingernails. Right now, she wished she had even half her sister's effortless charm—but Kaya tended to win people over with crude jokes and wild stories.

Trust your instincts, her father had said, before her first meeting with other industry partners. *Never say too much. Leave them curious.*

Asa gave a confident nod and spun her first lie. "Cerys has worked with both my father and me."

Reinhardt looked to Cerys. "So she knows why I'm here, then."

Cerys drummed long fingers on the edge of the table. "She can provide a recommendation."

"I'll need details first." He sat back in the seat. "What couldn't you tell me over comms?"

Cerys explained, and Asa pieced the details together. Reinhardt needed to smuggle Eisenhaut's contraband prototypes through Requiem; he'd been a client of Rio Oscuro's before their falling out with the Federation. But export controls had stepped up after the fallout, bringing more red tape than a crime scene.

Boneshiver had a chance to pick up some of Rio Oscuro's old clients. Cerys needed this deal.

"This is what I was trying to tell you earlier," Cerys continued. "Reopening the old routes risks provoking the Federation. To do so endangers other syndicates in a direct violation of the Code."

Reinhardt chewed on this as Cerys pulled up maps of satellites and safe houses, of routes across both star-systems. He didn't look pleased.

"The sanctity of Requiem's Code is the first tenet of our business there," Asa piped up, hoping it would help. "Otherwise the syndicates clash, the entire colony falls into anarchy, and all arrangements are null."

"I understand the Code's importance," Reinhardt snapped. "But I need hard proof you'll have everything in place on time. We only have a week before the new regulations go into effect."

"What you require demands extensive resources," Cerys said. "New warehouses and new contacts needing payment. Making the risk to my people worth it necessitates you paying up front."

"Your syndicate's reputation is for your networks—not for your shipping routes," Reinhardt said. "If you can't prove you already have the capabilities—"

"If I may," Asa said. Here was the clinch point, where one perfect lie could tip the scales. "After the Sanctum's Edge incident, Almeida Industries almost had to cease operations on Earth. But Boneshiver knew exactly how to remove the resulting red tape. They built us a new network of contacts within three days." It stung to speak so casually about Sanctum's Edge—the early test run for Project Winterdark that had cost Riven a friend and turned her life into a ticking time bomb. "And after what just happened with the Federation, you'll need something more precise than what Rio Oscuro ever offered."

"Hmm." Reinhardt gave an approving nod, lacing his fingers together. "Then I assume Boneshiver has been helping your father facilitate Winterdark's second phase, as well. Are these the new allies on Requiem he hinted at?"

Asa froze. Second phase of Winterdark? Allies? He knew something she didn't.

"He's been coy about it. But yes." She gave a shy smile, leveling her gaze at his unsettling eyes.

"I will say," Reinhardt said to Cerys, "I'd feel much more comfortable working with someone who knows this side of the business. Someone who's moved their own tech through Alpha Centauri's dark routes."

Cerys chewed her shiny bottom lip. Asa was the missing link here, and Cerys knew it.

"And luckily, you *will* be working with her." A sly grin split Cerys's lips. "Because not only will you have Boneshiver's resources, but we plan to put Miss Almeida on the Rio Oscuro throne."

BARGAINING CHIP

When Felix's bragging shifted to an entirely wrong tirade about low-gravity combat, Riven finally snapped.

"Hey, Felix." She interrupted his conversation with a savage grin. "You went to CAA? There's something I'm curious about." She planted her elbow on the table and wriggled her fingers in challenge. "Square up."

By the looks on the heirlings' faces, she might have spat in all their drinks.

"What do you mean by that?" Felix grimaced at Riven's open palm.

What I meant was, square up, bitch, she wanted to say, but bit her tongue. "Square up. You versus me. One of us grapples the other to the table. Arm-wise."

Nox gave a dark laugh. "That sounds like a challenge." Felix jumped, and she realized Nox had kicked him under the table.

"A friendly one. What, you scared?" Riven said. A small crowd of Felix's well-dressed friends had coalesced at their table. The girl in the crystal headpiece chuckled, making eyes at her.

Felix rolled his shoulder, likely deciding whether he felt ready to get beaten. "This really isn't the place."

"Oh, really? I hear there's a rooftop garden. We could take it up there if you wanted." Probably not the best idea. After his comments about Requiem, she'd be tempted to do a lot worse to him outside.

Felix's face cracked into a curt smile. "I'm here for the party, not to indulge some bodyguard's barbaric fantasy." He motioned to his friends. "What do you say we move tables? Closer to the dance floor?"

Nox's eyes darted from Felix to Riven to the expensive-as-hell whiskey bottle, looking a little betrayed.

"As expected," Riven said, loud enough for the crowd to hear. "You talk big about CAA and cleaning up Requiem, but I'm willing to bet you wouldn't last ten seconds in that city."

By now, Felix had turned heat-reactor red. "I've partied on Requiem. Last time, we had a run-in with some Staccato bruisers at Horrorshow. But Nox and I got them to back off."

She leaned back. Despite its name, Horrorshow was one of the tamest clubs on Requiem. A favorite among rich kids. "I highly doubt that."

"And how the hell would you know?"

She took another sip of the expensive whiskey—which she probably should've sold off for her *Boomslang* v2 fund, but it was already open. "Horrorshow is in the neutral sector patrolled by the Federation, where the salirium deals go down. None of the syndicates bother with that tourist trap—especially not Staccato. Most of their territory is on the southeast edge, anyway."

Felix got a strange, probing look in his eyes. "Aren't you supposed to be Asa's bodyguard?"

Right. She was supposed to be lying low. "I've been around the system a bit."

"You mean she pulled you out of a Requiem gutter?"

Something snapped. Whiskey buzzed at the back of her mind, and damn if she was going to let them push her around. "I pulled *her* out of a Requiem gutter." She kicked her ankles onto the table. *Riven Hawthorne, commander of the Boomslang Faction*, she wanted to say. *And next in line for the Rio Oscuro throne.*

"So it's true, then." A grin twisted across Felix's face. "I thought that might be the reason Asa's entourage was wearing scramblers tonight. A few rumors make sense now."

A chill banished some of the whiskey warmth. "You mean the rumors she's been outside Requiem's kiddie-pool zones?"

"I think you know which ones I'm referring to." He glanced over the others gathered. Low murmurs rippled among them. "You mentioned the rooftop garden. We could discuss there in private if you wanted."

Riven stared at him hard. Clearly he knew something about Asa and Requiem. And saying it in front of a bunch of gossiping heirlings might make things worse. "All right, then. We'll talk."

Nox stood up to follow, but Felix motioned for him to stay put.

The others murmured as she followed Felix. The pulse rose in her ears. The danger-prickle at the back of her mind, once drowned in whiskey, came shrieking back.

Maybe getting under his skin had been a mistake. But he'd already known something, and she couldn't let him have the upper hand. She could still smooth this over, maybe.

They passed the main stage, where a glitter-faced performer sang about *taking a bullet for your love*, though they'd clearly never been shot before. A crystal staircase, lit up acid green, twisted toward the roof.

Samir's voice came through her earpiece. "Riv. Where are you going?"

He must still be watching her. "Just cleaning up a mess," she said, prompting a side-eye from Felix.

"What kind of mess?"

"I've, uh, got it. How are things on your end?"

"Negotiation's in progress, as far as I can tell."

That was good. Though the bigger problem was currently sauntering up the steps ahead of her.

In the rooftop garden, the air was clean, almost sterile, above the alien city stretching around them. Sculpted trees surrounded an empty pool. Two people sipped champagne on a lounge couch, and a lone security guard waited by the door. Otherwise, the place seemed deserted.

Felix strode toward the edge overlooking the farthest expanse of city. Riven stole a glance at her wristlet—at the security camera locations and vantages Diego had sent them before they'd left. This place had one camera on each side and two stairwells, one attended by the suited security guard.

Riven took the lead, steering them toward the concrete balustrade next to the pool maintenance hut. The only spot out of the security cameras' lines of sight, just in case things went south.

They usually did.

"Glad you got serious about squaring up," she said to break the silence.

Felix sidled up next to her. "What do you think Luca Almeida would do if he knew you were here tonight?"

Well, damn.

Riven casually pressed her back to the balustrade and crossed her arms, keeping an eye on the security guard. "Why *wouldn't* he know his daughter's bodyguard is here?"

"He might not, if she were still shacking up with Requiem smugglers." Felix's kohl-rimmed eyes flicked over her vest. "The clothes are, admittedly, impressive. Burkhard's? Fits you perfectly."

Damn. Felix knew he was onto something. Whether he'd heard about his parents' bank account was another story.

There was a telltale lump beneath his jacket. A little too squat for a handgun—probably a stunner. She had one of her own since this place forbade guns. But the security guards—including the one near the door—were probably packing.

"I don't know what you're getting at," she said. "What the hell do you want?"

"I'm not out to get you. Truly. In fact, I have a proposition you might be interested in."

She lifted her chin but said nothing.

"Asa has been remarkably difficult to get ahold of, so I was thrilled when Nox said she'd be here tonight. There were whispers she'd skipped town during that Banshee business on Requiem, but then the story was that she reconciled with her dear old dad and came home after all. Still, she's been completely absent from the social scene for months now. She's still on the run, isn't she?"

"If she were on the run, this is the last place she would be,"

Riven said. But the bluff was getting harder. Seemed he'd had this on his mind even before he sauntered up to Asa's table.

"Truth be told, I'm still figuring out why she's here. Can't just be for *Nox*." He scowled. "Before she left, there was talk about the alliance of the century between rivals Almeida Industries and Ardesco. Both our families happen to have heirs around the same age. So I'm sure you understand my interest in making sure she gets back safely."

The implication turned Riven's guts to paste. "You want to *marry her* for a business arrangement?" It sounded worse than ridiculous. As if Asa were a bargaining chip to be traded.

"Is that a problem?" An oily slyness crept into his voice.

"She wants nothing to do with you."

"You don't know what she wants. You don't know what she *had*." His tongue clicked as he sized Riven up. "And you have no idea what I could offer for your help."

You don't know what she had. Riven was beginning to realize that, and it stung. But Asa had made her choice to leave this place. "Piss off."

"She can't hide out on Requiem forever. Her dad has pawns inside the syndicates, and he's not the only one with eyes on those salirium mines. Your matriarchs won't run that place for long." Felix shrugged. "And if you won't help, I could always call Luca and ask him to reconsider attending tonight."

Riven clenched her jaw. She was walking a razor's edge here.

Movement flickered at the corner of her eye. The security guard was walking to the stairwell—either for a shift change, or for an incident elsewhere.

"If you touch Asa, or *any* member of my crew," she murmured, "you won't be ready for the hell that follows."

"Big talk from a Requiem gutter rat." Felix's voice rose a panicked octave when she grabbed his lapel, pulling him close.

"You think I won't hurt you here?" A sick sense of satisfaction washed over her at the thought of breaking him open. If he thought decorum would protect him, he was dead wrong. "Clearly you've never met a *Requiem gutter rat* with a death wish."

His hand slid toward his stunner. "This place is packed with security guards. Think carefully."

"Maybe if you'd passed basic at CAA, you wouldn't need to count on everyone else to save your ass." Her fists wrung creases into his suit jacket. "But the biggest mistake you made tonight: I'm more than Asa's bodyguard."

Before he could respond, Riven grabbed the back of his head and slammed him against the balustrade.

Miss Almeida on the Rio Oscuro throne.

Asa's next breaths were a struggle, as if all the air had been sucked out of the booth. All that power. All that pressure. A position others would kill for, and a target on her back.

She steadied herself, fixating on the holographic fish swimming beneath the surface of the glass table, as Cerys and Reinhardt launched into a discussion of Rio Oscuro's previous leadership. She should speak up, tell Cerys the candidate shouldn't be *her*, but would that jeopardize everything she'd been working for?

"Miss Almeida is a bit young," Reinhardt said, mercifully. "Much taller than when I last saw her, but—"

"She wouldn't be running the syndicate for some time," Cerys said. "Our official candidate will be someone with more experience, but Asa has considerable influence with them. For now, she'll be close to the top, and it's possible she will take the throne herself, in time."

Tension uncoiled in Asa's chest. The contender wouldn't be her. But Cerys seemed to already have plans to make Asa her pawn.

"I'll confess . . . that's brilliant," Reinhardt said. "Requiem would be in good hands."

"Thank you for the confidence," Asa said, composing herself.

"I think that's all I need to hear tonight." Reinhardt stood, straightening his jacket. "I'll ensure you have everything you need to begin. We can work out the other details via holo."

"Of course." Cerys gave him a shark's grin. After they exchanged curt pleasantries, Reinhardt left.

She'd done it. Asa should be collapsing with relief, but her thoughts kept lingering on Reinhardt's mention of *Winterdark's second phase*. Her father's new allies. The tangled secrets lurking beneath Requiem's streets. And a throne her crew was now obligated to chase.

"It seems you were the ace I needed after all." Cerys peered over her flask. "Hawthorne made the right call in sending you tonight."

"But what you promised him . . ." Asa struggled with the words. "I never agreed to take over Rio Oscuro."

"I'll need you close to the top of the syndicate as a high-level contact for certain investors. It's a caveat. If I endorse Hawthorne, I'm making you her second."

A strange, bitter feeling washed over her, deep scratches of terror and yearning. "Her second? Like an advisor?" A promise to stay by Riven's side. A commitment she wished she could make.

"More a successor." Cerys tapped her fingers on the table, and her nail varnish dissolved from turquoise to deep red. "People have been *talking* about her and your crew. Not all good, but Hawthorne has a reputation for getting things done. These roles take a little more finesse than what she tends to exhibit, but as long as you're involved, I think it'll work out. Provided my assessment is correct and your father will be nowhere near any of this."

"He won't," Asa said. "I don't expect we'll be back on Corte for a while after tonight."

Cerys gave an approving hum. "Seconds aren't usually appointed until after a matriarch ascends, but we can choose alternates during the trial, provided the contender's entire retinue hasn't been eliminated. So if Hawthorne is ever unable to proceed . . ." Cerys quirked an eyebrow, and Asa knew exactly what she wouldn't say. "The nomination would fall to you."

The tension came flaring back. Riven's health was getting worse. Horrible as the thought was, who would take over the syndicate after her? Being on Requiem without her sounded like a death sentence, even more so with the responsibility of leadership. Asa would never be ready.

Still, that had been her life for the past few months—surviving things she wasn't prepared for.

"I'll make sure she succeeds," Asa said.

"You and the Boomslang Faction will be the underdogs in the trial," Cerys said. "But I do wonder. A Cortellion tech-princess becoming a Requiem matriarch . . . now *there's* a thought." She gave a secretive grin, and there was a small, pixelated ripple near her mouth. A holo-projector to conceal facial features. "I'll contact you and Hawthorne later tonight."

"We won't disappoint you." Asa bowed and slipped out of the booth.

There was a charge in the air among the murmuring crowds. This place felt different—like the tides here had shifted while she was away. Like she no longer belonged.

Like Cortellion wanted to chew her up and swallow her whole.

But she couldn't leave yet—she still had to meet with Nox about the biotech. Convincing a boy she barely knew to deliver her sensitive data might not be easy, but compared to winning Cerys over, it should be cake.

Sure enough, her wristlet had messages from him.

Sure, we're still at your table. Then, minutes later:

Have you seen Felix? I thought he left with your friend.

Asa frowned. With her *friend*?

On cue, Riven's voice came through her earpiece. "We need to get out of here. I might've just done something stupid."

Asa bit her tongue. Of course.

"Come in, Riven, Samir," Asa said into her wristlet. "Where are you?"

"Meet us at the west emergency exit. Now," Samir said. "Avoid our table, avoid the main doors, and avoid the reporters."

"What happened?" Asa steered herself away from the balcony and roving cameras, toward the edge of the crowd. Every pair of eyes on her now seemed threatening.

"Asa." Riven's breaths were hurried. "Don't panic. But, uh, your friend Felix is out cold in a pool supply closet."

"*What*"—Asa suppressed the shriek in her voice—"*is the heir to Ardesco doing unconscious in a closet*?!"

"She can explain later," Samir said. "We're waiting for you."

"I'm on my way," Asa said. "Two minutes."

Oh god. It was a frantic loop inside her head. Had Riven hurt the heir to her father's biggest rival? Had anyone seen?

Worse, did her father know they were here?

He'd find out eventually; that was inevitable. But to have him find out during the gala, with enough time to send people after her—that would be disaster.

The bar was straight ahead, filled with charcoal-black fountains and the sultry pulse of music from the stage speakers. Mercifully, Samir and Riven were there, behind the morphing spikes of a ferrofluid sculpture. They seemed to be chatting up one of the gold-clad bartenders.

"I'm not technically allowed to switch it off," the man said as she approached.

"I'm sorry it's an inconvenience." Samir's voice was smooth as silk. His arm rested protectively over Riven, whose hair was falling out of place. "But my wife had a bad experience with one of AlphaSpace's reporters last summer, and they are *swarming* the main entrance. We tried to get a restraining order, but you know how hard it is to enforce those." He gave a sly wince. "I'm sure you understand the need for discretion."

Asa kept her mouth shut. *Wife.* The word made her chest clench a bit. At least Samir seemed to have a plan.

The bartender relented. "I . . . I don't see why not, then."

"Ah, there you are." Samir finally made eye contact with Asa, beckoning her over. "She's with us. I hope that's not a problem."

The bartender shrugged and led them to the emergency exit, swiping a keycard to disable the door alarm. Samir shot him a wink as they slipped into the cool night.

"We probably still have eyes on us," he said, when the heavy door clicked shut. "Where's our port?"

"Three blocks east." Asa kicked off her painful shoes. The concrete snagged at her pantyhose, but flat ground felt like walking on clouds right now. "Though we'll be lucky to get something cheap to Requiem tonight."

"With what money?" Riven wriggled from Samir's grip.

Samir eyed his silver-embroidered cuffs. "I've got a designer jacket. We can figure something out."

<hr>

For the second time this year, Asa found herself on a transit ship bound for Requiem.

They'd pawned off Samir's cuff links for half what they were worth and booked a private booth on a ship a few trips shy of falling apart.

The stained benches faced each other, separated by a

window into space. Asa sat across from Riven and Samir, her pantyhose snagged to hell from hopping down the streets. Beneath the roar of the vent systems, they settled into uneasy silence. There were more of those lately.

Then Riven unfolded her rumpled jacket and produced a half-empty whiskey bottle. She removed the cork and waggled it. "Pass it around. We've earned this."

Asa frowned at the name embossed on the label. "Where did you get two-thousand-denar whiskey?"

"Ten thousand." Riven took a swig, but didn't elaborate.

What in all the stars.

"Does anyone care to tell me what happened?" Asa said. Sure, they'd gotten out unscathed, but Riven had thrown away her chance to fix what mattered most.

"Felix knew," Riven said. "About you. About us."

"And you *knocked him out*?"

"I did." Zero remorse. "He had it coming."

Once Nox found out, there was probably no way he'd even *speak* to Asa. "You couldn't have deflected somehow? This is how rumors and grudges start. This is how we get half the moguls on Cortellion looking for opportunities to–"

"I had to, okay?" Riven stared out the window. "He knew you were still on the run. He wanted to keep you on Corte. Wanted to *use* you." There was a hollow space between her words, something unsaid.

Asa shivered. *Use* her. So Riven had been keeping her safe– meaning something still burned between them. Something Asa couldn't let go of no matter how much it hurt.

And yet Riven had been willing to shove that aside, even while leaving teasing kisses that still lingered on Asa's knuckles.

"We could've found another way," Asa said softly. Riven was constantly sabotaging herself, even if she didn't realize what they'd lost tonight. *However I go, it'll be like a flare, on my own terms*, she'd told Asa once. Asa would never stop trying to save her, but Riven seemed determined to make that impossible.

Riven took another swig. "Felix implied some of the Corte bigwigs have a foothold in the factions. That the matriarchs can't touch them."

"You think they have eyes on the trial?" Samir's dark eyes were trained on the starfield.

"If they know it's happening, they probably do," Asa said. "This is going to be a bigger mess than we bargained for."

"Speaking of." Samir raised an eyebrow. "You sealed our deal, right? We're in?"

A Cortellion tech-princess becoming a Requiem matriarch... now there's a thought.

"Waiting on confirmation from Cerys," she said, "but yes. We'll have to make good on some favors if we win. If we want to back out, this is our last chance."

"Why the hell would we back out?" Riven said.

Because my dad has allies on Requiem, Asa thought. No doubt he'd interfere if he knew what she'd gotten herself into. And there was still Redline to contend with.

Samir nodded. "We all agreed to this. So far, it's just as planned." He crossed his arms over the harness. "Should probably try to get some sleep. Won't have much time to rest at the hideout before the trial kicks off."

Asa leaned back against the molded headrest. This trip would take the rest of the night, and they'd only have a few hours at the hideout.

Hours passed as Cortellion shrank into the distance. Riven fell asleep with her soft lips parted, and Samir scrolled through articles with earbuds in.

Asa was halfway asleep when her wristlet buzzed. A string of recent messages—from Nox.

so. not only did you stand me up, but now Felix is in medical with a mild concussion. delirious. won't shut up about your "hot/terrifying" bodyguard

seems we'll be missing the afterparties.

where'd you run off to? was this all to settle a grudge with Felix? you're sick

Asa hit the *delete* button. What could she possibly say to that?

There was another unread message too. An unknown number.

Well done. We've put you in the running.

Be ready next Duskday, 2:30PM GMT. Await further instructions.

2:30 Greenwich Mean Time—the standard on Requiem, corresponding to Earth's Prime Meridian. Only sixteen hours away.

"Cerys put us in," Asa whispered. A new power was in reach now, a way to sustain the life she'd chosen. She'd never be able to give her friends what she had on Cortellion, but she'd make sure they had the next best thing.

Before she could turn off the screen, another message

popped up. Skimming the text sent goose bumps across her arms.

You looked stunning at the gala tonight, Asanna. You certainly are my daughter.

It seems you miss home after all. Rest assured, there is always space at the table for you and your sister.

I'm sure I can make you see reason the next time we meet.

chapter 12

DOWN YOU GO

After last night, there had to be another bounty on her head.

Riven splashed tap water on her face, quelling some of the pounding heat in her skull. Her reflection glared from the mirror. The gala makeup had smeared from sweat and rubbing her eyes, and now watery black streaks rolled down her cheeks. She looked more like herself again, with her hair shaken out and the dress suit tossed onto the laundry pile.

She might've given that heirling brain damage, and who knew what kind of fire Cortellion's high society would return. Asa's dad had his sights on them already. But someone needed to put that Corte snob in his place.

It was good to be back on her own turf, playing by rules she understood. Tonight, they had a syndicate to capture.

As she toweled off her face, a smear of red appeared on the gray cloth. She touched her ear and brought her fingers away slick with blood.

The looming fear she could usually ignore came crashing over her. The white noise had gotten bad near the end of the trip, digging into her brain like claws—not as bad as a few weeks ago, when it laid her out for an entire job, but close.

Until recently, blood had been rare. It was getting worse.

But for tonight, she had to at least *look* like she had it

together. She tossed the towel away and started combing the tangle of her hair. The comb snagged on a nasty knot—no doubt the result of falling asleep against a ship harness wearing hair clips. It was so long now, too long. She imagined a competitor grabbing a fistful and ripping it out of her scalp.

Riven pulled a switchblade out of the cabinet and hacked her hair away at the collarbones. She let six inches of silver and magenta strands fall across the sink, then combed through what was left and tied it into a high ponytail. Better.

She was halfway composed when she strode out of the tiny bathroom, zipping her exosuit.

Through the hideout's single window, sunset bled over the streets. Colors of a city waking up, as their closest star disappeared over the horizon. Samir was a silhouette of deep-blue armor plating in his own exosuit.

"There's no telling when we'll be able to come back, so make sure you bring everything you need," he called to Asa and Kaya, who were zipping tools into Asa's duffel bag. "Water. Weapons. Protein, maybe."

"*If* we'll be able to come back." Asa crossed her arms over her red-and-gray suit.

"It'll be better than staying here, waiting for someone to collect one of our blood-debts and bounties." Riven leaned against the doorframe. Despite the alarm systems here, and Diego and Kaya monitoring their networks, it was only a matter of time before nowhere was safe to hide. At least in the Ascension Trial, there were rules about killing.

Asa's eyes widened as she looked Riven over. "Riven. Oh god, your—" She pointed to Riven's ear.

Riven daubed at it with a shaking hand. Shit. Still bleeding. The blood had mixed with stray splashes of water and trickled down her neck. "Yeah. We're running out of time."

Asa stared at her for a long moment before turning away. "I'm sorry," she whispered to nobody in particular.

"We need to move out," Diego said. "Our ride will be docking in twenty minutes."

Their ride. Normally Riven wouldn't jump on an unregistered train at an abandoned station, but Cerys's orders had been clear. She'd said nothing would be thrown at them until they'd received their first task, but Riven didn't plan to let her guard down.

"I'm ready," Kaya said. Her hummingbird drone was a blur of wings next to her, cocking its head at Riven.

"Glad *someone* is," Riven said.

"It's good to have you taking the lead." Something hollow passed over Kaya's eyes. "Entering this was the right call."

Asa didn't look so sure. Whether it was Riven's leadership or the trial itself that had her on edge, it was hard to read her.

Riven nodded at Kaya. "Hope you feel the same way after initiation." They'd be doing the matriarchs' dirty work, and based on info Dee had dredged up from every previous trial, some challenges would pit contenders directly against each other. Not everyone would make it out alive.

But not everyone had taken down Banshee and crossed Luca Almeida and lived to talk about it either. She'd have a damn good crew behind her. A chance to nullify the mess they were in, making history in the process.

So why wouldn't her nerves settle already?

Samir scooped Zephyr into his arms. "I hate leaving you behind, buddy," he said as the pup licked his cheek. "Xav will take great care of you, okay?"

A smile tugged at Diego's full lips. "I swear. You and that dog."

"Don't pretend you aren't whispering sweet nothings to him when you think nobody's watching." Samir held Zephyr close to Diego's face. "Look. Look at his little tongue. I think he wants to kiss you."

"Absolutely not." Diego flinched as Zephyr pawed at him, tail wiggling. "I've seen what he does with that tongue!"

As the two tussled—Samir attempting to lick Diego's face himself, while Diego made a half-assed effort to hold him off—Riven slung her pack over her shoulder. Bullets, a water canteen, a few medi-fibers for her healing left shoulder. "Samir, get your tongue out of Dee's throat and let's go. Galateo, power back on. Emergency mode only."

There was a friendly, synthy chirp from her wristlet. "Happy to be of service, my deathless queen."

They locked up the hideout, and Riven led them into the tangle of darkening streets, following Cerys's coordinates—a maze of encrypted data and code phrases that Diego and Asa had decoded. It was finally sunset, and the shimmering heat from the pavement had faded. The shadows fell like protective shrouds.

She slid her guns from their holsters. It felt like forever since she'd held them—slick and eager, ready to deal damage at her command.

Good to be back.

The five of them looked like a syndicate of their own—exosuits fitted with bulletproof plates, patchworks of dark tones with splashes of color. Samir brought up the rear, protecting the others behind Riven. Kaya's hummingbird matched her black-and-green exosuit; it flitted after her, controlled by some command inside her head, its scan-beam darting over dripping graffiti.

The streets seemed unsettled tonight. Too empty, as if the city were holding its breath for bloodshed.

Riven rechecked their instructions. A jumble of coordinates. Unmarked train, final car. And the last note:

When he asks where you're headed, tell him the Dreamers' Nexus.

She'd heard the name before, in rumors about Requiem's past. No doubt it was code.

"What's up with this place?" Asa whispered, as if paranoid the alleys were listening. "I don't like how quiet it is."

Riven peered into the abandoned station before beckoning them inside. The place smelled like trash and spray paint. Guns raised, she wove her way through the maze of busted-out terminals with their parts long salvaged, until she came to the broken escalators.

The dirty steps stretched into darkness and dripping pipes, with burned-out fluorescent lamps above them. Her heartbeat was a steady pulse, her nerves primed to fire.

The dark only intensified as they descended the stairs. There weren't even aux lights that Rio Oscuro sometimes kept on for their operatives. Riven kept her wristlet beam on, which cast stilted shadows of *Verdugo* on the walls in front of her.

Kaya's hummingbird turned its scan-beam to blacklight, ghosting over faded graffiti. A set of hidden letters lit up, shining pale blue over the pops of color. Fresher than the paint beneath it.

DOWN YOU GO. It was followed by a string of letters and numbers.

"Looks like this is right," Diego muttered. "I'll send them the code."

The minutes stretched like hours. Riven kept checking the time. Four minutes left. Three. She bit back the metallic taste on her tongue.

Then it came—so faint at first it was indistinguishable from the surrounding city noises. The sound rose to a roar. Scarnis chittered and leaped into the vines overhead.

A light appeared far down the tracks, brightening. As the train approached, its exterior screens were blank—no destinations, no times. The windows were deeply tinted, giving no indication anyone was on board. The flawless silver exterior suggested a train far too new for an abandoned station.

As the ghost train whined to a stop, Riven kept a firm grip on her revolvers. They weren't supposed to run into trouble this early, but her instincts were prickling.

Only one door slid open—the door to the final car.

"Looks like our ride," she said. Samir nodded, his rifle at the ready.

A figure waited inside the train car. He wore stealth armor and a helmet shielding his face—one of the Duchess's operatives.

The man cocked his head. "Not many people catch this train at nightfall. Where you headed?"

Riven lifted her chin and recited the other half of the code phrase. "The Dreamers' Nexus."

The man nodded and stepped backward. "Five of you, huh? I suppose there's room."

She stepped over the gap to the train car, followed by the others. The seats were all empty. No other competitors aboard—at least, not in this car.

"Now put your weapons away," the helmeted man barked, as the train doors slammed shut.

No. Instinct pounded at the back of her head. *Weapons up. Always. I don't like this.*

Samir holstered his rifle. "We'll keep them on us, if it's all the same to you."

The operative nodded and extended a gloved hand containing five tiny pills. "Swallow these. One for each of you."

Kaya tentatively took one. Diego picked his up in gloved fingers, grimacing at it like it was a dead bug.

"I don't think so," Riven said.

Samir gave her a warning glare. "Riv, just—"

"At least one of us needs to stay conscious." She stared into the operative's glassy helmet.

"The Nexus location is confidential," the operative said. "This train doesn't even take us all the way."

Asa settled into a subway seat, kicking back the pill and swallowing hard. That had better not hurt her. What if Cerys had lied, and this was a test too?

The operative crossed his arms. "I won't ask again."

"Riv," Samir said, pill in hand, "play along."

Riven caught the glimmer of a fade-suit at the corner of her eye. Immediately, strong arms grabbed her from behind.

Her instincts took over—the years of street brawls and training all screaming at her to free herself. She knocked an elbow backward into the attacker's throat, then kicked their legs out from under them. They hit the floor with a heavy *thud* as another grabbed for her wrist, earning a knee to his gut. As the two sprawled on the ground, Riven jabbed the barrels of her guns toward their throats.

"Stop this, Hawthorne," a voice called. "You're only one false move from getting cut."

"And you're one false move from getting shot," she said. They should know better than to grab her without warning.

"Should I tell Cerys you declined her invitation?"

The fight-or-flight high dampened. She was already breaking rules, and it could cost them the trial. Slowly, she slid her guns back into their holsters.

Before she could stand, a stun-shock hit the side of her neck. Her limbs locked up as gloved hands clamped her left arm into place, then her right. More armored figures lunged from the shadows, stunners crackling.

Assholes. She'd been complying.

And so had her crew. None of them were restrained, though—Samir was still on his feet, his dark eyes fixed on Riven as if he'd considered intervening. But he raised his palms in surrender as an operative pointed a stunner at him. Asa slumped half-conscious in a seat, her clever brown eyes fluttering shut.

"Don't you *dare* touch her," Riven hissed as her voice finally returned.

"Relax. It's all protocol." The operative's fingers pressed something sticky to the pulse-point on Riven's neck, and a strange numbness blossomed from it, dampening the fury. "Should've done this from the start."

The sedative crept through her, turning her blood to wet concrete. Soon her entire body felt limp, and her head slumped against the operative's cold helmet.

"That's a good girl." He chuckled next to her ear. "They did say you'd be a feisty one."

Riven wrenched an elbow backward, running on one last burst of adrenaline. "If you talk to me like that again, I'll–"

The ground lurched as the train began to move. Her head spun harder, further, until it seemed she was falling through space.

"You'll what?" the operative whispered as the world faded. "Welcome to the trial, chickling. Let's hope you're conscious by the time it starts."

Part II

THE ASCENSION
TRIAL

chapter 13
THE DREAMERS' NEXUS

Riven woke to stinging pain in her shoulder and a mouthful of grit.

She spat, leaving a dark spot in the blue-gray sand—the color of Requiem's deserts outside the city. How far had they taken her? Her head still spun from the sedative, and her bum left shoulder throbbed. Someone had just thrown her to the ground.

"Get up," said a voice behind her.

It was probably a bad idea to tell them to *piss off* when her hands were bound. She struggled to her knees and twisted to see over her shoulder. An armored guard stood over her, holding a rifle.

They weren't the only person here. Pairs of figures stood in an arc on the blue-gray sand—half of them handcuffed. Eight were contenders, she guessed, each with a guard attending them. Riven seemed to be the only one half-conscious and thrown into the sand.

"Ah, Miss Hawthorne," a familiar voice boomed. "Lovely of you to join us."

In the dim light, her eyes adjusted slowly. The room was a cavern of marbled-purple Etri crystal, with vertical runes carved into the arching, translucent walls. No stray beams of sunset shone through—they might be underground. Only footlights refracted through the crystal, and floating drones illuminated a dais next to a pair of massive doors. A vault.

Riven fought the spinning in her skull and stumbled to her feet. The other contenders looked alert. Maybe they'd taken the pills, and her sedative patch was taking longer to wear off. The bastards could've just blindfolded her and been done with it.

"Welcome to the Dreamers' Nexus." The Duchess's voice echoed through the room. "If you've heard the stories, you know this is the heart of Requiem itself. And if you want to earn a place in Rio Oscuro, you'll need to convince us you have an interest in protecting it."

In front of the arched vault doors stood the four current matriarchs, flanking the Duchess herself. Only a flare of pix-ilation revealed they were holos.

Cerys appraised Riven from the dais, her locks of blue-black hair trickling from beneath the hood of her jacket. Sokolov, Staccato's matriarch, paced restlessly in full body armor, a hunting knife twisting in her scarred hands. Fanged Invective's matriarch was a haze of holographic shadows, with a pair of green eyes glitching in and out as she watched the competitors. The Borealis matriarch stood next to her, their embroidered robes hanging to the floor, artful keyholes ex-posing white skin modded with crystals like human jewelry.

At their center was Duchess Reyala, in a crown of gold and black braids. Instead of elegant silk wraps, she wore a seg-mented carapace of fade-tech armor—a callback to the stealth missions that had first earned her fame in the underworld.

And at stage left was a void where the Rio Oscuro matriarch would've stood. Where Riven could be standing soon.

The ritual of it all was jarring after what had happened on the train: Asa's eyes fluttering shut, the hands on Riven's neck. Nausea rose in her throat. "What did you do with our crews?"

"They will be returned to you in time. Only those close to the matriarchate are allowed in this place."

Riven stole a glance at her wristlet screen. No messages. No external signal. Of course. This place was probably interfering with any tracking on them. She sensed the empty space behind her where her crew should have been, even worse than the lightness at her hips where her guns were missing. None of the contenders seemed to have weapons on them. A sick throb at the back of her mind whispered, *Will we have to fight? Now?*

She felt the press of eyes on her. The girl next to her, with tiny cybernetic horns poking through short hair the color of bruttore blood, was sizing her up with barely concealed smugness. She looked familiar, but Riven couldn't place her.

"The final test will be within the vault," a new voice said. "If any of you get that far."

A figure flickered to life in front of the Duchess. This woman's dark hair was threaded through a headpiece of crystals and circuits, and she wore translucent plates of body armor. The chrome-fanged skull symbol of Requiem's revolution was emblazoned on her chest.

Riven recognized her from old holos. Matriarch Huifang, the first Duchess of Requiem. The rebel leader who'd won this moon its independence and established the five syndicates with her lieutenants, the first matriarchs, as their leaders.

"The Dreamers' Nexus—this very room—is where I killed the Taskmaster in 2126. It marked a turning point in Requiem's independence, forcing the United Nations to recognize this colony's autonomy. Requiem has now been a sovereign territory for sixty-two years."

Another image appeared, a holo of a man on his knees, his helmet visor shattered to expose bloodied teeth. A younger Huifang dragged herself up from the sand in front of him, lifting a serrated blade and plunging it toward his neck. The holo cut before the blow landed.

"Under my guidance, we ousted the corporations seeking to exploit the lack of human-experimentation laws in Alpha Centauri."

Riven wondered who'd put these words in the first Duchess's mouth, or if she'd recorded parts of this before her death.

"I ensured the kidnappers and rapists found themselves ripped apart in anteleon pits. And I ensured Requiem's succession would be left in capable hands."

Riven bit her tongue. Not every matriarch was the paragon of revolutionary ideals Huifang had been. Sokolov would harvest the guts of anyone who looked at her funny. Requiem's desperation bred corruption—but unlike the corps, at least they were honest about it.

"Every matriarch leaves their mark on Requiem," Huifang finished.

Duchess Reyala strode to stand next to her predecessor. "Each of you will be given a chance to become an ally for us. Someone who shares our goal of carrying on Huifang's legacy."

Riven barely had time left to leave a mark. They'd all know her name, sure. But even if her crew had fond memories of her—even after all the shit she'd put them through—would that be enough?

She could do more, even in a few short years. With a syndicate's power at her command, maybe she could make sure assholes like Luca Almeida paid for the lives they'd taken. *That* would be a legacy.

Behind Reyala, Sokolov was staring furiously at the red-haired competitor next to Riven. Both women's faces slid together in her mind—their sharp chins and prominent brow-bones. It was rumored Matriarch Sokolov had a daughter. Riven guessed the girl next to her was none other than Jayde Sokolov.

Jayde would be one of the favorites here, for sure. Especially amid rumors that Staccato's elites were packing even more force, thanks to some shady new combat implants.

Riven stole a glance at the competitor on her other side—curvaceous, with a cascade of dark hair and a lethal scar over their full lips. *Shit.* She quickly turned away. That looked like Callista Aliu, one of Fanged Invective's most notorious assassins. They'd rounded up some of Requiem's deadliest.

The pulse rose in Riven's ears, bringing some of the white noise with it. She could barely make out the others in the dark—an older woman with steel glinting off her forearms, and someone with paint-tagged clothing and a half-shaven head. Including Riven, there were nine competitors. She'd only identified two of them, and both had the potential to rip her to pieces. Things would get ugly.

"You're here because we have work for you. *Assignments*,

to help us clean up in the wake of your predecessor's betrayal. During the first task, you're forbidden from killing each other."

Not a death match, at least. Riven was in no condition for it right now.

"You will be vying for similar objectives, however," the Duchess continued. "Work with the other contenders or betray them—you'll decide how to finish the first task. Some of you might encounter former allies or acquaintances over the next few Darkdays. If they're at odds with your objectives, your loyalty to Requiem's matriarchate will dictate the choices you make."

Reyala gestured to the room with a sweep of her long fingers. "I don't expect to see all of you on this side of the grave after the final task. I suspect you knew that coming in. But if needed, you may take one final chance to bow out."

The room was deadly silent.

"Nine it is," the Duchess said. "We expect to cull the pool of contenders to six or fewer in the first round. I'll see six of you next Darkday. Until then."

Without further explanation, the Duchess's holo dissolved into pixels. The muzzle of a gun prodded Riven's spine.

"Forward," the guard barked. "Single file. It's time we get you all to the tower."

The guards escorted them into a dark, narrow corridor. Soon, light illuminated the open passenger hold of a transit ship ahead, like a frogfish lying in wait for prey. Riven's wrists itched beneath the handcuffs, and sweat dripped down the side of her neck. She had better be getting her guns back soon.

As they passed beneath a floodlight, she glimpsed dark

spots on the arm of her exosuit. Blood. From her ear again, no doubt.

A low scoff came from behind her. She turned to see Jayde smirking.

"Word of warning, Hawthorne," Jayde said. "Don't bleed all over my boots when you get yourself killed."

Asa's legs were still tingling when the crew was loaded onto a ship at gunpoint.

"You're okay," Kaya whispered, steadying her against her shoulder. "I've got you."

The ship interior was riddled with handrails and holding bars, similar to a passenger train—clearly not designed to leave atmo. Their destination had to be within the city.

Asa shook off some of the sedative fog. "Where are they taking us?"

"I'm guessing it'll be another surprise," Samir said. "Tonight is just *full* of surprises." He leaned against one of the covered windows, shielding Diego from the crowd.

Asa scanned the crowd packed like prisoners into the ship's belly. Some were weighed down with guns and gear, bulletproof vests and masks. She saw cybernetic hands hiding knives and stunners. A man with filed teeth whose face changed as he tinkered with a holo-projector. A full crew wearing matching demon masks that glowed when they passed through shadow.

The signal on her wristlet was still scrambled, killing any location data or outside comms.

"Lots of chatter around here," Kaya murmured as the tiny

hummingbird drone perched on her shoulder. "Apparently a bar in the SilCaul was taking bets on contenders already. Nobody can decide whether we're wild cards worth betting on, or underdogs who'll get axed in the first round."

Diego pressed gently on his tight curls, fidgeting behind Samir. "The favorites are probably Callista and Jayde. Maybe Airen."

"Yep." Kaya nodded. "Listen to this."

The hummingbird cocked its head, and garbled voices came through Asa's earpiece. They phased into focus as Kaya tuned the drone's frequency.

"*. . . it's no-kill for round one. Not no-harm. Callista's team will try to hamstring some of us as soon as they turn us loose.*"

"*I'd be more worried about Jayde. She'll probably kill a few for sport. Thinks she's immune to the rules because her mommy's already a matriarch.*"

Asa's tongue was dry and twitchy. In her life before, there'd been nothing she couldn't prepare for—tests, tech shows, meetings. But she was going in blind here. At least there were rules. Rules, she could deal with.

"What do you think they're doing in there?" She had to hope Riven was still safe.

"No idea." Samir's dark eyes were distant. "But Riv knows what she got herself into."

The doors opened at the back end of the transit chamber, and guards loaded another group of people in at gunpoint. The contenders. Asa glimpsed Riven's choppy, purple-streaked ponytail.

"There she is." Relief coursed through her, and she slipped

through the crowd. "Riven!" Asa threw her arms around her, harder than she'd intended.

Riven stiffened. "Asa." Slowly, she pulled backward. A glimmer of violence waited behind her eyes, but it wasn't directed at Asa. "They didn't hurt you, did they?"

Asa's skin prickled at the thought of what Riven might do if she said yes. At least Riven seemed fine, even if she looked like she'd taken a beating. Blue-gray sand clung to her exosuit, and a bruise was darkening her left cheek. "I'm okay. I'm just glad you are too."

"Good." Riven's gaze pierced the crowd. "Looks like they want us to size each other up."

"Deadeye Riven, huh?" came an unfamiliar voice. "Thought I recognized you." An older woman—probably in her fifties, with cybernetic veins covering her forearms—stood at Riven's side. "You've been catching the rumor networks on *fire* over the past few months."

Riven's eyes lit up. "Oh. Oh, *damn.* You're Scrapper Tak."

The woman extended her cybernetic arm and caught Riven in a handshake. "In the flesh. Well, mostly."

Even Asa had heard the name Takara Goto, or Scrapper Tak. A legend in this city.

"Don't you hold the interstellar speed record for the Abraxas Run?" Riven was getting unusually flustered.

"That's right." Tak winked at Asa, but still didn't let go of Riven's hand. Weird. "Your girl's got strong hands. I'll bet she treats you right."

"My . . . ? Oh, Riven's not my—" *Treats you right.* Asa's cheeks heated as Tak's meaning sank in.

Tak turned Riven's hand over, probing the palm with her thumb. "No steel in your hands, huh? I expected you'd be modded to hell, with that aim I've heard about."

Riven looked a little dazed at the compliment. She finally pulled her hand back. "Nope. My aim's mine. Only mod is the hair grafts."

Tak laughed, deepening the creases around her eyes. "Well, word of advice: go visit the mod-doc on Hangman's Row. Not only can he make your hands steady as a planet core, but you can get a little something extra. Something to get your girl *really* flustered." She smirked, flexing her cybernetic index finger.

Asa felt her face would catch fire. She and Riven had never . . . well, they hadn't gone *that* far, and not that it mattered now anyway–

"We'll keep that in mind," Riven said dismissively, her freckled cheeks stained pink.

"Clearly she's got her tricks, too, if she's your second." The older woman smirked and swaggered off, mischief in her eyes. "See you both on the ground."

Once Tak was out of earshot, Riven turned to Asa. "My *second*? What was that supposed to mean?"

"I–" She hadn't told Riven. The past few hours had been a whirlwind, and she hadn't thought it would matter. But somehow, rumors had reached Tak already. "It was part of the deal with Cerys. A way to ensure I'd make good on her favors."

Riven looked like she'd been slapped. "And you couldn't have told me sooner?"

"How does this change anything? We're both still in this together."

"Because people will want to *hurt* you. More than they already do." Riven took a shuddering breath. "You really shouldn't have hugged me. Everyone here is looking for something they can exploit, and you're a target now. For more reasons than one."

Asa's heart sank, and she was suddenly conscious of the eyes on her. Of course. Tak had been sizing them up—the mods, the probing comments about *your girl*. Already Asa was breaking unspoken rules and becoming a liability.

But her bargain with Cerys was the reason they'd gotten in. They couldn't win this unless Asa held her own.

"You can't choose all my risks for me," she said. "If you want to protect me, then focus forward and stay alive."

Riven turned away with a resigned sigh. "Let's get back. Where are the others?"

Asa led her through the crowd of silent glares and holstered weapons toward the rest of the crew. But they weren't alone. Kaya was shrinking away from a man built like a bruttore, who looked like he'd once taken a jackhammer to the face.

The conversation became clearer as Asa approached.

"—you, isn't it? That Banshee bitch," he growled. "Why the hell are they letting you into this?"

Anger scalded away some of the fear. More of these rumors. Asa hadn't dragged herself through hell to let Kaya take the blame for Yllath's destruction.

"That wasn't me," Kaya said. "We got *rid* of Banshee."

"Got rid of it, huh? When none of the best hacker syndicates could touch it? I think whoever made it disappear was intimately familiar with it." The man edged closer, and his irises glinted with something metallic—a mod of some sort. "Can't believe the Duchess didn't string out your guts for that. You're lucky the first round is no-kill, because the group of you are already at the top of everyone's shit lists."

Shit lists. Exactly what Redline had wanted.

Asa slid in front of her sister, meeting the man almost nose to nose. Maybe it was her exosuit's bulletproof plating making her brave, but she raised her chin, channeling some of Riven's reckless confidence. "Banshee wasn't my sister. Don't you dare threaten her."

"Or what?" The deep scars across his cheeks twisted. "Nobody's money would be on you, girl."

"You're right. The safest money would be on *me*." The man's scowl disappeared as Samir shoved him back with one hand. Samir's voice had taken on a deadly edge, and the man had to crane his neck to look him in the eye. "It's not a good look to be making threats before the trial starts."

"Orsen, he's right," came a smooth voice. "This isn't the time." The newcomer had cropped blue-black hair falling to one side of a perfect jawline, and they approached flanked by Riven.

"What the hell is going on here?" Riven said. "Is that *your* attack dog, Nell?"

Seemed Riven had gotten sidetracked by another contender. The newcomer—Nell—motioned for Orsen to leave. "Go cool off, Orsen. This isn't the time for making enemies."

A little late for that, Asa thought. With one last glance at Nell, Orsen stomped off.

"Friendly guy," Samir muttered.

"Sorry. He's quite keen." Nell brushed some imaginary dust off her chrome-colored body armor. "Sometimes he's all bluster, but he's loyal when it counts."

"Nell Mikos. Nice to see they didn't get all of you." Diego turned to Asa. "She was one of Rio Oscuro's few remaining . . . good apples."

Nell nodded. "Good to finally meet your crew, Diego. Banshee rumors aside, you've made quite the names for yourselves."

A chime came through the overhead speakers. "*We're lifting off. Estimated fifteen minutes until we reach the starting point. Hang on to something.*"

"Looking forward to seeing you in action." Nell grabbed Riven's hand and lifted it near her lips, as if to kiss it. "Mods or no." With a knowing smirk, Nell flitted off to her team.

Riven swallowed hard, wiping her hand on her suit. "Great. Everyone's curious about us."

No matter how badly Asa wanted to trust Nell's smooth smile—to believe at least one of the other competitors wouldn't kill her in a heartbeat—she couldn't.

As the ship lurched, she stumbled, catching one of the poles. The chatter in the cabin had quieted to tense murmurs, an uneasy peace. The ship banked and turned until it was impossible to tell which direction they'd come from. Then the shields over the windows dissolved to reveal Requiem stretching below, in rivers of chromatic light and Etri crystals refracting the fading sunset. Dusk had ignited the city like a bonfire.

The first time Asa had seen Requiem from this angle, she hadn't known what she was getting into. She'd been a runaway on a malfunctioning ship, a girl who'd betrayed her father and left behind everything she'd ever known.

This was worse. The starting point was somewhere below, and it was too late to back out. No matter how far or how fast she ran, the city was out for her blood.

As she braced for the ship's descent, a blinking light on her wristlet caught her eye. A new message. Her wristlet signal and her wireless connections were still blocked, so whoever had sent it must be inside the ship.

Pawn or not, Asanna, you're not making it far. See you in the fray.

-RL

chapter 14
THE FIRST TASK

The adrenaline high surged like poison.

Riven leaned closer to the window as the ship banked into a corkscrew descent. They circled a massive landing pad with flickering lights—the top of a twisted glass tower. Their starting point.

Her crew had their guns and gear back. The air on the ship was ripe with anxious sweat and the promise of violence. Violence that might be coming Asa's way.

Nearby, Asa clung to one of the poles like a lifeline, probably still shaken from the message she'd just showed Riven. Not only was Redline threatening her—someone *inside this ship*—but there were even more eyes on her now.

Your second. What had Cerys been thinking? Riven could pick a different successor if she took the throne, but the dread twisted deeper into her chest. If the competition got messy, she'd cut Asa loose. All of them. She'd go it alone before she let any of them get hurt.

The thrusters kicked, buffeting the ship as it made the final drop. Then the doors opened, sending a dangerous gust whipping through the ship's cabin. Riven pushed the stray hairs out of her eyes. Her nerves were a gunpowder tang at the back of her throat.

Armored guards waved them out of the ship. The crowd

broke into small clusters among the floodlights, staking claim to different parts of the tarmac. Magazines slid into guns and holo-shields unfurled as crews waited for instructions.

Samir ushered their crew aside and planted his feet in front of Diego and Kaya. Close to the edge of the landing pad, where a gap separated the tarmac from the outer rim. Riven clicked the switch on her exosuit, and the holo-helm came up. Next to her, Asa did the same. The face-shield cast a glow over her light brown skin.

Finally, a voice echoed through the loudspeakers across the pad. The Duchess. "It seems you've all arrived in one piece."

Riven caught Callista's stare across the landing pad. Thick curls spilled out of Callista's hood, and their glossy lips quirked beneath its shadow. Callista had only two team members—a wispy figure covered entirely in black, and a square-jawed man with a segmented cybernetic tail. She let her gaze drift to the other contenders—the scrawny hacker Airen and her team of mech-heads, Jayde's crew of masked bruisers who called themselves the Skyrenders, and Nell's team in matching chrome-blue body-armor.

Even if the first task was no-kill, it was good to have the exosuits. The graphene-reinforced plates would stop a bullet, though there was still a hellish bruise on her ribs where one had caught her suit in the alley. Riven crossed her arms and squared her shoulders in warning. She'd be a faster draw than the other contenders.

"I'm sure you're all itching to get acquainted with your first task." A holo of the Duchess flickered into place at the center of the landing pad. "So we'll make the explanation quick."

Holoscreens appeared around the edges of the roof, forming a grid over the city streets. Greek letters popped onto the overlay.

"Consider this a retrieval mission. We placed tracking beacons in shipments of specialty tech that have been frequently preyed upon since Rio Oscuro's fall. These past few days, six of the shipments were stolen—all, we believe, by repeat offenders." On the holo, the street grids flashed, then zoomed in on the Greek letters. "Unbeknownst to their new owners, the beacons are transmitting their locations."

Diego's gaze traveled among the screens as he whispered silently to himself.

"Only six," Samir mused, "but nine groups."

"Precisely." The Duchess's holo appeared in front of Samir, and he staggered backward. "Every group who retrieves a shipment and activates the beacon within it will proceed."

"The beacons are lodged inside the shipment cases," Sokolov's holo said in her deep accent. In the middle of the tarmac, she held a small black canister with a ring of red at its center. "You can mark one with your fingerprint"—she gave it a twist and pressed the pad of her thumb within the red ring, and it hissed open with a shower of sparks—"and it's claimed."

"We've reviewed the beacon locations and are authorizing lethal force for their retrieval if necessary," a holo of Cerys said. "But you will adhere to the Code in every interaction, and you are not to kill any of the competitors here. Any team who violates these rules will be disqualified and subject to penalties as the Code provides."

Lethal force. Even if they couldn't kill competitors, there'd be blood spilled tonight.

"What about environmental hazards?" Jayde said loudly. "Like hitting the pavement at high velocity?" Muffled laughter erupted from behind the Skyrenders' masks.

"Galateo," Riven whispered, "pinpoint shields." The little drone split into three and brought up humming shields. Galateo couldn't protect them from getting shoved off the tower, but their competitors might have other tricks.

The Duchess snapped her fingers, and all the holoscreens disappeared at once. "Rest assured, Miss Sokolov, we'll be watching. You will need to rely on more than martial force to succeed. Any technology, vehicles, or resources at your disposal, you're free to call on."

If only Riven still had *Boomslang*. Her poor ship hadn't deserved to go out like that. They were already at a disadvantage—most of the other contenders could have ships docked nearby.

A holo of a blocky number 60 glared down at them. "Once the timer hits zero, you're all free to move."

Riven's pulse roared in her ears. Three beacons were within a few miles. Grabbing transit would cost precious minutes, and most beacons probably wouldn't last more than an hour unclaimed.

The teams burst into chatter as soon as the numbers began ticking down. *57. 56.*

"Any look promising?" she asked Diego.

On his wristlet screen, he'd tacked the locations onto a map. "There's still two I can't pinpoint. But we have options.

One is constantly moving, probably on a vehicle. One's in the SilCaul underzone. One is near the mechyard, close by—that's Indigo scav territory. Number four seems to be in Bullhound's sector, and he's been on Cerys's hit list for a while."

"Veto on that one." Samir pursed his lips. "'Don't tangle with drug lords' is high on my list of Rules for Not Getting Your Ass Handed to You on Requiem."

Riven shrugged. Samir *had* compiled that list, with over one hundred rules, but she'd broken several and wasn't dead yet. She also hadn't read all of them.

The numbers kept ticking down. *43. 42.*

"Let's go for the SilCaul," she said. "Nobody will be taking ships into the underzone."

"Three groups are already chattering about that one," Kaya murmured, watching her hummingbird hop across the tarmac.

"Next option, then. How do you feel about the mechyard?" Riven asked Asa, who was fidgeting with the straps on her exo-suit. "You should be able to make short work of any patrol tech."

Asa's gaze met hers through the helm. "Whatever you need. I'll do it." There was that determined glint in her eyes, the one Riven hadn't been able to shake from her dreams.

"I'm up for anything." Kaya, to her credit, looked excited. None of the other teams had an ace quite like her.

"The bigger question is: How are we getting down?" Asa cocked her head toward the roof's edge and the streets below, a nebula of tangled colors.

The numbers turned red, ticking louder. *15. 14.*

"I hate to say this," Samir said, "but we'll probably need to take the stairs."

Riven grimaced. They were probably close to one hundred floors up, and they had no ship and no descent plan. Stairs were going to suck, but it would be safer than getting stuck in a sabotaged elevator. "Let's run for it."

The final few seconds lasted an eternity. Tension spider-webbed through the air as every group waited—safeties clicking off guns, blades unfolding.

Then the timer hit zero.

The tarmac exploded to life as squads fanned out. Smoke grenades flew around Airen's group, erupting in a purple fog. A heavy, crackling *thoom* rang out as Nell fired a concussive shot at Jayde's tower shield. Ships approached with a low hum.

Riven dodged the crackle of a stun-blast and sprinted toward the stairwell. With any luck, most teams would be too busy hailing their ships and focusing on the beacons to sabotage her team.

A blur caught her eye—a trio of watery-looking figures sprinting across the tower's edge. Fade-suits. Callista and their team. Riven prepared to fire a stun-round, but Callista didn't seem to notice her. Instead, they ran and *dived*, disappearing over the edge of the building.

Whatever kind of tech Callista was running, it was ballsy.

Riven shoved open the door to the stairwell, guns raised. Nobody waited inside, so she kept running, descending the dizzying spiral. Diego lagged after the first twenty floors, but he picked up his pace after Samir threatened to carry him.

She barely heard the hiss of a tear-gas canister hurtling down at them, or the buzz of Galateo's drones intercepting it.

She reached the bottom first and shouldered the doors open. She'd never been happier to breathe the stink of street-level air.

"Beacon Gamma," she said between ragged breaths, surveying the empty streets. Whichever matriarch commanded this territory must've advised businesses to shutter their doors tonight. "Northeast?"

"Sounds right," Samir said. "Let's cut through the alleys. Prevent anyone getting a drop on us."

After several blocks of their boots pounding the concrete, they reached the mechyard. Scrap piles rose inside a barbed-wire fence and nestled between taller buildings riddled with rusted hulls and shattered windows. A shack stood near the busted-open gate, and a taller building covered in scaffolding loomed at the far corner.

Samir was already herding the others behind cover, a graffitied bus shelter that looked like nobody had stopped there for a decade. Riven slid between him and Diego.

Her nerves were primed to fire, burning a path up her throat. She was too hopped up on adrenaline to strategize.

"That shack seems to be a security outpost," Kaya whispered as her hummingbird drone flitted over the mechyard. "As for our beacon—"

With a whirr, a turret barrel extended from a hunk of scrap and erupted in a searing beam of blue. The bird flitted sideways, and the turret burned a line into the dirt.

"Looks like their security system is on an ask-questions-later setting." Samir clicked a mag into his rifle.

"There's at least a dozen turrets in there," Kaya said. "It'll take a while to shut them down."

"Oh, there's quicker ways to shut them down." Riven peered through a crack in the shelter's back panel.

"Turrets will be priority, then," Diego said. "But our beacon's transmitting from the warehouse on the other side, and the warehouse seems to have its own security system."

"Asa and I can handle that," Kaya said. "But we'll probably need to get inside the security outpost first. We'll need covering fire."

"Sounds like a plan." Riven gave *Blackjack* a spin on her finger to quell the tremor in her nerves. Every time, she had to wonder if it'd be her last time on her feet gunning.

Her other hand must've been quivering because Asa slid her hand over the knuckles. "Hey. Don't push yourself too hard."

Riven gripped Asa's hand, if only to prove she was under control. "I know my limits. And it's not like I've ever died before." Then she pulled away, drew *Verdugo*, and turned to Samir. "Ready when you are."

Samir counted off three, and they ran.

chapter 15
DOPPELGÄNGER

Splitting the crew always left Asa's nerves a smoldering wreck.

She crouched on the concrete, exosuit stretching taut over her knees. Beside her, Kaya's breaths were shallow; she could practically feel her sister's heartbeat, steady with anticipation. Ahead, Riven and Samir sprinted from the concrete to the mechyard gravel, jumping the busted gate as the turret heads swiveled toward them. Samir unfurled the holo-shield in the bracer of his exosuit.

Thoom. Thoom.

Riven's disruptor bullets did their work, sparking the turrets to pieces. Samir's heavy fire joined hers, the bass to her treble, sniping down the remaining turrets as they dodged the lines of plasma fire.

"Samir's going to clear the outpost." Diego peered through a crack in the graffiti-smeared wall. "Be ready to run."

With the lull in the gunfire, Asa's role was slotting into place. Time for her and Kaya's part.

When Samir gave the all-clear, they ran for the gate, and he ushered them into the outpost.

The control room looked like it'd spent a decade without a maintenance call. Dilapidated cardboard boxes were stacked in front of water-stained walls, and most of the control panels were powered down. A single unconscious human guard was zip-tied to the ratty desk chair—Samir's handiwork.

"Hooking in." Kaya connected a cord from the tiny node in her neck to the control panel—a more stable connection than anything wireless. Lines of code scrolled by on the console holoscreen. "You want to monitor the bird?"

"Sounds like fun." Asa pulled up the visual on the security networks, watching the hummingbird's camera feed on her wristlet.

Kaya made hacking jobs twice as fast. With her intuitive control and Asa's knowledge of code, there was no system they couldn't get into. But a new worry crept in. If they kept using Kaya like a machine, what would happen to her?

Sometimes being in the circuits makes me feel . . . a little less me.

"If you start feeling dizzy again," Asa said, "anything at all, let me know."

Kaya flicked her blue bangs aside with a mischievous grin. "I'm good. Pretty sure the adrenaline will keep me conscious for another week." She seemed fine for now, at least.

Asa was cracking the securities when Diego's voice came through.

"Hey. Two of the beacons have already been claimed by Tak and Callista. And I'm seeing a ship circling above us—looks like Jayde Sokolov's crew. Be on the defensive."

Not good. That meant four beacons left, and seven teams gunning for them.

"Jayde's going to have a lot of regrets if she tries to take it,"

Riven growled on the comm. "Is the warehouse clear? I need to grab this thing before they get here."

"A few tweaks, and . . . there," Asa said. The on-screen diagram of the lock system dimmed. "Warehouse is unlocked."

"Perfect timing," Kaya said. "I got the drones offline too."

"You're good to head in, Riv," Samir said. "I'll stay at the perimeter."

The next few minutes were agonizingly quiet. Asa could hear her own breaths rattling in the dark. *Come on, Riven.* They were so close to being finished with this task and on their way back to safety.

"Asa. Do you hear that?" Kaya was still plugged into the control panel, watching.

"Hear what?" From out here, the circuits seemed so quiet. Kaya had once described their rhythms, their symphony, another perspective Asa would never understand.

Kaya held a finger to her lips. Something shuffled in the darkened maze of control consoles.

Asa slid her stunner out of its holster and nodded. *It's probably just a spineback rooting through trash*, she tried to reassure herself.

Riven's voice came through the comm again. "Signal was coming from a lunchbox-looking thing. This contains our beacon?"

"I think so. Did you activate it?" Samir said.

"About to—" Her voice gave way to hard breathing and the crackle of her comm being jostled. Then swearing, plasma sizzling. "I thought you had security offline in here!"

Kaya stuttered. "I—I *did*. It should be—"

"I'll claim it when I'm not being shot at!" Riven said, breathless.

Oh no. Kaya should still have security locked down. Unless something had gone very wrong.

"Riven. Get to the roof hatch," Asa said. "Should be your closest exit!"

"*Already on it!*"

At the corner of Asa's eye, the light from one of the dead control panels flickered on. The static buzz was faint at first, then grew louder. "Kaya?"

Kaya held up a hand, her dark brows knitted in concentration. "Hang on. There's . . . something here."

Asa turned to the camera feed. Relief doused some of her nerves as Riven emerged from the warehouse roof hatch, unscathed, a silvery case under one arm.

But a whirring was building outside, growing louder, and a needle-shaped ship crawled into view on the screen. *Skyrenders* was scrawled on the side.

Riven swore on the comm as the ship stopped directly above her. She was hitting the latches on the beacon case when someone leaped from the ship hatch. Tiny cybernetic horns poked through red hair, glowing to match the fangs on her half-mask. Jayde.

Jayde slammed a crackling stun-bat down at Riven as she landed. Riven twisted out of the way, holding the beacon's case like a shield, but the bat smacked her square on the wrist, sending the case skittering across the concrete.

Diego swore. "They were waiting for us to take down those turrets!"

Riven scrambled back to her feet, drawing one revolver and her blade. The case lay between her and Jayde, and her back was to the rickety tower of maintenance scaffolding at the roof's edge.

"Riven's in trouble," Asa said. "Samir, are you nearby?"

"I'm on the ground. Don't have a visual on Jayde yet, but–" The rest of his words were drowned in static. On Asa's wristlet, the hummingbird's camera feed went out too. Kaya held a hand to her chest, gasping, as the control room lights flickered.

"Samir, Riven," Kaya murmured into her comm. "Someone's definitely here."

"You mean the Skyrenders?" Diego said.

"No," Asa said. "In here. With us." But the comm cut out, buzzing with static.

Something was drawing closer. Footsteps coursed through the dark.

"We need to go." Asa pointed to the door at the other side of the maze of consoles.

Kaya let out a choked gasp, bracing herself against the control panel. Fear trickled into Asa's bones. The control panel screens were locking up. Someone was trying to overload Kaya through her neural link–someone who knew the circuits like she did.

"They're back," Kaya whispered. "It's the same thing from the fighting pits–"

"I thought you'd learned your lesson, Kaya Almeida." The voice slithered through the dark corners of the room, eerily familiar.

The control panel gave a high-pitched whine. Kaya collapsed, clutching her temple. "Get out of my head."

Asa whirled toward the voice, raising her stunner. "Get away from her!" she said, hoping she sounded more threatening than she felt.

A black-clad figure materialized before her, the fade-suit darkening into armor like ink dropped into water. They surveyed Asa from behind a tinted helmet.

"Put the stunner away, Asanna." Their forearm splintered into metal shards and morphed into a crackling blade with a glowing red edge.

"And if you call for help . . ." An identical voice joined Redline's from the dark as a twin form materialized, wielding a rifle. "I'll destroy your friends like I destroyed your ship."

chapter 16
REDLINE

If Jayde expected her to back off, she was in for a nasty surprise.

Riven slid her finger onto *Verdugo*'s trigger and let the tech-blade unfold in her left hand. The beacon, their key to the first trial, lay on the concrete roof between her and Jayde.

"Callista swiped Beacon Epsilon from me," Jayde said, brandishing her stun-bat. In her other hand, a small staff spread into a pattern of gold hexagons—her tower shield. She glared through the translucent layer. "I'm paying it forward."

A rush of wind made the scaffolding creak behind Riven.

"Your ship would've been scrap metal if we hadn't disabled the turrets," Riven said. She'd need perfect shots to do anything to Jayde's armor. Riven was more mobile in her exosuit, but there wasn't much room to maneuver up here. Jayde would bull-rush her off the edge, and it'd be a long drop. "But it seems you're used to having everything handed to you. Your mommy probably makes sure of that."

Jayde looked ready to spit fire. "She hasn't given me anything. This trial's for *me*."

Then she charged, bludgeoning a hail of blows. Riven caught a few on her blade, leaving nicks on the bat's sparking edge, and leveled a shot at Jayde's shoulder.

But Jayde was good with a stick. Her next blow was a

feint—swinging wide of Riven's blade and slamming into her injured shoulder. The stun-blast dispersed over Riven's exo-suit, but the pain knocked her to her knees.

"Thought you were favoring that shoulder." Jayde wound up for another hit.

Riven rolled out of the way as Jayde's bat came down again, buzzing onto the concrete roof.

Now.

As Jayde lunged, her shield left an opening. Riven pointed her iron sights straight at the tiny gap where Jayde's thigh plates met her knee.

The bullet went just deep enough. Jayde howled in pain as dark blood burbled over her leg. She'd gotten blood on her boots after all.

Riven hurled another shot at Jayde's stick-jockeying hand. The bullet flattened on the armor but forced her to drop the bat. Riven lunged, grabbed it, and hurled it over the roof's edge.

She clipped the sword back onto her belt and snapped up the beacon case, wishing Samir were close enough to catch it on the ground. Jayde was already back on her feet, shield raised. Riven ran to the scaffold's edge and swung down.

The entire building rocked, seconds before a blast punched Riven's eardrums. Metal tore as the scaffold tilted viciously.

Then she was falling, twisting, lights blurring by. She groped desperately at the jungle of metal bars and caught one beneath her shoulder, sending pain rocketing through her.

She clung to the bars and looked up. The whole building had gone dark. An ugly hole had been torn in the scaffolding and the roof's concrete edge. Something had exploded.

Where had that come from? Spots crawled across her vision, and her ears rang as the white noise thrummed in her skull. She caught a glimmer of red in the balcony of a taller building nearby. A figure in a black helmet, staring through the sights of a rocket launcher.

That definitely wasn't a no-kill weapon.

Riven sidled across the bars, climbing her way down. A few more feet, and she could drop. Her instincts warred in indecision—*Get to cover. Keep your team safe. Get the beacon*—

The beacon.

She'd dropped the case. There it was below, a gleam of silver within the cage of metal at the scaffold's base. Jayde was limping toward it, her shield retracting.

Jayde opened the case and removed the beacon. She slammed her thumb against it until the light flashed. It was claimed.

Hell and a half. Riven dropped the last few feet to the ground, drawing *Verdugo.* That beacon had been *hers.* She should light Jayde up for the cheap trick—that explosion could've killed her.

A loud *thoom* rang from above, and Riven barely managed to duck as another rocket punched through the scaffold, tearing the metal apart and throwing shards of shrapnel.

"You've gotten your beacon," Riven called to Jayde, breaths ragged. "Why the hell are your teammates trying to kill us?"

"That isn't one of mine." Jayde aimed her shield at the roof, for all the good it'd do against a goddamn explosive. "I thought it was yours!"

Riven peered at the balcony. The black-clad figure still stared down at them. From this angle, she could see red glowing through the tinted helmet. Not a Skyrenders mask.

The name *Redline* came whispering back. Suddenly the beacon was the least of their problems.

The gunner wasn't after the beacon. Redline was after her crew.

Redline had them cornered.

The two figures loomed in front of the control room door like wraiths, blocking Asa and Kaya's escape. Asa's heart hammered. She wanted to tell her sister to send a mental message through their comm system, to call for help. But Kaya was barely clinging to consciousness, and Redline might intercept their signal either way.

They were trapped.

The first figure's crackling blade angled toward Asa. "Drop it."

The stunner probably wouldn't help her. Asa raised her palms, letting it fall from her fingers.

"Luca Almeida's heir, in the flesh," one Redline said. Behind both tinted helmets, pairs of red Xs lit up where eyes would be. "The culmination of so many aspirations."

The blade drew closer to her throat. Asa stepped backward until she hit the wall.

"Leave my sister out of this," she hissed. Whatever Redline's grudge against her—whether there was anything human controlling those suits at all—they had to know Kaya had only been a victim of her father's.

Redline barked a caustic laugh. "Your *sister*? It's not her you should be worried about." The figure surveyed her down the blade's edge. "You're the one at fault. Do you realize how many people your empire has killed, and how many more have suffered?"

"I renounced my father and everything his *empire* stood for," Asa said. Her legs felt impossibly weak. She should crumple to the floor and beg for her life, but a new instinct was taking over. *Keep them talking*, she told herself. *There's something here you're missing.*

"You still chose not to stop him. And even if you didn't choose to be, you're his spawn. His tool." The red Xs behind the visor flickered. "The world needs to know Banshee was his fault. And yours."

Asa felt a stab of indignation. It had been all she could do to escape with Kaya. Taking down the labs was unfathomable. "What could I have done?"

"You could have gone back for the one you lost," Redline said. "And no matter how you try to run, being his heir is in your bones. Echofall is coming, and you being alive makes it more likely he'll succeed."

Echofall. Reinhardt had mentioned a second phase of Winterdark, but she'd never heard the name Echofall. And what did Redline mean about the one she'd lost?

Before Asa could interject, Redline lunged, twisting the blade toward her throat.

Then they froze.

Kaya staggered to her feet, her teeth clenched as if she'd murder Redline with her gaze alone. Redline's head swiveled toward her—and then they jerked like a puppet, plunging the sizzling blade into their own stomach. It dug into the armor plates, bursting into a shower of red sparks.

"We're not *anyone's* tools," Kaya spat. The first Redline dropped to the ground, motionless, the ugly fissure on their stomach sparking. Kaya stumbled, and Asa ran to catch her.

"Oh my god, Asa." Kaya wiped the blood trickling from her mouth. "Are you okay?"

"Yes," Asa choked out. "But . . ." There was a corpse at their feet. She remembered the competition's no-kill rule, the Duchess's wrathful eyes.

But the wound on the corpse's stomach was riddled with severed wires and circuit boards. No blood. Not technically a kill.

"They're only mechs." Kaya's eyelids fluttered as she braced herself against a control panel. "Someone's still controlling them."

"Is that the best you can do?" came Redline's voice from the shadows. The second mech lifted its rifle. "This will only take a moment."

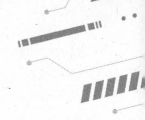

chapter 17
BARGAIN

The beacon was a lost cause, but they were about to lose a lot more.

Riven sprinted across the mechyard, tasting blood at the back of her throat. Samir's shots rang out, aimed for the rocketeer above them, but she couldn't focus on anything but the control room where Asa should be. Asa's and Kaya's comms had fizzled into static. Riven had a feeling their saboteur hadn't come alone.

She kicked open the door to the control room, guns out.

Kaya was barely conscious, collapsed near a control panel. On the ground next to her was a corpse with its stomach torn open, wires exposed, black armor identical to the figure on the roof.

And Asa was backed against the wall, facing another figure with red Xs for eyes. One whose rifle was leveled straight at her heart.

Riven didn't think twice before lighting Redline up.

Maybe a single bullet would've done the job, but they'd lost the beacon because of Redline. They were unsafe in their own city because of this creep. Redline deserved to be nothing but a smoking ruin.

Disruptors, live rounds, and stun bullets peppered Redline's form, punching smoldering holes through the black metal.

Even after Redline had dropped the rifle and collapsed, Riven fired until both her revolvers were empty.

"Bastard." She swung out one cylinder and let the empty bullet casings rain on the ground.

"*Riven.*" Asa uttered her name in soft relief. Then she ran to her sister's side. "Kaya. Talk to me, please—"

Samir burst through the door, followed by Diego. "Mechyard is clear." He swept the barrel of his rifle over the room, pausing at the two scrap-metal corpses. "Shit, there were more of them?"

"Did you get the one on the balcony?" Riven snapped the reloaded cylinder back into *Blackjack.*

"I tagged them. Got them to drop the weapon before they ran off. I didn't realize we were dealing with multiple." Samir's gaze snapped to Kaya on the ground. "What happened to Kay?"

Asa bit back tears. "Redline tried to trap her in the circuits again, but she fought back. She took down the first one. But then . . ." She brushed a lock of ocean-blue hair off her sister's cheek. "Come on, Kay. Tell me you're all right."

Samir knelt beside her. "Kaya. Hey." He patted Kaya's cheek. "You need to wake up. I'm about to put slugs in your toothpaste."

Kaya groaned, stirring slightly.

"That's it. Rise and shine, chickling." Samir gently lifted her limp form. "We need to get her out of here."

"Redline's not going to stop chasing us," Asa said, shivering. "They said my dad is working on something new. Something they think involves me."

"Then they're going to learn *fast* what happens when they

back us into a corner." Riven's skull pounded, and the pain trickled down her spine to her lungs. She'd beaten Jayde. She should've *had* that beacon. She fired another spiteful bullet into the nearest Redline corpse, making Asa wince.

She couldn't even think straight. Everything she'd fought for was falling through her fingers like water. No doubt getting cut from the trial would earn them worse than a *thanks for playing* message. Either they'd be stranded on the streets as Redline's thugs closed in, or the Duchess already had a fate planned for the contenders who didn't make it.

There had to be another way.

"Pull up the map, Dee," Riven said. "If there are any beacons left, we're taking one."

Diego rolled his eyes, mumbling something about *asking nicely* as he opened his holoscreen. "Looks like Callista's captured two. They're probably eliminating as many other teams as they can."

"Show-off."

"Jayde, Nell, and Tak have claimed beacons too. But Beacon Zeta is still up."

From his tone, there was a catch. "And? Where is it?"

"It's . . . moving. Toward us."

"Let me see that." Riven leaned closer to his screen layout. Sure enough, the zeta symbol was sliding through the street grid, just around the corner from them.

Riven thumbed the hammers of her revolvers. Something was on its way. "Get Kaya to safety. I'm going after that beacon." She had to finish this before the sickness pulled her under. Another episode was creeping up.

"Do you have a plan?" Asa said.

Riven shrugged. "Fight a bitch. Steal their beacon. Win."

"It could be a trap. What if Redline's messing with us?" *You're going to get yourself killed*, said the pleading look in Asa's eyes. But what else was new?

"Do any of you *want* to get eliminated?"

Nobody responded.

Outside the door was the growing hum of an approaching speeder. They wouldn't be able to catch it on foot. Riven grabbed the door handle, prepared to shoot out the speeder's thrusters, but Dee's map showed the zeta symbol *slowing*. As if the final beacon was paying them a visit.

Something was off. Riven motioned for the others to take cover, and they shuffled into place.

The speeder hum silenced. She pressed her back next to the door, her guns parallel to her head. Her team was dead quiet as footsteps approached, accompanied by the whir of a mech—or cybernetics.

The door burst open. A familiar, cloying scent drifted into the room. Riven's stomach dropped when she recognized it.

"Hmm. This is either a surprise party or an ambush," said the overly saccharine voice of Riven's worst nightmare. A nightmare she'd had the chance to stamp out, and didn't. "And it's not my birthday, so . . . come on out. I just want to talk."

Riven's pulse thundered. The scent of bubble gum and cigarettes was chokingly close. She shoved *Verdugo*'s business end into the woman's face. "You'd better talk fast, then."

The smaller woman's face lit up like the Crush after dark. She looked exactly how Riven remembered—bulletproof vest with pink buckles, butterfly clips on her hair buns. And there, clutched in her pink-taloned fingers, was Beacon Zeta's case.

"You're looking for this." A bubble grew between Morphett Slade's shimmery lips, then popped. "So let's make a bargain."

<hr />

Dread spiked through Asa at the sound of Morphett's voice.

She steadied her breathing as she crouched behind an old storage cabinet. Last time she'd seen Morphett, the woman had tried to kidnap her for her father's bounty, and attacked Riven and the crew for getting in her way. After Riven had left Morphett alive, Asa'd had the horrible feeling she'd be back eventually.

And now, somehow, Morphett had their final beacon. It'd taken several bullets and an EMP to get Morphett out of their hair last time. This wouldn't end well if it came to a fight.

"What the hell," Riven said. "You didn't kill anyone for that, did you?"

"Just a few drug lords." Morphett picked blood from under her bright fingernails. "None of the other teams, if that's what you're asking."

"And you did this just to bargain with us?" Riven said.

Samir slid out from cover near Asa, his rifle raised. Diego knelt next to Kaya, whose chest still rose and fell with breath. This would be a bad time for her to wake up.

"Word is you still have an open slot on your team. Your rosters aren't officially locked until you pass the first task." Morphett twisted one of her DNA-spiral curls—caramel brown, darker at the roots. "And I hate to admit it, but the group of you? Competent."

"You have to be *kidding* me," Samir said.

"Thought you would've formed your own team," Riven said.

"God no. I don't want to be a matriarch." Morphett spat her wad of gum onto the grimy floor. "But there's been a recent development in my search for a certain someone. Trail leads right into Rio Oscuro. Some nasty business there." Her eyes darkened, sobering. "Something I haven't gotten to finish."

"Sounds like revenge," Samir said.

"Doesn't concern you," Morphett snapped. With a mechanical whine, a surgical-steel arm segmented like a scorpion tail unfurled from her back. The claw at its end gently took the blood-streaked silver case from her hand, hanging it in front of her.

Riven glared at the claw. "How do you even have room for those?"

"Optimization. Ultralight materials. And a *really* good mod-doc." Morphett used her newly free hands to light a cigarette. "That's my offer though. I keep you in the competition, you let me on your team, and at the end of it all, you give me access to Rio Oscuro's networks, data, everything."

Riven narrowed her eyes. "Absolutely not. How about you hand it over because you owe me for not killing you?"

Morphett laughed. "I don't owe you *shit*. That was your choice, not mine." Her voice became a soft singsong. "You know, there's still four other groups without beacons. I know they'd *love* to have this fall into their laps—"

"Wait." Asa stood, holding her hands up to avoid provoking

any violence. "Riven. I think we need to give her a chance." They weren't in any position to fight Morphett. Not with Kaya vulnerable and unconscious. Not with Riven still staggering from those rocket blasts.

"Ah, your girlfriend has some sense," Morphett said.

"How do we know you're not affiliated with Redline?" Samir nudged one of the sparking mechs with his boot.

Morphett raised an eyebrow. "Red *what*, now?"

Asa pursed her lips. "Whoever sent the last Redline message was on the dropship. The signal was blocked, so it couldn't have been a proxy. And if Morphett isn't in the trial–"

"Yet," Morphett mumbled.

"–that, at least, wasn't her."

Samir chewed on the thought, then nodded slowly.

"I don't know what any of you are talking about," Morphett said. "But you've got enemies. I'm offering you the chance to have one less, and to keep your spot. This beacon's still tracking, you know—the other teams will be here any second."

Riven grumbled something under her breath. Her guns were still aimed at Morphett's skull. She was going to ruin this for them unless she held back, just *once*.

"Riven," Asa called. "Stand down."

Riven looked surprised at the command. But grudgingly, she took a step backward.

Asa approached Morphett, squaring her shoulders. This dangerous alliance was the only way to keep her crew safe. *Sometimes you need to make deals with demons*, her father had said. Asa hated that she was hearing his voice even now.

But to win, maybe she'd need to be a little more like him.

"We're willing to overlook your first impression if you're useful," she said. "So if you hand us the beacon—and help us through the next trials—we promise you'll get whatever data you need."

"It's on you if she tries to kill us," Riven rasped.

Asa bit her lip. The hum of engines was approaching outside. Shouts. Other teams were closing in.

If Morphett helped them through this trial, they might have a shot. With the right threats, she'd stay in line—everyone did. Asa just had to stay in control. Couldn't let Morphett sense her fear.

"If anything goes wrong . . ." Asa shrugged blithely. "I'm sure Morphett's heard about how Kaya destroyed Banshee. She must know her cybernetics aren't safe either."

"Maybe I'll check your bluff on that when she's conscious." Morphett chuckled. "Sounds like you have a deal." She tossed Asa the case. Asa fumbled a bit, but caught it.

"Welcome to the team." Asa opened the case and found the beacon among a collection of shimmering vials—the Duchess's cargo. She handed the beacon to her gunslinger. "Riven?"

"Fine," Riven grumbled, keeping her eyes on Morphett. "You're in." She tucked her guns away, then twisted the beacon and held her thumb to the scanner.

"*You've claimed Beacon Zeta,*" said a synthy voice in their comm channel. "*Well done. For the next phase, you'll convene at Tempest tonight. Instructions to follow.*"

As the voice cut out, a message appeared from a blocked number she was already sick of. A taunt.

Hope you're not afraid to get wet.

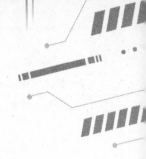

chapter 18
THE BOY IN
THE MIRROR

Victory had never tasted so bitter.

The rest of Riven's crew was trying to shake off their near-death experience, jostling and cracking jokes as they walked the night-shocked streets toward Tempest.

But she couldn't. Getting the beacon felt like cheating, and now they were indebted to Morphett Slade, of all people. Someone she wasn't looking forward to seeing again tonight.

Riven should have crushed that trial alone. And maybe she would've, if Redline hadn't interfered. It had been too close. Close enough that they might not survive this.

"I'm excited to finally see Tempest in all its slimy, chlorinated glory," Kaya said, lugging a duffel bag over her shoulder. "This is the first time it's been open since I've been here."

Samir gave her a lopsided grin. "Yeah. The water probably hasn't been filtered since then either. But if a cocktail of bodily fluids on the waterslides sounds like your idea of a good time, have at it."

"The new owners probably did *some* cleaning," Diego said. "The matriarchs and their envoys will be there tonight. Probably VIP and invite only, and anyone else the Duchess wants to keep an eye on us."

Riven carried their blood-streaked case of stolen cargo and hooked her thumb into the shallow pockets of her shorts. She regretted letting Kaya pick their outfits. Kaya'd insisted they didn't need exosuits for *one night* and dug up the gaudy techwear a previous client had gifted them. Purple diode lights speckled Riven's hooded vest, and Asa was as distracting as ever in a fitted carbon-silver jacket.

Diego was right—they'd be scrutinized tonight. Ever since they'd parked their beat-up speeder at the nearby garage, a charge had been building in the streets, as if demons traced in neon and greasy smoke waited in every alley.

"So it'll be a party, then." Kaya cracked her knuckles. Her hands were still trembling after Redline's attack. Asa had mentioned it was a side effect of her circuit dives, but she'd also mentioned her worry about how circuitspace was changing her sister. There might be a piece missing here, something Riven hadn't figured out yet. "Maybe I'll dunk you first," Kaya said to Samir, "to test the water."

"Would love to see you try," he said. "I'll probably throw Dee in first. He could use a cooling off."

"We still need to lie low, you know," Diego said. "Tempest isn't far from where I traced one of Samir's comm trackers. A small faction was monitoring us until I gave them a few compelling reasons to back off, but there's no telling how long they'll leave us alone."

More blackmail. Diego had been busy.

"Good to know," Samir said. "But we'll be fine for one night. Smaller factions are the least of our worries."

"Do what you want," Diego muttered. "But not all of us can

run away when this is over." His eyes widened, as if he realized he'd said too much.

Samir stopped. "What's that supposed to mean?" He threw Riven a questioning glare, and she shrugged. She hadn't mentioned his job offer to Diego, or anyone.

Diego wouldn't meet Samir's gaze, and a stifling quiet fizzed between them. Finally, Samir said, "I guess I shouldn't be surprised you know my mom contacted me."

"I had to monitor your comms," Diego said.

Samir drew closer to him. "*All* of them?"

"Why didn't you tell me?" Diego was receding into something steel-hard and impassable. His default. Riven hadn't seen it in a while.

"You think this would be an easy thing to break? While everything's so uncertain?" Samir swallowed hard. "It's not as if you've ever told *me* anything. Even your name—"

"Can we stop?" Asa said. "This is the last thing we need right now." She started walking again, leading them forward, her arms wrapped around herself in her *don't touch me* stance. "Redline will probably be there tonight. Or at least tied to someone who is."

Asa was right. None of their crew's stolen kisses would mean anything if they didn't get out of this alive. It was possible Redline was watching them even now.

Kaya's hummingbird flitted alongside Riven, its eye lenses glassy. A thought scraped at her. "Are we sure there isn't something we're not seeing here?" The message inside the competition ship. Kaya blacking out twice while trapped in the circuits.

"Redline had control of those mech bodies. And when Kaya took over the warehouse security system, it started firing on me."

Asa stopped dead in her tracks. "Are you accusing my sister of being Redline?"

"No," Riven said. "But if Redline is using her somehow—"

"The security system was an accident, and I'm sorry. But you've seen what Redline wants—they're trying to kill my sister." Kaya slid protectively in front of Asa. "I would never *think* of hurting her. And after everything you've all done for me—" A tremble racked her voice. "I wouldn't hide something like this."

The quiet fury in her voice seemed genuine, and Riven wished she could believe her. But what if Kaya didn't even know the whole truth? If Redline had more control than they knew?

"I believe her," Asa said.

Samir leveled his trademark glare at Riven. "Redline's rumors are already trying to connect Kaya and Banshee. They'd be pissing themselves with glee to see you suspecting her too."

"I know," Riven mumbled. "But nothing makes sense right now."

She kept walking, and the others followed. Maybe she should've kept her mouth shut and avoided this mess. If Ty were here, he'd scrape them back together—tell them to quit bickering, remind them why they'd all joined up in the first place. But he was dead, and so was part of her.

Tempest's doors loomed ahead, a wooden façade covered in blooming vines and false torches. Samir took the lead and greeted the bouncer. A quiet fell among the crew—they all knew better than to argue in front of their competitors. Even if Kaya wasn't in on Redline's plans, someone was. Someone who'd be here tonight.

After the bouncer took their names and scans, the doors opened, hitting them with the scent of chlorine and flashes of light through churning water.

On Requiem, excess water meant excess money, and the former smuggler matriarch's nightclub was overflowing. Requiem rarely had shortages of water—it was all recycled and filtered through systems a few decades old—but Rio Oscuro had extra, taken from asteroid ice shipments or smuggled in tankers from Corte's massive oceans.

Tempest had probably been built as some billionaire's wet dream before the syndicates took over. It was an homage to waterscapes on Cortellion and Phase I waterparks back on Earth. Glowing jungle plants, both plastic and organic, lined the maze of boardwalks and swim-up bars.

Kaya laughed into the swelling bass as holograms of fish flitted curiously around her ankles.

Riven reread the instructions on her wristlet. *Contenders only—meet in the anteroom to the shark lounge, fifteen minutes before the initiation.* Whatever the matriarchs needed them for remained to be seen. Between the steam, the holographic bubbles in the air, and the barrage of lights, it was hard to see anything resembling a shark lounge. It was more crowded tonight than she'd expected. Then, over the swimmers in the wave pool, she saw it.

A tank of live reef sharks formed a glass wall at the far end of the room. Lighting rigs shone behind it, glaring through the frosted glass. There must be a room back there. Riven didn't want to know who'd been feeding the sharks since the smuggler matriarch had been ousted, or who'd decided it was a good idea to bring sharks into a club in the first place.

"I need to head to the contenders' lounge," she said over the pounding music.

"Should we meet you there?" Asa said.

Riven stepped backward onto the boardwalk. "Stay here for now. But try to stick together." She turned and wove between clubgoers with water-smeared makeup and glowing swimwear. Even the volcanic hot tub seemed to be in operation tonight—a steaming, red-lit caldera. Hot water trickled like veins of lava down to the river that flowed through the club's darker caverns. No doubt these hidden passages and murky waters had hosted all sorts of clandestine meetings. Suddenly she didn't like the idea of Asa hanging out here.

When Riven found the entrance, she handed the cargo case to the guard, who let her in. In the anteroom, drone footage played on the holoscreens above the polycarbon couches, showing contenders reaching their beacons. On one screen, Callista's team split up and disappeared, never once drawing weapons. They captured not one, but two beacons, just to knock an extra group out of the running. Another screen showed Tak and her crew shearing through a gauntlet of mechs in the SilCaul underzone, hacking apart metal and circuits. On a third, Nell and Orsen double-teamed a beacon atop a cargo hauler, using some admittedly impressive ship maneuvers.

A fourth team failed to get into a drug lord's stronghold, and blood smeared the warehouse walls. Minutes later, Morphett Slade entered and tore through the guards like paper cutouts.

"So you've got that Slade girl on your team," Tak muttered from one of the couches, stirring a drink with her cybernetic fingers. "One hell of a twist."

Callista glared at Riven beneath their hood. They must be thinking Riven's crew hadn't earned this. She wanted to shove their faces in the footage where she had the beacon, but it wasn't playing. At least Jayde wasn't here to gloat yet.

"It looks like someone has it out for you." Nell sidled up to Riven, sinking onto the couch next to her. "They were just playing footage from Gamma. You should've had Jayde. The look on her face when you shot the bat out of her hand . . ."

"I'd been waiting for an excuse to do that," Riven said, vindicated that *someone* had seen.

Tak laughed. "Must be why she's making herself scarce. The girl was out by the dumpsters, hitting blunts. Smoking up like she'd short-circuited."

"Was that a competitor hurling the rockets?" Nell asked. "Or an *environmental hazard*?"

"Not sure yet," Riven said. Someone in this room might know what had happened. She looked Nell straight in her hazel-green eyes and said, loud enough for the other contenders to hear, "But I'll make sure to *thank them* as soon as I find out."

The others were silent, save for the whirr of Tak's fingers.

A sympathetic smirk inched over Nell's marble-smooth skin. "Seems you could use a drink."

"I'm good." The last thing she needed was to end up knocking someone unconscious on a rooftop again. And even if Nell had a strange, disarming charm Riven sometimes had trouble resisting, nobody here was worth trusting.

"Understandable. But we're between tasks—no hard feelings here." Nell tipped her own glass against her lips. "I think your crew has a real shot at this. So why'd you enter?"

Riven leaned back, slouching aggressively against the couch. "You first."

Nell gave a humorless laugh. "Fair." She glanced toward Callista, who was twisting a pair of earbuds into their ears, and her voice lowered. "Let's just say this might be my only way to get to the Federation. My former partner got himself into some trouble. Rio Oscuro owed me the resources to get him back, but . . . that arrangement fell through."

A hostage situation, not a power grab. Maybe Nell had a shred of decency.

"Your turn," Nell said.

"Don't pretend you haven't heard the rumors," Riven said. "We're as good as roadkill unless we get in with a syndicate."

"Protection under the Code, then. Unexpected. I would've pegged you as someone in this for the thrill of it."

"That's an added benefit."

The door swung open, and the exo-armored bouncer shouldered his way in. "Hey. Any of you seen the whinier Sokolov?"

Nell frowned. "You mean Jayde? Tak saw her outside."

He swore under his breath and cupped a hand over his comm receiver, mumbling something in the vein of *should've had that camera system replaced a decade ago*. Then he barked at them, "All of you. We're delayed, but be ready to head to the shark lounge. Matriarchs want to get a good look at you."

Riven was ready to get this over with, but something was off. "Is this holdup about Jayde?"

The bouncer worked his jaw, scowling, as if the news had a bad taste. "Yeah. She seems to have disappeared."

"We should head to the shark lounge," Asa said. "I want to keep an eye on Riven."

Kaya pressed her fingerprint to the pad on the locker, and it lit green. "Go ahead. I'll catch up. Need to sit for a few minutes." She stuffed her duffel bag inside, then settled onto one of the locker room benches. It was quieter in here, the bass only a muffled throb.

"Are you all right?" Kaya had seemed *off* since they'd entered the club. Asa was still shaken too. Of all their brushes with death on Requiem, this had been the closest—the red blade inching toward her neck, the awful intent in Redline's distorted voice. Whoever they were, they truly believed Asa was the key to something terrible.

Worse, Kaya might become collateral damage.

"It took a lot to shake off Redline this time," Kaya said. "And every time I have to push that hard . . . I think I slip a little further."

"Becoming a little less you?"

"Right. Being in there, detached from your body—it changes you." Kaya crossed her arms over the shifting geometric patterns on her cropped sweatshirt. "It's not as bad as before I got put back together. In there, it was hard to remember what made me human—there were no chemicals, no sensations. All urges and emotions were almost completely erased. But even now, sometimes it's tempting to stay. To never come back to this raging mess of a body trying to pull me in a thousand directions. Where things don't make sense."

Asa nodded slowly. Even working with computers from the outside required falling into another headspace. But circuitspace would be a different world entirely.

"And that's what worries me. What if Riven's right?" Kaya ran her fingertips over her brow. "This brain wasn't always mine. What if it's changing me? What if *Dad* already changed me? That other place I've been seeing . . ."

Fear prickled through Asa like static. "I don't think Riven really believes you're connected to Redline. You would've known *something*. And you'd never put us in danger on purpose." She felt a flicker of doubt, but she had to trust her sister. They were all each other had.

"I hope so." Kaya's eyes stared past her to the burned-out light on the wall that read *PARADISE FOUND*, and somewhere beyond it. "I just—I don't want to drag any of you down with me."

Asa sat beside her and squeezed her hand. "You won't. We need you. *I* need you."

But Kaya didn't respond. Didn't even react, as if she didn't even feel the touch.

"Kay?" Asa whispered.

Kaya's eyes were blown wide, blank and fearful. "It's happening again," she whispered. "I need to see." She stumbled to her feet. Her black-and-green high-top sneakers scuffed the tiles, and she caught herself against the dirty mirror.

"What are you talking about?" Asa's chest tightened.

Kaya stared into the mirror, past the crude phrases written in lip gloss, straight at her reflection—but she looked shocked, as if seeing herself for the first time. "Who are you?" Her fingertips brushed the glass.

"Kaya." Carefully, Asa held her sister's shoulders. "Kaya, talk to me."

Someone slammed a locker door behind them and laughed. "Your friend is *tripping*."

Kaya didn't even acknowledge them. "I know you," she said to the mirror.

Asa shouldn't try to pull her out of this—it might make things worse. "Can you tell me what you're seeing?"

Some of the clarity returned to Kaya's eyes. "It's your friend," she whispered. "It's Ty."

chapter 19

THE GIRL IN
THE MIRROR

I t was the first time he'd seen her face.

Ty barely felt the cold sweat breaking over his skin. The world had stretched and blurred, the tiny bathroom mirror fading, until it wasn't his reflection staring back at him, but *hers*— wisps of blue hair curling at her ears, full lips parted, curious.

Somehow, all those dreams—the careful hands he'd seen creating art, the view of climbing to a rooftop to watch the stars—they'd been her. The girl from the pictures and vidclips Asa had once shown him.

Now her eyes met his through the mirror, fierce and brilliant as burnished gold.

The girl next to her—Asa—steadied her. Asa's hair was longer than he'd ever seen it. This wasn't a memory; maybe this was *now*.

"What did they do to you?" Kaya addressed *him*, not Asa. There was an edge in her voice, as if she cared. As if she knew the hell he'd been through and would fight for him.

Ty opened his mouth to respond, but the words evaporated. What could he possibly say?

"Are you all safe?" he finally said.

But she was already disappearing. The broken neon and

lipstick-stained mirror bled back into the facility's washroom, and the muffled thrum of bass gave way to the hum of the lab vents. Ty caught himself against the sink, waiting for the vertigo to fade. In the mirror, he saw his own eyes—one sallow blue, one bright and cold.

"What the hell," he muttered. He pushed his mind further, hoping someone else would hear. *Yllath. What just happened? Was that the same thing I'm doing with you?*

A pause. "*Yes. Ntharen, but much stronger.*"

That Etri word again. *Stronger?* Ty's stomach twisted. *You mean when the psychiatrist said . . . same Etri tissue, subjects going mad—*

"*Exactly that. Normally it takes a mutual understanding of sorts to form a mental connection. But your mind and hers are linked with cells from the same creature.*" Ty sensed a quiet, simmering anger. "*Parts of my former body.*"

From the Progenitor, like the psychiatrist had said. *So that's really Kaya. They're alive.* A shiver racked him. Over the past few days, he'd had three more dreams through her eyes, each more vivid than the last. If she'd recognized him, then the crew had told her about him. They must have shown her pictures.

They still thought about him.

"*Have you forgotten what tonight is, Tyren? We do not have time for you to fixate on some female you've never met.*"

I know what tonight is. Ty splashed water on his face. *And I'm not fixating on anyone.*

"*I've glimpsed how you've felt, watching her. Her hands are distracting to you. Her thighs, even more so. Hopeless.*"

Ty sent Yllath as much annoyance as he could muster.

Don't you have anything better to do than probe my thoughts? He'd tried so hard to ignore Kaya's body when seeing through her eyes. It was an invasion of privacy, like everything Yllath was doing to him.

"*Truthfully, I don't. These surveillance networks are fairly dull.*"

Ty guessed he *had* been thinking about her. It was tempting to slip away to the safety and brightness of her world. But he barely knew her, and if by some miracle he ever saw his crew again, Kaya was definitely off-limits.

A new suspicion bubbled to the surface. The psychiatrist had asked about his dreams. Luca had to know what he'd created between Ty and Kaya. Either he was taunting his runaway daughter, or he wanted Ty to plead with his crew to come save him. Maybe he wanted Ty to get information about them, then break him until he talked. This might all be a trap.

He shouldn't have let Kaya know he was alive. From now on, no more letting his thoughts drift to her late-night climbs up the fire escape, or her skilled hands on the stylus–

"*Are you quite finished? The last thing we need is for these fantasies of yours to compromise our mission.*"

Ty pressed a towel to his warming cheeks. *Quit prying. I'm perfectly in control of my thoughts.*

"*I would hope so. Listen. Do you hear that?*"

Footsteps echoed beyond the door as one of the security guards passed. Ty quickly pulled his shirt on. Apprehension built in his chest. It was almost time.

"*Best steel yourself,*" came Yllath's voice. "*We have much to do, and little room for error.*"

I'm ready. Where do we start?

The lab doors slid open at Yllath's command.

If I don't do this, Ty told himself, *Riven is going to die.* He repeated the thought on a relentless loop as the sterile, overbright halls gave way to black marble corridors and pale footlights casting spidery shadows from atherblossom trees. Massive picture windows showed a city after dark, the ghosts of Himmeltor's white spires outlined in lights. Breathtaking, honestly. This wasn't the private lab Asa had described on the Almeida estate, where Kaya had been taken apart. This was Almeida Industries' headquarters, a temple with all the requisite blood tithes.

They need me, Ty told himself, to keep his thoughts from scalpels probing brain tissue, drills calibrating the metal in his body—from the punishments that might await if he got caught.

And what he might need to do to escape.

If Yllath heard Ty's thoughts, he ignored them. "*Take your next left. Past the lounge.*"

Ty squared his shoulders beneath the custodian's jacket he'd found in the washroom. A patch of gauze covered his cybernetic eye. With any luck, he wouldn't look like anyone important. He felt in his pocket for the tiny plastic chip containing a small piece of Yllath. A piece that could devastate this place, if he connected it to the lab's central network. His end of the pact.

His heart pounded as he passed a security guard, whose head turned toward him. *I'm nobody. Look away.* A few overtime workers nursed coffees in the lounge, but none of them turned to him as he passed.

"I hope you will be able to do this. It worried me when you would not kill the insect chirping in your bunk last night."

It was just hiding in the corner. Minding its own business. Ty had always been reluctant to kill harmless things; even when he'd been eight, and a honeybee had stung him while he was climbing a tree, he'd cried after the bee collapsed onto a branch and died. A few years later, when his dad had passed, the death had followed Ty like a shadow. He'd barely begun his studies in medicine when Emmett was killed a year and a half ago. Ty had sworn his hands would heal, never hurt.

But this place was ruled by Emmett's murderer, and that vow had begun to fray at the edges. Luca Almeida was far from harmless.

Yllath let out a growl of annoyance. *"This hesitation is why people take advantage of you."*

They usually don't, Ty thought. *You should see what Riven and Samir do to people who've tried.*

"A shame they aren't here, then." Yllath's voice grew smug. *"All you have is me."*

Ty shuddered. *Yeah. I'm aware.* Above, the tiny lights on the security cameras turned orange, a sign of Yllath's presence. He hoped the creature couldn't sense his reluctance. Last time Yllath had gotten into a body—a seven-foot-tall combat mech in Olympus nightclub—he'd kidnapped Ty and bruised him bloody before his friends found him again.

This time, Ty had to be in control.

"My kind revere those who can hear not only the thoughts of their kin, but the voices of gods. It is similar, no? For now, I am your protector. You pray to me, and I hear your voice."

You, a god? That's a flattering metaphor, Ty thought. *I think you forget which of us holds the power here.*

Yllath rumbled in surprised amusement. "*Cocky, for one so scrawny.*"

Says the one without a body.

He felt a current of deep laughter in their mental bond. "*Perhaps there is hope for you yet.*"

At the next door, Ty held the keycard against the pad, and the bolt clicked open. The door gave way to the prototype wing, eerily quiet. He stopped at the room Yllath pointed out—an unlabeled, entirely missable gray door.

Ty took a deep breath, staring at the handle. He could plug in Yllath and run to the landing pad, completing their bargain. He could escape now and never be scrutinized beneath lab lights again. Digging for information might mean throwing that chance away.

But it wasn't even a question. He opened the door to the Winterdark Archive.

The room was smaller than expected. Refrigerated vaults covered one wall, their serial numbers glaring in the dark. Opposite them, dimly lit plexicarbon panels held prototypes. Ty recognized one of the neural implants—it'd been affixed to the soldiers' necks that day at Sanctum's Edge. The AI-guided targeting system had led the soldiers to attack three kids on the beach nearby.

Blood in the sand. The wound bursting through Emmett's chest. Riven choking.

He steadied himself. This was definitely the right place.

Ty approached the row of control panels and entered the

passcode the psychiatrist had given him. Mercifully, it granted him access.

"*Everything you dreamed of?*" Yllath said.

"It's here," Ty whispered aloud. "It has to be."

"*Load me in. We don't have much time.*"

"I have one thing to look into first."

There was decades' worth of information to review—test-subject files, prototype schematics, chemical logs. He narrowed it down by test facilities and dates. *Sanctum's Edge, American Territories – Carolina Territory, September 2187.* Two months before Ty's seventeenth birthday, and weeks before Emmett's eighteenth—a birthday he'd never see. Ty was now older than his brother had ever been. Ever would be.

Ty forced himself to look at the logs. Objectives, outcomes, and numbers, so raw and indifferent. He'd been right; one of the augmentations on the soldiers had been an experimental bioengineered spore.

Targeted at reflex enhancement and symbiotic resilience, the log read. *13% survival rate after two weeks. Survivors have complications, most in the form of neural deterioration.*

His throat tightened. Most hadn't survived. But those who had . . .

. . . required subsequent stabilizer dosage to prevent uncontrolled progression, and consistent pain management thereafter. Trial concluded in late 2187. Further research needed.

The log described a second course of treatment that could stop the progression before it killed subjects. Ty scrolled through the notes, memorizing as much as he could. It was similar to what he'd suspected after all his blood sampling and studies of analogous diseases. Riven's condition could never be fully removed, but it could be helped.

She didn't have to die.

The file gave the serial number for sample formulations of the stabilizer dosage. Ty found the corresponding vault and cracked it open using the keycard.

Inside was a small, chilled collection of vials, all with the same label. Riven would only need one, but he pocketed three and a syringe, just in case. She'd need an injection to her brain stem, like the log noted. Now he'd just have to find her.

Somewhere in the ether, Yllath huffed impatiently. "*You will be noted as missing in eight minutes, Tyren. Do it now.*"

With hands trembling from nerves and relief, Ty plugged the chip into the terminal. He didn't have the skill to get Yllath deeper into the networks—Yllath would have to do that himself.

"*It will take me some time to get through the barriers,*" Yllath said. "*Something else guards the circuits here.*"

How long? Should I head toward the landing pad now?

Silence. Yllath was likely deep in concentration. Ty suddenly felt alone, cast adrift with nobody to guide him through the corridors or warn him of danger. How long would this take?

He should go back to his bunk and wait for Yllath's signal, but he risked getting locked there if Yllath didn't return. He could wait a few minutes longer. The Winterdark files were still open; curiosity urged him to look further.

Subject listings. Something titled Project Echofall. Names near the top of the list caught his eye. *Asanna Almeida. Kaya Almeida.*

Even if it was an intrusion, something compelled him to look at Kaya's file.

Kaya. The file began at her birth in 2170, which meant she'd been analyzed her entire life. From the overview notes and Asa's stories, he pictured Kaya ushered through the lab's halls as a child, dreaming of other worlds. She'd longed to run, to go to art school or anywhere she'd be free, but she couldn't bear to leave her little sister. Even though he'd never met her, Ty was glad he'd played a small part in helping her escape this place.

Kaya's file was linked to another labeled *[Precursor: Sofi Almeida].* A name he didn't recognize. A relative, maybe—though in the brief time he'd known Asa, she'd never mentioned her mother, or anyone else in her family. He clicked backward, to Asa's file.

Asanna Almeida. Her file was less detailed than Kaya's, with nothing but the words *Phase IV* under the notes section.

Ty's skin prickled. There were so many missing pieces here, and he was treading dangerous ground. He needed to go.

Yllath? Ty reached out with his mind. *Are you finished yet?*

Yllath didn't answer.

Yllath?

The door to the Archive slid open, as if Yllath were telling him to run. But two silhouettes blocked the doorway. One was a hulking, armored husk—an *Etri* husk—with his graying lips peeled back. *Iolus.*

The other was a man in a black-and-gold suit who had the confident bearing of a king. The man's dark eyes caught the array of screen lights, as if his sight extended through the wires of this place.

"Subject AV70," Luca Almeida said. "I was curious what you'd been up to."

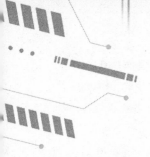

"They've been his hands," Kaya slurred, lying on the locker room bench. "All this time."

Asa handed her the water bottle. "Take another drink." She'd managed to catch Kaya when she fell unconscious at the mirror, and Kaya was slowly coming to.

Ty. It couldn't be. Why would Kaya's brain have conjured an image of someone who'd died before she was put back together? "You're sure it's him?" Asa said.

Kaya's eyes were as vacant as dead screens. "It looked just like him. Riven and Samir have all those pictures and vidclips, and . . . it's him. Same reddish-blond hair, light skin, blue eyes—well, one blue eye."

Asa's skin prickled. It sounded like a nightmare pieced together from stories. Ty had taken bullets in the smoke, but— "One eye?"

Kaya pointed to her left eye. "His left looked different. Probably cybernetic."

"So what do you think it was? A dream? Something worse?" There were still so many unknowns surrounding Etri brains. Etri fossils could link across spacetime—a quality that enabled the faster-than-light transit station, a folding point in space between Earth's solar system and Alpha Centauri. But as far as Asa knew, her father was the only one who'd ever managed to revive living Etri tissue and use it. Was anything Kaya had seen real, or was it a waking nightmare based on images she'd seen?

"I don't know," Kaya said. "I just got the sense he's been . . . hurting. Trapped."

"But he's dead." For the first time, though, there was a whisper of doubt. What if they'd left Ty behind to die, and he hadn't? What could they possibly do to help him?

Ty was the only person who'd accepted Asa without question during the worst days of her life. She was the last person he'd ever kissed, even though her feelings had been a mess. An awful, selfish thought surfaced: What would he think of her now?

Asa stifled the thought. "We need to tell Riven."

"No. Riven *cannot* know what's happening to me." Tears of frustration glimmered at the corners of Kaya's eyes. "She already thinks I'm connected to Redline. If she knew I was *seeing* things–"

"I'll make her understand. She might know something."

"Not yet. Maybe I'll tell her eventually, but this . . . it's too much right now."

All of this was too much. Maybe Kaya was right—it could wait until after the trial, after they had Redline sorted out. What Kaya was seeing likely wasn't real, and renewed guilt over Ty's death would only eat them all alive.

"We'll get through this." Asa settled onto the bench beside her sister. "We always have."

Kaya leaned against her. "Are we ever going to be able to stop fighting? To stop running?"

"I don't know. But I know we can make allies. Protect

ourselves." It started with the Rio Oscuro throne, in allying with the vicious, dangerous people who kept this city in line.

Would that make you any better than your father? a hollow voice deep within her asked. *Survival here will not allow you to be soft.*

The locker room door swung open. "There you are," said a sickly saccharine voice. "The initiation's starting."

Asa turned. Their unlikely team member stood in the doorway, looking startlingly harmless with her bulletproof vest traded for a ruffled pink club dress.

"If you want to see your girlfriend get her gold star or profound spanking or whatever they're planning for the contenders tonight," Morphett said, "you might want to get to the shark room."

"I guess we should go," Kaya said. Asa steadied her as they headed back toward the crash of overchlorinated waves.

The shark lounge was a small private dance hall, with slender sharks circling inside the tank that formed one wall. The tank jutted out near the floor, forming a stage. The back row of seats was shrouded in shadow, occupied by a few silhouettes. Matriarchs, watching.

As the sharks knifed through the water, Asa's thoughts drifted back to Ty. He'd been torn apart as she and Riven escaped Josiah's lab—but if he'd somehow survived . . .

She took a seat before her thoughts grew bleaker. But as the contenders stepped onto the stage, she swore something dark was clouding the water beneath them.

Blood.

Riven braced herself as sharks circled beneath her feet and the Duchess circled the stage around her and the other contenders. She couldn't decide which was more dangerous.

"You have our commendation for passing the first trial," the Duchess said, her silk skirts trailing on the glass tank. "We expected six to pass, but only five retrieved our cargo. And only four have brought themselves to the stage tonight."

Riven clasped her hands behind her back. Jayde was still AWOL, and they'd had to start without her. The sooner this was over, the better. The other matriarchs watched from the back row, behind Asa and the rest of the crew.

"For this, you are officially recognized as contenders for Rio Oscuro's leadership."

The Duchess gently rolled up Nell's sleeve to expose her inner forearm, pressed a bulky gun to Nell's skin, and—*click*. A small bump was anchored beneath the reddening skin. Nell grimaced and tugged her sleeve back down.

More tracking tech, just like on the first job they'd done for the Duchess.

"You have all proved your abilities in split-second, strategic assessment," the Duchess said, "in making the best use of your resources in a crisis." She moved to Callista, whose face didn't change as the chip clicked under their skin. "Next will be your test for true strategy. Without tracking beacons, you'll need to root out our more established enemies yourself."

Strategy. Not her forte. But Riven kept her face blank as the Duchess drew closer.

The Duchess lifted Riven's bare arm and pressed the gun

just below her inner elbow. Riven tilted her head back and squinted into the blinding lights.

Click. A dull sensation, then a rush of heat and pain. The Duchess wiped the traces of blood away, and Riven was marked.

Whispers erupted from the matriarchs and teams in the audience. Whispering about *her*? Riven shot them a glare. But she caught Asa's eyes, which had gone wide with panic.

"While any syndicate stronghold—this venue included—remains a neutral zone, the no-kill rule is lifted from here on out," the Duchess continued. "The Code still applies to the trial, and I will remind you that your aim will be, first and foremost, to complete your tasks. But if you wish to expend resources eliminating your competitors, that is for you to decide."

The murmurs in the audience turned to shouts, and people rose to their feet. Riven frowned. It was too big a reaction for the Duchess's words, since they all *knew* things would turn bloody at some point—

Next to her, Tak swore, scrambling backward.

The world seemed to slow as Riven looked down at the tank beneath her feet.

A human form drifted through the water, peaceful, as if suspended in space. As it floated to the top, she saw the face.

Blank horror was scrawled across Jayde's features. Her lifeless eyes stared through the glass, and a haze of red hair drifted around her face.

Riven stumbled backward as Jayde's corpse bumped the glass top. Tendrils of blood streamed from a pair of slices forming an X across her forehead, clouding the blue-lit water. Another burst of blood seemed to be leaking from her back.

In the audience, Matriarch Sokolov was screaming. "That's my daughter, you bastards! *Get her out of there!*"

A shark latched on to Jayde's arm, dragging her through the tank. A second retaliated by biting her other wrist.

The Duchess's lips pressed into a grim line as she ushered Riven and the other competitors off the stage. "We'll finish this later," she said.

Riven's pulse hammered as chatter raged among the teams.

"*—settled it before they lifted the no-kill order—*"

"*—must've really had it out for Jayde.*"

Most pairs of eyes were now locking on to *her*. The scalding lights and humid chemical air pulled inward, crushing. Jayde had to have dozens of enemies, but after her scrap with Riven . . . Redline must've known this would put a target on her. Maybe Redline's grudge against Jayde went deeper, but the implications here were no accident.

As Riven passed a shrieking Sokolov and guards rushing to rope off the stage, she caught the matriarch's eye.

Sokolov's glare could've torn her limb from limb.

chapter 21

WARNING SHOT

Nestled into the back-corner booth of Xav's bar, Riven saw Jayde's staring corpse every time she blinked.

Don't bleed all over my boots when you get yourself killed. Jayde had been nasty, but she hadn't deserved to end up a floating hunk of meat for sharks. Numbness crept over Riven, detaching her from the fear. When her time came, would anyone even care?

She hoped she'd at least go out fighting.

"Riv, you okay?"

She dragged her gaze away from the ceiling fans churning the greasy air. Samir watched her from across the table, concerned. Morphett, their regrettable tagalong, ordered another drink at the bar. Diego and Asa sat opposite each other, already deep into their assignment for the second trial—a tangled web of cryptic messages and location data.

Their mission was on the downlow, for now. *I know requesting you investigate another syndicate is a bit unconventional,* Cerys had said, *but I trust Diego, and if anything happens, I'll deal with the fallout.*

Seemed Staccato's operatives were up to something. There'd been a string of weird incidents, including a rough-sleeper camp cleared recently, and not even Cerys had learned where its residents went. If Sokolov was using them for organ fodder, or something worse, it might be against the Code.

Cerys had asked them to find evidence of what Sokolov was doing. To find out who'd been taken—and where, and why. Every team had received an assignment from their patron matriarch. Passing the second task would depend on whether Cerys was satisfied with their findings.

Still, the code-breaking part wasn't Riven's expertise, and being unable to help only made her wandering thoughts worse.

"I'm fine," Riven said. A glass of lukewarm, whiskey-free cola had miraculously appeared in front of her, and she took a tentative sip. "But I hope Cerys knows what she's doing. This is a hell of a time to ask us to probe into Sokolov's business. She's probably already digging for the proof she needs to gut us."

"Well, there's no proof linking us to Jayde," Samir said. "But there's also nothing to clear our names."

"Do you think Redline did that just to frame us?" Asa's pretty eyes were bloodshot as she looked up from the annotated maps on her wristlet. She looked like she'd run all night on raw determination. One task in, and all of them were exhausted. This place's typical bacon-grease-and-fried-onion scent usually felt like home, but tonight, the smell was nauseating.

"Could have. But they didn't leave anything behind to incriminate us." Diego tapped a stylus against his jaw. "Redline might have a bigger picture than we're seeing. We might not be the only ones in their crosshairs."

Riven stirred her drink with the straw. All the footage of Jayde had been cut from the security cameras, but Sokolov had sworn to find answers before the end of the second round.

Even if she didn't find real proof, Riven knew what the assumption would be.

"It's also possible Jayde was Redline's mole," Samir said. "Maybe she messed up royally in the first round, and they saw fit to dispose of her."

"Who knows," Riven mused. Her gaze slid to Kaya, whose head rested on Samir's shoulder, slipping as her eyes fluttered shut. Kaya barely caught herself before her face planted into her plate of spicy chicktrill wings. If anyone would know about glitchy camera footage, it was her. "Hey, Kaya. You didn't notice anything weird tonight, did you?"

Kaya's eyes snapped open.

Samir groaned. "Riv, this isn't the time."

"She was with me," Asa interjected. "She had a bit of an episode, but she's okay—"

"Really," Riven said. "What kind of episode?"

Asa froze, as if she'd said too much. Something *had* happened. Maybe something they should be worried about.

"You said it before, Asa. You're worried she's *slipping* in there."

"That's not what this is about," Asa said, but Kaya was shrinking, looking a little betrayed.

Riven cocked her head. "Surely if it's nothing—"

"It was *him*," Kaya blurted. "Okay? It was Ty. Every time I lose control, I see him."

The words scraped Riven's nerves like sandpaper. "Are you fucking with me?" Kaya didn't even know Ty.

The whole table had gone silent. Samir's vertical pupils zeroed in on Kaya.

The girl squirmed. "I sometimes see what he sees. Or saw. But then we looked in the mirror, and I saw him looking back, and I . . . I know it sounds ridiculous."

Riven was close to shattering the glass in her grip. It felt like the world had been kicked from under her.

"It's possible it's her new brain, making its own memories," Asa cut in. "Or . . . maybe it's something more."

"Are you suggesting he's alive?" Venom crept into Riven's voice. "You realize that would be a *very big fucking deal*?" Adrenaline forced her to her feet. She hated that it ignited a buried hope, and that it brought back the crushing guilt.

She leaned over the table, leveling with Kaya. "This is a hell of a bomb to drop on us. If there's the slightest chance of him being alive—" Her voice cracked. "You know I would *tear the universe apart* to get him back."

Kaya found her voice again. "I know. I . . . I'm sorry. I'm still adjusting to these dreams, or whatever they are." She met Riven's gaze. "But you need to know they have nothing to do with Redline, or Jayde. It's just . . . him. It always is."

"Do it again, then," Riven said. "However you've been see-ing him—do it. Find him."

Asa touched Kaya's shoulder. "Riven, she can't just—"

"And why not?" Riven stared at Kaya.

"It could hurt her," Asa said. "It's hard enough when she's in there—"

"Then how are we ever going to know?" After months of moving on, she couldn't throw herself into impossible hope again. She'd destroy herself trying to fix things.

Samir clutched the edge of the table in his carbon-knuckled grip. "Riv. Sit down."

Riven shook her head slowly. She shouldn't have pushed. This was another splinter beneath her armor, another crack widening the fissure. She slumped back onto the sticky booth cushion. "This is too much."

"Kaya, I'm not saying you should strain yourself," Samir said, "but this could be important. If this happens again, let us know what you see?"

Riven watched the bubbles rise in her cola. The guilt already woke her up thrashing some nights—nightmares of the smoke, of Ty's blue eyes fading. Losing anyone else would kill her, even before the white noise did.

All that lay ahead was the bloody path to the throne. The sole way to protect the rest of them before the city swallowed her whole.

No more distractions.

Nothing made sense.

Asa's hands shook from exhaustion as she took another swig of mango soda. She closed her too-dry eyes, waiting for the afterimages of the screen to fade. They'd been at it for hours, but while the rest of the crew had gone back into the hideout, Diego still parsed the data across the table. A modest crowd packed the bar, chatter blending with the slow bass over the speakers. Nobody was paying attention to the kids in the corner booth who were still dressed like nightclub trash.

Asa forced her eyes back to the cipher, to the signals gone

dark with no explanation. A maze of errant pings and missing persons with few existing records. She narrowed her focus, pushing away memories of Kaya's vacant eyes, the accusation in Riven's. Buried here somewhere was the key to keeping them all together. Winning this trial would depend on finishing the investigation for Cerys. But why did nothing *match*?

She buried her fingers into her hair and groaned.

Diego quirked an eyebrow from across the table. "You okay?"

"Fine," she grunted. It was hard to keep her eyes open. She wished there were ice cubes in her drink to smear across her sweaty forehead.

"Sometimes I think Cerys overestimates my capabilities. But every code cracks eventually." Diego had a series of maps layered on his screen. They'd matched eyewitness reports from Cerys with time stamps from other accounts of the night the rough-sleeper camp had disappeared. Asa had found a scattering of signal pings that dispersed in every direction. Diego had cracked a few victims' identities, but there was no sign of where they'd gone.

Diego knew what he was doing. Even if he was between factions—maybe even between identities—he'd been new to this path at some point. Like her.

"How did you end up here, working with Cerys?" Asa said.

"Where'd that come from?"

"Just curious." She could use any distraction right now.

He leaned backward. "I was useful to her. Had intel on some factions that didn't like how she was running things."

"Before that. Why did you want to join her?" Asa had caught

him digging, late nights when he didn't think anyone else was awake. Searching for something. "I . . . I shouldn't have seen. But I was checking for attempted security breaches on your hideout . . ." She felt her cheeks warming. "You have Federation records. Charts of exoplanetary missions."

Diego gave her a hard look. "I don't get to have my secrets?"

"You knew my biggest secret the moment I first walked through your door. And you kept it because you knew it might put me in danger."

"A secret for a secret, then." He sipped his water. "I'm looking for my parents."

The admission was so unexpected that all she could say was, "*Oh.*" It was the most personal thing Diego had ever told her. "Where do you think they are?"

"Anywhere? Nowhere? Dead, probably. But I need to know." Diego worked his jaw, as if it was hard to talk about himself.

A strange sadness settled over her. Diego was only a year or two older than Riven. Maybe he'd been a kid trying to find his way home. "If you tell me more, I can help. Kaya, too, once we're finished with this."

Diego stared into the compiling images and progress bars. "They were aerospace surveyors. Always promised to bring me along when I got older. They'd send pictures of deep space, notes on other worlds with potential for terraforming. Hell, sometimes my mom would call and read me bedtime stories from the station. Then, when I was fourteen, they were studying some energy traces that might be Etri in origin, from Gliese 667 in the Trappist system, when their messages just . . . stopped.

"I never learned what happened. And when you're a frustrated, lonely kid with nothing better to do, you dig into incident records. And when you hit walls, you teach yourself to dig deeper. Into confidential Federation databases. Got in big enough trouble that I had to skip Earth entirely. Bigger trouble when one of the shipments I hacked was a decoy–not Federation, but Boneshiver." Diego gave a thin smile. "That's when Cerys offered me a job. And a better database, to boot." He tapped his cybernetic arm.

The arm he'd lost. "I thought Samir saved you that day."

"That was before I connected with Cerys."

"Different story?"

"It's another secret. You'd owe me."

Asa narrowed her eyes. She doubted she had many secrets Diego didn't know. "That one's not really a secret. Samir's mentioned it before. I could ask him instead."

Diego mulled it over, then sighed. "Fine. I met him and Riven when I was on Laurizon station, fresh on the run from Earth. Someone had hired *Boomslang* to transport some contraband fuel, and they wanted help with docking codes. We ran into some trouble, and I ended up caught in the airlock of another ship that was trying to nab their cargo."

Asa winced. "And that's when . . ."

"Yeah. Samir ran into the firefight to get those doors open, the half-wit. Risked his life to save a boy he'd just met. It wasn't pretty, but I could've lost a lot more than this." He idly rubbed his elbow beneath his jacket sleeve. "On Laurizon, you just . . . you don't help someone without asking something in return. I barely knew Samir. Didn't trust his intentions. Thought it would've been better if he'd let me die there. I couldn't look him in the eye for a while afterward."

Asa understood. The reluctant gazes, the push and pull of longing and incompatible dreams. "You love him."

Diego's gaze fell back to the screens. "Sometimes, I wish I didn't. I think you understand that all too well."

The pit in her stomach deepened. "If you could go back with him, would you?"

He shook his head slowly. "I don't think I can ever leave this place. I'm in too deep."

Diego Valdez. Suddenly, his name seemed to fit wrong. Like a borrowed jacket, a temporary thing.

Asa was beginning to understand his world. The fragile balance of favors and secrets, the addictive pull of power and danger. If they took over Rio Oscuro, she'd recruit the best data brokers, track Redline down, and force them to admit they were lying about Banshee. Make them disappear. Redline wasn't getting her sister, or anyone else.

You're starting to think like Riven.

Maybe Diego was right. Once you were in too far, it was impossible to leave. This place—this life—had gotten into her blood.

She pulled up the map of the data points again. It showed different types of tracking signals, fanning outward to form a spiderweb. Frowning, she filtered them. Some from wristlets, some from mods. And she had an idea. "Wait. Doesn't this seem odd?"

Diego looked it over. "You're right," he finally said. "The

wristlets could be more easily confiscated. Taken away and then destroyed. Or used to throw any pursuers off their tail."

Asa nodded. "But the victims' cybernetics . . ." The cybernetic signals headed in the same direction before going dark. A location. "Oh god."

"You're onto something." Diego let out a shuddering breath. "And I don't like where this leads."

chapter 22

PROJECT ECHOFALL

I can't break. Not here.

Ty's heartbeat threatened to punch a hole through his chest. Padded restraints held him to a steel cot beneath a trickle of sickly golden light, which illuminated a round room with concrete walls. A private lab, for a single specimen.

"I expected a lot from you, Tyren. Escape attempts, maybe. Curiosity, of course." A silhouette cut into the light, and Luca Almeida's surgically perfect face came into focus. Iolus lurked near the door, steady as an armored boulder. "But it seems the incident at Sanctum's Edge is burned into your mind even more deeply than I'd imagined. You will do anything to revisit it."

Ty set his jaw. The last thing he wanted was to revisit that place.

Talons of cold metal pressed against his temples as Almeida anchored his head into place. "What if we remove that event from your memory?" Almeida's hand unfurled to reveal a glass tube containing a metallic node attached to a spidery swatch of Etri brain matter. "If we replace it with something . . . peaceful. What will you fight for afterward? Will you fight at all?"

Ty fought the urge to thrash. He was cornered, another lab animal taking its turn under the knife. He reached out with his mind, searching for the voice that had pulled him through these past few days.

Yllath. Where are you?

Silence.

"It seems we'll have to keep a closer eye on you," Almeida said, pulling up Ty's mental profile on the overhead screen. "Thankfully we have a surgeon available to conduct the transfer today. Earlier than expected."

Project Echofall, said the tiny letters at the top of the screen. The next phase of Winterdark. The project that had Asa's name beneath it.

"It seems you and my daughter were fairly close. I hope you two weren't doing anything . . . untoward." Ty flinched at a metallic snap, inches from his ear. His heartbeat was a frantic throb. "Asa is headstrong, isn't she?"

"You're going to change her next," Ty whispered.

Almeida's lips spread into a taut smile. "She had a chance to see reason." He set the tiny implant vial onto a surgical tray. "But now she will have a new snippet of memory—hazy, but pleasant. She will become what the world thinks she is. What she was always meant to be."

The words forced themselves out of Ty's throat. "How long do you think it'll take before she rediscovers the terrible things you've done?"

"I have nothing to hide from her. But if she misunderstands—if she falls onto the wrong path again—that area of her memory can be reset. As her friend, you'll be doing Asanna a great favor by ensuring Echofall works like a dream for her."

Ty's ribs were iron girders across his lungs. He couldn't

stop Almeida. The man would continue to take and use as he saw fit. But if all else failed, Kaya would try to save her. She'd already been through hell for her sister.

As the anesthesia machine chirped online, a hiss and a crackle came from the far end of the room. Almeida pulled backward, frowning. "Iolus, do we have an intruder?"

"*I have control*," a voice boomed at the back of Ty's mind. A voice he'd never been so glad to hear. "*In a few seconds, I will pop your restraints open. You must kill him quickly.*"

Every ounce of hope quickly dissolved. *Why do I need to be the one to do it?* Ty thought.

"*I need to contend with Iolus. You're the only thing close enough to kill Almeida before he activates the next layer of security.*"

Iolus lumbered past Ty, cricking his neck and pulling a long data cable from somewhere beneath his armor. A wired connection in a lab with few wireless networks. Maybe he *did* control the circuits here.

"Fix that," Almeida said as his bodyguard plugged himself into the sterilizing chambers, where control panels hissed with static. Almeida's back was turned, and Iolus was occupied. Nearby, Riven's vials sat atop a lab table with a tray of sharp surgical tools.

"*He is distracted*," Yllath said. "*It must be now.*"

The tools were within reach—a surgical drill, a scalpel, a slim pair of scissors. Biopsy tools. Any of them could find the right artery in Almeida's neck.

Okay. Free me, Ty thought, and immediately the restraints

released. He trembled as he swung his feet, soundlessly, to the concrete floor. His mech hand closed around the scissors.

The skin of Almeida's neck was exposed. Soft, vulnerable. How easy it would be: a quick stab to the carotid, a twist to widen the cut. The tool in Ty's hand felt like a dark promise, a vow waiting to be spoken.

He imagined Almeida's hollow gasps, his heartbeat pulsing lifeblood over the joints of Ty's mech fingers. Asa's father, dying. Like his own father had.

Taking a life would stain him permanently. A choice he could never undo.

I can't do this, Ty thought as nausea rose in his throat.

"*You must*," Yllath rumbled. "*Stop being a coward.*"

Ty moved the scissors into his flesh hand. Out of the hand Yllath might try to control. *I'm not a killer. I can't.*

"*Do you think it makes you a good person, to have others kill in your stead? Whom are you protecting?*"

Ty could barely think straight. He'd never harmed others to save himself. Unlike Yllath, who'd laid waste to Requiem—

"*Your people bring enough destruction upon themselves. After everything he's done, does this man really deserve your sympathy?*"

Luca didn't. But killing felt like more power than Ty ought to have.

"I'm sorry," he said through oncoming tears. Almeida whirled toward him, and he realized he'd spoken aloud.

"What have you done?" Almeida's eyes narrowed at the open restraints. "You released the Progenitor, didn't you?"

The lights plunged with an electrical whine, then flickered back on.

Yllath gave a frustrated roar, then his voice disappeared from Ty's mind.

"I'm not the only one you've wronged," Ty said, backing toward the table. He grabbed Riven's vials, tucking them into his pocket.

He's yours, Ty thought to Yllath. *I got you where you needed to be. Take your revenge, but leave me out of this.*

He braced himself for Yllath to attack—for mechs to burst through the doors—but nothing happened. And Almeida didn't look afraid, or surprised. Iolus loomed next to him, his attention fixed on Ty.

"I hope you understand what you've done, Tyren," Almeida said.

Through the overhead speakers trickled a familiar voice in an unfamiliar language. Sharp sibilants and guttural vowels. In response, a low growl rose in Iolus's throat. Something surprised, reverent.

Etri speech. Whatever Yllath was saying, Ty had to run.

He fumbled with the latch and hurled the lab door open. The halls echoed with the shriek of alarms. Somewhere, he sensed Yllath clashing with Iolus's uncanny control of circuitspace. Against another Etri, Yllath would have a fight on his hands.

Ty ran through the maze of hallways until his chest ached, trying to match the layout to the maps burned into his mind. Almeida's offices would be this way—and so would the landing pad. His escape route, if Yllath would let him go.

The halls were dimmer than usual, footlights flickering across the marble floors. It brought back a remembered fear of Banshee flooding docking bays and nightclub halls. A corruption that'd tried to kill his friends. Ty was worthless to Yllath now, and all bets were off.

He kept sprinting, his breaths a ragged rhythm. The security mechs were at war with themselves—some flickering and dead, others awakening with orange eyes. Ty ran past glass offices, where Almeida's desk rose like an empty throne. Ahead was the glass wall overlooking the landing pad. The door slid open when he pressed the switch, then slammed shut when he'd barely passed through.

Outside, weak rays of sunlight crawled over the city. It had to be here somewhere. Somewhere—

There. The emergency escape pod. Ty brushed condensation off the outer panel. The security systems were all in flux—lights scrolling, screens flickering. It took three tries, but Ty managed to coax the latch open. The pod door rose, welcoming him inside.

He slid onto the seat and pulled the harness over his head, with one last second of hesitation before he clicked the buckle. There was no telling where this thing would take him when activated—a safe house somewhere, likely offworld. His odds of survival would be better there than here.

He engaged the emergency launch and closed his eyes. There was a lurch, a hiss, and a high-pitched, rising whine. A progress bar on the dashboard read *ENGAGING LIFT*.

Please work, he begged silently, as if Yllath would still help. *Please.*

The whine rose to a fever pitch, and a rush of vertigo sent his head spinning as the pod lifted off.

He braced himself as the lab shrank beneath him. But with the shaky relief came a strange tug at his cybernetics, then pain slicing through his shoulder. Ty tried readjusting his arm, relaxing his tense carbon-fiber muscles, but the pain only worsened, accompanied by a shattering headache behind his cybernetic eye. Something was wrong.

The farther the pod took him, the more the searing heat erupted. Until his mind tried to wall it away, forcing the world into merciful nothingness.

Ty regained consciousness somewhere among the stars.

He felt like a sledgehammer had cracked his ribs, and pain scythed from his mech arm as sparks of light floated by outside the portholes. He was powerless here, at the mercy of the escape pod's trajectory and whatever was wrong with his cybernetics. Maybe the pain was a fail-safe to prevent him from escaping the lab. Maybe it was punishment for failing to stop Almeida.

Maybe it would keep getting worse, until the lab decided he was no longer worth recovering. And then . . .

Ty couldn't think about that. His world alternated between blurs of nova-bright pain and the softness of a place blank and dark and empty. Occasionally, he worked up the strength to open his eyes. Requiem crept closer, a dusty blue-gray moon with a patch of light stretching over its surface.

Something else came into view too—a tiny satellite station.

It evolved from a blinking point of light to a ramp and a small building covered in a hazy atmo-dome. Eventually the ship lurched as docking arms pulled it into place.

When Ty unbuckled his harness, something stabbing-hot pierced his ribs, and he almost fainted again. But somewhere in that mass of light below, he'd find his friends. He'd find Riven. He just had to get *down*.

As he stumbled out of the escape pod, footlights flickered on, illuminating a walkway lined by plants. Oxygen concentrators whirred around him, but the air was still thin, forcing his breaths into gasps. A boxy white building loomed ahead. Almeida's safe house.

As another crushing pulse erupted from his shoulder, Ty pushed open the safe house door. The space was tiny but palatial compared to his cell. Inside were white couches, a pantry stocked with MREs, and a deep freezer. Some water rations, a cot. But he didn't have time to linger here.

Eventually, he found a comms console in the kitchen. There had to be a way to call his crew. He tried to pull up a keypad, to enter Riven's messaging code.

NOT AUTHORIZED, the console read. *ENTER PASSCODE.*

He clicked through the available screens again. He found Almeida's contact list, but he couldn't enter Riven's messaging code. Or Samir's. Or anyone's.

Ty's head throbbed, his good eye blurring with tears as he scrolled through the list of contacts. He could reach out to Kaya, but it was hard enough to focus that ability at the best of times, and right now, he couldn't think straight.

It was a long shot, but maybe one of Almeida's contacts could help him.

Some names on the list were concealed in code. Most of them he didn't recognize—and worse, some of them he did. Nobody he wanted to meet.

Ty collapsed against the control panel. He didn't have much time. Luca would have seen he'd activated the pod. Someone would come for him. He just had to make sure the right someone showed up first.

Then one name on the list made his heart drop. A true gamble, but maybe she'd help him. He hit the *call* button, bile rising in his throat.

It felt like eternity between the ringtones. Then—

"Hey. Didn't think I'd be hearing from you again." Her voice was missing its deadly lilt. She sounded . . . friendly, almost.

Ty leaned over the microphone. "This isn't Luca Almeida. But I've never been gladder to hear your voice, Morphett."

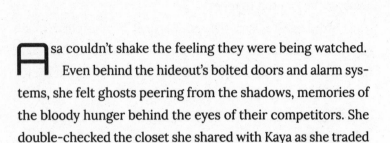

chapter 23
PREDATOR

Asa couldn't shake the feeling they were being watched. Even behind the hideout's bolted doors and alarm systems, she felt ghosts peering from the shadows, memories of the bloody hunger behind the eyes of their competitors. She double-checked the closet she shared with Kaya as she traded her clubwear for the constrictive comfort of her exosuit.

The second round was underway, and the no-kill guardrail had been lifted. Cracking the location might've been the easy part.

Out in the living room, Riven paced in her half-unzipped exosuit. "I'm sick of waiting for Redline to make their next move. We might need to take the fight to them first."

"We've only got a day to finish the second task." Diego sprawled on the couch, chewing a licorice stick. "Giving chase will cost us time."

Samir peered out the solar blinds. "It might also require splitting the crew—and we should keep everyone together from here on out."

Riven grumbled as she shook out her rough-cropped hair and tied it into a ponytail. Asa's breath caught at the sight of her hands trembling. No doubt the anger and stress were breaking her at the seams. As usual, Asa was helpless to stop the thing eating Riven, the thing her father had started.

She had to make sure they won tonight.

"Samir's right," Asa said. "Most of us aren't great in a fight, and we shouldn't split him and Riven up, but—"

"Um, you could send a few of the nerds with *me*." Morphett popped her gum, leaning against the kitchen wall. "If you think even Callista could get through me—"

"No," Riven snapped. "Ugh, you have a point, Samir. Her being here is reason enough for us all to stick together."

Thank the stars for that. Morphett still sent tremors rippling over Asa's skin. They had her word, but Redline might still offer her a bounty. Or worse, Asa's *father* might offer her a bounty. Again.

"Such hostility, after all I've done for you." Morphett sighed. "Still. You owe me a victory. I think I'll sit this round out." She pulled out a cigarette and poked it with the smoldering tip of a cybernetic finger.

Samir immediately pointed down at her. "Not in here. Take that outside."

Morphett rolled her eyes. "Fine, fine." Then she looked at her wristlet, and her eyebrows shot up in surprise. "I guess I need to take a call anyway." Her eyes met Asa's briefly, calculating, as she tapped her earpiece and headed toward the door. "Hey. Didn't think I'd be hearing from you again . . . The hell. Who is this? . . . Oh. Oh, *shit*. Does she know?" She shot Riven a strange look as the door closed.

"Should we be worried about that?" Kaya said.

"I haven't trusted her for a second," Riven said. "I say we bolt the door and forget about her."

"Or we stay on her good side until we've gotten through

this." Samir frowned at something out the window, his jaw twitching.

"She's a candy-coated gremlin made of Swiss Army knives. I don't even know what it *means* to be on her good side." Riven settled behind the coffee table and reassembled one of her revolvers, which she'd taken apart for cleaning. "I just hope we don't need her. Other crews are probably splitting up to hunt us. Hell, Jayde was killed in a safe zone. Someone isn't messing around."

"Which is why it's even more important we stay together," Asa said.

Riven screwed the last piece of *Blackjack* into place and stood up. The air grew warmer as she approached Asa, and it wasn't from the broken air-con unit. Her ponytail exposed the soft, translucent-pale skin of her neck.

"I know," Riven rasped, igniting a familiar tingle behind Asa's ribs. "I'll feel a lot better if you're behind me."

I'd follow you anywhere, a naïve, hopeful part of Asa whispered. But Riven was a time bomb, and until she went off, Asa was tethered to the inevitability of losing her.

"I'll be wherever I need to be," Asa murmured.

Riven's gaze fell, making her heavy lashes flutter. Not for the first time, Asa wished she could tell her how little she cared the future was uncertain. But they were past that. Riven had made it clear where she stood, and she wasn't Asa's to lose.

Asa was pulling away when the lights cut.

"Get away from the window," Samir's voice came through the dark. "Down on the floor. *Now.*"

Asa had learned to comply without question whenever

Samir used that voice. She crouched, but Riven was faster, dragging her into the hallway and lowering her firmly to the ground. Riven's body covered hers, pressing close, so close.

Dazed, Asa looked up, barely registering the others clustering around them. Stray locks from Riven's bangs tickled Asa's cheeks as Riven held her in place—

A horrific blast rocked the ground. Colors flared behind Riven, bursting through the dark, followed by a boom like a gunshot too close to her ears. Then the world went muffled, like being underwater, as smoke rushed through the air.

Riven rose into a crouch. "What the hell was that?!"

Samir slid a mag into his rifle. "Saw something on Galateo's camlink. A speeder circled the building three times. Guess they gave us our warning shot."

Asa mustered the courage to peek into the living room. Where the window had been, there was only a gaping hole. Beams of colored light from the street shone through clouds of drywall dust, and glass shrapnel had impaled Riven's water-stained posters.

"Is there anything they *haven't* ruined?" Riven poked a gun around the living room corner.

Samir shushed her. "Hear that?"

A clicking against the exterior brick, like mechanical claws. A soft *clink* like a canister opening. The blast hadn't been aimed to kill—it had made an opening. Someone was on their way.

Kaya gestured to the closet where hidden stairs descended to the abandoned subway tunnel. *Go*, Samir mouthed, ushering them toward it. Riven kept one revolver up as Diego scooped up Zephyr, a trembling ball of golden fur.

Just as Samir pulled the door open, reddish smoke drifted through the hole in the wall, clouding over the city lights. Tear gas. Asa hesitated until Riven shouted at her to "*Move!*" She didn't breathe until she'd slipped into the musty familiarity of the subway tunnels, Kaya close behind.

Gunshots rang out in the hideout, and Samir grabbed Riven's arm and pulled her inside the hidden exit, slamming the door.

"Why aren't we fighting?" Riven spat.

"It's not the time to engage," Samir said. "They came prepared for us."

"To the garage?" Asa said. The ladder to its lower hatch was a few tunnels over.

Samir nodded, rifle in hand. "We'll sweep the tunnels and run for it."

Diego handed the dog off to Kaya, then aimed his wristlet light down the tunnel. "Has anyone heard from Morphett?"

Riven narrowed her eyes. "If she had anything to do with this, she's dead."

No, Asa knew. If Morphett wanted to take their crew down, she'd had opportunities. This was bigger than any grudge of Morphett's.

Redline was closing in, and the target was on her.

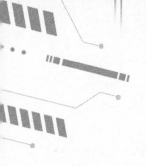

chapter 24

CIRCUITS & CONCRETE

Asa ran until the ladder rungs were cold within her grip. Until the hatch to the garage opened and her crew scrambled among the vehicles. Until her bike kicked to life beneath her.

She twisted the throttle, gunning for the skyway. The air tugged at her exosuit's straps and armor plates. The others were in Samir's speeder and close on her tail—but Riven was at her back, arms tightening around her. Here to shoot their way out if things got messier. They'd agreed to take two vehicles in case their attackers gave chase.

"Caught sight of our friend rounding the north exit," came Samir's voice over the comm. "We're going to split, see if we can drop off their radar. Meet you a few blocks from the coordinates."

The display on her bike's dash highlighted the coordinates she and Diego had found. The lead for the Staccato operatives was underground. They were running from danger, and possibly into something worse.

In the rearview mirror, Samir's speeder hit the blue holo of the skyway ramp, lifting from two to ten feet off the ground as it engaged the magnetic field. Then it took the opposite fork, arcing toward the dizzying sprawl of the tower markets.

"We'll keep an eye out." Riven's voice came through Asa's earpiece. "Galateo. Pinpoint shields?"

"They would not be able to keep up with you at these speeds, my deathless queen."

Riven grumbled, "I guess we're going commando, then."

Asa threaded around the ground traffic—the three lanes of cruisers and bikes treading directly on the blue holo. She was the reason they were all in danger again. She should've left months ago, when she'd had the chance. Even if Cortellion wasn't safe, she could've gone to Earth—maybe São Paulo, where her great-grandmother had grown up. The city where scientists developing restoration tech for the world's largest rainforest had made the breakthrough for terraforming new planets.

Now everything was slipping through her fingers. Even the girl at her back.

Asa twisted the throttle, taking a hard left as the skyway branched. No looking back. The coordinates were only two miles off now. The bike climbed into a narrow tunnel that rose above towering palms and broken balconies. Traffic thinned out, and only one other speeder moved in the two-lane stretch of road ahead.

For a moment, one of the billboards seemed to change. A woman with metallic-blue skin grinned, showing off HUD optics—and then her eyes were replaced by red Xs, melting black ooze. At next glance, it was back to normal. As if she'd imagined it.

A message appeared on her bike's dash: *Where do you think you're going?*

A ripple of light flared across the skyway beneath her tires. Warning symbols flashed above, and farther down the tunnel, an emergency barricade appeared. Layers of steel and holos snapped shut like a maw, sealing the tunnel ahead.

Asa hit the brakes. The speeder ahead of her attempted the same, brake lights flaring, but it was too late. The vehicle collided with the barrier, crumpling like a soda can.

Asa bit out a curse as her bike grated to a stop, a few speeder-lengths from the wreck. Even the traffic grid hadn't stopped it in time. Something else was in control.

"Asa." Riven's voice was hurried. "I think our tail is back."

Asa peered into the rearview mirror. A pair of lights grew as a dark gray speeder—a Spectre model—approached behind her, fast.

Her heartbeat surged. If it were connected to the traffic grid, it would slow automatically as it approached the sealed tunnel. But instead it hurtled up the hill, cutting a path straight toward them.

"I think this asshole wants to play chicken," Riven said as her blade unfolded next to Asa's thigh. She fired one revolver at the Spectre's lower thrusters. Perfect shots tore through the metal. Sparks flew, and the speeder's lift dropped—but it never swerved, never flinched.

Asa's palms grew sweaty on the handlebars. They were trapped at a dead end with a speeder that seemed determined to smash them both into shrapnel.

She backed up, wheeling the bike in an arc until they faced the speeder head-on. She'd need a burst of speed to dodge it, but that would propel her straight into the guardrail. Unless . . .

She saw it then—a gap between the holo-shielding of the tunnel and the guardrail of the skyway's carbon skeleton, barely wide enough for her bike. Another layer of skyway ran perpendicular beneath them.

Their only way out.

"You have a plan, mechanist?" There was no panic in Riven's voice.

"I do," Asa said. "And it's terrible."

Riven's arm tightened on her waist. "Sounds perfect."

The headlights flared brighter. As the Spectre passed beneath a streetlamp, Asa glimpsed empty seats beneath the windshield. No passengers, and nothing to lose.

"Come on," she challenged under her breath. "Get me. Let's do this."

When the Spectre was so close she could feel the breeze from its thrusters, she gunned it.

Asa steered toward the edge, and the world seemed to slow. She imagined the projected path of the speeder, flying toward inevitable impact. The arc of her own jump, and a thousand ways to land her bike wrong.

This was something Riven would do. But Asa had built up years' worth of reckless chances not taken, and she had to hope luck would tilt the dice in her favor. Just once.

The bike sped over the edge, and the wheels lifted from the holo. The world slowed. Electrical fire spread through her, the descent pulling at her every fiber.

Her tires hit the lower skyway with a teeth-chattering bounce, and then she was zipping forward again, hurtling toward traffic. She kicked the brake, turning the bike into a drift curve. It lurched to a stop on the skyway's shoulder, shuddering with every vehicle that whizzed by. Asa vaguely registered a metallic rumble somewhere above. But they'd made it.

"Oh, damn," Riven gasped, pressing her forehead to Asa's shoulder. "Thought *I* was the one with a death wish."

Kaya's shouts came over the comm. "What the hell did you do? Your tracker just flipped between skyways, and—*que merda*, Asa, say something!"

"We're fine," Asa said. "But . . ."

Greasy smoke bloomed from the skyway they'd leaped off. The wrecks of two speeders now lay smashed against the emergency barrier.

Redline's speeder was a sparking ruin. It'd been unoccupied, but the other probably hadn't been. Whoever'd been inside was now collateral damage, like everything else Asa was leaving in her wake.

Maybe Riven had been right. The two of them together were primed like a nuclear reactor, and they were burning everything to ash.

Samir's voice came over the comm, and Riven gave a breathless explanation. When her gloved hands gripped Asa's waist again, Asa hesitated to turn the engine back on.

For a brief moment, they were safe. The city sprawled around them, wild and menacing, and it hit her how small and desperate they were, fighting to survive in the belly of a beast made of circuits and concrete. Where nothing was certain except the road beneath her and the tech at her command.

But if she didn't keep moving, she'd be swallowed whole.

"Hang on," Asa said, revving the engine again. "We're getting out of here."

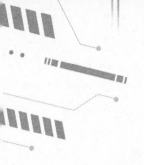

Riven would finish this job if it killed her.

Now that she was back on solid ground, rage seeped through her, vicious and intoxicating. Her ship, her hideout–everything was turning to ash in her hands. Redline had spread lies and made them homeless.

So if they had to bust down the door of this boarded-up shack, so be it. Asa and Diego's coordinates had led to a shabby building in the underground market. Even now, Redline might be watching from the musty pawnshops and sketchy brothels.

"What do you think they're hiding in there?" Asa said, fidgeting with her suit's gloves. "Do you think it's a server farm?"

"Maybe," Riven said. The peeling posters behind the window well grates suggested a defunct electronics shop. "Definitely looks like a place where they breed computers for slaughter."

Diego rolled his eyes and let out the longest, most exhausted sigh she'd ever heard.

"We should kick the door in," she said. *Knock-knock, assholes.*

"No." Samir slid his hands into the pockets of his worn jacket, aggressively casual. "This is clearly a front. Stay cool." He wasn't wrong. No way Sokolov's operatives were dealing in secondhand speakers.

The crowds were sparse in this corner of the lower

markets. Steam rose from the vents, smearing the overblown colors outside the recycled cybernetics stalls and VR dens. Cheap speakers blared chipper bubble-rock music from the 2160s. She thought of Morphett again—strangely absent now, with no messages to update them where she'd gone.

"I'm not waiting for Redline's lackeys to catch up," Riven said. "How else are we getting in?"

"I feel . . . a hum." Kaya headed around the corner with Zephyr wriggling under one arm, then stopped before a dented alley door. Gently, she touched the keypad. Her lips twitched as her brown eyes seemed to stare through the door. Then the keypad chirped as it unlocked. "Something is watching this place. And it really doesn't want to be disturbed."

"A little late for that." Riven quelled the shudder that threatened to rip through her and put up her holo-helm.

Samir shouldered the door open, rifle at the ready. Riven guided the others in. When the door closed behind them, the dark was stifling.

There wasn't much here but an old, still-glowing vending machine. The electronics demo tables were long since looted. Riven kept her guns trained on the shadows. She had a nasty feeling about this place.

Kaya trailed her fingertips along the walls, her eyes glassy and wide. "There's a lot more on the lower level than bootleg copies of *Death Raider IV.*"

"How do we get down there?" Asa said.

"We could take the stairs," Kaya mumbled, setting Zephyr in Samir's arms. Then she moved her hand over a peeling poster of a chainsaw-wielding demon. "Here."

A holo shimmered, revealing a steel door behind the false posters. Kaya unlocked it, and Riven pushed through.

Dim lights clicked on as she entered, revealing a narrow staircase. A moldering reek crept through the vent in her holo-helm, like sweat and old urine, and she had to stop herself from imagining what condition their missing people might be in.

"That's not a good smell," Samir said. He slid past Riven, a new intensity crackling off his skin. Where there were hostages concerned—people getting hurt on his turf—Samir always had to stick his neck out.

Riven followed him down the stairs, and every breath sent the world spinning. The sickness was ejecting its talons into her skull, her spine. The bottom of the staircase opened to an underground warehouse illuminated by deep red light that seemed to emanate from nowhere. The tang of filth sharpened.

Her eyes adjusted to rows of shipping crates and make-shift curtains pulled back to reveal surgical chairs and vats of viscous black fluid. In the faint light, she saw some of the shipping containers were barred, like portable prison cells. And there were silhouettes inside. Silhouettes that weren't moving.

"What is this place?" Asa whispered into the unearthly quiet. Somewhere in the dark, Zephyr whined.

Eyes up, every instinct screamed at Riven. *Be ready.* She clicked on her wristlet light and forced herself forward.

The beam of light caught a face pressed to the bars—staring, jaundiced eyes, and a bloody slash opening a throat.

Riven staggered backward. "Oh, *shit*."

In the shipping containers were people. And if the quiet was any indication, they were all dead.

Asa let out a choked cry.

"What is this?" Samir's voice broke. "Organ piracy?"

"No," Riven said, forcing herself to look again. In the other cages were more of the same—people slaughtered, sloppy, wounds still oozing. "They were just . . . stabbed. Left here to rot. All the wounds are fresh." Something didn't add up. Nothing had been harvested, and none of the cuts resembled surgical precision. What the hell was Staccato *doing*?

"Hello?" Asa called, a little louder. "If you're conscious, call out. We're here to help."

Only her own echo answered.

Diego's wristlet scanner ghosted over one of the corpses. He looked at the result, frowned, and moved to the next. "None of these people are registered with a syndicate. But this man— he went missing from a SilCaul brothel a few weeks ago."

"They're collecting people who wouldn't be missed," Samir said.

Diego nodded. "Certainly knew what they could get away with." Then, with grim determination, he flicked his wristlet light on and began snapping photos and vidclips. Evidence. They'd found almost everything Cerys had wanted, except for *why*.

"Just one botched job, one slip," Samir said. "Only takes one person in this city to decide you're worth more dead." Riven knew the edge in his voice. Samir's anger was a slow, forceful thing. Even if it wasn't directed at her, it sent a shiver crawling across her skin. "I think we have a lot to tell Cerys."

It was a Samir she hadn't seen in a long time. The military had never been his dream, but he'd excelled at CAA because he excelled at everything. And whenever he had a good reason, he became one of the scariest damn people in this city. It was the Samir they'd need if they were getting through this alive.

Riven's fuse was much shorter. *Any of these could've been you*, part of her whispered. *Broke and desperate, and on the matriarchs' hit lists. Selling yourself to survive.*

Maybe it still would be, if she didn't finish this.

"Either Staccato is responsible, or they're covering this up," she said. Whoever had done this would pay, whether or not Cerys wanted them alive. Whether or not there'd be fallout.

At her feet was a bloody smear on the concrete, as if someone had crawled while bleeding. Riven's flashlight followed the dark smudge to a corpse in a surgical smock, curled up near one of the vats. Next to the scientist was a dead operative wearing a helmet with Staccato's signature serrated jawline. The operative's chest was slashed open, and a gun had fallen from their hands, as if they'd died protecting the scientist. From what?

She pulled the light away before the wounds could burn themselves into her mind. "There's a dead scientist and an operative over here. What the hell happened?"

"There's something in that operative's head," Kaya whispered. "Some kind of tech attached to the brain. Offline now, but—"

The air seemed to freeze as something creaked in the dark behind them. Bending metal. The *snick* of a latch pulling shut. All of them went dead silent, not daring to breathe.

Then came the slow tap of footsteps.

"Staccato didn't kill them," a familiar whisper trickled. "*I did.*"

Riven's fingers slid onto triggers. The voice echoed from everywhere, hitting her nerves like a tremor.

"I intercepted your communications," Redline said. "Thank you, Valdez, for helping me find this place. I thought I was onto something with Jayde, but she was only the tip of the iceberg."

Diego swore under his breath.

Riven's head spun. So Jayde *wasn't* just a warning shot. She was the daughter of Staccato's matriarch, and if Redline had business here . . . "Why are you after Staccato?"

"They're working with *him*." The voice seemed to slink closer. "All of them, corrupted."

Him. There was only one *him* Redline seemed to hate, and he was the reason they were after Asa.

Riven nodded to Samir, and they urged the other three into a gap between storage crates, giving them some cover. Riven could already taste gunpowder on her tongue.

"You're saying my dad was experimenting on these people?" Kaya said. "And you killed the victims?"

"I *freed* them. A mercy killing." Rage seeped into Redline's voice, human and real. The shell of a humanoid mech glittered in the dark, then disappeared behind one of the crates. Another set of slow, heavy footsteps clung to the shadows. "Staccato captured and tampered with them as tools for him. Echofall was already inside their heads."

"Oh, fuck you," Riven spat. "Almeida didn't do this—you did."

From one of the shipping containers, a blank-eyed stare

met hers. A girl with matted brown hair and ripped shorts, a worn plush puppy clutched in one hand. The mismatched clothes and small comforts reminded Riven of herself a handful of years ago, the first time her luck had run out.

This is for your own good, the patrol officer had spat as twelve-year-old Riven dropped the spray-paint can to clutch her split lip and throbbing teeth. *Maybe you'll learn this time.* She'd always been a target then—a girl who'd kept getting herself in trouble to feel something, who would've burned herself to ash if she hadn't found the few people who cared about her.

These people weren't as lucky. Nobody had come to save them. The dead girl in the cell reminded her why she'd dreamed of becoming a matriarch in the first place.

"Galateo," Riven whispered. "Can you tell where the signal on that mech is transmitting from?" If Redline was a technomancer like Kaya, they'd be camped somewhere to circuit dive. Vulnerable.

There was a pause. Then: "There," Galateo said in her earpiece. Her wristlet screen showed signal paths pointing to her left, close by. Across the room was a sliding door, jammed half-open.

"This is a necessary consequence of your father's actions," Redline said. "These people were a lost cause. Do you see what your empire caused, Asanna? If you want to avenge these people, start by cutting your own throat."

"I'm going in," Riven whispered. "Don't wait up."

Samir grabbed her wrist. "Don't." His voice was barely above a breath. "If we separate, they'll try to pick us off."

Asa nudged Kaya, and Kaya's voice echoed in Riven's

earpiece—heavily processed, like it was whenever she used her mind and not her mouth to send messages. "Just wait. We need to stick together. Find out what Redline knows."

But she couldn't wait. Riven had tried to hollow herself out long ago, to scoop out her emotions and splatter them in the dirt. Now she was far past fear. In those hollow parts, the anger was slow and unstoppable, taking root.

Riven pulled her hand out of Samir's grip. "There's no reasoning with them."

"Riv." Samir's eyes were staring past her, tracking something in the dark. "I need twenty seconds. Wait—"

"I know where the threat is. I can make this fast. Keep them safe."

With that, she crouched and ran. Past the crates of corpses, through the half-open door, and into the corridor beyond. She didn't flinch even as the door snapped shut behind her.

The memories of Sanctum's Edge roiled like an undertow. The blank eyes of the human experiments who'd killed Emmett.

This time, she had a chance to stop them.

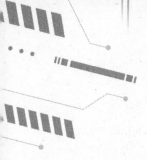

ALIAS

With Riven gone, the crawling sensation on Asa's skin grew worse.

"She's going to get herself killed," Samir murmured. Asa sidled closer to Kaya, who held their trembling dog. Only Samir stood between them and the creatures in the dark.

"Riven, come back," Asa said into her comm, but only static responded. So much for sticking together. The steel door had snapped shut behind Riven, and an electromagnetic barrier now hummed over its surface.

"All the comms are cutting," Diego said. "Something's interfering."

Redline was in control here, separating them. All in pursuit of her.

"Why do you think this is my fault?" Asa called into the dark. "I told you, I don't know what Echofall *is.*" The bloodstains and haunted eyes remained burned into her mind, even when she looked away. Was this how the test subjects in her father's lab had looked? At Sanctum's Edge?

If you want to avenge these people, start by cutting your own throat.

"He doesn't plan for you to know yet," the voice purred. Every time it spoke, she heard the footsteps moving closer, as if Redline's speaking were meant as a distraction. "You're not only a pawn, but you fled to let his empire fester."

"We need to get out of here," Kaya's mental whisper came in her earpiece. "There's a prickle in my head. And I'm pinging some mechs and mods over there."

"I'm not leaving Riven behind," Asa said, even if they might not have much choice.

"What kinds of mods?" Diego whispered to Kaya.

"Carbon skeletal reinforcements and dark vision oculars," Kaya said. "Though I think it's all just one person. Human."

Asa stared at the flickering shadows among the corpses in the crates. The darkness now seemed to have eyes everywhere, leaving them all vulnerable.

Beside her, Samir's breathing shifted. It was subtle, but she knew that steady, coiling tension. "That *human* is guarding our way out."

"Kaya, can you scramble his oculars?" Diego whispered.

"I can try. Might only be able to give you a few seconds."

"If you can," Samir said, "just say when."

For a few moments, Asa heard nothing but her own breaths and a ventilation hum. Then, on Kaya's signal, Samir broke into a run, disappearing around the corner of the nearest container.

What came next were grunts and gunshots.

Through the bars, Asa could barely see the commotion. Sparks flew as bullets met body armor. A flare of molten orange scythed toward Samir, searing metal bars. His opponent had a plasma blade.

Asa gripped her stunner, willing herself to move. Riven should be backing him up.

"Where are the mechs?" Diego hissed. He'd drawn a tiny pistol from his jacket.

"I . . . I can't tell," Kaya said. "Everything's scrambling."

With a loud clatter, the plasma blade fell to the ground, smoking on the concrete. In the wan light, Asa saw Samir grip the other figure from behind, his hands on their neck. A quick yank, and with a grunt and a horrific crack, the figure fell limp.

Samir panted, locks of hair falling out of place. With a deep breath, he stepped over the body, not looking back. The corpse's face glared, slack-jawed, just as the plasma blade winked out.

"How disappointing," Redline snarled. "Orsen had been salivating to give you a try. I knew he'd be all talk." More scraping in the dark, clanking of metal on concrete.

Orsen. Nell's teammate. Asa's heart pounded. Did Redline's trap have something to do with the trial, or was Orsen trying to snuff them as revenge for Banshee? It wasn't adding up.

Samir crouched beside her. "We need to get to Riven. Now." He jabbed his rifle toward the sealed door, signaling her and the others to follow. Diego covered Kaya, and Asa clung tight to her stunner.

"Come closer, Asa," Redline called, harsher this time. "I can tell you how Echofall works. I can *cut it out* for you."

Cut it out. The fear dug cold fingers into Asa's chest, prying her ribs apart. Her father had created Kaya for Winterdark, and his work hadn't ended there.

Samir grabbed the metal latch on the door, then yanked his hand away as if shocked. Then he tucked his hand into his sleeve and pulled again, but it wouldn't budge.

"Kaya, Dee, it would be great if someone could get this door open!" he called. Nearby, the murky surfaces of the vats began to shiver.

Kaya was stroking Zephyr's fur, murmuring under her breath, when her eyes snapped open. "Samir. Behind you!"

A creature burst from the fluid, dark liquid sluicing over its edges. One arm of Redline's mech stretched into a metallic garotte, wrapping around Samir's neck.

Samir reacted immediately, grabbing the appendage and shifting his weight as he struggled against its grip.

Asa almost missed the splash behind her. She whirled just as another mech rose from the fluid, red Xs flickering under its helmet.

Its arms morphed into metallic claws as it reached for her throat.

Riven ran through the maintenance tunnel of hissing pipes. If Redline had a body, it was somewhere close. Almost close enough to eat bullets. She could *feel* it.

"My deathless queen," Galateo piped up. "The door has electromagnetically sealed behind you. This does not bode well."

"Then I guess I have to keep moving." The tunnel twisted into a hairpin curve, and she pressed her back to the wall, catching her breath, listening.

Only a phantom dripping echoed, so she slowly turned the corner, letting *Blackjack* lead. A series of mangled lumps littered the floor ahead. A flicker of light caught body armor, blood. Three of Sokolov's operatives, dead on the ground.

They're working with him, Redline had said. *All of them, corrupted.*

The sting in Riven's skull tightened its grip. Cerys wouldn't be happy about this—and neither would Sokolov.

The slightest tremor pulsed through the air, a shiver of instinct. She immediately whipped *Blackjack*'s barrel toward the ceiling and fired.

The mech dropped like a spider, landing on its feet with one arm sparking. A pair of red Xs lit up behind its visor as it cocked its head. This mech was covered with bullet holes, now welded shut. It was the one she'd taken out before, back from the dead.

Riven hurled more bullets into the mech's joints as its hands morphed into claws, swinging like scythes. One latched on to her thigh, tearing the seam of her exosuit and forcing a cry from her throat. She clicked her tech-blade to life and carved upward, shearing the claw off at the elbow.

Her thigh stung like hell, and then her whole leg sank into warm numbness. No time to dwell on it. She brought *Blackjack* into a cross with her blade arm, sending disruptors tearing through the mech's neck and chest.

"Should've cut you to pieces and burned them," she muttered to the smoking ruin, sliding a few fresh bullets into *Blackjack* and twisting the cylinder back into place. Someone had repaired this thing. Probably a pair of *human* hands.

As the red lights on the mech faded, bright trails lingered in their wake. Dizziness washed over her, compounding the white noise. Something had been on that mech's claws—*in* them.

She crouched next to the dead mech. A thick needle was mounted within the claw—a combat-grade injector, designed for fast, imprecise hits. The dizziness amplified, and the world refracted into geometric colors. Every edge was so bright, and the room stuttered like a slowing frame rate when she turned her head.

"What did you do to me?" she murmured. She felt heavy, like her blood was turning to tar. But there was an electrifying giddiness there too. Not just a sedative.

Riven hacked the mech's head off and carried it in her palm like a gravball. If Redline thought one mech would stop her, they were dead wrong.

Ahead, the path plunged downward, and the tunnel deadended in a small room lit by glowing screens. A figure sat in front of them, motionless in concentration. They didn't need keystrokes to issue commands. Just like Kaya.

When they lifted their head, the light caught the harsh angles of Nell's face.

What the hell.

"Hello, Riven," Nell said. Blood ran from the corners of her mouth, like Kaya during a hard circuit dive.

"I think this is yours." Riven wound back and hurled the mech's head at her.

Nell caught it effortlessly in one hand and observed it with mechanical precision. "After all the time I spent repairing it." She clicked her tongue and threw it back at Riven with unnerving force. Riven swerved aside, and it clanged against the wall. "I expected you'd come alone. Dying makes you reckless, I suppose."

"Redline should've learned by now that I'm going to rip them apart every time they get close to Asa." Riven raised her gun, even as her vision blurred. "So what is this? This whole time, Redline's lackey has been you?"

A grin split Nell's razor-perfect face. And then her voice changed, becoming deeper, richer. "I don't answer to anyone." The voice spilling from her lips was Redline's.

Riven's breaths came ragged. *How?* If Nell was Redline, then she'd been responsible for all of it—destroying *Boomslang*, blowing up the hideout, killing Jayde.

There was a thread here she wasn't seeing. On the screens, tangles of wires from the power-system diagrams seemed to float and twist, forming mocking faces.

"You spent years working your way up through Rio Oscuro," Riven said. "Then you woke up one day and decided to go after Luca Almeida and his daughters? Why are you so obsessed with Asa?"

"You're not in much condition for an interrogation." Redline's voice came from behind her. *Dammit.* Something was wrong with Riven's head, the pain gripping her like a fist. She steadied *Blackjack*'s barrel. *Focus!*

Her bullet smashed through Nell's collarbone, a little left of where she'd aimed.

The disruptor had hit its mark, but no blood splattered from the fragmenting bullet. Instead, Nell moved with inhuman speed. Her gauntleted fist hit Riven's helm once at the temple, then again as she fired another shot at Nell's shoulder.

The holo-shield in front of her eyes flickered, and her helm disappeared as the battery died, letting her hair fall loose.

The air hit her sweaty skin, and she gulped in a breath. The world spun beneath her.

"It's the glitch, isn't it?" Nell said, in Redline's voice. Riven managed to dodge her next punch, catching the wrist in her free hand. "Only a mild neurotoxin, but with an affliction like yours, it reacts *quite* badly."

She knew about Riven's sickness. The one thing that made her weak.

Riven pressed *Blackjack*'s muzzle under Nell's chin. "You don't know a damned thing about me. I told you to talk. Now, *talk*."

Even at gunpoint, Nell didn't flinch. "Some addicts say glitch can help you hear the voices of dead Etri, or whispers from distant worlds. What will you see as you die?" Nell's voice was silken calm.

Droplets of blood mottled the ground, blindingly bright. There was an itch at her ear. Blood on her suit, her arm. The white noise was getting worse by the second. Somehow, her gun had fallen to the ground, slipped from her quivering fingers.

Rage simmered up her throat. She ejected the blade in her right hand and jammed it through Nell's stomach.

Or, at least, she would've, if the world hadn't shifted.

Riven felt the blade make contact, heard Nell's sharp intake of breath. Then pain rocked through her knees, her elbows, and she was on the ground. Another sharp pain lanced her ribs as a kick landed, then two.

She coughed, sputtering on the lab floor. Colors twisted

and blurred violently. Both her hands were empty now. With a shaking hand, she groped for *Verdugo*, still in its holster.

Nell's boot came down on her wrist. "You were so close to figuring it out, Riven. Nell Mikos died a month ago. Maybe I'll show you my face—my real one."

Riven could only grunt as not-Nell clicked a tiny holo-projector on her neck and her features shifted subtly. Scars deepened beneath her jawline. Her nose became wider, cheeks higher. Her skin melded with metal at her neck and scalp, making it impossible to tell how much of her body was flesh. Her face now had bow lips and deep, searching eyes. It was a face Riven recognized.

Her pulse roared. She blinked away the illusion, but this was *real*. Even through the glitch haze, it was undeniable.

Staring back at her was Kaya's face.

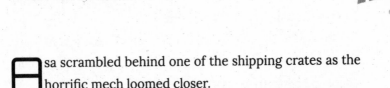

chapter 27
SISTER

Asa scrambled behind one of the shipping crates as the horrific mech loomed closer.

"Even now, you're running." Its claws dripped rust-black fluid onto the concrete. "Even as your girl succumbs to the disease eating her nerves—another part of *Winterdark* you failed to stop. You cling to the shadows while our father continues doing horrible things."

"I want him gone as much as you do!" Asa choked. "He doesn't even consider me his heir. He wanted me dead!" She pulled the trigger on her stunner. The blast crackled, sending the mech stuttering.

"Don't mistake his silence for him forgetting." It lunged. Asa barely managed to roll out of the way as its claws scraped the floor, leaving sparks in their wake. The mech rose to its full height, swaggering toward her. "He considers you his prodigal daughter. And after you attended that gala, he no longer must explain your disappearance. What do you think he'll do to ensure you remain his successor?"

"*Stop*," Kaya hissed. "Leave my sister alone." Kaya's focus was coalescing. A charge built in the air, raising goose bumps on Asa's skin.

"Oh, Kaya," Redline murmured. "Rely on clever tricks all

you want, but you're inexperienced. The circuits are my world, not yours."

With Redline's attention elsewhere, Asa ran toward Samir on instinct. He had the upper hand now, plugging bullets into the monster he'd hurled to the ground. But before she could reach him, a set of claws fastened around her ankle. The mech yanked, and Asa's heart skipped before she hit the ground. She fought and kicked, scuffing her exosuit's elbows as the concrete dragged by beneath her. Until she was behind a shipping container, and Samir was out of view.

"He'll stop at nothing until he's reprogrammed human minds on a mass scale." Redline's mech loomed over her, pinning her. "Pretending to save the world while distributing a new means of control. The final piece of his plan is you. It's *always* been you." The helmet split into a maw of shattered glass, a horrible grin edging closer to her face. "He needs his successor, very soon. You were always destined to be more brilliant and ruthless than him. No matter how far you run, he will use you to subjugate Requiem. He's already implanted Echofall inside your head."

"No," Asa whispered. The world tunneled. *Inside your head.* Redline seemed to know so much about her father. All the memories of home, the seductive pull of Cortellion—how much of that was really her? Did her father pull the bounties because he knew she'd return?

He would've had to open her skull to change her. A chill wormed through her stomach as she felt for the small scar behind her ear—one she'd had since she was a kid and had fallen from a tree in the water-gardens. But she couldn't remember falling, she'd been so young . . .

"It's not true." Kaya's digitized voice was strained in her earpiece. "Echofall is recent. An extension of Winterdark. You wouldn't have run away if he controlled you. They're just trying to bait you!"

"The files for Echofall show you're to be his prime test subject," Redline said.

Asa grasped the last threads holding herself together. She had to believe Kaya. "You don't even know me. I am *not* like him."

"Aren't you? I've seen the spark in your eyes, ever since you were a child." Redline's claw traced a stinging line across her throat.

Asa cried out, seeing spots from the pain. Redline knew so much, as if they'd grown up with her. Grown up with her father. Fragments of memories surfaced—the strange messages hounding her when she'd first learned to program as a child. *Shut it down, Asa*, one had said. *Listen to me.*

Her father had pulled her away from the computer system, warning her about cyber-stalkers who'd pursue their family for being in the public eye. Asa had diligently shut down anomalous messages after that, but had it been *Redline* trying to reach her?

Something else Redline had said finally clicked.

Our father.

"I know who you are," Asa whispered.

An inconclusive file in the Winterdark vault, ending in the

year 2168. A girl with Kaya's face. A discovery Asa had tried to forget.

The claws released a fraction. "Say it, then. Name me." Vitriol laced Redline's voice. "Nobody else will."

"You're my oldest sister," Asa said. "Sofi Almeida."

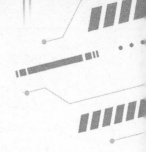

chapter 28
THE FACE IN
THE DARK

My oldest sister.

The girl she'd thought lost in the circuits. A girl Kaya might've become, if Asa hadn't saved her from Winterdark.

The claw of Redline's—*Sofi's*—mech pulled away from Asa's throat. The glass-shard teeth smoothed back into the helmet. "So you know."

I learned from her, Asa's father had said. *Used her as a foundation for my second daughter.*

How alike were Sofi and Kaya? Would Sofi have been an artist, a prankster, a girl who loved the glimmering city streets like her own bones?

"He tampered with you," Asa whispered. "Like he wanted to change Kaya."

"He *tried* to," Sofi's mech seethed. "And if your other sister understood what you were responsible for, she wouldn't be protecting you. We're the same, after all—" The mech sputtered, freezing in place.

Asa tilted her head and saw Kaya stagger to her feet, her eyes aflame.

"You aren't me," Kaya whispered. "I would *never* have done this."

Kaya sliced her hand downward, and the mech slammed against the concrete. Immediately, Samir's bullets tore through its helmet, its shoulders, until it was still.

"Asa. Are you okay?" Samir was breathing hard, and a cut bled on one cheek. The second mech was a dead, sparking tangle of limbs behind him.

"Yes," Asa said weakly as Samir pulled her to her feet. Her head still spun. Sofi wasn't dead, but changed. Lost. How much of her was still human?

Kaya struggled from her brief delves into circuitspace, but to be lost there for decades . . . what would it do to someone? And how much of what Sofi said was true?

The lights stuttered overhead. Somewhere, Riven was still trapped. Asa ran back toward the sealed door but stopped short of grabbing the electrified handle. It still hummed with an electromagnet.

"Riven," Asa begged into her static-laced comm channel. "Come in. Are you okay?"

A few seconds of silence stretched by. Then another voice answered.

"*Don't bother*," Sofi whispered. "*She's as good as dead.*"

As Riven faded in and out of consciousness, the monster watched her with Kaya's eyes.

"What the hell *are* you?" Riven slurred. Maybe she couldn't trust her perception right now. She'd left Kaya back with the others. But if Nell was dead, and Redline had taken *her* identity– "Are you going to kill Kaya like you killed Nell?"

The not-Nell gave a bitter laugh as she pulled her boot off Riven's wrist. "I didn't kill Nell. She knew what she was getting into when we began working together. I was helping her find her former partner in exchange for her connections in Rio Oscuro, but she had a nasty accident during a job. Since she'd already been accepted into the Ascension Trial, I figured I could still use her."

Riven reached for *Verdugo* again, but found its holster empty. "So why–" Her throat was so dry it hurt to speak. "Why Kaya's face?"

"This face was mine first." Redline scowled with Kaya's lips. "Kaya wasn't the only sister Asanna had. And she would've known that, if she hadn't turned a blind eye to her empire's crimes."

Sisters. Almeida's test-subject daughters. Riven didn't want to admit it was possible, even as the glitch sucked her under.

The light caught the blue-black of Redline's hair, and it refracted into spikes like frost spiderwebbing across glass, into blue feathers of the winged nebula. Suddenly Riven was sitting with Emmett in the starfield again, as he told her the Etri myth of the nebula's creation–a bird that wove its wings from sorrow in the void of space.

"Asanna doesn't care about anyone but herself," a distant voice was saying. "You always had some time before your affliction killed you, but she just kept running. She left you to die, like she left me to rot."

Riven coughed. Maybe Redline was right. Maybe this whole time, Asa'd had answers within reach, but lying low had been more important than finding a way to fix her.

With her senses failing, it no longer mattered. Redline needed to die, or she'd be wearing Riven's face next. Using her like she'd used Nell.

The pain was a furious throb shooting up her spine, and the world blurred between reality and echoes in her head. There was no standing up this time. Her sickness was reacting to the drug, the stress.

It's over.

So many times she'd imagined this—slipping into a place deep and hollow and empty, where the pain and dread simply *faded* and nothing mattered anymore. And here it finally was, pulling her under. But a small, furious thought thrashed back.

No. If I go now, they've won.

Everyone who'd told her she'd never be anything more, everyone who'd wanted to see her fail—it would be a victory for them. And she'd scatter shrapnel in her wake, leaving scars and broken shards stuck in everyone she cared about: Asa. Samir. And that tiny, buried hope, somehow, *maybe*, Ty.

One more minute, she told herself. *That's all I need. Please.*

Riven opened her eyes. Redline had turned on her heel to walk back toward the control consoles. Riven pushed herself into a crouch. Stumbled. Then grabbed the woman's ankle and yanked, throwing her to the ground.

Not dead yet. You piece of shit.

Her tech-blade was barely within reach. She rolled onto Redline's prone body, pinning her throat, squeezing. Whoever this asshole was, she didn't have military training. Not hours spent on the training mats, learning to subdue people bigger than her, grappling on the ground and twisting, choking—

Riven drove the buzzing blade straight into Redline's metallic guts.

Redline gasped. Thrashed. Sparks flew from the wound, blood burbled, and then . . . she went still.

Riven collapsed next to the half-machine corpse, and the world went dark.

Asa and Samir were both tugging on the sealed door, the handle wrapped in Samir's jacket, when the lights plunged overhead.

With a descending hum, the room went completely dark. Then came a sucking *pop*, like an electromagnet disengaging.

"Um." Samir took a step backward and flicked on his wristlet light. "Did we do that?"

"Wasn't me," Kaya's voice came through the dark. "The circuits just got . . . quieter."

Asa's throat closed in a hard, choking lump. Did this have something to do with Riven?

Samir gave the door another heave, and it reluctantly whined open. He shone his wristlet light down the maintenance tunnel. "Riven?" he called. When there was no answer, he ran ahead.

Asa struggled to keep up on shaky legs. The tunnel was quiet. No gunshots, no shouting, nothing. *She's as good as dead.* No. No, no, no—

Samir stepped over bodies, and it took a heart-squeezing moment to recognize Sokolov's operatives and another mech, the latter in pieces and riddled with bullet holes. Riven's work. She had to be close. They continued into a room lit by static-filled holoscreens, and Samir stopped near two prone forms on the ground.

His flashlight caught shining blood on Riven's lip. Her gray-green eyes were blown bright and stared into nothing.

"Oh, shit." He crouched next to her. "Riv. Talk to me."

"Riven," Asa whispered, falling to her knees. "Oh god . . ."

Samir's fingers gently pressed against Riven's pulse points. "She's alive. But I don't know for how much longer."

"She needs immediate medical attention," Galateo said from Riven's wristlet, startling Asa. "Her opponent used a neurotoxin that has exacerbated her condition."

Diego hung back, whispering a prayer in Spanish. Asa almost didn't dare to look at the corpse next to Riven, but she had to know if it was true.

The corpse's chrome-blue body armor was spattered with blood. A gaping scar across the midsection revealed innards of shattered metal where Riven's blade had struck home. And the half-machine girl had Kaya's face.

Sofi's face. Scarred human skin—maybe the only part of her original body she'd clung to.

"My sister," Asa whispered. All the secrets she hadn't delved into, too afraid of becoming her father: Riven's affliction, her father's prisoners, a sister she'd never known. Just another way Asa had failed.

"We need to go." Kaya wouldn't look at Sofi, at the face uncannily similar to hers. "I don't doubt Redline has a backup somewhere."

Samir slung Riven's arm over his shoulder. "Riv. We're here. We need you to hang on a bit longer."

Riven let out a strangled moan, her head hanging against her carbon chest plates. A bloody gash had opened on her thigh.

"We need to get help." Asa's voice cracked. "Where can we take her?"

"There's a clinic a few blocks over," Diego muttered. "They might have a drug antagonist to treat overdoses. But with her condition . . ." He trailed off. Nobody wanted to say it.

Maybe Riven had been right. This was inevitable—Riven's fate, and hers.

"Stay with me," Asa whispered as they left the tunnel. She trailed her hands over Riven's shoulders, through her hair. Anything to keep her conscious. "Just a little longer."

chapter 29

RESCUER

Moments of pain stretched into hours, maybe *years*, and Ty was still alone.

Sometimes he opened his eyes to the plain white walls and portholes offering a slow-drifting view of the stars. Sometimes he retreated to a small burrow deep within himself. Everything still hurt, but in the quiet, he could pretend the pain wasn't real.

Sometimes he saw flashes through someone else's eyes—blood shimmering beneath mechanical claws, blank stares between metal bars, Asa whispering *please wake up* over Riven's glassy eyes as she rushed through familiar alleys.

It was ending. He'd been so close to saving her.

Ty pulled back into himself, shivering in his cold sweat. Even if he could stand, he wasn't getting out of here. His cybernetics were feeding off his body's electrical currents to hurt him. He could only hope it would end soon.

When the floor shook and a ship engine whirred outside the safe house, his first instinct was that it was another dream. But he managed to roll into a sitting position against the wall, and the noise sharpened into voices.

"Didn't get very far." Through the transparent door, Ty saw two helmeted figures on the walkway, anchored by the artificial gravity.

"Kid didn't know what he was getting into," the other figure responded, rapping the empty escape pod with their knuckles. "He's probably in bad shape."

Almeida's forces, come to retrieve the fugitive. Seemed Yllath hadn't managed to stop them.

Ty closed his eyes. The best he could do now was surrender. The vials in his pocket might never make it to Riven. He began to drift, ears ringing, pulse racing. Somewhere beyond it, the guards' chatter turned to swearing. He heard a hum as another ship arrived, a hiss as a door depressurized. Voices rising. An argument.

Slowly, Ty opened his eyes.

The operatives were raising rifles at a newcomer. "There's no bounty on him. He's property of Almeida Labs. You should leave."

The girl sauntering toward them was five-foot-nothing and pear-shaped, with curly hair tangled into buns. She gave them a delicate shrug, and her forearms parted to eject long blades sweeping into wicked points. "I don't think you were listening. I *did* ask nicely."

"We have permission to use force if you—"

Morphett cricked her neck, and two slim metal appendages unfurled from her back, extending like an insect's legs. Then she was on them—her talons ripping their helmets off, her forearm blades arcing toward their throats.

Ty couldn't watch as more blood was spilled to protect him.

Soon the screams and whirring went silent, and there were only light footsteps on the walkway. Ty gripped his cybernetic arm as the door to the safe house slid open.

In the white lights, a deadly grin beamed down at him.

"Hello, Princess," Morphett said. "You called for a rescuer?"

The next thing Ty knew, he was tossed ass-first into a passenger seat.

"There you go," Morphett grunted, pulling the harness tight across him. "Don't need you flopping around when we hit atmo."

"Where are you taking me?"

"Passengers get to sit tight and shut up." Morphett tugged up the hem of his pantleg. He felt a brief pressure as something clicked over his ankle. "She still thinks you're dead. I am *so* excited to see her face when I throw you at her feet."

Please don't throw me, he thought. But some of the fog lifted. "You're taking me back to them?"

"Eventually." Her gum popped.

For Morphett, it seemed too good to be true. He turned his ankle. It had to be a tracker, or something worse. As if he didn't already have enough tech trying to kill him. "Riven's in trouble. I don't know what you want in exchange, but if you take me to her, I'll do whatever you want."

"Anything?" She snorted. "What, are you going to scrub my ship for a year? Bring me the eyeballs of my enemies? No, I think you being alive is enough. At least until Hawthorne wins this thing."

"Wins *what* thing? Look, I don't have a lot of time—" Ty cut off with a gasp as pain exploded from behind his left eye, sending a tremor through his skull.

A silicone-soft hand patted his cheek. "What's wrong with you?" Her voice softened. "Are you hurting?"

"Yes," he said through gritted teeth.

Morphett sighed and placed a hand on his jaw. "Open."

He was too exhausted to question it, so he complied. Something small and peppermint-sweet landed on his tongue.

"Chew that."

He hesitated, then worked his jaw. A mint sharpness flooded his mouth, his throat. Something soft and numbing spread through him, dampening the pain to an ache.

Finally, he opened his eyes. With the pain receding, the world came back into focus. "What was that?"

Morphett crouched next to the seat, her eyes faraway. "New cybernetics hurt, huh?"

"I think it's more than that."

Her glossy lips pursed. "Well. If you need more, there's a med-cabinet on the wall, and water in the kitchenette at the back of the cabin."

Ty winced. "Why are you being so nice to me?"

"I'm *not*," Morphett snapped. "Got it?"

She settled into the pilot seat, and soon the ship roared to life. It was a while before she spoke again. "I know what it's like to have metal you didn't ask for." She ejected one of her wrist blades. "Best you can do is grow into it, make it yours. Get more. And then impale the guts of the asshole who gave it to you."

Ty didn't think he wanted more steel. Or vengeance. Before everything had gone to hell, all he'd wanted was to finish school and get a job at a clinic somewhere. But it was so hard to see Morphett as an unwilling cyborg.

"Who gave you yours?" he asked.

"General Antioch, the jackass who headed my division. Kids with cybernetics. Some experimental Federation shit." She rubbed a trace of drying blood off her blade. "I'm working out a deal to track him down."

Ty shuddered. Morphett had unfinished business, and it sounded bloody. "I don't think I can go back for Almeida."

"Maybe that's not your battle to fight, then." Morphett shrugged. "You survived. I'm sure that pisses him off plenty."

Ty wasn't sure. He should already be dead a hundred times over. As soon as he'd stepped off that lift, letting Asa and Riven escape, he'd expected to fade into the dark. He'd been terrified, hoping to be swallowed quickly, retreating inward as he tried to ignore the brightness of his own blood. He wondered if Riven felt the same way, living with something slowly eating her, never knowing whether she'd wake up again.

Maybe Morphett knew this. Maybe she'd sympathize. "I know it's a lot to ask," he said. "But I need you to take me to Riven as soon as possible."

She sighed. "You're probably used to getting your way, just because you're so damned pretty. But puppy eyes don't work on me."

"She's *dying*." Ty let the word echo through the cockpit. "Whatever you want from her, it's not going to be worth anything soon."

Morphett narrowed her eyes. "And what are you going to do about it?"

Ty dug the vials out of his pocket. "Etri-cell infusion, from Almeida's lab. It might be the only thing that can stabilize her."

Morphett stared at him searchingly, then turned away with a soft *hmph*. "This is a hell of a favor, Buttercup. I think you're going to owe me double."

chapter 30

ROT

The sickness flared through Riven, tendrils reaching into her throat to choke her.

One moment she was leaning against Samir, and the next she was floating in space, somewhere between colliding galaxies and stars winking and shimmering, cold but furious, too far for warmth.

"*Riven.*" A face stared back at her—her own. The not-Riven's body was faded to shadow, nothing recognizable except her exhausted eyes and the frayed silver-blonde braid she used to see in the mirror every day.

"Am I still drugged?" Riven moaned. "I hate this."

The face shifted and duplicated into a row of mirrored reflections. All the different versions of her that would never be.

The girl from Sanctum's Edge, light in her eyes, reached into Riven's chest, running her fingers along the rot within her. Riven choked as blood burbled over her stomach.

"*You're pathetic,*" the not-Riven whispered. "*You might've had more time, if you hadn't been so reckless.*"

"I did what I had to," Riven said. "I saved them." If she'd gotten them out alive, it was worth it.

"*And if Redline's still out there? If you left them behind to fend for themselves? You couldn't protect them because you kept acting like you were already dead. And now you're too far gone to hear their voices one last time."*

Riven gasped as the girl who wasn't her pulled at the rot like a cutting wire. She'd always been alone. Unwanted. A girl with no birth parents to speak of—left in an artificial womb facility and forgotten, then dumped in her first group home with a family who'd only taken her for the tax credits.

Now she'd failed the only people who wanted her around.

The fingers grazed her brain, her spine, pulling her apart. But then . . . they stopped.

Riven sensed voices above her, pressure on her pulse points. Something vast as an ocean waited above her, separating her from them. But one voice was familiar. So familiar it made her bones ache.

"I've got you, Riv," he whispered. "I've got you." She felt a pain on the back of her neck, then a feather-light touch as someone pressed a kiss to her forehead.

And as everything faded, she glimpsed a face that was unmistakably Ty's.

━━━━━━━━━━

Riven jolted awake in an expanse of darkness and pink.

"Ah, hell." She sat up, sinking deeper into the too-soft bed. The sleep fog was lifting, and the fresh bruises and the slice on her thigh burned. The back of her neck was sore, like she'd taken a carbon-knuckled punch. But everything else felt lighter, and the crushing white noise that had clawed at her nerves for over a year . . . wasn't there.

Am I dead?

She didn't recognize this room. It was barely bigger than a closet, lit by a neon lightning bolt on the shiny black wall. Plush animals with threateningly huge eyes stared from the edges of a window, and a fake berry scent pricked the air. The world looked sharper, all rough edges.

A soft hum—the light buffet of turbulence—suggested she was on a ship. A *moving* ship that hadn't left atmo.

She stumbled to her feet, catching a view of lights stretching beneath the window. With some relief, and mild disappointment, she recognized the bends and arcs of those streets. Not an afterlife, just Requiem.

Something stirred at the corner of her eye. In the dim light, she hadn't noticed the girl dozing in the chair next to the bed.

"*Riven.*" Asa stood up, rubbing tearstained eyes that glimmered with something like hope. "Oh god, it worked. I thought you were dead."

"I thought so too." How had she woken up at all? Everything was a blur—Nell with Kaya's face, her sword ramming into Redline's guts, the nasty memories dredged up from some drug-induced haze. "But what do you mean, it worked?"

"You ran off, and—" Asa's voice was tinged in worry, but maybe anger too. "We didn't know what Redline did to you. You were coughing up blood and wouldn't respond, and then Morphett found us, and Ty—" Her breath hitched. "He saved you."

"What the hell are you talking about?" A pit deepened in her stomach, filling with sour, fragile hope. "How would Ty—"

"That call Morphett got . . ." Asa twisted her hands together. "He's in the next room."

From the waver in Asa's voice, something was wrong. Riven moved toward the door in a detached blur. The faint reek of cigarettes hung in the air, suggesting this ship was Morphett's, but that was the least of her worries.

Voices rose behind the door. Samir's: "They hurt him *bad*. If there's any way to fix this . . ."

"Maybe we can get her to call her mod-doc," Diego said.

Riven burst through the door into a tiny lounge. "What's going on?"

Samir's and Diego's heads swiveled toward her. Between them, someone was lying on the couch.

It couldn't be. She stumbled forward. "No. How?"

Lying on the couch, one eye closed as if asleep, was *Ty*.

His other eye stared into nothing—an ink-black sclera with a faint blue iris. Kaya had said she'd seen him with a cybernetic eye, and—

Oh god. This was real.

"Ty." Riven knelt next to the couch. "Oh, damn. Is he—"

"He's alive," Samir said. "But he's not doing too well."

She pulled back the edge of the thin blanket and grabbed for his wrist to check his pulse, but found a rod of cold metal instead. A mech arm, where his left arm used to be.

She choked back a gasp. "What the hell happened to him? How is he *here*?"

"Almeida had him all that time," Samir said. He wouldn't look Riven in the eye. "Morphett brought him back. Somehow, he knew where to find us."

It punched Riven in the gut. *All that time.* "Ty? Can you hear me?"

Only a few months had passed, but he looked older—the same delicate features seemed sharper, his good eye sunken. Shit, he hadn't died a kid. She'd sometimes cursed that she'd made it to eighteen, six months before him, and he hadn't. Last month she'd lit a flare on the roof of the old SkyNav building—one of Ty's favorite city views—on what would've been his birthday, not realizing he was still out there.

He must have suffered. One hundred nineteen days, and she'd never tried to find him.

"I think you should let him rest," Asa said. "He's woken up screaming a few times, and we don't know how to help him."

"What did they do to him?" She remembered the bullets carving through his arm. "How much of him is still—"

Her heart jumped as Ty stirred. One eye fluttered open—the same piercing blue Emmett's had been, a boy dragged up from the grave. It was hard to look at him.

"Riv," he whispered, then gave a small, delirious laugh. "You're okay."

Riven strained against the sob building in her throat. She pressed her face into the blanket covering Ty's chest. "Where the hell have you been? Dammit, Ty, I—"

Ty's chest shuddered. After soft gasps, he began to convulse.

Riven held him to prevent him from thrashing. He was listless, cold sweat breaking over his skin.

Samir swore as he dug through a med-kit. "Morphett brought us painkillers, but I don't think they're helping much anymore. It's getting worse, and I think it's coming from his cybernetics."

A sudden worry hounded her. If Ty had escaped with some of Almeida's tech, and the lab still controlled his cybernetics . . . they might try to dispose of him.

"I could try removing them," Asa said, "but I've never worked with parts of a person. I don't want to risk making it worse."

Diego had rolled up his own sleeve and was carefully working his cybernetic elbow. "My arm has an easy release switch, but his doesn't."

"We have to do *something*." Panic bubbled up Riven's throat. She was useless at everything except wrecking things. Useless at protecting them when it mattered.

The door hissed open and soft footsteps padded in. "Can I try something?"

Riven recoiled at the girl in the doorway, whose face had stared down at her as she'd been dying. But this face was softer, lacking the ragged scars and haunted fury. Kaya's.

Kaya rubbed the steel glinting on her neck. Her mind-link node. Just like Ty, she'd been a lab rat of Luca Almeida's. And she'd claimed to have seen Ty before. She knew something they didn't.

"Do whatever you can," Samir said. "Nothing has worked."

Kaya knelt next to Riven and set a hand on Ty's shoulder. "Hey. Your cybernetics are hurting you. I'm going to try to fix them, okay?"

Ty shuddered. Riven grudgingly moved aside as Kaya leaned over him.

Kaya closed her eyes and let out a sharp gasp. She sat there for a few minutes, whispering in concentration. Whatever she was doing—working her way through Ty's tech, maybe—it seemed to be working. His body slowly went slack, and his face was no longer contorted in pain.

Eventually, Ty spoke. "Kaya?"

"Right. It's me." Kaya brushed a lock of blond hair out of his eye, strangely tender for someone who'd never met him. "I'm sorry I can't do more. But is that better?"

Ty nodded and fell asleep. Somehow, he'd recognized Kaya, even though her brain had been in a biocapsule when he'd given himself up.

"He'll be okay," Kaya said. "Something's messing with his nerves. It seems to be proximity-based, getting worse as he gets farther from the lab. It might take me another few tries to undo it, but the pain should stop for at least a while."

"Good. Let him sleep," Samir said.

Whatever Kaya's brain could do, she hadn't been lying about seeing Ty, or about his eye being cybernetic. She'd never betrayed them.

"Kaya." Riven stood up. "I . . . I shouldn't have accused you of working with Redline. You've done more for us than we can repay."

"Ah, um. Thanks." Kaya looked down at Ty. "I probably should have told you more from the start, but I wasn't sure what my head was doing. It's been a weird few days. I'm just glad you took care of"—she stumbled on the name—"Redline."

"For now." There were still some pieces missing here. "Do you think that's over?"

"Probably not," Kaya said. "Knowing her, she has a backup somewhere."

The door opened again. "Hmm. So Banshee fixed him?" said that irritating voice. "I was just about to call my mod-doc."

Morphett. Come to think of it, they were on *her* ship, headed stars knew where. Riven had a feeling they owed some heavy favors.

"How did you find him?" Riven said.

"He called *me*, for the record," Morphett said. "Seems Luca Almeida still has me on his contact list. For now, I think we need to talk about the trial. And what you're going to do for me before I let him leave."

The trial. It had barely crossed her mind since she'd woken up. As for the second bit—

Riven stood, taking a small measure of satisfaction from being a head taller than Morphett. "I don't think he needs your permission to go anywhere."

"Sorry to break it to you." Morphett lifted the end of the blanket, revealing a bulky cuff on Ty's ankle. "Your girlfriend says we have to drop off our data with Matriarch Cerys to complete the second task. And until you've gotten through all three . . . he's not leaving this ship without my say-so."

chapter 31

CAPTIVE

sa's hackles rose as Riven's fury rolled through the room. "Riven, calm down," she warned. This wasn't the time to pick a fight with Morphett.

But Riven edged Morphett into the hallway, away from the rest of the crew. Asa slipped after her and closed the door.

"He's been some asshole's captive for months now," Riven snarled. "No way in hell is he yours now."

"You should've thought of that before accepting my help. And last I checked, you'd both be dead if I hadn't brought him to you." Morphett pricked the scalpels at her fingertips. "So, I think I'll keep him until your hot buttered ass is on that throne. You still owe me access to Rio Oscuro's networks."

"We're holding up our end of the bargain," Asa said. "That hasn't changed."

"Right. Leave Ty out of this." Riven's words crackled like stun-bolts. "You're going to take that thing off him. *Now.*" A terrifying calm had come over her. The threat of violence hung in the air—a steady, stinging thing.

Not here, Asa thought. *Please.* She'd already almost lost Riven once tonight—held her in her arms while she twitched and bled, until Ty had stumbled to her prone form and administered an injection to her brain stem.

"Come try me, Deadeye." Morphett's right forearm split,

and her horrific blade snapped out. "You were three steps from the grave an hour ago, and you don't have a single weapon on you."

Asa had barely noticed the narrowing of Riven's eyes before Riven grabbed Morphett's left wrist and twisted, flipping the smaller woman onto the shimmering carpet.

Morphett should've landed hard on her back, but her spine-talons caught her, setting her delicately back onto her feet. More of Morphett's blades unfolded.

"Don't you dare try to intimidate me," Riven said.

But Morphett was right—Riven didn't stand a chance in her territory, unarmed. This was only getting worse, and Asa couldn't run away this time.

Guilt had shadowed her for months because of the black hole of problems she'd brought from Cortellion. But now everything had turned on its head. Ty wasn't dead. Neither was her oldest sister, who'd uncovered the mess taking root beneath Requiem's streets.

This time, Asa had to stand her ground.

With a sudden burst of bravery, she threw herself between them—face-to-face with Morphett's array of gleaming blades.

"Stop and *listen*," she said, her voice cracking. "Both of you."

Morphett stared her down, pure venom.

"We made a promise," Asa said. "And my word is as good as my father's. We are *not* fighting right now." She looked pointedly at Riven.

Riven grumbled to herself, rolling her shoulder.

Asa straightened. They *would* listen. People seemed to listen to her, more than she expected. "I know you're angry.

But it's not Morphett you should be mad at." She turned to Morphett next. "And Riven's right. Ty is hurt, and the last thing he needs right now is to be a bargaining chip."

There was the smaller matter of what Asa would say to him when he woke up. Whether he'd ever be conscious enough to care remained to be seen. She risked hurting him even worse. But she'd have to own up to that too.

Morphett stared past her to Riven. "You're lucky for his puppy-dog eyes. I was going to lock him up and not let him see you at all until you were matriarch."

"We owe you more than we can give right now," Asa said. "But no matter what happens, we'll get you the information you need. I promise."

"Promises are sweet. Insurance is better." Morphett retracted her blades. "But, fine. If you don't get cut from the second task, I'll *think* about letting Buttercup go before the third."

That was something. Some of the tension uncoiled from Riven's posture. Then Morphett continued: "That's a big *if*. Your mech-head filled me in, you know. Sounds like you not only found your marks dead, but you also killed the one person who might've known what Staccato was up to. Great move. You really think Cerys is going to call that a job well done?"

"We found exactly what we needed for the second task," Asa said. "We found the missing people Cerys was looking for, ran ID scans, and—" She hesitated. Redline had told them what Staccato had been doing, but could they trust her word? "We finished the investigation. Whether it's sufficient proof will be up to Cerys."

"Then why haven't you sent it yet?"

"Because it's sensitive data, and we need more processing power to encrypt it." Redline had beaten them to the Staccato operation, and who knew who else was spying on them? "If you have a computer I can use, it'll make things faster."

Morphett sighed. "I suppose you can plug into my rig. But none of you had better get comfortable. This is my castle, not *Morphett's Home for Wayward Teenagers*." With a flick of her wrist, she led Asa back toward the bedroom where Riven had been resting. Riven followed them through the aggressively colorful interior of Morphett's ship—pink lights mounted near the ceilings, racks of polished guns on the walls, a cabinet of cybernetics calibration tools that made Asa's mouth water.

When they reached the control panel of rainbow keyboards and holoscreens, Riven crossed her arms. "*Tch.* I need to find a window. This place is going to make my teeth rot."

For a moment, Asa almost asked her to stay. There were a thousand things she wanted to say. If Ty really *had* stopped Riven's condition from progressing . . . how would that change things between them?

But Asa stopped herself from hoping. Even if her nerve condition was stable, Riven's fuse was still ticking. She'd stopped Redline—for now—but the cost had almost been too steep.

So Asa simply watched her leave: hair falling across her bare shoulders like spider silk, her half-unzipped exosuit swishing at her hips.

As Asa settled into Morphett's highbacked chair, Diego sauntered in, flipping a foil-wrapped candy between his fingers. "So how do you distinguish your drugged candy from your not-drugged candy?"

"Who's to say it's not all drugged?" Morphett popped a bright bubble. Then she whipped her hand toward Kaya, who was eyeing the cat-eared headset at the VR deck. "Hey, Banshee. Touch it and die."

Kaya backed away, hands raised defensively.

"Okay, heiress," Morphett said, "I'm going to route us for landing at the west docks. If you touch any of my files, I'll know. Let me know when you get that data sent." With that, she headed off toward the cockpit.

Kaya popped open a bag of raspberry fruit crisps she'd probably pilfered from the lounge. "Well. She's . . . accommodating." She tossed a crisp to Zephyr, who sat attentively at her feet.

"We're lucky she's still on our side." Diego leaned against the desk next to Asa. "I talked to Cerys again. She doesn't want us sending the data wirelessly."

"You told her we were hacked?"

"Had to. Can't hide anything from her. Once we get it cleaned, she wants us to meet her in person."

Kaya kept staring at the door to the side room. "I'm going to check on Ty again." Asa recognized the protective edge in her voice. "Call me if you need help."

"Will do. But I think we've got this." Asa booted up the rig and opened the face-scans Diego had taken, along with the footage. It was hard to look at the blank faces of people her father's empire had killed. Everyone she should've saved.

Even if she couldn't have saved Sofi, maybe she could have saved Ty. Or Riven, if she'd only searched more. Leveraged her father's connections to delve into the dark corners of the world she'd been running from.

Diego stepped in when she hesitated. "Hey. I can take over, if needed. You can go see Riven."

Asa shook her head. "I think she needs some space right now."

"Does she?" His voice softened. "She's been acting weird lately. Probably thought you were going to skip off to Cortellion when you had the chance. People with a safety net tend to leave this place eventually."

From the far-off way he spoke, he wasn't talking about *her* anymore. "You worry about Samir leaving too?"

"No, that's not—" He sighed. "Well, I knew he would from the start. Doesn't make it any easier." His knobby fingers drummed against the keys in an uneven rhythm. "And I can't exactly leave with him."

Not until he'd used his syndicate connections to find his parents, because it would eat him alive otherwise. "We'll find out whatever we can," Asa said. "I know you need that closure."

"I can't see it being good closure after all this time." His brown eyes were so distant. "My best guess is the Feds were covering up an accident on the station. An embarrassment they quietly swept behind some red tape." He twisted his candy wrapper open. "I don't know what it matters. But even if the news is bad . . . it'll be like removing a splinter. One shard of hope can hurt if you hold on to it for too long."

"Maybe," she said. "But sometimes, that's all you have." When Kaya had been in pieces, a tiny, impossible hope had kept Asa alive, pushing her to do impossible things. They'd need it to get through this mess too.

"I'm glad you're here," she continued. Diego made a small, surprised grunt as she hugged him. "We'd be dead a thousand times over without you."

Slowly, astonishingly, he hugged her back. "Nice that someone appreciates me."

"You *know* we all do."

Much as he tried to hide it, Diego had a striking smile. He pulled away and cleared his throat. "It's been good to have you in our corner, Asa." Diego's wristlet chirped, and his face sobered as he scanned the messages. "Hmm. Looks like Cerys has coordinates for us already."

"Oh. When does she want us?"

"As soon as possible. She wants us to meet her across town. Should be a twenty-minute trip or so. I'll let Morphett know."

At least they had a way forward—if Cerys accepted their data. Asa didn't want to think about the alternatives. The streets below were getting more dangerous every hour.

She only hoped Cerys could make sense of what Staccato was doing, what Redline had been after. Even now, the words hounded her: *The final piece of his plan is you. It's always been you.*

The trial might be the least of their problems.

chapter 32
LAB RATS

Ty faded in and out of nightmares—cold sweat, tremors, visions of Almeida's scientists ripping away more pieces of him to replace.

Had he hallucinated escaping, helping Riven? As far as he could tell, he was alone. He tried to focus on the harrowing clarity of his left eye—on every string of dust clinging to the ceiling, the light creeping between the solar blinds. Whenever he squeezed his eyes shut, making his mech-eye's vision go dark, he saw scenes from the simulator again, the memories etched like afterimages.

You're on Morphett's ship, he told himself. *They found you. You're safe.*

But what if he was still in the simulator, in a loop of endless decisions before he'd be spat back into the cold gray of the lab?

Despite the pain in his cybernetics, he'd do it again. He would fail this sim, over and over, just to keep seeing Riven and Samir and even Zephyr. That would be a good way to go.

The door slid open, then shut again. He heard soft footsteps on the carpet, and a girl approached from the shadows.

"You're awake," said the voice from his restless dreams. "How are you feeling?"

Kaya. Somehow, they were in the same room. The strange

pulse between them—part of her mind, calling to part of him—felt real.

"Not great," he said, and an uneasy silence stretched after the words. "I, uh, I don't think we were ever properly introduced."

"Yeah. Weird, right?" She sat down next to the couch, folding her long legs. Zephyr scurried after her, wagging his tail furiously. He hopped onto the couch, and his small paws pressed against Ty's stomach as he sniffed Ty's cybernetic arm. Then his rough tongue found Ty's cheeks.

"Someone's missed you," Kaya said.

"Hey, buddy." Ty ran his fingers over the pup's soft fur. "Been a while."

"He kept waiting for you to wake up." Kaya studied him. Shifting city lights through the blinds formed stripes across her blue fringe, her elegant jaw. "This doesn't feel like the first time we've met. They talk about you so much." She paused. "They said you were the reason I'm in one piece again."

Ty still had no idea how they'd beaten Banshee, Almeida's mercenaries, *and* Morphett. "Blame your sister for that. And, well, all of them. They went through hell for you."

"I know. They always do." Kaya turned away to hide her smile. He wondered what other stories they'd told her—no doubt Asa had mentioned the kissing. But from the terror in Asa's eyes when Riven had almost gone under . . . it seemed she'd found her person.

"I couldn't fix you completely last time," Kaya said. "If you're still hurting, I thought I'd try again. Work on the programming for the nerve connections." She idly rubbed the metal node on her neck. "Would that be okay?"

"Yeah. It really would be." Ty set Zephyr on the floor and let his head fall back against the pillow. "Whenever you're ready. Do your worst."

Kaya sat on the couch's edge next to his hip, then braced her hands against his upper arms—artificial nerves on one side, skin on the other. His first instinct was to flinch from memories of being grabbed and shoved into the sim room, of the Watcher strangling him. Memories of gloved hands analyzing him like a specimen.

Kaya seemed to know exactly what he was thinking. "You're safe. They can't hurt us anymore."

Her touch was gentle, and he focused on that instead of the memories, forcing away the urge to thrash. The burning in his nerves calmed, replaced by something cool and featherlight. Kaya's touch amplified through the artificial nerves, and he shivered.

With her hip brushing his torso, she was so close—closer than anyone he trusted had been in a long time. As she leaned over him, her touch arced through him like lightning, into every nerve connected to his cybernetics. Maybe she hadn't meant for it to feel quite like *this*, but—

By the time Ty realized what was happening, it was too late. "Um. Kaya . . ."

"Almost done. You okay?" Another tingling surge came from his shoulder. It shot down his spine, and he let out a sharp gasp.

Oh, no.

"I—" His voice came out strained. "I think you should stop."

Immediately Kaya let go, and the sensation faded. "Shit. Was that hurting you?"

"No. It wasn't." He tugged the blanket into his lap and rolled onto his side, hoping she wouldn't notice his burning cheeks. Or his other embarrassing symptoms. "It, uh. It felt . . . nice."

"Nice? Oh. *Oh*." She clenched a hand over her mouth, holding back laughter. "I am so sorry, I didn't realize—"

"It's fine." Ty winced.

Kaya snorted.

"Good to see you find my pain amusing."

"It's not your pain, it's your—" She cut herself off with a soft snicker.

"You know that's worse, right?" Ty managed a sidelong smile. "I might need a minute."

He desperately willed his mind to go blank, to focus on *anything* but the memory of her touch clinging to his nerves. It didn't help that Kaya was kind and fascinating, even if she was *Asa's sister, dammit.*

"Um. I think I managed to remove the tracker attached to your pain receptors." Kaya sat back on the floor next to him. "That should help for now. But there's still something in there I can't make sense of. Asa might need to help me deprogram it so I don't have to keep poking at you."

He wasn't sure he minded the poking, but he would never admit that. Having her here banished some of the spiraling thoughts. It quieted the constant, shrieking survival instinct telling him to run and keep running.

Even before they'd met, and whether or not Kaya realized it, seeing through her eyes had kept him from breaking. She'd shown him the vibrant, vicious city with the bright spot at its heart. They might never be able to control this connection spilling between them, but it'd helped guide him home.

It was Kaya who broke the silence. "I don't know exactly how this works—if you see through my eyes every time I see through yours. But . . . I saw flashes of you confronting my dad. You chose not to hurt him."

Was that an accusation in her voice? By now, Almeida was far behind him. He'd never have the chance to kill him again.

"I couldn't do it." Slowly, testing every muscle, Ty sat up. "But maybe we'd all be better off if I had."

Kaya stared out the window, seeming lost in thought. He could try to reach for her mind to see whether she was judging him, but that would be too intrusive.

"What would you have done?" he said.

"That's never been easy to think about." She crossed her ankles, and Zephyr curled into her lap. "I don't blame you, you know. Sometimes you can only save yourself."

They sat in communal silence, a pair of lab rats with metal in their skulls. Kaya's thoughts slipped toward his, faint outlines of memories. Of empty circuits, of seeing her own comatose body from the outside, of far-flung dreams anchored by a father's disapproval.

"Do you think it'll ever go away?" Ty said.

"I don't know. But it gets better."

Voices drifted through the door—Asa laughing, Diego groaning and mumbling *didn't expect such a low blow from you, Miss Almeida*. Asa challenging him to a rematch in some game Ty had never heard of.

Kaya's thoughts came as a mental whisper. "*You're lucky to have them.*"

"I think you have them now too," he said.

The ship lurched as it descended. He vaguely heard Morphett calling to *hang on to something, brats.*

Kaya held Zephyr close as she gripped the couch. "Hey. I don't know if they filled you in, but this whole mess is for–"

"The Ascension Trial. Yeah, Morphett told me." Maybe he'd always known Riven would attempt this, dying or not.

He couldn't lose her again. Riven had looked so fragile, bleeding from her mouth. He'd almost been too late in administering the cell vials, and he still needed to check her symptoms. But being back here again–to patch up wounds and break up arguments, just like before–was far more than he'd dared hope for.

"I guess this is my mess now too," he said. "Whatever I can do, count me in."

With a grating whine, the ship jolted. Then it was motionless, grounded. Zephyr whimpered softly.

Morphett's voice came through the speaker by the door. "Hey. Banshee. Your sister wants you on deck. Leave Buttercup here."

"I should be going with you," Ty whispered. He could probably walk well enough to help if anyone got injured.

Kaya looked to the door. "*You might want to rest a little more,*" her voice echoed in his head. "*It's probably safer if you stay. At least for now.*"

Ty sighed. She wasn't wrong. The last thing they needed

was another fight with Morphett, and Zephyr and Diego would probably appreciate the company.

But as Kaya left the room, he reached for her mind. *If anyone gets hurt*, he thought, *find me*. A soft, affirmative flush came from her end of their link.

He'd be here for them, again. Where he belonged.

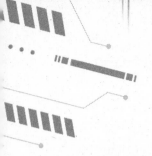

chapter 33

THE EDGE

Being back from the dead had left Riven's head a throbbing mess.

She pulled a jacket over her exosuit as the *Nephilim*'s hatch snapped shut behind them. Asa, Samir, and Kaya did the same-keeping low profiles as they headed into the streets, toward the edge of Requiem where the atmo-dome met the sand. The meeting point was nearby.

For the first time in a long while, her whole crew was together. An uneasy comfort hinged on whether Ty got better, and whether their data was good enough for Cerys.

Planetlight from Cortellion cast a glow on the stretching desert and sandy gusts pounding the atmo-dome's edge. The lights of the mining outposts were strewn across the wastes like beacons in a snowstorm. Sometimes, when the sand shifted, the hull ridges of derelict war machines protruded like teeth, relics of the revolution that marked the end of a bloody corporate reign and the beginning of a matriarchy.

"Are we good to head in?" Asa said. A faint scratch marred her neck, just above the exosuit collar. The sight turned Riven's stomach.

After everything, Asa was still at her side. And with the poison in Riven's nerves ebbing, things could be different between them. But maybe that was too much to hope for.

"Looks like it's just the four of us," Riven said. "Five blocks west."

"I need to say something before you go," Samir said.

"Before what?" Riven turned.

Samir stared down at her with an icy-sharp intensity that made her stagger. He hadn't looked her in the eye since she'd woken up.

"I didn't want to say this on Morphett's ship," he said, "but you really fucked up back there."

Riven set her jaw. Maybe she'd been a little too gung-ho in running after Redline, but she'd beaten her. "This isn't the time for a lecture. We have a job to finish."

"So you can take over Rio Oscuro, and we can keep following your lead? So you can keep rushing off and leaving your crew to get killed?" His voice cracked, like he'd burned through all his anger and had nothing left.

"I *saved* us. I went after our enemy, and I got rid of her. We don't finish jobs by holding hands all the damn time. We've always trusted each other to make split-second decisions."

Asa pulled her jacket tighter as the wind stirred her hair. Kaya looked like she was bracing for a fight. But Samir was focused on Riven alone.

"We all got extremely lucky back there," Samir said. "Especially you. You were an inch from death before Ty showed up, by some goddamn miracle. And Redline almost got Asa too. Had her by the throat. You weren't even there."

Asa's gaze fell to the concrete as she ran her fingers along the scab. She let the silence hang there. Maybe she blamed Riven too.

But this was a bad time for Samir's preaching. "Samir—"

"You've done this before, countless times," he cut her off. "Trying to negotiate with Banshee, getting us in hot water with other syndicates . . . and maybe we got out this time, but what about next time? Or the time after that?" He was as still as a statue, impassable, his metal-plated hands in his jacket pockets. "Reckless leadership is how crews *die*, Riven. I've been there, at CAA. I was less lucky when I made my mistake, and I can't let you keep making it."

"This sounds like it's about you, not me," Riven said.

"It's not. You aren't even listening!" In an instant, Samir's calm had evaporated, and he wound back, kicking an empty shipping barrel across the sidewalk. The rusted metal made a hollow clatter. He straightened with a shuddering breath, hiding his old scars once again. "The way I see it . . . we have a chance to walk away now." His voice was quiet. "Redline's gone. You're alive, and so is Ty. So we can go back to the *Nephilim*. I'll grab my dog, and we'll get Ty away from Morphett. And we'll leave this whole goddamn mess behind."

"Kaya said Redline could still be out there!" Riven said. "We still have people calling for our blood. And we're too close to back out now."

"It doesn't matter. I can't do this anymore." He gave Asa and Kaya an apologetic look. "Half an hour ago, I booked myself a ticket off this rock."

Riven's throat felt like a mound of concrete was lodged there. "You said you'd see this through."

"I also said you had to be careful about risking your crew's necks. Honestly . . . maybe Cerys should've swapped it. Made Asa our contender instead."

"Seriously?" After everything Riven had fought for—the jobs she'd pulled them through—those words cut like a bonesaw. She shot a glance at Asa, whose gaze was still fixed on her boots.

"I never wanted that," Asa said. "Even being second felt like too much—"

"And what if worse had come to worst back there, and you'd needed to take over?" Samir said to Asa. "What if we were following your lead now, instead of hers?"

"I . . . I don't know." Asa straightened. "But I don't think we should quit now, after all the enemies we've made." Her eyes met Kaya's briefly. "And if my dad's really aligned with Staccato, then Requiem has bigger problems than the succession. We at least need to tell Cerys. If nothing else, she'll know what to do."

Riven nodded. There was so much at stake still. "We aren't backing out of this."

"Then I guess I know my choice. Your bad decisions aren't my business anymore." Samir turned, as if he couldn't face her any longer. As if his path was set. "If any of you make it to Earth, let me know, and I'll find a way to keep you safe." His voice was a coarse whisper. "Goodbye, Riv."

He sauntered back toward Morphett's ship.

"Asshole," Riven murmured. "*Asshole!*" she called after him, louder.

He didn't look back.

Wind screamed in the desert, throwing whirlwinds of stinging sand at the dome. Raging, violent, but ebbing without a trace.

Samir had lost faith in her. And despite Asa's reassurance, she probably felt she had no choice but to keep going.

Maybe Riven would never be more than an impulsive mess, with the world falling away beneath her feet. But, sickness or not, she only knew one way forward.

Asa and Kaya were huddled close, whispering. It was Kaya who pulled away to speak. "Are we still going to—"

"Yes." Riven thumbed her revolvers. There was no backing out now, not even without Samir at her side. "We're going to finish this. And we're going to do it right."

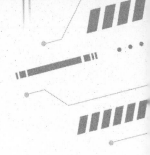

chapter 34
THE DROP

Asa couldn't exhale the bramble of thorns in her chest. With Samir gone, their next few days were even less certain. Every time she looked at Kaya, she saw her other sister's face, peeled and replanted onto a mech body. The sister who'd never forgive her. Who might return to finish what she'd started.

They stopped at the side gate of the abandoned salirium refinery—a monstrosity of towering pipes, broken concrete, and yawning vents.

"Did they design this place to be creepy?" Kaya muttered.

Riven gave a noncommittal grunt. "Either way, *creepy* keeps trespassers out. One reason it makes a good shortcut." She heaved up the bottom of the roll-up metal door, releasing a cloud of dust. She was still shaky, much as she was trying to hide it. "After you?"

Kaya hesitated, then crawled under and urged Asa to follow.

Asa thumbed the tiny pistol at her hip, one Morphett had reluctantly loaned her, *just in case*. Once they were through the refinery, it would be two blocks to the meeting point.

Staying in the trial was risky, but they had to see this through. Cerys would take care of Staccato, and they'd be one step closer to her father's plans. Still, Asa wished they'd gotten a few hours to sort things out with Riven's condition and Ty's uncertain fate. For too brief a moment, they'd all been together.

Asa crawled on the concrete, then dusted herself off as Kaya helped Riven through. They let the heavy door fall behind them.

The slam echoed through the building. Above, shafts of planetlight cut through the ceiling panels, illuminating burned-out fluorescent lights, empty vats, and ropes of fungus snaking along broken glass. A chrome fanged-skull logo was graffitied onto the walls—the symbol of Requiem's uprising.

This place felt like sacred ground. It had been one of Requiem's main refineries sixty years ago, before it was bombed and claimed by the revolution. Asa kept close to Kaya's heels as they climbed the steel steps to the main floor.

Diego's breathy voice came through their comms. "Well. Things are a shitshow here."

Samir must've said his goodbyes. It'd probably hurt Diego worse than anyone. "Sorry, Dee," Asa said. "It was his choice."

"I know. I'm still here though. Always am." His whisper was resigned, almost relieved. Then she heard the click of keys. "Thought you should know—I've picked up tracers nearby. Someone's following you."

"What kind of someone?" Riven said.

Asa shivered. Even if Redline were truly gone, the enemies Sofi had dragged into their wake weren't.

"No way to tell," Diego said. "They've got stealth tech. It's not as if they're broadcasting their affiliations."

"Maybe Cerys has scouts monitoring us." Riven kept her guns up, leading them into a labyrinth of crates and dead assembly equipment in the central atrium. Somewhere in the dark, a loud *creak* resounded.

The building's settling, Asa told herself. Never mind that it'd been multiple night-cycles since the dark had fallen and the temperature dropped.

Suddenly, Riven held an arm out to stop them. Three heartbeats went by. Four. Riven turned back and mouthed something, and one of Kaya's hands was on Asa's shoulder, guiding her behind a concrete pillar. Asa crouched next to her sister, listening.

The creaking became more regular. Footsteps, tromping from side corridors in both directions. On the steel scaffolds above them.

Behind them.

Armored figures came into view. Three, then five, then seven. One of them stepped into the light, and Asa's stomach dropped.

A helmet with a serrated metal jawline. Not Cerys's people—Staccato forces.

"So this is where those kids ran off to." Someone emerged from the shadows ahead of them, blocking the way forward.

Matriarch Sokolov. Flanked by her personal guard, her face hidden behind her signature horned rebreather helm. Always one to do her own dirty work.

Asa pressed back into the pillar. Riven crouched behind a shipping container close by, looked thoroughly stunned.

"I hear you've brought something for me, Hawthorne," Sokolov called.

Asa's heart thudded. The data was in her pocket—info for

Cerys about Sokolov's involvement with Echofall. With her father.

Riven shifted toward the edge of her makeshift cover, re-volvers at the ready. Deadly calm radiated off her skin, and Asa knew she was preparing to go out shooting.

"Riven, don't," Asa whispered.

Kaya's mind-link voice crackled in Asa's earpiece. "*Diego, call Cerys. We're in deep shit here.*"

"What's going on?" Diego said.

"*It's Sokolov.*"

Diego hissed a curse in Spanish.

"This doesn't need to be a bloodbath," Sokolov said. Her heavy footsteps continued moving. "We're arresting the group of you for the murder of Jayde Sokolov in violation of the Code. Not to mention the deaths of my operatives."

"We didn't kill Jayde," Riven called. "*Or* your operatives!"

"Camera footage from the warehouse showed the lot of you entering and leaving, right about when the operatives were slaughtered. The cameras were glitchy, the same way they were the night Jayde died."

Sofi must have tampered with the footage to conceal herself, Asa thought. *Both nights she killed.*

"My daughter," Sokolov continued. "Always trying to prove she wasn't an embarrassment. But you had to kill her in front of the whole damn trial and make my syndicate look like a joke. That's been your goal all along, hasn't it? To free up another throne to put your grimy hands on."

A gunshot rang out from the upper scaffolds. Sparks flew

as the bullet pinged against Riven's shipping container, inches from her head.

"*They're trying to flush us out,*" Kaya said in the comm. "*Can we make a break for the door?*"

Asa's pulse surged. Escape wasn't likely with at least seven operatives skulking the room, waiting for Sokolov's signal.

"I've already talked to Reyala," Sokolov said. "Your whole team is out of the trial, whether or not you come quietly. So you have no reason to hold on to that data."

Asa saw a fire ignite in Riven's eyes at something else being taken from her.

"Does Reyala know you've turned traitor like Rio Oscuro?" Riven said. "We know you've been working with Luca Almeida."

Kaya's metallic voice came through. "*Asa. Sokolov has an implant in her head, same as the operatives we found. I can sense it.*"

A chill crept over Asa, intensifying. Sokolov had an implant. Redline had said Jayde was only the tip of the iceberg in Staccato. Had her father compromised the entire syndicate?

Before she could say anything, Riven stuck her gun out and fired blind.

Two warning shots. The bullets took chunks out of the concrete wall. Sokolov and her operatives ducked behind some pillars.

Asa didn't doubt Riven could take most of them down. But picking a fight with a matriarch and her personal guard would be a declaration of war. If not here, then very soon, someone would make sure she paid for this. Getting out of here without casualties would require Samir's strategic maneuvering and shielding, but he was probably on a transit ship to Earth.

Asa had to stop this before it came to blows.

"This is a little more complicated than you're making it, Sokolov," Asa called. A warning for Riven as much as the matriarch. "Weapons down. Please. We can talk."

"No," Riven growled. "She's made up her mind."

"Riven–" *Stop and wait*, Asa wanted to plead. *We can negotiate. There might be another way.*

But Riven's eyes connected with hers, and she saw the fear there. The calculated violence. Riven was going to get them out of here, the only way she knew how.

Riven's bullets flew, and Sokolov returned fire. Two of the operatives dropped, one clutching a bleeding hole where his helmet met his neck.

"You two, run for it," Riven said. More gunfire. A bullet from the upper tiers caught the shoulder of Riven's exosuit, and she stumbled.

No. Echoes of the night Ty sacrificed himself came flooding back–the guilt, the helplessness, memories tightening a vise around her neck. As Kaya ushered her to cover behind crates and old pieces of machinery, the world was a blur of gunshots and shouts and her pulse roaring in her ears.

Riven took another operative down, kicking out their knees and riddling them with bullets. Three more now lay unmoving near the exits. "You have a path, Asa. *Go!*"

Two operatives approached behind Riven, and she lowered her stance, bracing for bullets against her exosuit. But bullets didn't come. Instead, their weapons hurled a mesh of red wires, pinning her left arm to the wall like an electrified spiderweb. She squirmed, shooting down the first with her right-hand revolver just as the other fired a mesh that anchored her torso in place.

"Riven!" Asa screamed.

Voices and footsteps approached behind them. Kaya yelled, and two of the operatives' weapons went dark. One swore, tossing their gun aside and pulling a stun-baton from their jacket. But when Asa whirled back, her sister's leg was tangled in red wires, and more operatives were rushing up to flank them.

"Weapons down!" one shouted.

Asa clung tight to the pistol, willing her fingers to unclench. But she couldn't. It felt like the last thing in her control.

"Bring her to me," Sokolov barked. "The prodigal daughter. The others are expendable."

Prodigal daughter. Asa's heart pounded. Redline had used those same words. *He calls you his prodigal daughter.* Sofi was convinced their father wanted Asa back.

You'll be his heir, and there's nothing you can do to stop it.

Redline had been right. If Sokolov had an implant, then Luca Almeida had a matriarch under his control. He'd already won, and Asa's friends were going to take the fall with her. This time, he wouldn't let them live. That left only one option.

Asa lifted the gun and pressed the muzzle to her temple.

"What the hell is she doing?" one of the operatives shouted.

"If it's me he wants," she called, "then let them go, and I'll come with you."

"Asa. Don't you *dare*," Riven grunted, struggling against the mesh pinning her to the wall.

The muzzle was cold against Asa's temple. She kept her finger off the trigger. She wouldn't be able to pull it, but this was a bluff.

"Sokolov," Asa said. "I know he's in your head. It's been a slow drip, but he's changing you."

Sokolov's face twisted in concentration, as if there were something deep and buried she'd forgotten.

"I don't know if Luca Almeida can hear me right now." If her father was in control, he likely had a mic in Sokolov's helmet, or on one of her operatives. "But I can promise he's getting nothing out of me unless I cooperate."

When her father had tried to reprogram Kaya, he'd had trouble forcing her to cooperate. *Minds are so much easier to work with when they're willing*, he'd said.

Asa might still have leverage here.

Sokolov was silent, her arms crossed over her bulletproof vest. Her head tilted as if she were listening to another voice, one Asa couldn't hear.

"I would die before I let you take them," Asa said. "And even if you took me to him, I would destroy his empire from the inside out, no matter how much he tried to change me. One moment of clarity, and I'd undo everything he built."

Kaya was stock-still, held in place by two operatives. Her eyes were wide as distant moons. "*Don't do this*," her digitized voice came in Asa's earpiece.

Asa didn't stop. "So, Dad, I'll give you a chance to convince me. To hear you out on *your* terms about becoming the heir you always wanted. My condition is that you let Kaya and Riven walk out of here, and you never follow my crew again."

"No," Riven whispered. The waver in her voice struck Asa like a dagger. Riven's lips on her knuckles at the gala might've been their last kiss. Their last embrace was when Riven was letting her go. She might never see Riven again.

But she couldn't let her die.

"This is my choice, Riven. I need you to accept that." Asa lifted her chin at Sokolov. "You have my word."

Sokolov mumbled something into her helmet comm, then waited. The creaking pipes and the hum of the vents filled the silence. Then: "You have a deal, Miss Almeida."

The operatives released Kaya, shoving her to the floor. Riven struggled, cursing. Kaya let out a muffled sob.

The muzzle of a gun nudged Asa's spine, and she dropped the pistol, holding up her hands. The remaining operatives formed up around Sokolov. They escorted Asa to the far door, toward a roar that sounded like a ship landing.

She was done running from her father. Now she had to face him.

"Luca Almeida," Riven shouted behind them, still restrained. "I will tear you to a thousand *fucking* pieces and shove them down your disembodied throat!"

Trust me, Asa mouthed over her shoulder. Then the door slammed behind her. Beyond it, Riven was still yelling after her. The sound ripped at Asa's chest.

Maybe Sofi was right. Maybe this had always been inevitable. But if there was any chance of stopping Luca, it would be close to him.

One last time.

chapter 35

HEARTBEAT

Riven punched the drywall until her knuckles were raw and bleeding.

The wall was a mess of blood and powder, but it didn't matter. Her hideout was already blasted to hell. Even if she was only here to load up gear and extra bullets, coming back had been a mistake.

A hole still gaped where the window had been, letting in the fry-grease-and-exhaust stink of the streets and a polluted rainbow of light. Scavengers had looted their juicier electronics, but the safe containing their ammo was intact. Light trickled over the living room and the personal items left behind—Asa's tools, Kaya's spray paints, Samir's vintage galaxy maps. Plastic noodle cartons and powered-down pieces from some holo strategy game.

So many of Asa's things. *Asa*, her steady spark of hope over the past few months. And Samir, whose absence now ached like an open sore.

Riven had screwed up. Spectacularly. Maybe Samir was right that her years of bad decisions had gotten them here. She'd led her crew along a razor's edge, and it'd taken only a few missteps to lose everything.

Asa had left her the way Ty once had. Putting herself in harm's way, to *protect* Riven. One last message from Asa had confirmed that her father was here, on Requiem. Meeting with a contact before he'd take her back to Corte.

The ship had taken Asa toward the city's north edge, the Fed-patrolled district—toward Solus Tower, the embassy for salirium trade. Riven didn't have the beginning of a plan to get her back.

Riven gave the wall one last hit, letting some of the frustration out through her fist. The worst part had been watching Kaya choke back tears as she broke the news. Diego had tried to shoulder the blame for Sokolov's attack. Morphett had gone into Ty's room, emerged with his tracking cuff, and hurled it at Riven. *Unless you have a damn good plan, get off my ship*, she'd said.

Riven knew they all blamed her—and maybe she deserved it. They'd been pulled apart by a leader who couldn't strategize about the future, because there wasn't one.

Riven couldn't find the rest of that overpriced whiskey, so she headed to the fire escape sober and climbed the stairs to the roof. Leave it to Requiem's enormous sea of city lights to make her failures feel a little smaller.

The city was in its third day cycle of darkness—the apex of night. Intersections were calderas of light, tangled marquees of twisting crystal and neon. Somewhere, the hollow knock of distant gunshots rang out.

A living map of hundreds of stories being created every second. Heists she'd never hear about. Adrenaline rushes surging and disappearing. Smugglers whose names nobody would remember. A city she couldn't escape, no matter how hard it tried to spit her out.

But Requiem was alive. And, against all odds, so was she.

She'd been so hung up on dying that she'd never imagined Asa could be taken first. Maybe she owed it to her to do better this time, whatever that meant.

The roof door creaked behind her. Riven tried to ignore it—it had either blown open or one of the building's other residents had come up to smoke. Then steady footsteps grew louder, closer.

Reluctantly, she turned. Her heart stuttered.

Striding toward her was Samir.

He had his usual brick-wall posture, hands buried in his jacket pockets. Not a hallucination.

"Crawling back already, huh?" After everything she'd said, this was probably just a temporary stopover on his way out. "You forget your hair gel or something?"

"No. I just couldn't live without your constant heckling." His cat eyes shimmered in the dark. "May I join you?"

"Not like I can stop you." The last thing she needed was another lecture, but she was too exhausted to resist. She probably *did* need someone to punch her in the jaw and tell her how to make things right, but Samir would never do that. "What are you doing here, really?"

Samir set down his duffel bag and leaned against the balcony next to her. "When I went back to get Zeph, I had a talk with Morphett, of all people. Turns out she overheard a lot of our outburst." The unzipped bag squirmed, and Zephyr's head poked out. "She's familiar with some of the Fed's test programs. Said they took in kids from desperate families and experimented on them. Her included."

Riven tamped down the stab of sympathy. Morphett probably didn't want her pity.

"The general she's after is the same one who sanctioned my squad's test run," Samir said. "Which led me to wonder whether that mission was planned to go south. Maybe it wasn't my fault."

"Of course it wasn't," Riven said. "I've been saying that this whole time." After that accident, the guilt had sent Samir running to Requiem. Running from his certain future, from the military hierarchy his family had wanted him to rise within.

"It made me realize I can't work for them again. I'd always be bound by orders and red tape, knowing my higher-ups condone shit like this. My mom's done a good job working around it all, but even though she's a bit of an idealist, she's also a hardass. Subtle and gradual change. I don't think that's enough." He sighed. "And then Dee called and told me what happened to Asa. I should've gone with you."

Riven remembered blind firing at Sokolov without the steadiness of Samir at her back. The gun against Asa's temple, something ripped from a nightmare. "I doubt it would've changed much. Wasn't your fault Sokolov chose to screw us over." But maybe he'd been right about her leadership, much as it stung. It was partially her fault they were in this deep.

Quiet stretched between them, as if he were waiting for something. Seemed she was going to have to apologize first.

"I'm sorry, you know," she choked out. "I should've listened."

"Yeah," he said. "You probably should've."

"I always thought if I was the one to take the risks, you'd all be better off."

"And bigger risks mean more glory for you." He gave her a sidelong smirk. "Tell me I'm wrong."

"Well . . . not entirely," she admitted. "It's not just glory though. Guns blazing is the only way I've ever gotten things done."

"You *have* gotten us out of tough shit as often as you've gotten us into it." Samir ran a thumb over his carbon-plated knuckles. His punches had backed her up countless times. "But leadership doesn't mean shouldering all those risks yourself. There's a bigger picture you need to account for. And you can't keep acting like it wouldn't destroy the rest of us if something happened to you. Seeing you like that . . . it was rough."

After having Emmett and Ty and now Asa taken away, Riven could guess how they'd all felt when Redline's attack had laid her out. They really did give a damn about her.

"I can't do this without you," she said. "None of us can."

Samir watched the lights from a patrol cruiser streak across a distant skyway. "You were right too," he continued. "I was projecting some of my mistakes onto you. But Asa needs us now, and I'm pretty sure I have an unfinished prank war with Kaya."

"So you'll see this through?"

"For now." The riotous lights winked back at them. "Maybe there's still a lot of good we can do here. But it's going to be a hard path, and we can't stay here forever. Requiem's somewhere to fight and die, but it's not a place to settle down."

"We won't have forever." Riven rubbed her sore knuckles. "Getting Asa back might be a suicide mission." If Samir wanted to back out now, he still could. "I just don't know where the hell to go from here. It's like some big cosmic prank. *You're no longer dying, Riven!* Great, thanks. Now I have an entire city's worth of shit to wade through."

"You really think we're out of options?" Samir said. The air seemed to freeze between them.

"I'm not giving up. But I think our odds are pretty bad. Even with you here."

Solus Tower was the worst place Almeida could've taken Asa. It was one of the few Fed-controlled spaces, where business suits from Corte and Earth met for salirium deals—guarded by mechs and killer drones. Going in guns blazing wouldn't only be risky, but it could create an interstellar incident.

A breeze tugged at a lock of Samir's dark hair. "I don't know how we're going to save her either. But if you're not going to dig in and figure it out, how did you ever plan to be a matriarch?"

"What's that supposed to mean?" Riven said.

"Even if you *were* a matriarch—if they'd picked you after the trial—you'd still have Luca Almeida and his peers to contend with. Having power in this city is playing a long game. Thinking five steps ahead. I've never seen you do that." Samir gave her a shattering gaze. "There's more in your control than you realize. You just need to start acting like you have a future."

"Playing a long game, huh?" The not-dying thing hadn't sunk in yet. Any of them could still die tonight. "Hard when the decks have been stacked against all of us from the start."

"Maybe they have been. But even *Ty* came back. From one of the worst places in the system, because he wanted to make sure you were okay."

She gripped the railing, breaking apart the dried blood on

her knuckles. Samir was usually right. The anger burned, so unpredictable and formless, that she hadn't stopped to consider a better way. "I don't know what those bastards put him through. Or what they're going to put Asa through. But if we still have a shot . . ."

"You know what I think, Riv? You're impulsive, but you're also a fucking survivor. We haven't followed you through hell just because you had a ship, or because you and I were friends at CAA. We've followed you because you do shit nobody else would try. Because you fight like nobody I've ever met. Like you could cleave the world in half on spite alone."

She had to smile at that. He wasn't wrong.

"But now it's time to get strategic. You can't shoot your way out of everything. There has to be something we haven't considered."

"Something Luca Almeida would never expect us to pull," she mused. "We'd need a small army to get in there." He'd never expected his sheltered daughter to end up gun-running and stealing kisses in the galaxy's darkest gutter. And he'd never expected a tiny group of Requiem smugglers to tackle him head-on.

Tonight, he probably wouldn't expect Riven to get into Solus—or actually steal his daughter. Hell, she didn't expect herself half the time.

"Is the third trial happening already?" she said.

"Yeah," Samir said. "Dee says it's down to Callista and Tak."

"I guess we knew Nell was out. What's their assignment?"

"To hunt down one of the matriarchs' greatest enemies

and bring in their head. Not sure if it's metaphorical or just gruesome."

Oh, hell and a half. A grin tugged at Riven's mouth.

"I know that look," Samir said. "Don't tell me you're going to try jumping back into the trial. Even if there's a loophole–"

"That's not what I'm thinking. We're going to get Asa back, and that's priority." Samir was right. The Boomslang Faction always got through hell. They made things work when there was no hope otherwise. Maybe Riven had a few cards left after all.

"Whatever stunt we're going to pull . . ." Samir drew something slender from his pocket. One of his shiny Gliflex pistols. "Things are probably going to get worse before dawn."

Riven thumbed *Verdugo* and *Blackjack* in their holsters. Her old-tech Smith & Wesson revolvers, built sometime in the 2090s, which she'd won in a shooting competition during her first week on Requiem–when she'd brought her nickname and her reputation to this city. "Mine have never let me down."

He shook his head. "This has a bigger mag. Aim assist. Fewer reloads, and it'd be a split-second faster, even for you. Sometimes it's not about pride–you take any edge you can get."

Riven took the pistol and gave it an experimental spin on her finger. Clunky, but she could make it work.

Even now, Samir was looking out for her. He'd kept her together for the past few years, like he'd kept her together at CAA.

"Hey. Thanks. Really." She rested her head on his shoulder. "This place needs you. And I do too. You keep my ego from suffocating everyone–your words."

He laughed, wrapping an arm around her. "Someone's got to."

She tilted her head back to look at him. Big damn hero, as usual. Something about this place fit him. Requiem was his home too—a place where he had friends in every bar, a place that had sheltered him at his lowest point. A place that had gotten under his skin like it had hers.

Maybe Samir wouldn't stick around forever, but for now, he might be the ace they needed.

"Here's what I'm thinking," she said. "It won't be easy, but we can still steal that stubborn heiress back."

When Riven split from Samir to make one final sweep of the hideout, she'd already envisioned half a dozen ways to break into Solus, and twice as many ways to fail.

Things were getting ugly tonight, but there was no avoiding it.

She was wading through the minefield of dirty clothes and empty pizza packets when the latches on the door began clicking.

Her hands froze halfway to her revolvers. Whoever was opening the door knew all the combinations.

The door creaked open, slow and tentative. Riven recognized that hesitation—a warmth that had been missing from this place even before it had been blown apart.

Then Ty walked in.

Half his silhouette was hard edges and smooth curves. His new arm reflected the light trickling in from the window. One eye was a pale blue light swimming within an oil-black sclera, rimmed in surgical steel.

Riven's heart stuck in her throat. She'd been avoiding him—avoiding the possibility he might never get off that couch. It was too hard to face the awful things Almeida must have put him through. But Ty had found his way back home.

"Riven," he whispered.

She threw her arms around him. Harder than she'd ever hugged anyone, probably.

He laughed softly. "Um. I can't breathe."

She loosened her grip but didn't let go. "Ty. Oh, shit. I'm so sorry."

"You've got nothing to be sorry about," he said into her hair. He clung to her as if he hadn't been held by anyone in months. "That was all my choice."

"It was a bad choice. You were *dead*. Dammit, Ty—" For so long, she'd accepted that he was gone. That when he had a split second to decide between his life and hers, he'd picked hers. That he'd probably made that decision long before, so when the time came, he knew exactly what to do.

She could never repay him.

"You deserve better than this," she said. "You came back just as soon as we got ourselves in deep shit again."

"Wouldn't have it any other way." He took her face, so gently, in both hands, as if she were something broken he was trying to hold together. "How are you feeling?"

One set of his fingers was colder, silicone pads over slick mechanical joints. New and unfamiliar. It wasn't just his body that had changed. He was frayed at the edges. Their Ty, but different.

"I'm . . . a lot better," she said. "The pain's fading in and out.

No more blood though." She didn't know what Ty had done, but somehow, despite everything, he'd saved her.

"Good. It might never be gone completely, but we have meds for that. Still, you haven't noticed anything weird, have you?"

"Weird how?"

He stiffened. "It's . . . complicated. The thing you got hit with at Sanctum's Edge—it was a nerve spore. An experimental trial, supposed to increase your rate of neural firing. Derived from some Etri symbiotic plant that syncs with your nervous system."

"What do you mean, neural firing?"

"I don't entirely know. They discontinued the project because most of the original subjects died. There was a missing piece, a stabilizer dosage, which I brought back for you." He paused, and Riven's heartbeats filled the silence. "I don't know if the treatment is working the way it's supposed to, but at least the spore shouldn't be spreading anymore."

Revulsion crept through her like the rot that had grown for so long—rot that might never be gone. But now a longer future stretched ahead, twisted and uncertain.

"I'll still need to give you a quick once-over, to make sure," Ty said. "You might need to have a subdermal mod installed to keep it under control. Still, so far . . . this is better than I could've hoped for. I guess it was worth it."

It couldn't have been worth him being cut apart and imprisoned and god knew what else. "What happened to you, Ty?"

He went quiet. Maybe he wasn't ready to talk about it. Maybe he never would be.

And the people who hurt him were still out there, hurting others.

"I'm going to end them," she said, the words so scalding they almost burned her tongue. "After we save Asa, I'm going to rain hellfire on every single one."

"That's the Riven I know." She heard resignation in his voice. He knew he couldn't stop her. "I'm getting better though. I, uh, I think Kaya fixed the fail-safe in my cybernetics. It was supposed to prevent me from leaving the lab." A blush began staining his cheeks. "She's been . . . great."

Better was something. But the way he said Kaya's name was hesitant, hopeful. Ty was always quick to offer his heart on a platter. The few times Riven had seen him drunk, he was in love with everyone within ten feet of him. It had sometimes brought unwanted attention, which Riven deterred by breaking fingers.

Right now, he was especially vulnerable. He'd follow Kaya like a lost puppy now that she'd helped him when he was hurting.

"She'd better be careful with you," Riven said.

He scrubbed a hand through his hair. "It's not like *that*, it's just . . ."

It was good to see something about Ty hadn't changed. Part flesh, part steel, still completely flustered around girls. "You don't need my permission, you know."

"I guess I survived without it." His smile faded. "I only wish we could've been done with Almeida by now."

"I know," Riven said. Almeida hadn't broken Ty, and he

wouldn't break Asa. "But we're getting Asa back, and we're doing it right this time."

With a knock on the kitchen doorframe, Samir strode around the corner.

"I'm ready to go," he said. "Seems some bastard ran off with my espresso machine, but not much to be done there."

Ty nodded. "I'm coming to Solus too. Need to make sure you both walk out of there." When Riven opened her mouth to object, Ty kept going. "You said I didn't need your permission."

Not what she'd meant, but she supposed it was his choice. "If you even *think* of trying to play hero again . . . I'm not losing you twice."

"I lost you both too," Ty murmured, looking at her like he was willing to jump into the smoke all over again. He grabbed Samir's wrist and pulled them both close, and suddenly it felt like their first nights on Requiem, when they had nothing at all and nothing to lose. Before the weight of the world had come crushing in.

"The three of us again, huh?" Samir's arms wreathed them both in. "Beat-down, hopeless, desperately needing showers . . ."

"The way it should be," Riven said.

If it came down to their lives versus hers, she knew what she was picking. But this time, they needed an edge. Possibilities strung themselves together, tangling like spider threads.

"I think we have a call to make, Samir," she said. "And I don't think they'll be able to refuse."

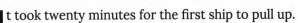

chapter 36
HEAT

It took twenty minutes for the first ship to pull up.

"They're here," Samir's voice echoed into the comm. He was a shadow at the far corner of the roof, his rifle a glint in the dark.

Finally. Riven dangled her legs off the air-con unit. The looping ads on the VR gaming den across the street were starting to make her twitch.

"Sounds good." Ty's voice came in her earpiece. "Keep us updated."

A tiny hummingbird perched on Riven's knee, then flitted to land on the chain-link fence behind her. Kaya was watching, too, in case things went to hell.

A quiet hum rose as the first ship reached the roof's edge. The claw-shaped gunship was stealth class, though the stealth drive wasn't engaged. Damn, Riven missed *Boomslang*.

Callista's curvy silhouette leaped from the hatch and landed on the roof. The ship stayed in place. No doubt their crew was waiting on board with heat.

The rickety roar of a second ship came moments later. The splashy red-and-gray doors of *Charybdis* irised open, and a small foot ramp slid out.

Tak ambled down it, giving Callista a lopsided grin. "Huh. You brought me Callista? From the way you made it sound, you had some Fed officer's ass on a silver platter. Expected more, *Deadeye Hawthorne*." Tak's ship scudded off, but Riven didn't doubt she had tricks up her sleeves.

"You didn't say she would be here," Callista snarled, hand on a pistol beneath their jacket. "What's the meaning of this?"

Riven leaned back against the chain-link fence and cracked open a soda can. "Just wanted a front-row seat to the two of you duking it out." They both shifted uncomfortably before her laugh echoed over the concrete. "Nah, joking. Honestly, though, I have a deal I think you'll both be interested in."

"*Tread carefully*, Riv," Samir murmured.

"I have a proposition," she said. "A target. Whoever gets this will win the trial, guaranteed."

"Thought you were out of the competition," Callista said.

"I am." Riven idly scratched at her nails. "To you, I might as well be a nobody."

"And if I kill Tak first?"

Riven shrugged. "You could. But this job's big, and none of us can go it alone. So you'll need to work with us for a bit. My condition is, you save the backstabbing for after we've won. Then you can make bullet-sponges of each other to your hearts' content."

Callista glared from beneath their hood, but they were listening. Good.

"So, the third trial. It's about finding the head of the biggest enemy, yeah? Now, I don't know if the two of you had your sights on some small-time Fed moles or glitch dealers gone rogue, but I've got one better."

"Going to need harder details than that," Callista said.

Riven took a swig of the cola. "Luca Almeida is on Requiem, right now."

Stunned silence fell over them.

"Yeah." Riven hopped off the air-con unit. In the glow of the ship headlights, her legs cut long shadows across the roof. "Guy responsible for Banshee. And he's got worse planned—something that concerns the whole city. Whoever's going to run Rio Oscuro will have to deal with him either way."

"Why not tell the Duchess?" Tak said.

"I doubt she'll listen. She kicked me out, after all." After her crew's expulsion from the trial—and without hard evidence about Sokolov—it was probably best not to approach the Duchess directly.

"And why should we trust you?" Callista said. "Forgive me, Hawthorne, if I don't trust a girl with your kill count and hard-on for bullets. The matriarchs have already been whispering you've gone traitor. The fact you're still alive means you're either absurdly lucky or you're a slippery bitch with an agenda."

"Callista's right," Tak said. "If you're not in the trial, what's in this for you?"

Riven dug her nails into her arm. Damn, she was going to have to tell them, wasn't she?

"Because," she said grudgingly, "he's got Asa."

Callista's arm holding the gun went slack.

"Oh, damn, I knew it." Tak gave a guttural laugh. "You are absolutely *whipped* for that girl."

"I didn't ask for commentary," Riven snapped. "But if you want Luca Almeida's head, I can take you there. It's going to be tough—maybe one of the biggest jobs Requiem's ever seen. But you help me, and there will still be a Requiem to lead."

"If Tak doesn't skewer us in the backs first," Callista said.

Tak clicked her tongue. "You're one to talk, chickling."

"Save it," Riven said. "You can fight it out afterward. But for now, if you're in, put the guns down and shake on it."

Grudgingly, Callista tucked the gun away. "Fine, Hawthorne. You have yourself a deal."

Tak extended her skeletal metal fingers toward Callista. Her sleeve slipped, revealing the scars where wires melded with tattooed flesh. If the stories were true, Tak had survived worse than what lay ahead.

Damn. Maybe Riven would be older someday too.

"What next?" Tak said as Callista dropped her hand like a dead snake.

Riven grinned. "Here's where the hard part begins."

Part III

THE WHISPER &
THE ECHO

chapter 37
RAISON D'ÊTRE

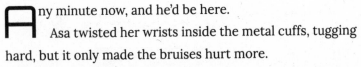

Any minute now, and he'd be here.

Asa twisted her wrists inside the metal cuffs, tugging hard, but it only made the bruises hurt more.

Not that she was going anywhere. Solus Tower's penthouse felt nauseatingly familiar, with potted atherblossom trees, translucent gel couches suffused with golden light, and floating steps disappearing toward the rooftop. A slice of Cortellion out of place on Requiem, like Asa had been.

She'd tried to memorize the tower layout when the guards marched her toward the elevators, but they'd led her in circles. And their only keys were kept subdermally.

Now even looking out the glass felt like vertigo, as if she'd fall past the wall separating her from the north side of Requiem and back into the rusted scaffolds, smoke-stuffed alleys, and guttering neon. Her city, her home. A world that seemed so far removed from up here.

At least Riven and the rest of the crew would be free of her problems forever.

With a soft hiss, the door at the far end of the room irised open. Her father gave a shallow bow as he approached, flanked by two guards and tailed by another. "My Asanna."

Asa forced herself to look him in the eye. Statuesque posture, skin flawless as silicone. She hadn't seen him in the flesh since he'd shown her Kaya's comatose body with her mind removed. He hadn't even been physically present when he'd tried to kill her on Earth.

Deep breaths. She had to stay alert.

The bodyguard behind her father had to be eight feet tall and covered in plates of armor. Eyes masked in a mirrored face-shield, cracked lips that seemed almost blue. Her father's prior bodyguards had been stocky, stoic, and forgettable, but there was something unsettling about this one.

She focused her glare on her father alone. "Dad."

He tapped his wristlet, and instantly her cuffs released, falling with a heavy thud. She rubbed her sweaty wrists.

"You're on your way home," he said. "I don't want you to feel like a prisoner."

"It's a bit late for that. You went through a lot of trouble to get me back." He'd infiltrated Staccato. He could've found her so much sooner. Looking back, it was laughable how powerless she'd been. Especially now, with her wristlet confiscated.

"It was never just about you, Asa." Her father motioned the tall bodyguard to hold position near the door, then he strode toward the glass at the far wall. "Come here. I want to show you something."

She glanced warily around the room, at the cameras observing her every step and the holo-projector near the couches. Aside from the tall bodyguard—so motionless he might as well have been stone—two more guards in carbon armor flanked the door, rifles slung across their backs. There was no easy way out. And she could only pray to any deity among the stars that Riven wouldn't try to free her.

Reluctantly, Asa squared her shoulders and walked to join her father. If this was the last time her mind was fully hers, she wouldn't spend it cowering.

"Out the window, Asa," he said. "What do you see?"

"It's Requiem," she said flatly. Whatever answer he was digging for, she wasn't giving it. "Do you see something different?"

He chuckled. "Evasive. I suppose it was inevitable that you'd grow up. Though I believe I have a mistake to correct."

"A mistake like me?"

"No. My daughter, you were never a mistake." He turned toward her, and the city lights made his skin translucent. She envisioned what he must look like without his anti-aging mods. Older than she knew. "My mistake was not telling you sooner—about Winterdark's evolution, Requiem's future. I was reluctant to accept you'd grown up, when I should have treated you like an equal. That's what you wanted, yes?"

What she'd wanted once, yes. The promise of the stage lights had been intoxicating. The dream of breaking free of the shell he'd packed her into. Of earning her own respect. But she'd found more of that in the past four months than in seventeen years with him.

And nothing could undo the last words he'd said to her. *I only hope my next child is less of a disappointment.*

"If you want to treat me like an equal, you'll stop condescending by pretending you didn't try to kill me," she said. "Or have you forgotten? Saying you'd make yourself another heir?"

"It was an empty threat. While other heirs are a possibility, you are extraordinary. The world already knows your name and anticipates you."

An empty threat. That was a lie. His guards had been shooting to kill when they took Ty away. They might've killed her too.

But her father had used Ty instead. Like he wanted to do to her.

"Having a successor who has bled on this city's concrete . . . you've surprised me, Asa. You're cleverer than I gave you credit for." His slow footsteps crossed behind her, and she instinctively whirled. The skin on the back of her neck still prickled when he was near. "You got what you wanted—your sister, whole—but then you stayed. It was more than Kaya, wasn't it? You wanted to prove your independence by scraping by in this city's gutters. And now you're vying for power. It's already in your blood."

I stayed for the rest of them. For Riven. Asa swallowed the words like a mouthful of sand. There was no use telling him that.

Right now she was close to the heart of his plans for Requiem. Closer than she'd been since she'd left home with Kaya's brain in tow.

She had to play along. Learn the truth.

"The trial was Hawthorne's idea," she said. "Power is the only way to stay safe in this city. You must understand that."

"I do. But you're destined for much bigger things than a city where even savvy matriarchs rarely live to their thirtieth birthdays."

"I know." Asa summoned tears, let the quaver creep into her voice. It came easily right now. "I've been running for so long. All this time, I thought you'd meant to kill me too."

"I'm so sorry, Asa." His arms settled around her. "I did whatever I could to get you to come home. I would never hurt you."

Lies, again.

"I should apologize too," she said. Her father smelled inhumanly fresh, like sharp cologne and sterile detergent. "You offered to put Kaya together, to let me come back without consequences. I should have taken it. This city is . . ." She let the implication trail off.

He stroked her hair. "Echofall will help you forget."

Revulsion crawled across her skin. If not for Kaya, she wouldn't have discovered the blood covering his empire. Forgetting the bad things wouldn't erase them—the hollow-eyed test subjects, the bodies strewn in alleyways, Jayde's lifeless eyes.

"What *is* Echofall?" she said.

"Echofall is Winterdark's successor." Her father pulled away and brought his fingertips to the glass wall. "Simpler, less invasive, easier to replicate on a larger scale. Made with lab-grown pieces of Etri brains instead of whole ones. Echofall lets us target specific memories and drives using only partial brain implants." The glass lit up with an overlay, a map of Requiem that glowed across the view of the streets beyond. "This city is a pit of human corruption, but therein lies its potential. Even if I don't have much time left, you're the one. You have the empathy, and the resolve, and the brilliance to make it happen. I should have told you all this earlier."

Not much time left. Sofi had been lost since before Kaya was born. Luca was old, and not even mods could extend his life forever. But he'd use Asa to continue his work.

"You're rewriting parts of people's minds?" Asa said. That had to be what he'd done to Sokolov.

"In a way. The rewriting is a slow process of suggestion. Gradual but steady, like moving a glacier. It took months for Sokolov to cooperate." He looked thoughtful. "Sokolov reached out to me when our escaped Etri wreaked havoc, seeking a deal to remove Banshee. I supplied her with combat implants in exchange for test subjects. She had enough enemies, enough failed operatives, that they were in good supply. Eventually, Sokolov accepted an implant herself—a piece of Echofall. Before she knew the implications, we were able to begin changing her. Slowly, she has given us the rest of what we need."

Asa's heart hammered. Whether her façade had worked, or Luca simply knew he had her trapped, at least he was talking. "And what has she given us?"

"You remember how Winterdark originated, yes? We recovered a single Etri specimen in a small bunker beneath the outskirts of Requiem. The Progenitor was cryo-preserved in technology from a civilization we'd thought completely extinct. He was not alone though. We salvaged a second and third with him, though neither brain was as complete." He gave his hulking bodyguard a sidelong glance. "Most of their species still slumber deep within this moon, beneath the mines. Waiting for a more hospitable climate that never came."

"More Etri?" Yllath. The Progenitor. The brain that was currently sewn into Kaya's head.

"Yes. They will provide the diversity of Etri genetic material we need. But the hurdle lies in *getting* to them." Out the window, transit ships crawled across the sky. A web of cargo, departing and arriving. "The salirium mines are protected by interstellar treaty. Though the Federation taxes the reserve, the mines are owned by Requiem itself. And the matriarchs have been reluctant to cooperate."

"So we needed a way through the mines," Asa said. "That's where Sokolov came in."

Her father nodded, his profile stark against the city lights. "One challenge still remains. The last thing keeping Requiem under syndicate control, aside from peace treaties. The Dreamers' Nexus."

Asa braced herself against the glass. So *that* was what the matriarchs guarded so viciously. Something protecting Requiem?

"It is a weapon system protecting the cryo-chambers, controlled by a virtual intelligence of Huifang, the first matriarch," he continued. "Not a true uploaded consciousness—that technology didn't exist in the 2120s—but an artificial approximation of her. Now that Sokolov is on our side, we have access. We're prepared to act tonight."

Asa's heart was in her throat. *Tonight.* That was the reason he'd infiltrated the syndicates. He had the key to taking over Requiem itself.

"That's . . . an accomplishment," she said. "So what happens after harvesting the specimens? Shouldn't we pull out of Requiem, to avoid provoking the Federation?"

He gave a soft chuckle. "There's a much bigger picture here, Asa. The Federation will be swayed once they understand that Echofall can address human civilization's biggest catastrophes—Earth's pollution, Requiem's violence. The unchecked impulses that have led to rampant crime and overpopulation and climate disasters. It all starts with slow suggestion." He fidgeted with one of his cufflinks. The bodyguard near the door immediately straightened. "Requiem lacks Federation regulations. It will become the starting point for a better world."

The horror chipped at her calm façade. "You'd be taking away what makes them human."

"Requiem has *thousands* dead due to violence every year." Annoyance crept into his voice. "You've seen the cruelty here. It is impossible to fix the world without conflict."

"And what do you gain from fixing the world?" No doubt he had other motives.

"You can imagine history would remember the elimination of violent crime without eliminating the criminals. We would be the ones who fixed two star-systems." He stared down at her. "They will name us their saviors. The greatest minds among them."

He would do it. Harvest Requiem's people like animals in a mass laboratory. He didn't care about the people he used and destroyed in the process, as long as he left a legacy. One that he'd make sure Asa carried forward.

She swallowed the urge to vomit on his polished shoes. "I think I need to shower. It's been a long few days."

"Asa. I know this is much to take in, but thank you for hearing me out." He cupped her cheek in one stiff hand. "Echofall will work perfectly for you. If you'd like, I can give you an advanced implant, like my own. It carries the potential for great things, such as remote technical control, like what your sister commands. The process will be easy. You need only sleep for a while. The world will be brighter on the other side."

Asa backed out of his grasp. If he was implying he could now do what Kaya could . . . this was worse by the minute. "Um. The bathroom?"

He nodded curtly. "It's left of the rooftop stairs. The ship is fueling and will be prepared to take us home in half an hour."

Half an hour. Barely time to escape.

Asa slipped into the bathroom, let the door slide closed behind her, and all but collapsed against the sink.

The reflection in the bathroom mirror taunted her. In her own face, she saw his. The dark eyes flecked with gold, the delicate chin and peaked lips.

You're your father's daughter.

All this time, Sofi had known his plans. Knew he'd planned to change her.

She splashed water onto her sweat-streaked skin. Her father wanted her to forget Riven, and Kaya, and the rest of the crew—all burned so deeply into her. Without them, she'd be nothing but a pawn in his legacy, ignorant of his empire's atrocities. Maybe she'd spend the rest of her life with the hollow, infinite sense of something missing.

Somehow, she had to warn her crew.

Asa scanned the bathroom. Adjustable lighting settings above the mirror, control panels for shower settings, an entertainment holoscreen set into the tile. All connected to Solus's internal network—but all the outgoing signals were probably monitored.

She remembered the fury in Kaya's eyes as Staccato had

dragged her away. The sister she knew would never give up on her. Riven too. Maybe they were already looking for her.

Asa could create a signal. Something only Kaya would know to look for.

She pulled up the diagnostic files on the shower's screen. Found the screen's name in the network:

HOLOSCREEN_RM_245A

A simple name change might be enough. She took a deep breath and tapped the touch screen.

ABYSSQUEST_HOME

She settled onto the marble rim of the bathtub, peeling away the sweaty top half of her exosuit. Minutes stretched into a small eternity. After everything she could have done, this seemed laughably small. Her father would pull her brain apart like he'd done to Kaya and Sofi and countless others.

The holoscreen fizzed into static.

"Asa," a familiar voice said. "Is that you?"

Her heart leaped. On the screen was Kaya's face, shaky, as if she were using the self-camera on her own wristlet.

Kaya probably couldn't see her. Asa pulled up the keyboard on the holoscreen and opened the text box on the entertainment search bar.

I'm here, she typed.

"Oh, thank god you're safe." The screen flickered, and Kaya's brow furrowed like she was concentrating hard. It was probably a strain to break through the security here. "We're coming to get you. And Dad."

Asa almost sobbed in relief. But there were mechs waiting

outside the tower, and guards in every hallway. Coming here would be a death sentence for her crew.

Footsteps creaked by in the hall, stopping outside the door. She turned on the shower and went back to typing.

don't talk. someone's listening.

Kaya nodded. Letters began to appear on the screen below her face. *I don't have much time before they notice the intrusion*, Kaya said. *There's something else watching this place.*

Listen—Dad's ship is leaving soon. Asa kept typing, stumbling over the letters and backspacing after Kaya nodded. *He's taking me back to Corte. As for Requiem . . .* She typed it all out in broken snippets—what their father had confessed about Sokolov, about the Dreamers' Nexus. That the whole city was in danger.

"*Meu Deus*," Kaya said. "Are you sure?"

Asa nodded. *Yes. You need to warn the Duchess as soon as possible.*

Kaya was quiet. Then: *She hasn't responded since we got kicked out. I don't know if it's the trial, or if something's gone wrong, but . . . you're my first priority. We aren't leaving you behind.*

I don't think even Riven could get me out of here. There was something profoundly unsettling about her father's new bodyguard.

Well, we're not alone. Riven got help, and she threatened to vacuum Tak's brains out her ass for suggesting we leave you behind. On-screen, Kaya smirked. *Maybe it's my turn to save you.*

You've done that plenty of times already, Asa typed.

Doesn't matter. I'm going to keep doing it as long as you're my sister. Even if we couldn't save Sofi.

Kaya was right. Sofi had been taken before Asa was even born. Now Asa had others to protect—and a vicious city to awaken. If Tak was in on this, Riven must have pulled some strings. Maybe they had a chance after all.

If you can get me out, she typed, *I might have a way to stop Dad.*

You always do. But don't do anything reckless before we get there. Kaya's face on the screen blurred with distortion. *You'll need to take the elevator down to us. I'll see if I can get it for you, but—*

The static nearly drowned Kaya's final words. *I have to go. Love you, Asa.*

"Love you too," Asa whispered.

But Kaya was already gone, and the holoscreen in the shower was blank blue. Outside the door, her father's voice rose, issuing commands to his guards. There was no easy way out, but she had to try.

Asa finished toweling off her face. It was time to betray him once again.

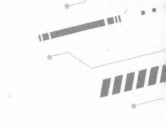

chapter 38
ENEMY

"She's okay, for now," Kaya announced as the door to Morphett's ship lounge slid open. "But we don't have much time."

Riven was on her feet in an instant, nearly knocking her reheated bacon-cheddar fries off the coffee table. "What's going on? Where's he keeping her?"

Kaya sank onto the couch and propped her head in her hands. "Give me a minute." She'd been at it for half an hour now, finding an access point into Solus Tower. Seemed she'd found something.

Ty settled onto the couch next to Kaya. He'd been flitting around the ship since waking up, looking for things to fix and people to help, maybe to distract from his own hurt.

"Your dad's not going to wait for us." Riven was already starting to regret taking responsibility for a mission that could get them all killed. And it still stung to help the other contenders vie for the matriarchy.

"We know." Ty unwrapped some medicated gauze and dabbed at the blood on Kaya's ear. "But it's been hard on her."

Riven huffed. She knew what it was like to have nerves that wouldn't cooperate, but they couldn't afford any delays.

"Asa says he plans to take her back to Corte in half an hour. Probably to rework her mind." Kaya looked up, her brown eyes glassy. She looked so much like her sister when her imp-ish smile was gone. "She might be able to meet us inside the tower. As for Dad . . . he has plans tonight. About much more than just Asa."

Asa would be *reprogrammed*. Riven's trigger-fingers itched. "Let's focus on Solus first. How do we get to Asa?"

Kaya pulled a stylus out of her pocket and scribbled patterns on her wristlet's pop-out holoscreen. "Here. I got a rough floor plan and mapped the security networks. There are some complications."

Riven watched the sketches scroll into place. Normally, she'd let Samir or Diego handle this. But she'd made the deal with Callista and Tak, and she was seeing it through. "Seems like our best plan will be to split up. Have a ground-floor diversion outside the building for those mechs. Then an extraction squad for Asa, and another group to intercept Almeida's ship. As for the security systems inside . . ."

"Right," Kaya said. "I might be able to trigger a lockdown and keep the embassy guests in their rooms. But honestly, it was hard to get in the first time. It's not just an AI system in those circuits."

Ty shifted uneasily. "What do you mean?"

"There's something guarding that place that feels a little like Banshee, but *isn't* Banshee, if that makes sense. I could feel it staring at me from every direction. Like I was an intruder. Like it was deciding whether to rip me apart." Kaya shivered. "And then its attention just . . . wandered. Like it couldn't see me anymore."

"You think it was Redline?" Riven said. None of this sounded good. Usually Kaya could skate right past any AI security systems. But even if Redline were still intact, she wouldn't be protecting her father.

"No, I think I know what she's talking about," Ty said quietly. "Almeida has two circuit divers protecting him."

"I don't like where this is going," Riven muttered. She pulled a soggy fry from the pile and crammed it in her mouth.

"One of them, I know only as the Watcher. He guards the lab." Ty fidgeted with one of his cybernetic knuckles, as if the limb was still foreign to him. "The other is the armored Etri, Iolus. He guards Almeida himself and is . . . tied to him somehow."

"Another Etri?" Kaya said. "We suspected, but it's true?"

"At least a shell of one. Sounds like Almeida's been using bits and pieces of them lately." Ty shivered. "Be careful. Both of you. There's something *off* about them."

Kaya nodded. "I'll do my best. But I'm not sure how much more I have in me."

"Whatever you can do, we owe you," Riven said. "Your recon is already a huge help. The crew's not the same without you and your sister."

Kaya managed a weak smile. "Damn right it's not. That's why we're getting her back."

When Riven stepped into the hallway, Morphett emerged from the cockpit, where frantic music pulsed from the speakers.

"I hope you've got a plan, Hawthorne." Morphett shoved raspberry crisps into her mouth and licked pink dust off her fingers. "If we stall here forever, Solus's security is going to get suspicious."

Behind Morphett, the horizon was visible through the cockpit windshield, with Solus Tower jutting above the jagged skyline of lights and smog.

"Yeah. I get it," Riven said. "Maybe we could all think straight if you'd turn down the sugar-pop crap." She dialed up Tak and Callista on the cabin's main holoscreen.

Callista answered first. "So? Has that Banshee girl figured it out yet?"

"That's not her name." Riven crossed her arms. Tak's image popped onto the screen a second later. "And yeah, we have a pretty good idea what we're dealing with. We need at least one crew on the ground to draw out the mechs. One crew to intercept Almeida when he tries to ship off. And one to help us grab Asa and get out."

Tak gave a humorless laugh. "Well. That certainly complicates things."

"I hope you mean my squad will be collecting Almeida," Callista said, their voice cutting like a plasma blade. "My ship and crew are designed for extractions."

"Doubtful," Tak said. "I'm not about to play decoy while you pack Luca Almeida into your cargo bay."

Callista glared into the camera. "Hawthorne. You know I'm right."

Everyone was acting like Riven had all the answers, and it kind of sucked. But someone had to keep them in line. Maybe this was how Samir felt most of the time.

"You know what?" Riven said. "Someone's going to have a

chance to put a bullet through Luca Almeida's skull. And believe me, I'd *love* to be the one to do it." It still felt like she was walking away from a fight that should be hers. All the nights she'd dreamed of putting that asshole in the ground as payback for what he'd done.

Hell, if Riven brought Luca Almeida's head to the Duchess, she'd *have* to let her back into the trial.

"But this isn't about shoving one of your asses onto Rio Oscuro's throne," Riven continued. "It's about stopping him from screwing over our city. A city one of you will have to help lead. You both agreed to shut up and follow our plan, so until we work something out, I'm not forwarding you Kaya's schematics."

They were quiet. At least they agreed on that.

Riven squared her shoulders. "Here's the deal. Divide up your crews—they'll have to work together without you to set the ground distraction. Then the two of you go after Almeida. Together."

"Seriously?"

"Yeah. Cut the guy in half if you need to. Because divvying him up will be *your* problem." Riven let out a shaky breath, exhaling some of the nerves and uncertainty. "Meet us on the *Nephilim*'s docking ramp in seven minutes. We're almost prepped for launch."

She clicked off the holo. Responsibility sucked. She wished Samir had been there—he'd have handled that more gracefully.

Either way, it was time to get her crew together.

She stumbled through the ship and found Samir with Diego in the side hall, two silhouettes beneath lights tinted like sunset. Diego was saying something in his taut, *this-stays-between-us-or-you're-dead* tone, and Samir leaned against the wall next to him. Not much privacy on this ship, even if it was a little roomier than *Boomslang*.

She turned on her heel and stopped around the corner, waiting.

"I'm not going to chase you," Diego was saying.

"I'd never ask you to." Samir's voice. "And I understand. But as long as our paths align, I'll do everything I can to be here for you."

"How long will that be?" There was a hopeful undercurrent in Diego's voice.

"I don't know. A good while longer, at least. I have a lot of work to do here."

A grin tugged at Riven's mouth. Maybe Samir would eventually call this place home for good.

Diego murmured something she couldn't make out.

"You don't owe me anything," Samir said. "You've done more for me than I can ever repay. But I really hope we're beyond quid pro quo."

"It's not that." Diego sighed. "You used to talk about marking every corner of the star-system. You sure you won't get bored of me?"

Samir chuckled. "Never. And there's still a thousand things we haven't done. Dragging you onstage at poetry night, for one." Diego groaned. "And I can't forget covering you in glow-paint and throwing you onto a—"

He cut off with a soft grunt. Then their breaths turned to stifled gasps, and hell, Riven *really* shouldn't be listening to this.

She was turning back toward the cockpit when Diego rounded the corner and pushed past her, bright-eyed and a little smug.

"Eavesdropping?" Samir sidled up to her, straightening the collar on his exosuit. His hair was mussed.

"I believe that was defined as *sucking face*," Galateo chirped proudly.

Riven smothered her wristlet speaker with a gloved hand. "Just making sure you're not trying to steal my informant." When Diego was out of earshot, she asked, "Everything okay?"

"Yeah, just the usual. 'Don't get killed.' 'You're an asshole.' 'Maybe I'll come home with you eventually.' I think we'll figure things out, if we get through this." Samir cleared his throat awkwardly. "Speaking of—did you get the squads ready?"

"I think so. I'm sending Tak and Callista up together." She blew out a breath. "That leaves the two of us going in for Asa."

He listened to the rest of her plan, taking it in without interruption. "Sounds tough. You up for it?"

"Have to be." She tightened Samir's pistol strap on her thigh. "I just hope this isn't a bad idea."

"I think it's the closest we're getting to a *good* idea." Samir lifted his chin. "Just another Darkday-III, huh?"

"Never easy. That's for sure."

As usual, the future was a blur. In a few minutes, it would be her and Samir again, facing odds that seemed impossible. But if there was one thing she'd ever wanted to gamble on, it was Asa.

"There was one person your plan didn't account for

though." Samir inclined his head toward the cockpit. "We could use a third in there."

As if she'd been waiting, Morphett rounded the corner, grinning like a monster with pink-stained teeth. "Yeah. Forgetting someone, Hawthorne?"

"You really want to be involved in screwing over your former employer?" Morphett hadn't earned her trust quite yet.

"Of course. Every potential Rio Oscuro matriarch is in on this, and I need *someone* indebted to me. Plus, someone needs to make sure you don't mess up." Morphett popped a blue gumball into her mouth. "So the plan is to save your tech-princess from the glass tower? Hopefully then you'll quit all this pining–it's nauseating, honestly. Makes me *so* glad I'm immune to all that."

They'd already racked up too many favors with Morphett. But with her cybernetics against Almeida's thugs, they might actually stand a chance.

"Fine," Riven said. "Hope you're ready to raise some hell."

"Come on, come *on*," Asa hissed at the screen.

The smart-system control panel winked back at her. Somewhere in here was footage to make the Duchess pay attention. Everything her father had said about Sokolov, about Echofall–everything that could save them.

Her father and his unnerving bodyguard were just outside the penthouse bedroom. Asa was feigning a trip to the mini-ifridge as she worked on the control panel, but if she took too long, they'd get suspicious. She shifted her weight, crouching on the hardwood floor.

"Yes, I realize," her father's voice drifted from the other room. Asa leaned to peer out the door. He was pacing by the waterfall wall, speaking into his wristlet.

She scrolled through more of the system accesses, then pulled up the emergency dialer—outgoing comms had been disabled, because of *course* they had. But what she needed was internal. She began chipping through the CCTV encryption.

"Tell them the Nexus will be secure by sunrise," her father said from the other room. "We can meet tomorrow to discuss the next phase."

By sunrise. Oh, damn. Even if she got the data out before he took her back to Corte, there might not be enough time.

Words scrolled onto the screen, blocking her windows. *Looking for something?*

Asa's breath caught. Someone had noticed her.

Our sister is having some trouble getting in, the text continued. *You played right into his hand, like I knew you would.*

It had to be Sofi, watching her. Asa recoiled from the control panel.

Admittedly, Sofi's messages continued, *it would be hard to kill you within there. And for now, it seems we have a common enemy. What matters now is getting you away from him. He needs you, or Echofall will die with him when he inevitably crumbles to dust.*

Asa glanced at the door. Nobody was peering in. "What are you proposing?" she whispered.

I saw you put that gun to your head. You were willfully ignorant for so long, but there might still be hope for you.

You want to prove you're not a pawn? Stop him.

A file appeared on-screen. Brief snippets of text, encrypted like passcodes. It had to be the Nexus key codes, the ones Sokolov had given her father.

This can be your atonement, Sofi's text said. *Take this, hail the elevator, and head to the Nexus. Your friends are coming for you.*

Succeed, and I'll consider letting you live afterward.

Asa braced herself against the wall. Her lost sister was offering a pact. After Sofi had incited violence in every alley, had almost killed the fire in Riven's eyes, Asa couldn't forgive her. Everything Sofi had done was calculated, this included.

But Asa could play along. Sofi might be her only hope of stopping their father.

"All right," Asa whispered. "I'll take it."

Then quit drooling and go, Sofi's message said. *Quickly.* The tiny data card clicked, ejecting from the edge of the panel. Asa slipped it into her pocket.

With a loud *pop*, the holoscreen above the bed—which had been playing some talking-head channel discussing Corte stock markets—cut to static. Then it displayed a security feed. A familiar room. A girl with black hair, crouched in front of a control panel—

Asa froze. It was footage of *her*. Someone had switched the display, as if to say *I see you*.

Just outside the room, a quiet shuffle of footsteps

approached. A *slither*, almost. And as she moved toward the bedroom door, heart pounding a hole through her ribs, someone blocked the entrance.

Her father's bodyguard. He cocked his head, his mirrored helmet reflecting Asa's panicked eyes.

"Excuse me," she said.

He stood frozen, as if deciding what to do with her. It slowly clicked—he was the one guarding her father's circuits, watching her in the security feeds. She could only hope Sofi had kept her messages hidden.

The lights dimmed overhead. There was a flash, then a blare of alarms. The bodyguard whirled toward her father.

Her father clicked off his wristlet, cursing. "We have a security breach. Iolus, go greet our intruders."

Her friends. They'd come through.

The bodyguard—Iolus—let his hidden gaze linger on Asa a moment longer, then he glided toward the penthouse elevator. He held his webbed fingers near the keypad, and the door slid open to admit him.

Asa finally stepped out of the bedroom. Her father was pacing furiously as he watched the wall holoscreen. Security footage showed mechs warring at street level.

Riven had to be behind this. But they'd have a hell of a fight on their hands.

"Asa," her father said. "Do you know anything about this *complication*?"

She shifted on her feet. "Seems like a normal day on Requiem."

He narrowed his eyes. "I'm going to check on the ship." He nodded to one of the guards by the elevator. "Costa. Keep an eye on her." The second guard followed him up the floating stairs to the rooftop, and the first took his post by the elevator.

Asa was alone with one guard and blaring alarms. Redline had told her to hail the elevator, but that wouldn't be easy. She'd either need to take the guard's key or hack the keypad, but she doubted the guard would let her do either.

She slowly approached the elevator.

"Can I help you?" the guard said icily through his rebreather.

"Just jittery. Moving around a bit."

Static came over the guard's earpiece. "Yes?" he said into his comm. He glanced at Asa, then he turned toward the glass wall. "I thought they were on the lower level. How many?"

While Asa debated how to lie her way out, the elevator dinged. Impossibly, the doors slid open. Empty, as if beckoning her.

Her heart pounded. Either Kaya or Sofi had to be behind this. Her two sisters. Maybe part of Sofi was still like Kaya, watching over her.

Asa had only a split second before the guard noticed. Even if this was Sofi, Asa had to trust her.

The guard's head snapped toward her as she slipped into the elevator. "Wait, what the—"

As soon as the door slid shut behind her, the elevator lurched and began moving.

A chuckle fizzed over the speakers. Kaya's voice, but rougher. Jaded.

"I hope you're ready to do this," Sofi said. "Go prove you're his worst enemy."

The speaker cut out. And Asa watched the numbers tick down.

chapter 39

HOT CHAOS

Getting into Solus Tower meant they'd have to jump.

Riven leaned out the *Nephilim*'s open docking hatch, stray wisps of hair whipping at her face. The streets scrolled by below, a dizzying drop over torn metal scaffolds and steaming gutters. The balcony on the fifty-eighth floor drew closer—an eerily empty pool deck, with half-full champagne glasses left on the bar tables. The evacuation must've been fast, after Kaya triggered the security lockdown.

As planned, the streets surrounding the tower were hot chaos.

One of Tak's patchwork mechs hurled a speeder toward the main entrance. Alarms blared over the tarmac, and security drones streamed from the building's lower level to answer them. So far, so good.

"Looks like Tak's crew has this on lock," Samir called over the whir of the thrusters. "Ready?"

A familiar thrill built in Riven's chest, the rush of adrenaline hotter, faster. It felt like waking up. "Always am."

"Riv." Ty gripped the bar behind her. He squinted against the rush of air, one eye unflinching. "You'd better come back."

"Nobody's dying. I promise." Not even her. This time, they had a plan. "Keep our mech-head from short-circuiting, yeah?"

He nodded. "She'll be safe."

"And . . . we're clear." Morphett snapped on a visor, bracing herself in the rush of the open hatch. "Ready for freefall."

The tilted glass of the bar awning loomed just below. The ship couldn't get much closer without skimming the outer railing.

It was time for the drop.

Riven fell from the hatch into the night air, her gut spinning from the vertigo. Half a second later, her boots hit the glass at an angle and skidded. She ran down the awning above the bar, leaped off the edge, and hit the concrete of the pool deck.

She sprinted off the momentum, ducking behind a palm planter. Morphett and Samir touched down and slid into place beside her.

"I'll see if I can break you into the penthouse," Kaya's voice said into her earpiece. "Doubt Dad will cooperate."

"We'll be ready when you are," Riven said.

She thumbed her revolvers, listening to the alarms and the clash of metal in the street below. Slow bass still pulsed through the bar speakers, and shards of glass littered the deck. The surface of the pool rippled as a tremor tore through the building. She suppressed a shudder. Things were about to get ugly.

"This way," Samir said. A pair of plexicarbon doors led inside the building. With a few shots from Riven and metal-plated punches from Samir, the doors shattered, activating another alarm. Not that it would draw much attention, with the building already on high alert. With any luck, most of the security would be engaging Tak's crew on the ground.

Remain in rooms, a voice droned over the hallway speaker. *Threat located on premises.*

The elevator to the penthouse would be around the next corner—

A squadron of whirring drones and armored, humanoid mechs rushed down the hall toward them.

Morphett cackled. If there was a way to snap gum menacingly, she had it perfected. "Seems they've got some cavalry left. Want to wager, Hawthorne?"

"Wager on what?" Riven's guns kicked in her hands. Bullets dented the metal cladding, making the first mechs stagger. She shot for the joints, the lenses. Her 44-cal bullets tore the first mech apart.

"Kill count. Loser walks naked through the Crush." Morphett ripped another mech apart with her wrist blades and scorpion tails.

Riven swore as the first salvo of bullets burst from their enemies, but Samir was already diving in front of her, a holo-shield materializing from the bracer on his exosuit. The shield shimmered with the impacts, and he fired his pistol over its edge.

"These things barely count as kills," Riven said. She exhaled adrenaline, and the world seemed to slow as she peered down *Blackjack*'s iron sights.

Crack. Crack.

The drones' targeting lenses shattered, and they fell in worthless heaps of scrap. Three more combat mechs, taller than Samir and wielding riot-shields, barreled toward her.

She leaped from behind Samir's shield and pulled out her blade, forcing the singing carbon fiber through one mech's shield and ducking beneath the precision turret of another. Morphett's blades whirred to life, chopping the androids to bits.

Samir's gunshots took care of the rest. Just as quickly as they'd appeared, the mechs were nothing but a mess on the carpet.

"Clear." Samir let out a whistle. "Damn. Hope they had those insured."

Morphett pulled the wad of gum out of her mouth and crammed it into the card-reader slot of a security room. "Hawthorne's not such a half-wit bitch when she puts her mind to it."

"I'll pretend I didn't hear that," Riven said. Either Morphett wanted a reaction, or she was attempting to give a compliment. "We need to keep moving." Her hands twitched from the combat high. Her unspent adrenaline rushed hotter. The pricks of pain were muted now, not strong enough to pull her down.

As she headed toward the elevators, the throb of the alarms seemed to slow. Even the whirring and folding of Morphett's cybernetics seemed to move at half speed. *What in hell?*

There was a *high* in her veins. Like she could pulverize this tower with her bare hands, crushing Luca Almeida and his thugs into the dirt.

Riven rolled her shoulders. Something was off with her head. Maybe it was just nerves.

Samir's hand clapped onto her shoulder. "Something's ahead."

She peered around the corner, revolver raised. Lights flickered in the hall leading to the penthouse elevator, illuminating a massive silhouette. Huge, lumbering, built like a tank and covered in chrome.

Her comm channel fizzed with static. Then Ty's voice came through. "Riv. You need to get out of there."

"What the hell is that?" she murmured, though she had a feeling she already knew.

"Something–" Kaya's voice crackled. "–there's interference. Ty says–" Static. "–don't try to engage–"

Then her comm went out completely.

The armored silhouette had to be eight feet tall. As he approached, the lights guttered out. His webbed hands twitched, as if preparing to clench a throat.

Iolus. Almeida's Etri bodyguard. He was blocking her way to Asa.

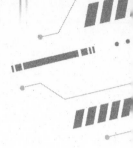

chapter 40
IOLUS

A growl built in Iolus's throat as the hulking creature stared down at her.

"Hey, there." Riven's fingers slid onto her triggers. "We're here to pick up my girlfriend. Seen her?"

Iolus—a tank in black-and-gold body armor—cocked his head. The only visible part of him was his mouth, cracked and deadened gray, a perpetual grimace.

"She's about five foot five," Riven continued. "Gorgeous. Probably half-covered in grease if you let her anywhere near a wrench."

A Morphett-shaped blur whirled past her, steel extending, blades scything toward his armor—

And almost instantly, Morphett was flying backward. Iolus had thrown her, so fast Riven had barely seen him move. Morphett skidded into a crouch, her scorpion tails shuddering.

Riven fired. Bullets pelted from both hands, pinpoint shots at the joints in Iolus's armor.

Iolus was already moving again, fluid as a snake but *faster*. Her bullets flattened and fell. The points of articulation, the armor's weak spots, shimmered with holo-shielding.

As Riven ducked out of the way, she spun *Verdugo* back into its holster and unfolded her blade. But Iolus was lunging past her, jamming a massive fist against Samir's shield and sending him sprawling.

Ty's voice came back in her comm, small and pained. "Kaya's having trouble. You need to get out of there."

"We still don't have Asa," Riven grunted.

"Don't engage with Iolus. He's—" Ty's voice went in and out. "—to Almeida. Even if your condition is stable—" Static. "—dangerous to push yourself."

Your condition. Was that what was happening to her? Her head swam, her blood coursing hotter. She fired a few more bullets at Iolus's holo-shielded chin. Even bulletproof, the impacts made him stagger.

Morphett jumped and wedged one of her wrist-blades into Iolus's neck. It pierced the outer cladding, and the creature whirled, wrenching her aside and slamming her against the ground.

Samir's gunshots pinged Iolus's armor. Riven saw every impact, the ripples in the air as the bullets discharged. "That's right," Samir said, his voice too slow. "Over here, big guy."

Iolus's gaze snapped toward Samir, part of Morphett's blade still lodged in his neck. Behind him, Morphett groaned in pain. Her forearm gaped where the cybernetic should be attached, and blood leaked down her metal-scarred skin.

Oh, hell. They might not be able to take down this asshole without casualties. They had to grab Asa and go.

"Hey," Kaya said over the comm. "Dealing with two other entities here. Something else seems to be drawing their attention. But the penthouse elevator, it's—"

Light spilled into the hallway as the elevator doors opened. They revealed a wide-eyed, frantic girl in an exosuit.

"Riven!" Asa slipped out of the elevator, as dauntless as ever. Unchanged.

Riven's chest shuddered in relief. "Samir. Cover her. We're getting out of here."

Morphett stood, her ruined forearm sparking. "I'll hold him off."

"Not alone," Riven said. She'd promised Ty they'd all come back.

Samir urged Asa behind his shield, pointing her toward the pool deck where Morphett's ship waited.

Iolus cricked his neck, and the lights in the hallway blew out, cutting the alarms into eerie quiet. Riven's eardrums throbbed as her covering fire and Morphett's clanging blades rang out. Iolus was injured, but he *charged.* Samir intercepted him, letting Asa run while Morphett wrenched Iolus's helmet backward.

Whatever Iolus was—some augmented, beefed-up experiment of Almeida's—he wasn't their target.

Security mechs fired at Morphett's ship as the docking hatch opened. Those, Riven could handle. She lunged with her tech-blade, tearing them to shrapnel. "Let's *go!*"

She let Samir and Asa on first. Morphett grabbed a sparking mech in her scorpion-claws and hurled it at Iolus, stalling him—if only for a moment.

The ship's thrusters roared, and it began to lift. Riven grabbed Morphett's good arm and pulled her on just before the docking hatch slammed shut behind them.

Riven caught her breath, delirious from the combat high. Morphett swore, punching the wall with a bloodied fist. They hadn't gotten Iolus, but they'd gotten out alive.

Asa was already at Riven's side, steadying her when her legs threatened to collapse. "You came for me," Asa whispered. "Even though I said not to."

Riven lifted Asa's perfect chin. "Did you expect me to sit on my ass and wait for you?"

Then Tak's frantic voice came through her earpiece. "We're hit. Almeida's ship got away."

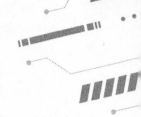

chapter 41
NOW OR NEVER

"What do you *mean*, he got away?" Riven hissed into her wristlet comm. "I thought your ship had a stealth drive!"

As the *Nephilim* rocked forward, Asa eased Riven into one of the pink-and-black harness seats. Riven was bleeding and battered, but alive. From what Asa could tell, the whole crew was.

It'd been so reckless for Riven to come back. But she'd somehow rallied help. The alarms, the diversion outside, the squad covering Asa—had Riven orchestrated all this?

Whatever she'd done had *worked.* Still, whether they could stop Asa's father tonight was still in question.

"Seems we're not the only ones with stealth drives," Callista said. "Almeida had some cloaked turrets. Killed our main thrusters. We're making an emergency landing."

"Speaking of which," Morphett hissed, "we'd better hope those turrets aren't aimed at us."

The lounge door slid open, and Ty stumbled in with Kaya braced against his shoulder. She looked exhausted, and her blue hair was a mess, but her eyes lit up. "Asa." She let go of Ty, sank into the seat next to Asa, and threw her arms around her. "I was so sure he'd turned your brain to gelatin. I should have done more. Those turrets, I didn't even—"

"Nothing you could've done," Riven muttered. "Crossing your dad was always going to be a shitshow."

"How'd you get out?" Kaya said. "It took everything in me to keep the main security force off us."

"I . . . had help, somehow." Asa opened her palm, and the tiny data card shimmered. "From someone who wanted me out of Dad's hands. She said we shared a common enemy."

Kaya's eyebrows shot up. "You don't mean—"

Asa nodded. "I also learned a lot more. Dad met with Sokolov tonight, set his gears into motion, and took off."

"Dare I ask what gears?" Samir was pacing, too restless to sit. "What has he been doing with Staccato? Something big enough to make *Redline* help you?"

Asa told them, as quickly as she could, about the Nexus and its weapon. About Echofall.

Ty's eyes were haunted as she explained, as if he'd already known. "That's probably why he brought Iolus here. If anyone can break into the Nexus, it's him. And the Watcher will be guarding him."

The ice in Asa's veins thickened. "He's doing it tonight, while the matriarchs are split up. While there's still one matriarch missing, and Sokolov is listening to him."

Riven swore, kicking the seat next to her.

"We need to tell the Duchess about this," Samir said. "If the other syndicates turn up, we might have a fighting chance."

"I have footage of Dad describing it all. It'll make them listen." Asa pinched the data card between her fingers. "Diego. Can you get this information to Bria or Cerys?"

Diego had his wristlet plugged into his cybernetic forearm. "Calling up Bria now. We'll see if they answer."

He settled into one of the cabin seats, waiting. When Bria's comm didn't pick up, he tried again.

"No response," Diego muttered. "All right, we'll try Cerys. Rare that she'll answer a direct line, but it won't hurt to try."

He dialed and waited. Outside the ship, an alarm shrieked to life, echoed by others in the distance. Asa shivered.

Soon, she heard a *click* and a shuffling noise at the other end of the line. A rasping breath, and then waiting silence.

"Need to speak to Cerys," Diego said. "Tell her Valdez has information concerning the Nexus."

There was a low grunt. Then a few more pops of static, and a voice came through—Cerys's, but pitched lower. "Valdez. This had better be important."

Cerys's voice held a coldness Asa hadn't heard before. No doubt the matriarch knew every detail of their expulsion, and the charges over Jayde's death.

Diego didn't waste a moment. "Sokolov's compromised. We have evidence."

Cerys paused. "Scan your surroundings for me."

"The rest of the Boomslang Faction is here, and another ally," Diego said.

As the scan-beam rotated, Morphett yanked open the med-kit on the wall, her ruined arm hanging limp. Ty reached for the torn steel of her cybernetic blade, and she reflexively smacked his hand away. She stared him down for a long moment, but finally relented and offered her arm.

When Diego finished the scan, Cerys continued. "*Sokolov's*

compromised. That's a dramatic way of putting it. We're aware of her syndicate's infractions. The whole city is."

"Whole city?" Diego said. "What do you mean?"

A high-pitched whine pierced the cabin, and Asa clapped her palms over her ears. A transmission crackled from somewhere in the cockpit ahead. "*You're entering a restricted zone. Land immediately,*" it demanded. "*Turrets are online.*"

"Hell. Since when is this a no-fly area?" Morphett said as Ty worked on her arm.

Cerys's voice came through patchy. "Have you been under a rock for the past hour, Valdez? The barricades and blackouts are all Staccato's doing."

"Blackouts?" Asa said.

As the navigation rerouted, the ship lurched, and Asa had to grab one of the bars for support. Samir toppled, catching himself in the seat next to Diego.

"Dee," Samir murmured. "What's going on?"

Kaya hit the button beneath the window, and the blinds retracted, letting in a flood of city lights—with a few patches missing.

"Shit." Riven braced herself against the window.

Asa's gut churned. Below, the skyways were barricaded in red holos flashing warning messages. Emergency lights glared from speeders on the ground, and armored Staccato forces waited near the alleys. Whole city blocks were blacked out—and comms towers with them.

"Staccato's done all this?" Diego said.

"As far as we can tell, Sokolov is trying to force a negotiation with the Duchess in line with the Code, claiming negligence over Jayde's death." Cerys's comm hissed with static, louder this time. "It seems there are a few fundamental details you've missed. Now why are you wasting my time?"

Asa was about to jump in, to beg Cerys to listen, but Diego quickly collected himself. "No, it's more than that. Sokolov is in league with Almeida. She's looking to override the Nexus itself. I'll send you the footage—Asa retrieved it all."

"Most of our resources are already focused on bringing Sokolov into custody," Cerys said. "Callista and Tak have been called back for support, and the trial is on hold. As for the Nexus, it can protect itself."

"Sokolov isn't the primary threat," Diego said. "Almeida's new circuit divers—"

Before he could finish, the comm line dissolved into static. The feed cut.

"Dammit." Diego fiddled with his wristlet, brow scrunched. "Dammit!"

"The nearest comms tower looks like it's gone dark." Kaya pressed a hand to the window as the ship lowered.

"Did you get her the footage?" Asa said, panic bubbling up her throat.

"No," Diego said. "It didn't go through. Not that it seems to matter. Boneshiver isn't going to help us."

Sokolov was making a move—challenging the Duchess herself. Treading on the Code, tying up the comm lines, and distracting the other syndicates from the Nexus. Help wasn't coming. Maybe Sofi had known that.

"He's trying to start a syndicate war," Asa said. "This is

exactly what he wanted. And once he gets into the Nexus, all bets are off."

"He said he'd have it under control before sunrise," Kaya said. "Guess he's won after all." Whatever Kaya was capable of, Iolus was probably engineered to do it better.

It was quiet in the ship's cabin, save for the alarms outside and the hum of the thrusters. Asa couldn't look out at the city she'd failed, couldn't even look at Riven. She'd let all of this happen.

The ship lurched to a stop on the roof of an apartment complex overridden with fungal vines. High above a city still fighting.

The only thing Asa had left was to fulfill her promise to Sofi.

"If they won't listen," she said, "Sofi also gave me the location of the Nexus. And the passcodes for its outer chamber."

Silence stretched after the words. It was so much to ask. So much to risk. The entire crew was gathered now—Ty dabbing numbing salve on Morphett's arm, Riven brooding by the window, Kaya beside her, and Samir and Diego huddled together. They were all far from home, on an unfamiliar ship reeking of bubble gum and cigarettes. The places Asa had called home for the past few months were a venom-green ship in smithereens somewhere, and a bombed hideout that might be overrun with scavengers.

But compared to what she had left, those losses were unimaginably small.

"Right now, we're the only ones who know the truth," she said. "The only ones who might be able to shut this down in time."

"You think we can trust Sofi's word?" Samir said.

"I think we can. She said she'd consider letting me live if I helped stop Dad."

"Is this really all going to be on us?" Ty said. "Again?"

"We've had too many near-misses lately." Riven pressed her fist against the window. "The matriarchs wouldn't give two shits if we died for something that should be their problem."

"And what do you think happens to *us* if Almeida wins?" Samir said.

Kaya was wrapping Zephyr in someone's hoodie. "I don't want to imagine what this place would become."

"Ty and Kaya managed to escape my dad's labs," Asa said, "but the rest of Requiem might not be so lucky." Other crews just like hers would be picked apart. Maybe her friends eventually too.

"I'm not going to lose any of you. Not again." Riven scowled, a storm brewing behind her eyes. "But this isn't about the goddamn matriarchs," she finally said. "We can't let Almeida do this."

Kaya set a hand on Asa's shoulder. "I don't have much left in me, but I'll do whatever you need."

"You said you have the codes for the outer sanctum. And the inner?" Diego said. "There have always been whispers that the Nexus is intelligent. You heard what Cerys said—it protects itself. Even if you have a passcode, it might see you as a threat."

"We can only hope my dad doesn't get that far. But if it comes to that, we'll have to make the Nexus listen." If the Nexus was truly connected to Huifang, the first matriarch, and the fate of Requiem itself, Asa might be able to negotiate with it.

A charge filled the air as an understanding grew among

them. They all knew the risks, but they'd faced impossible odds before.

"It's really not fair this ended up our responsibility, is it?" Samir sighed.

"This'll either be Requiem's last hurrah or ours," Morphett said as Ty finished the stitches on her arm. "I suppose I'm re-routing the ship."

Samir gave her a *look*. "You're still coming? We wouldn't turn down the help." He rubbed the stubble on his cheek, which was becoming a proper beard. "Nice not to be on the wrong side of those blades."

Morphett's wicked grin returned. "We'll see how long that lasts."

Riven waited for Morphett to slink back into the cockpit, then turned to Asa. She'd tugged her ponytail out, and silvery hair hung loose over her shoulders. "You just keep throwing yourself into the fire, huh?"

"Have to," Asa said softly.

Riven's gaze slid over Asa's exosuit, which probably needed an acid wash by now. Riven had a way of staring through her, seeing past all her insecurities and mistakes.

After a few heartbeats, Riven took her hand and pulled her into the lounge room.

"Asa." As the door closed, Riven traced Asa's jawline with her fingertips. "I . . ."

Asa set her hands on Riven's wrists, her heart racing.

"When they took you, it almost killed me," Riven finally said. "I kept wishing I could take it all back. I should've trusted you to make the decision about us." Her hand cupped Asa's cheek. "All this time, you've been in as much danger as me."

"I wanted to save you too," Asa said. "Kaya and I, we . . . we kept hitting dead ends, so I never told you. But I never would've stopped trying." She couldn't meet Riven's eyes. "I should've faced my dad's plans earlier. I'm just glad Ty fixed you."

"For what it's worth, you're still the bravest person I've ever known." The intensity in Riven's voice suggested she meant every word.

Asa felt her cheeks flushing. "I haven't had much choice but to be brave."

"You *did*. And you still do. And you're still here, fighting." Riven stepped backward, just enough to look Asa dead in the eyes. "I can't promise we'll ever be safe. But say the word, and I'm yours. However long this lasts."

They might have years, or maybe days. Maybe only hours. But Asa wanted all of it.

"I'd like that," was all she managed to say.

It was enough. Riven smothered her with a hard kiss. Most of her rational thought drained away as Riven's chest pressed her to the wall. Being in the arms of her dangerous, riotously beautiful girl again was surreal. Whatever they'd be when the sun rose, Asa would take it.

Asa threaded her hand into Riven's hair, trying to pull her closer. Riven lifted the back of Asa's knee to her muscular waist, and Asa eagerly wrapped her legs there. The ship could be crashing right now and Asa wasn't sure she'd care.

Riven finally broke the kiss, gasping. Still intertwined with Asa—messy hair and grasping fingers. "I'm playing a long game now," Riven murmured, pressing her forehead against Asa's. "And tonight, I'm wagering on you."

Asa ran her thumb over Riven's cheek. "You would've made a good matriarch. Maybe you still will."

Riven chuckled. "We'll see. Definitely not priority right now." She let Asa's feet slip back onto the ground. "If we're going to see the other side of this, we need to get into the Nexus and blast your dad's forces into next Duskday."

The ship rumbled as it changed course. Asa's knee trembled, restless, at the thought of whatever chaos lay ahead. But Riven kept her steady. After everything they'd been through, the two of them could face it.

Asa gave her one last kiss, nipping at Riven's bottom lip. "For luck."

Riven's smile was hard and fierce. "For luck."

As the *Nephilim* began its descent, Asa tied back her tangled hair and stumbled into the main cabin.

Her breaths constricted from more than just the cabin pressure. They were all risking everything to right her wrongs. To fix what she'd fled from.

Her skin still burned with the memory of Riven's hands, Riven's lips. But some of it turned cold when she saw the only other person in the half-lit cabin.

Ty was hunched in one of the seats, his elbows resting on his knees. He twisted a rag between his fingers, smeared red with blood.

She'd been avoiding him, not entirely on purpose. It awoke

the stinging guilt whenever she saw the scars around his eye socket, the hollow of his cheeks, the quiet sobriety that now covered him like a shroud. He looked like a patchwork doll, something lost and found again, new parts and healing scars. Something she could never make right.

She had to say something eventually. "Hey. Is everything all right?"

Ty met her eyes for a split second, then pretended to be interested in the bloody rag again. "Oh, the blood's not mine. Had to give Morphett stitches. But she might need a mechanist's eye. Cybernetics aren't my department."

"I'll check on her soon," Asa said. Voices drifted, muffled from the cockpit. The rest of them must be plotting. Kaya was probably in there too.

Tentatively, Asa settled into the seat across from him. It had to be now. "I didn't think I'd ever get a chance to thank you." God, that was inadequate, after what he'd been through. "I'm sorry I brought you into this mess. And that we didn't come back for you."

Ty was quiet, likely processing the deep hurt that had sunk into his bones. It wasn't something that could be brushed off. Maybe he'd already forgiven them, but it had left scars.

"I'm glad you didn't," he finally said. "For all you knew, I was dead. Hell, I should've been. Even if you'd known the truth, there's not much you could've done."

Ty set the cloth aside. His top-of-the-line mech hand was clean—carbon fiber with neural linking, next-gen cybernetics. But the rest of him looked haunted.

"Maybe not," Asa said softly. Whatever he'd done to escape

that place, he'd done because he desperately wanted to come back.

"I'm glad you're okay. And Riven too. Seems you two have gotten . . . close." An unspoken question lay beneath his words.

"Yeah." She had to say it. Now or never. "Look. I was an indecisive mess when we first met, and I didn't think about what I was doing. I thought I'd never see any of you again after you helped me save Kaya."

"Oh." A small smile crept across his face.

"So . . . I'm sorry," she said, for about the thousandth time. "For that too."

"Well, it was fun while it lasted, right?" His grin brightened, and there was a trace of the Ty she knew. Kind and beautiful and lots of things she'd never deserved. "None of us thought you'd be on the crew long-term. At least at first."

"You're not mad?"

"No. Honestly, those days are . . . a bit of a blur now."

Kaya's laughter echoed from the cockpit, and Ty's head snapped toward the door. More of the fatigue lifted off his features. A few things made sense now.

"You have it bad, huh?" Asa said.

"What?"

"You've been making eyes at my sister all night."

For a split second, terror passed over his face, and then it softened. "Well. You've been doing worse than making eyes at mine."

Asa fought the urge to cover her messy hair, but Ty was still smiling. She snorted, and soon they'd both broken into awkward laughter.

It felt like the most natural thing in the world. Like their paths were intertwined, no matter how short-lived. Nothing was certain tonight except the risks they'd chosen to take, and the people they were taking them for.

"You're kind of stuck with us," Asa said.

Ty squinted with his right eye. "Couldn't be in better hands."

The intercom beeped, and Morphett's voice came through. "Hey. You'd all better strap in for landing. The place we're headed seems to have already gone dark."

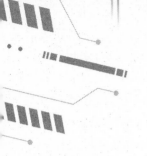

DESCENT

The channel leading toward the Dreamers' Nexus descended into shadow.

Riven's footsteps echoed as the walls slowly rose around them. Rusted scaffolds hung from the buildings on either side, and old trash bags and ratted blankets littered the basin, the remnants of a rough-sleeper camp that'd been cleared out.

They were nearing the western edge of the city and the heart of the mines. Wherever Asa's coordinates led, it felt like they were walking toward the edge of the world.

Riven fidgeted with the grips on her revolvers, keeping pace with Samir's longer strides. He'd encased himself in a soldier's calm, the one that numbed you to all fear.

The fear still hung heavy among them, though nobody seemed to want to acknowledge they might not all get through this. But they'd all chosen to be here for Requiem. For their sweat-slicked, filthy cradle. The only refuge they'd ever had together.

Riven's breaths were ragged. It was harder to face the shadow of death when it wasn't constantly brushing her neck like the muzzle of a gun. Now she had more to lose.

Gunshots mingled with the scream of far-off sirens. A ship passed overhead, sending a beam of light that made their shadows warp and stretch.

"No sign of Dad yet," Kaya said. The light flared in her gold-flecked eyes. "He might already be in there."

Riven's wristlet light caught the shine of metal, and she crept closer. The light slid over a strangely shaped drone with an opalescent sheen. It looked like Etri tech, except plasma-scarred and dead. Next to it, an android like the ones guarding Solus Tower lay motionless.

"Well, there's your sign," Riven said. "Looks like the Nexus has been fighting back. If it's already on alert, it might see us as a threat too." They still had to get in and find Kaya an access point.

Asa nudged the dead android with her foot. "I think something EMPed this mech. Maybe that's what the Nexus does to intruders."

Electromagnetic pulses. That was bad news, when half their team had cybernetics.

"Ty," Riven said. "What would an EMP do to you?"

"I . . . don't actually know," he said.

She turned to Morphett, who'd been prowling behind them. "And you, Tiny?"

"I've taken worse." Morphett had survived the EMP Riven had thrown at her, back before this bizarre alliance had taken hold. She'd probably had the time—and the cash—to get her cybernetics backed up again.

Diego had rolled up his sleeve and was punching something into the keypad on his cybernetic forearm.

"I'm not leaving," Ty said, adjusting the med-kit slung over his shoulder. "Most of our tech probably has hardened back-ups, right?"

Morphett shrugged. "Even backups will be toast if there's enough of a barrage. We'll just have to work fast."

"Ty, if we catch even the *smallest* hint that the Nexus doesn't want us here—" Riven cut herself off when a crash of metal resounded through the alley, like cans knocking over.

Samir held up a hand, his yellow eyes flashing. "Something's here."

Riven turned her light toward an overturned shipping container, its red paint peeling into rust. Ragged bedrolls littered the ground around it. A hairbrush threaded with red hair. The remains of a rough-sleeper camp.

The only living things were a pair of scarni rooting through takeout containers, but two sets of worn sneakers lay next to the beds. Someone had been here recently. Someone who hadn't had time to run.

Ty's voice was hoarse. "Do you think Almeida . . ."

"Is pulling people from their beds who can't fight back?" Riven said. "Yeah, that's what it looks like." Something vicious unfurled in her chest. This could've been her as a kid, when she'd spent the night on the floor of a bus station, trying to get away from home. When she'd stumbled through town the morning after one of her parents' tantrums, wishing she had just enough money for an energy bar after a night of gnawing hunger.

Almeida and his allies saw Requiem as expendable. As fodder. And the whole city would soon be theirs.

Asa's lithe fingers intertwined with Riven's and squeezed gently. She was one of the few people Riven had told about her days on Earth.

"We'll fix this," Asa said softly. "But we need to keep moving."

Riven's fury quietly grew as Asa led them deeper, toward the Nexus. The path grew darker with the descent. Things would only get worse before they finished this.

But she wasn't ready to die yet. Requiem had survived out of spite and sheltered expendables like her crew. If this city had a future, maybe she'd be part of it. And if Almeida and his cronies tried to take any of her friends—trap them and pick them apart like they'd done with Ty and Kaya—she'd burn them all.

The channel dead-ended into a wet, jagged wall like the inside of a cave. Asa skimmed her hands along the rock.

"Here," she breathed, pulling aside a curtain of slimy mosses. Underneath, a tiny lens stared back. "Kay. Hand me your wristlet."

Kaya did, and Asa loaded up the Nexus's passcode. The screen flashed a sequence of colors onto the lens before going dark.

For a few seconds, it was quiet. Then, with a heavy lurch that shook the ground beneath their feet, a crack appeared in the stone. A door.

Asa's eyes widened as she peered into the crevice. "Dust and bones," she whispered. "It's beautiful."

chapter 43
OVERRIDE

A sa held her breath as the door opened and the darkness gave way to stars.

The tunnel glimmered beneath her wristlet light, like the inside of a geode. Faint Etri glyphs were carved across the walls, and as the corridor arced into shadow, facets of crystal reflected ghosts of her crew members. This was certainly the Dreamers' Nexus—an ancient Etri ruin, built like the dreams of a slumbering god.

Requiem's deepest secret, and its defender.

"Hear that?" Riven whispered, her footsteps silent against the bluish sand. "No gunfire. Nothing."

Asa *felt* the silence too. As if something were lying in wait.

"Maybe the Nexus fought off the attack," Ty said uneasily. "Maybe everyone went home?"

A sickening grinding rose from farther down the tunnel, and Ty staggered backward, bumping into Riven. She steadied him as the whirring quieted.

Samir stopped them at the end of the tunnel, holding a finger to his lips. Beyond him, the hall gave way to a cavernous room with a sandy floor and other branching tunnels. It looked like what Riven had described from the trial's initiation—a massive pair of vaulted doors hewn in opaque purple crystal. But now, the doors were open, leading into shadowy nothingness.

"Looks like not all of them made it in," Samir murmured. Behind him, Diego muttered a curse, reaching for the pistol beneath his jacket.

Asa took a step closer. Strewn in the sand were armored corpses, disfigured like dropped puppets. Dark blood pooled beneath their armor. A pair of blank eyes stared from beneath a broken visor.

"Riven," Ty whispered. "Those soldiers are . . ." He trailed off, but Asa recognized the metal implants snaking from their eyes to the backs of their necks.

Winterdark subjects. Soldiers augmented by her father's work. No doubt he'd made them better, deadlier, since the test runs at Sanctum's Edge.

"Shh." Samir held up a hand.

Asa stilled her breaths and heard the padding of footsteps in the sand.

Beyond the mouth of the tunnel, something came into view—a massive feline mech, a fusion of many-clawed metal and living crystal. It stalked among the corpses, spikes of energy undulating beneath the translucent spines at the back of its neck. Asa couldn't look away. It was beautiful, horrifying, something not created by human hands.

The creature stopped near one of the corpses. A tiny drone scudded alongside it, its lenses racking focus as it inspected the body. Asa recognized the drone as the same kind they'd seen dead outside—maybe the thing that'd released the EMP.

The corpse twitched, and the creature immediately latched

on to its throat with scrap-grinder jaws, shaking its head and *tearing* until the neck was only shreds. A loud whirring rang out, like the one that had echoed down the tunnel moments ago. Blood spattered the creature's crystalline spines as it finished off the intruder.

"Those things must be the Nexus's defense system." Samir's voice was barely louder than a breath. "Almeida already pissed this place off."

With a faint whirr, the drone's lens swiveled toward the tunnel entrance, zeroing in on them.

Hands clasped Asa's shoulders as Kaya yanked her back around the tunnel's curve. It wasn't much use, though; they'd been spotted. The padding of steel claws on sand drew closer.

Asa leaned against the jutting crystals and groped for the stunner at her hip. Riven counted off on her fingers, nodding to Samir and Morphett. Ty chewed his lip as he looked over their weapons—something he still wasn't carrying.

Then Asa winced as a high-pitched whine sheared through the air. With it was a rumble that seemed to come from within the center of the moon itself. When it stilled, the mechs went silent.

Riven rounded the corner with her revolvers out. The momentary quiet stretched forever. Then: "It's gone dark."

Asa peered into the cavern. Sure enough, the crystalline beast—nearly as tall as Riven, even on all fours—was motionless. Faint light still glowed within its core. Its companion drone had crashed to the floor.

"Kaya," Diego said, "please tell me that was *you* shutting them down."

"Not me." Kaya gingerly picked up the fallen drone. "But it's not dead. It's . . . rebooting. There's something in the networks here." She closed her eyes, her brow furrowing. "It's turning the Nexus against itself."

"Hell and a *half*," Riven muttered.

Asa tried not to imagine these things tearing through the streets under her father's control. Even if he took his prize at the Nexus's heart, he wouldn't waste the opportunity to use its weapons too.

The clash of gunshots rang through the cavern as Riven plugged bullets into the creature's eye lenses. For good measure, her tech-blade extended to slice its circuits to pieces. When the creature lay on its side in a sparking heap, she pointed toward the vault. "We can't stay here. They'll be at the heart of this thing."

"You want to follow them down the murder hallway?" Ty winced. "What do you think's down there?"

"More mechs, for one," Diego said. "Nothing sheltering the Etri will see us as friendly."

"But that's where Almeida will be." Riven faced the doors, as if to challenge the dark beyond them.

"Riven—" Asa grabbed her hand. "Be careful."

Riven turned toward her, a sorrowful determination behind her eyes. "Trust me this time. Calculated risks only. And I have backup."

Morphett unfolded her one good blade. "I'm not about to let her have all the fun."

"Kaya should stay back here," Samir said. "The second she starts breaking into the Nexus, it could draw Almeida's attention *and* more of these things. And Dee—" He gave Diego a long look. "Where will you be?"

"I'll stay with Kaya too. It's possible I can keep her breach invisible, at least for a few minutes."

"They'll need you here, Samir. It's just Morphett and me, then." Riven slid her hand out of Asa's and pressed a kiss to her forehead. "See you on the other side."

"Wait—" Asa's stomach knotted as Riven headed toward the inner sanctum doors. With Samir staying behind, Riven would be in more danger. But Asa had been turning the Nexus over in her head like a puzzle-box. *It protects itself.* It protected Requiem.

There had to be another way to leverage its power. Something she could use.

"Kaya," Asa said. "I'm going with them. Promise you'll be safe?"

"I think we're both in good hands." Kaya nodded toward Riven and Morphett.

Asa gave her sister one last crushing hug. Then she glanced at Ty, who'd stayed within five feet of Kaya since they'd left the ship. "Don't let her get hurt."

Asa gave a small salute and ran to catch up with Riven. She had nothing but a tiny stunner in her grip and a reckless idea forming in her head, but it would have to be enough.

*   *   *

The darkness swallowed them as soon as they'd crept through the crystal-cut Nexus doors.

Asa could barely see her own feet. The air in the corridor prickled along her skin, like the aftershocks of an EMP blast or the charge before a thunderstorm. Dread rose in her throat like bile, but they'd come too far to stop now.

"I'm still waiting on that bet," Morphett murmured into the dark. "What do you say, Hawthorne?"

"If we get out of here alive, we're *all* going streaking through the Crush," Riven said. "Bet on that."

"*What?*" Asa said.

"Uh . . . long story. Tell you later."

Asa didn't ask. She didn't have time to. A light was growing at the end of the path, and with it came an unnerving silence. *The fight can't be over already.*

Ahead was a massive spherical room, decked out like an armory. Small, translucent pods covered the curving walls, with more feline mechs curled inside. Black stone stairs and scaffolds led up to a network of platforms and bridges connected to slumbering mechs on higher tiers.

"There they are," Riven snarled, her revolvers snapping out.

Asa looked up, and the sight turned her stomach. On one of the higher platforms was a mass of armor plates and data cables, plugged into an exposed control system: Iolus, flanked by a small cadre of Winterdark soldiers.

Her father's forces were here, in the Nexus's heart. A place created to defend a city of slumbering Etri. But instead of fighting off the intrusion, the Nexus was deadly still, as if in quiet acceptance.

No, Asa thought. *Where is she?*

At the far end of the room, Asa saw what she'd been looking

for: an arched door, a panel with a humanoid silhouette flickering behind its surface.

The guardian of the Dreamers' Nexus, a digital consciousness of the first matriarch. Why wasn't she fighting back?

On a lower platform, a feline mech saw them and snapped to attention. Riven immediately shoved Asa behind a tall metallic obelisk. A matrix of blue hexagons materialized across Morphett's body as her shield went online, and Riven's helm went up.

"Hey, ugly," Riven called to Iolus, her voice echoing through the room. "High time for a rematch, huh?"

All four of the soldiers flanking him raised their rifles. Morphett cackled as she rushed the stairs, bullets pinging her shield.

Asa dared to peer out as Riven darted after Morphett. On the surrounding platforms, more of the Nexus's feline mechs shuddered to life. Instead of attacking the soldiers, they chased Riven and Morphett.

Iolus was awakening them. *Turning the Nexus against itself.*

Hundreds of mechs lined these walls. If they all woke up under her father's control, it was over. He'd have his Etri to harvest, and more.

Riven dodged a mech's swiping paws and jammed her techblade into its maw. A hovering drone accosted Morphett on the stairs, shooting a tethered claw with electrical discharge crackling along it. So this was the Nexus's EMP system: precision tethers to attack intruding tech, without a blast radius that could damage the other mechs.

Thankfully, Morphett was faster. Down one blade, but still a whirl of cutting steel running on spite and sucrose.

Soon, though, there'd be too many. The Nexus should be stopping Almeida's forces, not Asa's friends. And that was the key. Asa ran toward the Nexus's innermost door.

"Huifang." She pressed her palm against the door's holographic silhouette. "It's you in there, isn't it?"

Nothing. The figure shimmered beneath the surface. Hiding, useless, while a threat raged above.

"Please *listen!*" Asa said. "You're supposed to be protecting Requiem, but it's in danger. I want to help you."

Gunfire rang above. Sweat dampened the insides of her gloves.

The holo shifted. Then: "*Access code not recognized.*"

It could hear her, at least. Asa stood straighter. "You need to stop this reboot. This was *your* city, and it's being overridden by someone who wants to undo everything you started."

There was a thoughtful pause. Then Huifang's voice came, curt and pointed. "Interaction request refused. I answer only to Requiem's matriarchs."

Matriarchs like Sokolov. The whole reason her father's forces had gotten in here.

All this time, Asa had been too afraid of becoming like him, with his dangerous lies and deadly gambles. But he hadn't taught her to survive here, hadn't taught her to navigate Requiem's Code. Everything she'd fought for—every skill she fought *with*—was hers alone.

"Then how about this." Asa's adrenaline sharpened, replacing her fear. "I received Matriarch Cerys's blessing to enter the Ascension Trial as a second. My crew passed the first task and completed the job we were assigned for the next. And even if Riven Hawthorne was expelled—on unfair grounds, mind you—I wasn't."

"You would qualify as a contender," Huifang said. "But that does not make you a matriarch."

"The third task is underway, yes? To bring the head of one of Requiem's greatest enemies? In that case . . ." Asa let out a shaky breath. "I'm offering you mine."

She braced herself. All she needed was the AI's attention; with the weapon systems compromised, Huifang probably couldn't strike her down. But if that was what it took for Riven and the rest of them to get the help they needed, so be it.

Huifang studied her. "On what grounds do you make such a claim?"

"Because I brought Banshee," Asa said. "I enabled Project Winterdark, and my family created Project Echofall. But I know how to bring it down and I want to help."

"Even after you claim to have doomed us?"

"Consider this my atonement. An offer of alliance." Like she'd done with Redline. "The Duchess's forces might not get here in time. My team is fighting, but we need an edge. If you want to save Requiem, I know how to help you."

Huifang's silence lingered, as if the Nexus was mocking her. Asa suddenly felt exposed, surrounded by empty-eyed mechs, with gunfire ringing above her.

Then Huifang spoke again. "An unconventional offer. But an intriguing one." The translucent panel slid aside, revealing an inner chamber. "Come in, *Asanna.*"

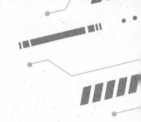

chapter 44
MALFUNCTION

There was a shadow breathing down Ty's neck. Ever since they'd entered this place, it'd been creeping closer.

Ty tried to blink away the throb at the back of his head, a pain in his cybernetic eye that made the shadows stir. He leaned against the tunnel wall, unable to look out at the broken Winterdark soldiers in the blue-gray sand.

He couldn't shake the feeling that the Nexus's spines of crystal hid pairs of eyes. He'd gone through an Etri phase as a kid, poring over every docuseries and article he could get his hands on, dreaming of visiting the ruins in Alpha Centauri. But this place, lurking beneath the most dangerous city in the star-system, felt like a tomb.

Farther down the tunnel, Diego fidgeted with a handgun, and Kaya sat cross-legged and motionless, holding the inert drone like a scrying bowl. The dead mech lay sparking next to her. Ty wondered whether she felt the same scraping at the back of her skull, the undercurrent of *wrongness* in this place, but he didn't dare reach for her thoughts. Especially not while she was fighting for control of the Nexus. So much hinged on her, like usual.

Samir's cussing echoed from the central chamber, followed by the clank of metal on stone. Then, gunshots. Ty peered around the corner.

Samir was brandishing his shield, holding his own against more of the feline mechs. He deflected one of the lunging creatures and rolled off the momentum, firing from the hip as he came back up. With a few well-placed bullets, the first mech crashed—but the second leaped for his throat.

Gunshots fired near Ty's ear. Diego's bullets pinged the mech's crystalline hide. The distraction was enough for Samir to put it down for good.

Then Samir was back on his feet, straightening the plates of his exosuit like he hadn't broken a sweat. "Saving my ass, like usual." He flashed his signature grin at Diego.

Ty should've felt relief, but dizziness washed over him, and he had to catch himself against the wall. Somehow, the mechs had slipped past Riven and Morphett and Asa, but they hadn't called for help.

"Is the signal in here scrambled?" he managed to say.

Diego shook his head. "There was a magnetic field interrupting signals before, but Almeida must've brought it down." He clicked the safety on his pistol and tucked the gun beneath his jacket. "I uploaded our footage for Cerys. She might be pissed I'm still bothering her, but at least she has a chance to act."

If Cerys didn't help, it would all depend on Kaya. Her lips parted as she took a breath, her long eyelashes fluttering. As Ty watched her, a tendril of pain sliced behind his cybernetic eye, like a needle into his brain. He recoiled, clutching the lens.

"You all right, O'Shea?" Diego said.

"Yeah." Ty rubbed his temples. "Residual pain, I think."

But something was off. A strange, dull pain was spreading

from his cybernetic shoulder. He tried to sit, but his legs were going numb.

"Looks like more than *residual*." Diego's voice faded to a tinny echo.

The vision in Ty's good eye blurred, until only darkness and throbbing red-orange veins spiderwebbed across his vision. His cybernetic eye winked into static.

Then he was slipping, fading.

Ty wasn't sure how long he was out. The next thing in his awareness was the aching throb of his cybernetics and bruise-colored afterimages when he opened his right eye.

His cybernetic eye came back online, blurring and focusing. Dim fluorescent lights illuminated steel grates and blank walls. He was lying on the floor of a familiar room.

"No," Ty gasped, cold sweat breaking on his neck.

The simulator room. They'd taken him back.

Almeida's cronies must've been waiting for the right moment to override Ty's cybernetics. And maybe chasing him had led them right to his friends.

Where are they? Ty thought, reaching desperately into the ether. Yllath must have failed to destroy the lab, but if he was still alive . . . *Yllath. What happened while I was out?*

Yllath was quiet. Ty sensed him clawing against digital restraints, trapped somewhere far away. His fate was Ty's fault too. In failing to kill Luca, Ty had doomed his friends, and maybe Requiem itself.

Ty lifted his cybernetic hand. Blood seeped through the joints.

"Easy now," a voice was saying. Familiar, but somehow out of place. "Can you stand?"

Ty let his head loll backward. Standing over him was the guard who'd escorted him to and from the simulator. At the far wall, the Watcher waited behind tinted glass. And there, cross-legged on the floor across from him, sat Luca Almeida. Kaya lay next to her father, unmoving.

"Get away from her." Ty's head pounded. If Almeida had taken Kaya, he'd taken the rest of them too. They'd all be picked apart. "What did you do with them?" He pushed himself to his feet and staggered toward Almeida.

"You should sit back down," the guard said. "Something's wrong." Suspicion edged the voice, a voice that wasn't like Ty remembered.

A throb was shooting through his nerves, a numbing buzz. It was hard to see straight, think straight. If he didn't act now, he might fall unconscious and never have the chance again.

The guard held an arm out to block him. Ty didn't let himself hesitate. His cybernetic arm shot out, latching on to the guard's wrist. He let his fingers constrict, twisting.

The guard cried out as metal—not bone—crumpled beneath Ty's fingers. He ignored the nausea. The next thing he had to do would be worse.

"What's wrong with you?" the guard shouted.

"I should have done this before," Ty murmured, even as something within him said he *couldn't*. He moved toward Almeida, who still sat motionless. Extended his hand—

"*Stop.*" Then, a click. The guard's remaining hand pointed a gun at him. "Don't make me do this, O'Shea," the man whispered in that familiar-but-unfamiliar voice. His chest shook with surprising regret. "You know they'll never forgive me."

Ty stared down the barrel of the gun. *How many times are they going to kill me before I do this right?*

Then he lunged toward Almeida.

A gunshot cracked, barely missing his heels. Almeida jerked to his feet, scrambling backward. The guard said, "Kaya, stop him!" and everything spun and Ty had to do this *now–*

He wrapped his cybernetic fingers around Almeida's neck and heard a soft whimper. He'd remembered Luca being *taller*.

Ty paused. Was there something he'd forgotten? Something wasn't right, but the angry pulse in his cybernetics made it impossible to focus. He shouldn't stop, shouldn't hesitate–

Something collided with the side of his head.

Rough hands grabbed him, and Ty's mech arm unlatched from Almeida's throat. His cybernetic fingers jabbed at his attacker's eyes, acting on their own accord.

The attacker grunted as Ty struggled within their grip. Taut plates of carbon, a suit covered in data ports–the Watcher. But for someone so slender, they felt sturdy as a tree, and held him like a vise. The Watcher wrenched his cybernetic arm backward and shoved him against the wall. Pain erupted at the back of his head.

Some of the spots cleared from his right eye, and against his cheek was rough crystal, not sterile lab walls. And it wasn't the Watcher wrestling him aside but Samir, and where Almeida had been standing–

Kaya. Panting, touching her throat.

Oh, no. His vision was flickering again, and the world around him kept changing–

"*–has control of his cybernetics,*" someone was saying. "*Might be disrupting his other nerves too.*"

And Kaya's voice– "*I'm going to help him*"–and Diego's– "*It's too dangerous.*" And more hands were on his shoulders, jostling him. And–

A strong hand squeezed his neck. His head spun. "*Ty. Kid. I'm sorry.*"

The world went dark.

chapter 45
VERSUS

Riven supposed she should be afraid.

There were a hundred things in this trippy-as-hell bunker that would love to rip her to pieces. But as she climbed the winding stairs, revolvers kicking in both hands, something electric surged through her. A powerful stillness drowned the white-noise pain, and her fear sank beneath an impenetrable, lethal calm. Her nerves came to life, a wicked pulse that made even her double-action firing mechanisms seem slow.

Monsters unfurled around her, roaring constructs of steel bones and crystal, charging across the platforms. Two flights of stairs above, Iolus was plugged into the Nexus, trying to corrupt her city from the inside out. The homeless kids ripped from the streets, the torture Ty had endured—all of it tied back here.

It was time to end this.

Riven's bullets ripped through the oculars of the snapping creatures. When one got too close, she unfolded her blade, cleaving the creature through the skull and sending it tumbling off the platform's edge.

The pulse in her veins was the scariest thing in this room. Every matriarch on Requiem could mark her for dead right now, and she'd turn their syndicates to gunpowder.

Morphett fought on another platform nearby, a storm of flesh and steel, turning the creatures to scraps and crystal shards. One of the drones fired an EMP tether at her wrist. She hissed as it buzzed through her, then swiped her blade to sever the line. No telling how long her cybernetics would hold up.

And no telling how Asa was doing on the ground floor. But knowing her, she had a plan.

Riven swung out her revolvers' cylinders, letting spent shells rain down before she reloaded. She approached Iolus, who stood near a half-circle protruding from the wall. Cables snaked through his armor and under his skin, plugging him into a control panel.

"Hawthorne." He didn't even turn toward her. "Such a waste that a rat survived one of my most promising projects." Something about the inflection was familiar: haughty and articulate.

When she placed it, the rage in her gut boiled hotter. Somehow, Luca Almeida was in control of this Etri.

"That's the thing about gutter rats. We just don't know when to roll over and die." Riven lined up her guns and pelted his armor with bullets, denting the chest seams and shoulders.

Iolus swung a metal-plated fist at her, and she caught it against her blade, leaving a shallow fissure on his armor.

The Nexus lights flickered. Whatever he'd taken here, he wasn't keeping it.

Before he could sink his claws into her eye sockets, Riven lunged behind him, hacking at the cable ports with her blade. He thrashed at her, but she twisted aside and kept stabbing.

With two hissing *pops*, she sawed off the cables in his shoulder blades. The cables flopped to the ground like dead snakes.

Iolus's laugh was hollow. "I don't need those to finish this."

She shifted her grip on the blade, chest burning from exertion. He'd been using those wires for a reason—it had to be like Kaya's tech connection, which was stronger with a physical tether. His takeover should be slower now.

It'd give her time to get through his armor. Break his concentration and destroy him.

Untethered, Iolus charged for her, impossibly fast. But right now, so was she. Riven whirled away from his bullrush and fired at the cable ports on his armor. He let out an inhuman howl as gray-blue blood burbled from the wounds.

She almost felt sorry for the Etri he'd once been. Another test subject, another casualty.

Climbing the stairs behind her were other mechs shuddering to life. When Riven turned to fire, Iolus's massive hand swiped the back of her head. A dull thud reverberated through her as she hit the platform, then pain erupted. Her exosuit's helm stopped her head from being crushed, but hot blood trickled down her temple.

Her right hand was limp on *Verdugo*'s grip, but her left was empty. *Blackjack* had been knocked a few feet away. She staggered to her feet just as Iolus kicked the black revolver off the platform.

"Are you finally ready to stay down?" he said.

Riven laughed as something with claws dragged itself from deep within her. "Your entire life, you've taken and mutilated and *killed* people you think are beneath you." She slid Samir's gun out of the holster on her thigh. "But you're not used to them fighting back, are you?"

Iolus didn't flinch. "Some have tried. They are utterly forgettable. Specks of dust in the course of history."

If she could take him down, it wouldn't matter who forgot her. Matriarchy or no. Legacy or no. The pain still whispered—fainter, but never gone. It was still part of her, and maybe it always would be. But her fate wasn't set in stone anymore, and she had a chance to turn the tide here.

We've followed you because you do shit nobody else would try, Samir had said. *Because you fight like nobody I've ever met.*

Like you could cleave the world in half on spite alone.

She wasn't alone this time. And right now, she had to trust them all to play their roles.

Hers was right in front of her.

"I think it's time for you to square up," she bit out. "Bitch."

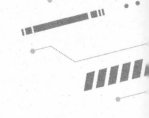

Asa was alone in a pitch-dark chamber with an AI that might decide to kill her.

"Come closer, Miss Almeida." A faint light flicked on, illuminating rough-hewn stairs of violet-colored stone. The edges of the room faded, darkened to nothingness. The heavy *thoom* of Riven's revolvers was muffled.

Slowly, Asa climbed the uneven steps. She'd accepted a life on the edge of a blade. Now she gambled with the fate of her city.

At the top of the stairs, a platform held a pedestal beneath a pool of blue light. A holo flickered to life when Asa reached it: a woman wearing a helm of metal and circuits, her eyes so brilliant they were nothing but light.

"Matriarch Huifang," Asa breathed. Or at least an AI approximation of her, like Asa's father had mentioned. "Is that really you?"

"In a way." Huifang smiled. "Tell me: Do you know how Requiem's freedom was won?"

Asa gnawed her lip. Was this a test? "I know Requiem was a salirium mining colony, but the miners were dying of salirium poisoning, stuck under predatory contracts . . . until they organized and rebelled."

"Correct. And do you know *how* they managed to destroy the Federation armies?"

Asa shifted on her feet. She didn't have time for this. But she couldn't risk pissing Huifang off. "With this place?"

The holo nodded slowly. "When Huifang's troops were run ragged, she sought cover deep within the mines. And here, she found *me*. She was trying to protect her people, as I protect mine."

The AI spoke as if it weren't Huifang at all. "Your people?"

"Yes. After this moon became inhospitable, the Etri created me as a guardian of their slumber. They wait for the others to arrive to make this star-system livable again. Unfortunately, it seems we might have centuries left to wait." Huifang's robes drifted around her, as if underwater. "When Huifang found me, both our peoples were in danger. I agreed to fuse her consciousness with mine so we both might protect this place. And so it has been, for decades. For every matriarch."

That was why the Nexus was a weapon. And as for the matriarchs . . . "They're all accepted by you?"

"They are. Otherwise, they are destroyed."

Asa's breath hitched. She'd never considered what the final test for Requiem's matriarchs might be. As much as the syndicates fought—as much as their subfactions clashed—the matriarchs' common goal was always to protect their city. She wondered how Sokolov must've changed since her first meeting with Huifang.

"In some ways, this city has strayed from my vision." Huifang sounded startlingly human now. "But I suppose that is inevitable. Human desires are chaotic. And in a city that must fight for its life between powerful governments and corporations that wish to devour it, violence is all but a given. Still, I need to know . . ."

Huifang's face drew closer to Asa's, growing impossibly large, until she could see the pixilation at its edges. A ripple of glitches ran over it as the lights guttered out again. The Nexus was still under attack. Her father must have slipped past Huifang's awareness and isolated the weapon systems. Asa hoped Kaya was giving him the fight of his life for control of them.

"What is it you desire here, Asanna Almeida? Why leave Cortellion to pursue power on Requiem?"

"I never set out for power," Asa said, and it was the truth. "I left to save my sister. To stop my father."

"And what do you seek now, if you were once an enemy of ours?"

The question stuck in her throat. "My father wants to make Requiem his test lab, since he'll have no interstellar ethics laws to contend with. He'll use the Etri as a source of genetic material for experimentation. He considers everyone on this moon disposable. He already has an Etri under his control, and once he has the Nexus weapons under his command, he'll try to take the secrets you protect." Asa squared her shoulders. "My goal is to stop him." *And to keep Riven safe. And to stay here, with the truest family I've ever known.* "Nothing more."

Huifang considered this, unflinching. "What would you request of me, then?"

"I want you to let me help you. I can reconnect you to the

weapon systems before he takes full control. My sister is trying to flush the invader out, but she'll need help."

More muffled gunshots rang outside, and the lights
dimmed and flickered. Asa stilled a quiver in one of her knees.

"I had sensed an Etri consciousness earlier," Huifang said.
"It seemed . . . altered, anomalous, and in my curiosity, I did
not immediately engage. Soon after, my sensors went offline.
I believe you are telling the truth."

The pedestal in front of Asa lit up, revealing a flat panel
screen.

"Very well, Asanna. If what you say is genuine, you may
access the Nexus's central command. Succeed, and I may consider this a task fulfilled. I will be watching."

Asa's heart pounded as she tugged off the glove of her
exosuit and pressed her palm to the warm panel.

"I'll do my best," she promised. "Thank you, Huifang."

The dynamic particles of the pedestal shifted, and an interface appeared around her in a curving holopanel. It took
a moment for the Etri glyphs to switch to the English alpha-
bet. Then she saw the expanse of systems, the power at her
command. Mechs and defenses and components she had no
name for.

Asa could turn the tide, if she could figure out how.

She could make some sense of the heat-map and network
modules. The weapon systems that weren't yet corrupted had
been disabled. But the underlying source code was ancient,
unreadable. She needed help from someone with a more intuitive understanding of the network.

She clicked on her comm. "Kaya? Kaya, come in."

Kaya didn't answer. Instead, Diego's voice came through. "Asa. Are you safe? Because I think we have a problem."

"What's going on?" Asa said, but the comm fizzed to static.

Another voice replaced the hissing. "They're having trouble. It's me you need." Kaya's voice, but not Kaya.

You again. Asa tamped down the trickle of fear. "I don't want to ask anything else of you, Sofi." No more bargains to fulfill.

"You did what I asked of you last time," Redline said. "So I'll help you make sure this is the last thing he ever does."

chapter 47
CIRCUITSPACE

Something with teeth chased Ty through the dark.

The world had faded to night on all sides, but a strange twilight followed him. Ty ran, stumbling over roots and vines he could only see once they were under him. Sometimes he heard a sickening clatter underfoot, and the debris at his feet wasn't wood, but bone.

He'd lost consciousness somewhere in the Nexus. The last he remembered was the buzz in his skull, his cybernetics under someone else's command. Illusions conjured by his metal eye. His hands on a throat that hadn't been Luca Almeida's—

His captors were still in control. Using him to hurt his friends.

Ty couldn't close his eyes. Every memory from the simulator was being dredged up at once.

Something slithered behind him, hot breath on his neck. Black scales glinting, reflective pupils watching, waiting for him to fall. A horrifying slickness crawled up his flesh arm as fungal pores opened on his skin. On his other side, his cybernetic arm was gone, leaving a bloody stump behind. He didn't dare feel for his cybernetic eye.

He'd doomed them all by coming back. This was his fault for not stopping Almeida's work when he had the chance.

Ty's foot caught on a root and he fell, landing on his one

hand in the stinging dirt. He should get up. Keep running. The creature in the shadows would destroy him.

But he'd never be free of this. And maybe the others would be better off with him gone.

"Come get me." Ty stared into the dark, breaths shaky. "Get it over with."

A guttural snarl responded, accompanied by a glint of reflective irises.

Ty pushed himself to his feet. "I'm not going to run forever."

The creature drew closer, out of the murky dusk. Jaws opening, strands of spittle dripping from stalactite teeth—

Something crashed into Ty, shoving him out of the way.

A hand clasped his and dragged him forward until the forest floor gave way to stone. He blinked, and gradually the world brightened. He was no longer in the woods, but beneath a rock overhang, a tiny chamber filled with warm light. An old LED lantern hung from the ceiling—like ones from the summer camp he'd gone to with Emmett.

Someone was here with him. A girl, panting, within the pool of light.

Kaya.

"What's going on?" he said. "Where are we?"

"Samir had to knock you unconscious. Someone else has control of your cybernetics—and I think it's your Watcher." She swallowed hard. "They planted a program to control your cybernetics. I'm trying to get rid of it."

So the Watcher was still in control. But the hand on Almeida's throat—*Kaya's* throat—had been his.

"I'm so sorry," Ty said. "None of that was real, was it?"

"You weren't thinking straight. It was your nerves going haywire, and the illusions, and—" Her eyes followed something slithering outside the cave. "They really hurt you, huh?"

He steadied his breaths. This place was in his head. His dreams. "I should've stayed behind. Or—"

"This isn't your fault. They try to break you a thousand different ways." There was a fire in Kaya's eyes as she carefully touched his bloodied shoulder where the arm was missing. Her nearness—even in a dream—made him shiver. She wasn't wearing the exosuit he'd last seen her in, but a hooded sweatshirt and thick-soled boots. This must be how she saw herself.

"They succeeded," he said. "For me, anyway."

"No, they didn't. You're still *you*. You wouldn't knowingly hurt your friends." Her eyes met his. Blood trickled from the corner of her mouth. Whatever she was doing, it was straining her. "My dad was the one who did this to you."

He hardly dared to ask: "How much has he changed me? If Echofall is in my head—"

"It's not Echofall. Your cybernetics were bugged, but your mind is yours. Monsters and all." Kaya's eyes fluttered closed. "I've been in a place like this before too. Mine feels more like drowning."

"How'd you get out?"

"You need to trust there's shelter somewhere. Even if sometimes you need help finding it."

Shelter. Like this place, with her. Inexplicably safe.

Kaya gave a hard breath, then her eyes opened. "That should do it. Your cybernetics are clear. They're yours again."

Tentatively, Ty crossed his arms and felt the cybernetic back in place. His chest shook in unexpected relief.

"The Watcher might still try to break in, if he's not focused on what I'm about to do." Kaya's form blurred. "I have to go."

"Where? Do you need help?" Ty reached for her and sensed pain somewhere in the dark, where her mind called to his.

"The Nexus is still under attack." She smiled sadly. "Hope to see you on the other side."

"Wait—"

Kaya was gone, taking some of the light with her.

Ty opened his eyes. He was hunched over and staring into his lap, back in the crystal tunnel. A pressure held his wrists, and he realized they were zip-tied together.

He looked up. Kaya was still sitting across from him. But her expression was pained, and blood leaked from her ear down her neck.

"Kaya," he whispered. "Can you hear me?" He felt for her mind and hissed at the shock of pain.

She was fading. There had to be something he could do.

"Hang on," he whispered, and reached for her.

⸺⸺⸺⸺⸺

With a burst of fizzing pain, the world shifted, like falling back into a dream.

A speck on the horizon grew until it enveloped him—lines of colors across a dark, infinite expanse. Pulses of light, data spiking and disappearing across networks spiderwebbing around him—like lines on a graph, outlining a world without concrete form.

Circuitspace. The heart of the Nexus itself.

Around him, circuits tilted and linked like neurons. This place teemed with something brilliant but unalive.

"You shouldn't be here, Ty," came Kaya's voice from everywhere and nowhere. "You could lose yourself."

He knew what she meant. This place had a strange, eerie peace that numbed all his anxieties. No cortisol, no adrenaline—none of the chemicals that made people who they were, concoctions of synapses and receptors and molecules and *emotions.* There was only order and logic; something far less than human, and far more.

Even without the rush of chemicals, something steady and concrete urged him on. A fact he knew with absolute certainty: everything depended on Kaya.

Ahead was a towering sprawl of nodes connected to a central hub. Some nodes were faded to ultraviolet, like burned-out bulbs, and something was swallowing them, creeping over the wires like an infection.

That had to be the Nexus. Through Kaya's eyes, he saw her tangled in ultraviolet rot. It flashed through the circuits toward her, threatening to knock her into the black and liminal space between.

At the other side of the central node, amid the center of the rot, two shadows waited.

Is that . . . Iolus? Ty thought to her. *And the Watcher?*

"Sort of," she bit out. "Iolus has already turned parts of the Nexus against itself." She gritted her teeth, and a pulse of greenish light arced through the pathways surrounding her, sparking at the Nexus's center.

Sort of?

"My dad's in control of him. He's altered his own mind with Iolus's brain tissue. Iolus's mind is a vessel. A mess of wires and flesh. No idea what my dad has done to it, but it's given him complete control."

A vessel. If Kaya's own father had Etri cells in his head, she or Ty should be able to mind-speak with him. But Ty had never sensed Almeida the way he could sense Yllath, or Kaya. As if whatever Almeida had done to his and Iolus's minds had closed them off.

Kaya cried out as one of the deep violet shards buried itself in her shoulder. Ty felt it, too, a burning shock somewhere at the back of his mind.

It had come from the Watcher. His presence loomed over circuitspace, trying to fry them both.

If Kaya was destroyed in here, what would happen? Would she ever wake up again? Ty forced away the image of her lifeless eyes. *You need to pull back*, he thought to her. *You're straining yourself.*

"No," she seethed. "I have to do this. I'm the only one who can."

The circuit maze was a puzzle Ty couldn't make sense of. He almost wished Yllath's voice were still guiding him. But he was alone, like he'd been after losing his dad, losing Emmett, losing everyone when he'd been taken by Almeida. In here, not even Riven could protect him.

But Kaya was in danger, and he had to try to help.

Let me help, he thought. *I've got you.*

Kaya gasped as the circuits lit green around her again and flowed toward the corruption. If Ty could take the brunt of the strain, she could focus.

The Watcher must have returned fire, because something sharp sank into her chest with a horrid *sluck*. The flood of pain was shockingly real. Energy or radiation or something else, attempting to burn her nerves.

Ty focused on the pain, tried to suppress it like he'd done when his cybernetics had betrayed him. Siphoned away the sensation so she felt less of it.

"Ty," Kaya whispered.

Keep going, he thought.

And she did. Blasts fizzled against them. Another stab of pain, two.

It's all in your head, he told himself. But it still hurt, and it burned hotter until he was sure he'd shatter into a thousand pieces. There was a clarity beneath it all, a resurgence of what he'd known before he'd hopped off the lift to let Asa and Riven escape.

Whatever I can do for them, I will. Even if he couldn't help Kaya fight, he could protect her.

"Ty," she whispered. "That one is—"

A charge gathered in the air. A massive storm cloud of rot was building at the other side, a void waiting to devour. It was directed straight at them.

Ty clung tighter to her. He tried to close his eyes, but it was impossible in this place. And then it hit, surging through him like boiling water poured over his scalp. He couldn't shrink away. He focused inward, trying to keep it from touching Kaya—

Suddenly, it released. Kaya was forcing him out.

"Get out, Ty," she whispered. "Before you fade."

Everything tunneled, and the world gave way beneath his feet. He was back in the Nexus corridor again, covered in a cold sweat, his hands bound and head pounding. Kaya's arms were wrapped around him now, her forehead pressed against his.

"No," Ty whispered. When he listened for her thoughts, Kaya was faint but fighting. She'd forced him out, even though she was outmatched. She was one test subject against two of her father's most advanced circuit divers. He couldn't do what she did, but . . .

He'd seen the Watcher there, in the maze of circuitspace. If Iolus was connected near the Nexus's heart, the Watcher was hidden away nearby, in a northwest cavern.

He knew what he had to do.

He twisted the zip-ties over his cybernetic fingers, stretching the plastic until it snapped and freed his wrists. Then, carefully, he eased Kaya's arms off him and rested her back against the wall. *I'll be back*, he thought. *Keep fighting.*

He trudged onto the sand of the Nexus cavern, where Samir was patrolling.

"Ty." The muzzle of Samir's gun rose an inch. "That had better be *you* in there."

Ty held up his palms. "Kaya fixed my cybernetics. They're mine again." When Samir relaxed his gun, Ty continued. "Someone's hurting her in circuitspace. And I know where to find him."

"Lots of things are trying to kill her *here* too." Samir looked to Diego, who was holding the pieces of his cybernetic arm that Ty must've crushed. "And it hasn't just been the Nexus."

The guilt came surging back. More reason he had to do this. "Maybe it's better if I go, then."

"You're safer here with me too," Samir said. "And I can't leave them here alone."

"Then I won't ask you to come with me."

Before Samir could protest, Ty headed into the branching corridors of broken crystal. He knew where he'd find the Watcher, but it was impossibly dark between caverns.

The dark dredged up his worst thoughts again. *You could die for real this time.* He was numb to the idea now. He'd never be free of what that lab had done to him. But now was another chance to make things right.

Ahead was a light at the foot of the wall. A still-glowing flashlight lay in the sand, illuminating a tangle of limbs. He quelled the bile in his throat, forcing himself to look.

Two soldiers lay with their throats torn, likely the work of the Nexus guardians. Blood shone on their armor. Holstered at one corpse's hip was a handgun.

A grim thought dawned on him. A gun would be faster, more precise than the crushing grip of his cybernetic arm—like a scalpel excising a cancer. One bullet, and then silence.

Carefully, he slid the gun from the leather. He'd watched Riven and Samir use these a thousand times. Even though Ty had never fired one, Samir had lectured him on gun safety. These things were frighteningly easy to use.

The safety was already off. The HUD screen showed it was

loaded—three bullets left in the mag. No fingerprint authorization would prevent him from firing it.

Ty held it loosely as he resumed running, trying to pretend it was only a toy. The trigger guard was cold against his fingertip.

When he rounded the next passage, his heart crawled into his throat. The room was quiet, dimmed red as twilight. Three more soldier corpses lay strewn on the floor, next to the cracked remains of two Nexus mechs. Remnants of a struggle.

The man they'd been guarding was sheltered inside a half-domed holo-shield. A jack in his neck was plugged into the wall, and he stood motionless in concentration, seeming oblivious his entourage of guards was down.

The Watcher.

The gun was sweaty in Ty's palm as he drew closer. An EMP drone lay sparking, bullet holes in its hull. Above it, one hexagonal panel of the Watcher's shield glitched in and out. The gap was slightly smaller than Ty's head. He couldn't crawl through—but a bullet could.

I have to do this. Before I lose the will.

Ty slid the gun's muzzle through the downed panel, aiming at the Watcher. Whenever the shield flickered to life, it held the gun in place. Steadier than Ty's hands.

"Unplug yourself," he called, his voice hoarse. "Or I'll shoot."

The man didn't react, as if he hadn't even heard. He gripped the control board like a prayer vessel, arms quivering. Ty recognized those tremors—they came from too many dives in the simulator.

Ty's finger slid onto the trigger. He stared down the iron

sights at the Watcher's head. This close, it would be an easy shot—simple, irreversible. The bullet would tear through, brain and bone shards splattering. Like the exit wound through Emmett's ribs—

Kaya needs you, Ty told himself. *Pull the trigger. Save her.*

He could make it fast. Painless. The back of the skull, or the temple.

Then he looked closer. The Watcher was no longer a silhouette behind a plexicarbon panel, and the hood of his exosuit was down. Affixed behind his ear was a metal node like Kaya's. He had scars from the sim-jack on his neck, like Ty's. Deep lines under his eyes.

But most striking was how young he looked. Ty's age—maybe even a few years younger. A boy too young to have endured this voluntarily. Something had weathered him beyond his years.

Ty's chest sank. *You were another victim of Almeida's*, he thought.

Something scratched at the back of his mind. Then an unfamiliar voice answered him. A thought. *"Who are you?"*

The Watcher had heard him.

He'd seen Ty's face before, encountered him in their simulated nightmares. And now Ty understood him a little too. Enough to connect their minds and reach him.

Subject AV70, Ty thought back. *Those simulations—those were your nightmares, weren't they?*

He sensed a spike of anxiety. Confusion.

"Nobody in the simulator is real. Only me," the voice said. There were images behind the thought—endless feedback

loops of terror, of safety in the corner of a dimly lit lab cell. The Watcher had been someone else once, a child given away by desperate parents, but the scientists had hollowed him out. Given him promises of escape, of a contract to fulfill, and roadblocks every time.

The gun was steady in Ty's hands. But what if he could save this boy?

You're not the only one Almeida has done this to, Ty thought. *He's changed you. Forced you to trap us and test us.* He poured images through the connection—deep, terrible truths he couldn't convey through words alone. The dead-end maze of the simulators. The Echofall specimen in Almeida's hands. The expanse of lights stretching beneath the laboratory windows, and the unkillable hope that there was something beyond the lab worth fighting for.

The Watcher opened his milky, colorless eyes. He turned to stare at Ty and the gun aimed at his forehead.

Somewhere in the ether, Ty felt a stab of pain from Kaya.

"You have to stop this," Ty whispered down the barrel of the gun. "I don't want to kill you. But if I have to, I will." With startling clarity, he knew he meant it. Death would come at the press of his finger, if it meant saving the others.

But no matter what the lab had done to him, no matter how much they'd tried to crush and break and change him, he'd always try to find another way.

The Watcher yanked the plug from his neck.

As soon as the connection broke, the shield flickered and disappeared. The Watcher's eyes dimmed with fatigue, and blood trickled from his mouth as he staggered, half-conscious.

"Easy," Ty whispered, dropping the gun and catching him. The boy barely struggled as Ty pulled him into a blood choke. With an elbow over his neck, Ty eased him unconscious and gently set his limp form down. He couldn't say whether the boy would be safe here, but if they succeeded tonight, Almeida wouldn't be able to take him back.

Kaya? Ty thought to the darkness.

"*He's gone*," came Kaya's voice, and her exhaustion and relief flooded into him. "*Whatever you did, it worked.*"

You're the one fighting, Ty responded. *I'm just glad you're okay.*

"*Iolus is still here, but . . . I think I have help now.*" She gasped. "*We still have a fight on our hands though.*"

From deep within the caverns, a loud boom shook the corridor.

I'm coming back, he thought. *Stay safe.*

Ty picked up the gun and ran, leaving the Watcher behind.

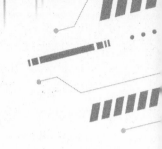

chapter 48
FINALE

Riven's nerves were on fire, a grenade someone had bitten the pin out of. As she wove between Iolus's heavy blows, her footsteps seemed to send shockwaves through the floor.

Supersoldier or no, Iolus had cracks in his armor. Repeated impacts from her bullets and blade had opened small, bloody gashes. Holo-shielding still shimmered beneath some joints—but with enough force, every shield went down eventually.

It might take a hundred more stabs, but this was a long game.

Iolus hurled punches at her. She dodged and slashed as the world blurred by, faster than she'd ever moved, her muscles firing with an energy that surged like a drug.

"I already have a connection," he purred. "You're only burning yourself out."

The lights sputtered overhead, and a *thoom* reverberated from deep within the moon, like hundreds of circuits blowing at once. Kaya might be losing.

Morphett was shouting. Riven stole a glance across the room to see her facing down two tall, slender mechs, six-clawed like Etri gods.

Seemed Iolus had dug up a few more of the Nexus's toys.

Riven gritted her teeth and slid aside as Iolus lunged, trying to pin her again. If she could keep his attention off Kaya, they might still have a chance.

"Riven." Kaya's voice came through the comm, metallic and strained. "I broke through. My dad's connected his consciousness to Iolus's, and I'm keeping him anchored by a thread."

"What do you mean?" Riven managed to say as she jumped and landed, skidding.

"If you kill Iolus while my dad is in there, he might not be able to get out. Ever."

"Shit," Riven said.

"Yeah. I don't know what would happen to his body, but his mind . . ."

Kaya didn't need to say it. Asa had gone through hell for her sister when Kaya's mind had been uploaded, leaving her body a comatose husk. If Kaya's mind had been destroyed while outside her body, she'd have never woken up.

If Riven killed Almeida here, she wouldn't get to watch his smugness turn to fear when she put a bullet in his skull. But her city would be safe. Whether or not she'd ever lead it.

"Are you telling me not to do it?" Riven said.

Kaya took a shaky breath. Then: "No. I'm not."

Riven returned fire, punching another hole in Iolus's armor. Maybe this should be Asa's kill, or Kaya's, or Ty's. But Almeida had been hers since the day he'd killed Emmett.

She landed another hard stab at Iolus's armpit, and he grunted as dark blood sloshed over his armor. Before she could strike again, a barrage of sharp pain dug into her injured shoulder.

Three needles protruded through her exosuit like

spineback quills—no doubt from the slender mechs making their way up the steps. One cricked its neck, unleashing another onslaught of needles.

Even if they'd broken Iolus's connection, he still had mechs under his control.

"Come and get me, you piece of shit," she growled.

Riven steadied her hands and shot like her life depended on it, because it definitely did. But as she fought both the clawed mechs and Iolus, a numbing realization settled over her: she couldn't do this forever.

And the grin spreading within Iolus's helm suggested he knew it.

She made one sloppy swipe, and Iolus took the opening, kicking her feet from under her and pinning her neck with a massive fist.

"Perhaps I should keep you," he said. "You've survived this long. You might be our missing piece."

Choking, Riven stabbed at his neck, but it wasn't enough. No room to move—

"We could lock you up and let Asanna run the tests," he said. "You'd like that, wouldn't you?"

Spots crawled across her vision. *Steady*, she told herself. If she could wriggle enough to leverage herself, she could kick his knee out. *Steady*—

"Neither of us are going with you," said another voice, soft but deadly calm.

"You." Iolus's grip relaxed, and his head snapped toward the platform steps. "I was wondering where you were."

Riven's head lolled toward the steps. Coming up the

staircase was the most beautiful goddamn thing she'd ever seen.

In her sleek exosuit, red and black curves stark against the sparking chaos behind her, was Asa. Her feathery dark hair whipped in a gust from the vents, and a cadre of EMP drones scudded around her.

Nexus weapons, at her command.

"I think we're done here." Asa raised her fist. The drones fired their EMP tethers.

Iolus convulsed, and his grip loosened. Riven kicked and wriggled out from under him, then staggered back to her feet, her vision clearing.

"Riven," Asa said.

"Hey, gorgeous." Riven slid in front of her, angling the blade to defend her.

"Still fighting for the people who've brainwashed you," Iolus—Almeida—said, rising to his full height. "But that you've survived this long . . . it makes me proud."

Proud. What a load of garbage.

He lashed out with a steel-edged claw, but Asa's EMPs had done their work. The layer of holo-shielding beneath his armor was gone.

Riven caught his hand on her blade, tearing the webbing between his fingers. From her other hand, *Verdugo*'s bullets punched through the holes she'd made in the armor. As the Etri stumbled, she made a brutal stab at his chin.

The world slowed to a crawl as the blow landed.

The blade buzzed through his cracked lips and serrated

teeth. Droplets of blue-black blood burst free, splattering across her exosuit.

And though his eyes were hidden beneath the mirrored shield, there was something like shock on his face as the blade jammed straight into his throat.

"Choke," Riven rasped.

Iolus fell to his knees. Blood fountained over his armor. Then he was still, and the Nexus was silent.

Riven doubled over with her hands on her knees.

A final gunshot rang out below, near the room's entrance. Samir was surrounded by a cluster of broken mechs, his exosuit helm down from a dead battery. He kicked one of the sparking heaps, chest heaving, looking every bit the hardened general his parents had wanted him to be.

Morphett was near him, spitting at one of the dead EMP drones, looking absolutely pissed that her remaining cybernetic blade wouldn't retract.

And behind Samir were the others. Diego's cybernetic arm was broken off, but he looked fine otherwise. Kaya limped after him, followed by a squadron of feline mechs at her command. It was a heart-stopping moment before Ty finally entered the room, his med-kit slung over his shoulder.

Her whole crew was alive.

"We did it," Riven whispered.

She pulled her blade out of Iolus's corpse. Fatigue crashed over her, after everything that'd happened tonight—this goddamned Etri bunker, the Ascension Trial from hell, Asa's dad showing up in a proxy Etri body in the worst family reunion in history.

It was all suddenly hilarious.

Delirious laughter burbled out her throat as she clicked off her helm, letting air hit her sweaty face. The sound echoed through the chamber. She fell to her knees, then slumped onto her back, staring into the light overhead.

"Riven," Asa said. "Are you okay?"

"I'm not dead. After all that, I'm *not fucking dead*."

Asa knelt next to her, tugging one of the spines out of her shoulder. "You're hurt."

"I know." She lifted her fingers, twisting them in Asa's hair.

Footsteps tromped up the staircase as the rest of her team arrived. Kaya let out a soft gasp, and her footsteps paused. "Is he—"

"Yeah." Asa wouldn't look back at Iolus's corpse. "I think so."

Seemed she knew her dad wasn't coming back. That made one fewer awkward conversation.

"Hey. Looks like you took a beating." Ty eased himself onto the floor next to Riven and opened his med-kit, producing a tin of numbing salve and getting to work on the spines in her shoulder. "Where else are you hurt?"

"You really want me to answer that question?" She tilted her head toward him. "Everywhere. Ugh, I can't even tell. Let me nap first?"

Ty chuckled. "I could go for that right now." Then he winced at Iolus's corpse on its knees. "Just . . . maybe not next to the dead guy."

"We certainly made a mess of this place." Diego approached behind Asa. "We should move out before the Duchess's forces get here."

Samir smirked. It looked like he'd taken a pair of claws to the thigh. A blood-spotted bandage was already affixed beneath the tears in his exosuit. "You should've seen Dee back there. Lighting up those mechs like a turret."

Diego rolled his eyes but threaded his fingers into Samir's hair and kissed him.

"Gross," Riven moaned, but then Asa leaned in and kissed *her*, so she supposed she had to shut up.

And then Ty was checking Riven's vitals, and Kaya was snapping wristlet photos of the Nexus, and Morphett was bitching about her cybernetics, and even though they were surrounded by a mess of sparking mechs and blood and dead soldiers, everything suddenly seemed . . . normal.

Like a job well done. They could all go home, wherever home was now.

As Riven got to her feet, a familiar voice boomed through the Dreamers' Nexus.

"Well done, Matriarch Almeida," Huifang said. "The head of an enemy, indeed."

Riven nearly choked on her surprise.

"Wait." Samir's eyes flicked from Asa to Kaya. "Matriarch? What did you do?"

Asa gave a little shrug. "I made an appeal."

It was Morphett's turn to break into laughter. "Well, damn. It seems our princess has a pair on her after all."

chapter 49

ANOTHER DAWN

"Have to admit—I'll miss this place." Kaya stuffed a fox plushie into her duffel bag, which was already too full to zip. "Only a few months, and it already felt like home."

"Yeah. The new place will be bigger, but it won't really be the same." Asa carefully slipped a few of Riven's rolled-up posters into a storage box. The other bins held Ty's guitar, Samir's ancient paperbacks, Kaya's art prints and well-loved plushies. The hideout's green carpets were riddled with drywall dust but barer than she'd ever seen them, and it felt *wrong*. They were leaving the place where they'd watched terrible movies while bandaging each other's wounds, where Asa had introduced her crew to AbyssQuest, where they'd made a disastrous attempt to cook Corte desserts after scrounging ingredients with extra job money.

It was so hard to move on.

Asa had woken up here an hour ago, for what might've been a final time. After they'd returned from the Nexus, they boarded up the hideout's wall, and Asa had a twelve-hour sleep in the top bunk, with Riven curled against her back. Riven was gone when she woke up, and the thought of seeing her again made Asa's nerves flutter.

Say the word, and I'm yours.

"Maybe we can convince Xav to let us keep this place as an

extra safe house," Asa said. "I'm sure we'll manage rent money somehow."

Kaya snorted. "If he doesn't kill us for the hole in the wall. But I'm sure *Matriarch Almeida* can pull some strings."

Matriarch Almeida. The name still didn't quite fit.

Huifang had notified the other matriarchs that she'd given Asa her blessing. They were still dealing with Sokolov's betrayal, but the Duchess had summoned Asa to an underground safe house and given her what she'd need to study over the next few months—coordinates of routes branching from Alpha Centauri to Earth, Federation drop points, hideouts and armories on Requiem. Enough resources and personnel to make her head spin. She had a lot of work to do before her position became official, though Morphett was already hounding her for the data she owed.

"I hope you'll still have time for AbyssQuest," Kaya said, "because I have *ideas*. What do you think—a biomech crystal cavern zone, like the Dreamers' Nexus? I've already done two concept sketches."

"Sounds great. I haven't thought that far ahead though." Asa smiled, but a strange sadness stuck to her throat. It felt like she'd jumped off a foggy cliff and couldn't see what lay below. "This all feels surreal."

She checked the closet and found her old stack of laminated comic books, the ones Kaya had bought her for her seventeenth birthday. "Remember these?"

"Glad you saved them. Dad probably would've shredded them if you left them back—" Kaya caught herself, probably reconsidering the word *home*. "On Cortellion."

Stars only knew what had happened to the rest of Asa's fan posters and gaming gear in her old bedroom. The thought of the estate emptied—sold off, taken over by someone else—was strangely upsetting. "Do you think he's really gone?"

Kaya pursed her lips. "I don't know. You and Riven might've taken him down before he pulled out of that body."

Asa swallowed the tightness in her throat. She shouldn't be sad, after everything he'd put them through. After what he'd tried to do to Kaya and her friends. Luca Almeida might still be alive, or comatose, or a hundred other things. He might've chosen a successor. But it didn't matter now.

"We'll have to ask Diego to keep an eye on things," she said. "Though I'd be lying if I said I felt ready for any of this."

"Maybe this city needs you right now," Kaya said. "To undo some of the damage."

"I think I owe them that much. And at least I'm not handling this alone." She had work to do, for sure. Logistics. Patrols and whisper networks. Her first priority would be rooting out Echofall and shutting down any extant test labs on Requiem.

She'd have to talk it through with Riven. And there was another request Asa needed to make of her. The thought sent the pit of her stomach fizzing again.

At a knock on the doorframe, Asa looked up.

"Hey." Ty leaned against it, hands in the pockets of his frayed jeans. "Seems you finally cleaned up my room."

"You weren't using it." Kaya gave an impish grin, her cheeks reddening. "Someone had to keep it warm."

Ty gave Kaya a look Asa recognized. Secret mischief,

nervous hope. "Samir has the new ship parked on the roof. Might want to head up before your new bodyguards get testy."

"Gotcha," Kaya said. "Our *Boomslang* v2, with the godawful camo paint job?"

"That's the one."

"Guess we'd better go." Kaya turned to Asa. "Is there anything else you wanted to do here?"

"No. I think we need to leave before I rethink everything." Leaving this place felt like an ending, even if it was the beginning of something else.

Ty grunted as he lifted a stack of boxes, shifting most of the weight onto his mech arm.

Kaya waited for him to head out, then slung her duffel bag over her shoulder. A rare nervous energy radiated off her. "So, Asa."

"So, Kaya."

"What would you think if, you know. Would it be weird—I mean, I know you and Ty weren't technically . . ."

So it went both ways.

Asa had given her the details once during a night out, when Kaya had bought her a quad mango sour. She'd spilled that Ty looked like their elf rogue concept art, and a hundred other embarrassing things.

Not that it mattered now. After a few intense, adrenaline-fueled kisses, Asa and Ty had been short-lived.

"Are you asking if it would be weird if you and Ty were together?" she said.

Kaya's cheeks turned burgundy. "Yeah. It would be . . .

complicated. We haven't even talked about it yet. But, you know, in case anything were to happen . . ."

"I think it'd be hard for him *not* to fall for you. And you two will need each other."

"Thanks." Kaya threw her arms around Asa. "Hey. Whatever happens—whoever you become—I hope I can always talk to you like this."

"This isn't changing," Asa murmured against Kaya's shoulder. "I promise."

They headed to the hall elevator and up to the roof. A breeze from their new ship's thrusters gusted across the rooftop, and some of Rio Oscuro's security detail waited for her near the docking ramp. The ship's green camo paint job glinted in the sunrise—pointless, since it didn't blend with the sky, and it already had a powerful stealth drive. Still, Asa couldn't wait to modify its engines, and she was sure Riven was excited to be in the cockpit. It'd make a good second home in the skies.

"You two ready?" Samir called from the cockpit, as they carried their boxes up the cargo ramp. "I think you'll like the new place."

Asa strapped into one of the cabin seats, a thrill building in her chest.

It was time to see what the future held.

The city shrank beneath Asa's feet.

Glass panels sped by as the elevator climbed higher, pulling them above the mess of crystals and crooked streets and city lights fading against the rising sun. The Rio Oscuro matriarch's personal safe house was perched above Olympus nightclub. It was weird to come back here after the Banshee mess.

"This place had better have a gaming deck," Kaya said when the elevator shuddered to a stop.

"It's got more than that," Samir said. "What do you say, Matriarch Almeida? Going to let your personal advisors camp out here?"

"Wouldn't have it any other way." Asa's stomach fluttered as the doors slid open.

A squadron of guards wearing the syndicate's turquoise-and-black body armor greeted them. Lights flickered on as they entered, illuminating a walkway lined with biolumines-cent cacti. The safe house was eerily empty, a void waiting to be filled. It'd been furnished by a dead woman whose mistakes had turned her allies against her. Asa would have to be cleverer.

Her crew explored the place together, dropping off boxes and claiming rooms, and then Samir stopped by the loft staircase.

"Riven's probably up there," he said. "She got here early. Said she'd wait for you."

So this was where Riven had snuck off to.

Ty handed Asa a packet of medi-fiber bandages. "Tell her to use these. She probably needs them by now."

"You're not coming up?" she said.

"Um." Ty wrinkled his nose. "Those are your . . . personal quarters."

Samir turned, giving a small wave over his shoulder. "I'm going to catch up with Dee. Meet us on the second-floor bar in a few hours?"

"Uh, sure."

Kaya left with them, leaving Asa alone.

As she ascended the translucent steps, the weight of responsibility settled over her. This was everything Riven had wanted, handed to her instead.

She swiped her key in one of the loft doors, and it slid open to a chamber flooded with sunrise. Black lounge couches lined a tinted window-wall revealing the stretching skyline. At the room's center was a hot tub with deep violet lights under its churning surface.

And someone was in it, watching the rising dawn. Silver-blonde hair fell onto muscular shoulders.

Oh. *Oh.*

Riven didn't seem to be wearing a swimsuit. Asa's cheeks felt like they would catch fire. No wonder the crew had left them alone.

Her mind tumbled through all the things she needed to say and ask. Where they stood, and where they'd go next.

Riven turned toward her then. She swam to the edge of the tub and rested her forearms on the black tile. "Hey. How'd you sleep?"

"Fine. You left early."

"Wanted to get a look at the new ship. And to soak the wounds I took for you." Riven closed one eye, giving her that heart-shattering smirk. "Worth it."

Asa kicked off her boots and rolled up her pants, then lowered herself onto the tub's edge, letting the warm water slide up to her calves. The fizz tickled her knees. It took everything not to stare below Riven's neck, so she focused instead on the blood-soaked medi-fibers on Riven's shoulder.

"Here. Ty said you might need these." She held out the fresh bandages.

"You came up here just to check on me? I'm touched."

"Maybe I *like* taking care of you."

"Well, in that case . . ." Riven stretched her arms behind her head, and water sluiced over her breasts. "You'll have to get in here."

Asa was losing the ability to think. "I don't have a suit."

"Neither do I."

Something electric shot up her spine. After the terror and heartbreaks of the past few days, the solace here seemed unreal. Riven's eyes met hers, reflecting light on the surface of the water and studying her with a quiet intensity. Like Asa was the sole star in a universe gone dark.

The rest of Asa's hesitation melted away.

Carefully, she peeled off her favorite jacket. There was no point in getting the rest of her clothes wet, either, so she shucked them off.

Riven waited, chewing her bottom lip. She didn't stare, but kept sneaking glances, as if unsure whether she was allowed. She'd seen Asa without a shirt, but never without the rest.

Asa lowered herself into the glowing tub, letting the warmth slide up to her chest. The roiling water made her feel weightless. She could float here in a space free of danger, at least until the next obligation came crashing down.

"This was all supposed to be yours," she said. "I don't know if I'm ready for it."

"It was never *supposed* to be mine. Hell, no matter what I might've gotten, I'd never have stopped clawing my way up. But after the past few days . . . I'm not in a rush to leave my mark." Riven drew closer, so close Asa could hardly breathe, and traced a wet finger along Asa's jawline. "You've got all of us, you know. Me, Samir, Ty, Dee, your technomancer sister—even Morphett, maybe. And we're going to make sure nobody lays a finger on you." Riven grinned. "Sounds like Tak's swearing allegiance to Rio Oscuro too."

Asa nodded, even as her vision was tunneling on Riven. She'd heard Callista was in consideration to take over Staccato. But Rio Oscuro would have some incredible people in its ranks. "What I wanted to say is . . . I don't think I can do this alone. I need you as more than just a bodyguard. Are co-matriarchs a thing?"

Riven's eyes widened. "With you? Like, making decisions?"

"Yeah. We never would've gotten through that without you."

"If that's really what you want." Riven's gray-green eyes were stormy. "Whatever you want to call me. Co-matriarch. Lieutenant. Partner. Girlfriend. Like I said—yours."

Asa shivered despite the warm water. "I want you somewhere at my side. In whatever role you'll accept."

Riven stood up, her wet hair plastering her collarbones. "I could get used to the idea of running a syndicate with you." She set her hands on Asa's waist. "But for the record, I think Huifang was right to choose you."

Asa tilted her head back, and Riven's lips met hers. The universe melted away until it was only her, Riven, and the steam rising between them.

"Riven." Asa broke the kiss to say it. Something she'd wanted to say for so long, *too* long. "Whatever we are. Whatever this is . . . I love you. Always will."

Riven drew her closer, encouraging her with soft gasps and hard kisses. She pulled Asa into her lap on the underwater ledge, and Asa's hands wandered over every inch of her firm, freckled skin. Riven's touch slid over Asa's waist and lower, an invitation Asa readily accepted. Then Riven was touching her under the water, and Asa was whispering Riven's name into the steam, and they were pressed so close she could feel Riven's heartbeat.

Soon she guided Riven's hips onto the edge of the tub, and Riven leaned backward, her silver-and-purple hair leaving wet trails on the starfield-black tile. A blush rose across her cheekbones and her soft lips parted as she watched Asa kiss a path up her thigh. It was a side of Riven nobody else saw, something Asa would hide away and protect.

They ended up intertwined on one of the couches, and Asa's breaths came harder as the world faded to Riven's touch, Riven's limbs tangled with hers. She traced promises on Riven's skin, unspoken reminders that they had a home in each other, no matter where home was. Steam rose over the neon in the distance, and amid the distant cries of the city, it was only the two of them.

It seemed like an eternity later that Asa found herself lying against Riven's chest, wrapped in a damp towel.

Riven idly ran her fingers through Asa's semi-soaked hair. "I can't believe we didn't even know each other earlier this year. What the hell."

"Yeah. Four months, and we're already *here*." From a run-away and her kidnapper to a pair of matriarchs-apparent.

Riven gave a dramatic sigh. "Guess we have to think about the future now. There're still so many crews in this city risking their lives for their next meals or selling themselves to some corporate lab."

Asa had always thought life on Requiem was freer than on Cortellion, but freedom was harder for people bound to desperation. She and Riven had both been trapped growing up—Riven in a group home with parents who saw her as a tax break and not a child, and Asa with a collection of maids, tutors, surveillance drones, and a father who'd raised her for his own aspirations.

Requiem was an escape for them, but like the rest of the star-system, it was broken.

"We'll just have to fix this place," Asa said. "I need to clean up Echofall and make sure my dad's allies know better than to touch this place."

"Spoken like a goddamn matriarch." Riven's fingertips ghosted over the back of Asa's neck. "And if we make it that far? What next?"

"That'll be up to us. Half the fun will be figuring it out." Asa brought her lips crashing against Riven's again, and Riven grabbed her like she'd never let go.

Loving her would never be safe, or convenient, or uncomplicated. Asa could only trust it would be worthwhile.

Asa's wristlet pinged from the pile of discarded clothes. It was probably Samir or Kaya, asking where they were.

"Oh," she said against Riven's mouth. "Forgot the crew's

waiting for us down at the bar. They've been there a while, and–"

Riven sat up, pulling Asa onto her lap. "We can be late."

chapter 50

BOOMSLANG

When Ty opened the door to the roof landing pad, Kaya was silhouetted against the sunrise.

His heart slid into his throat. For some reason, being alone with her—after everything that had happened—was almost as scary as facing Iolus.

The wind carried the acrid scent of spray paint. Kaya crouched near the camo-painted ship, spraying a set of hull scraps.

Zephyr noticed Ty before Kaya did. The pup took a break from yapping at passing air traffic to greet him, tail wagging frantically.

"Zeph?" Kaya whirled around, lifting the safety glasses off her face. Stray splashes of paint stained the tarmac around her. "Oh. Hey, Ty."

"Already defacing a matriarch's property, huh? Bold move."

Kaya shook the black paint can, rattling the pea inside. "I have it on good authority that the new matriarch would let me get away with murder." She grinned up at him, and something swelled inside his chest. "Thought you'd be down at the bar."

"I needed some air. My last night here didn't end so well."

The last time he'd been at this club, he'd been drugged unconscious in the bathroom, and a service android with orange eyes had dragged him away as a hostage. Yllath had been a true enemy then, and not a reluctant ally.

But last night, he'd heard Yllath's voice again—hopefully for a final time.

"*I haven't forgotten how you fled. Left me here to rot,*" Yllath's voice had boomed at the back of Ty's mind, startling him off the hideout couch. "*They had other fail-safes waiting for me. Bespoke digital restraints.*"

Are you trapped? Ty had asked. *Is Almeida still there?*

Silence had stretched then. As if it had exhausted Yllath simply to speak. Then: "*I have not sensed him anywhere nearby. But if what we have discovered these past few days is true—if there really are others slumbering beneath Requiem—keep them safe. You owe me, after all.*"

Then Yllath had gone silent, no matter how Ty tried to reach him with questions. Maybe it was for the best if he never heard from Yllath again. He didn't miss being at that creature's mercy.

But if Yllath ever demanded too much, Kaya was more than a match for him. He could only hope the same would be true for Redline, if she set her sights on them again. Aside from a cryptic message on their way back from the Nexus, they hadn't heard from her.

He realized Kaya was still watching him with a sympathetic frown, as if waiting for him to say more.

"I also wanted to check on you." Ty slid fidgety hands into his pockets. "You had me worried back there."

"Me? *You* were the one running after the Watcher. And I think you took the brunt of that in circuitspace." In the early sun, Kaya's eyes were the deep gold of hardened amber. "I thought you'd be unconscious afterward, or worse. But you just . . . got back up, worrying over everyone else."

It still felt like his brain had been sucked out through a straw. But he didn't regret it. "It was all I could do."

"I don't think it would've worked otherwise." Kaya crossed her arms, and it was hard to look away from the paint smears on her bare shoulders. "I'd probably be lost somewhere in circuitspace. And everyone else might not have made it out. So . . . thanks."

"Kaya . . ." He should tell her how much he'd needed her, how much he *still* needed her, but he couldn't say it. Even if Asa had given him permission, he couldn't stand to ruin whatever trust Kaya had put in him. So instead he stood there, slack-jawed. Maybe someday, he'd be braver.

"Um." He cleared his throat. "What are you working on?"

"Oh." Kaya looked a bit disappointed, then collected herself. "Paint job samples, for the new ship. What do you think?" Three hunks of scrap metal lay in front of her, sprayed in three different patterns of bright green, magenta, and black. Like *Boomslang*'s old colors, but with splashes of purple.

"They all look great, honestly. You've got a knack for this."

Kaya tucked her hair behind her ear, near her mind-link node. Metal beneath her skin, so much like his own. She'd pulled him from some dark places recently, because she understood.

And it slipped.

For just a moment, Ty imagined brushing his lips against that spot on her neck where flesh met metal. Immediately

Kaya froze, as if she'd *felt* the thought. Her eyes bored into his, alight with surprise.

Oh no.

He swiveled toward the door as his cheeks caught fire. "I'll, uh, let you get back to work–"

"I don't think so." Kaya grabbed his shoulder, turning him to face her. "You're very distracting, but it's a welcome distraction." She dragged her thumb across his cheek, and he shuddered. "Too pretty for your own good, Ty O'Shea."

Then she pulled her fingers away, frowning, smearing wet green paint between them. "Shit."

Ty reached up to wipe the paint off his face, but Kaya grabbed his wrist, giggling. And then he was laughing with her, and she was closing the space between them, her lips pressing against his. And she was kissing him and he was kissing her back, and it all felt *right.*

Ty's control ebbed and flowed, spilling his thoughts into Kaya's as he kissed her deeper. The apprehension, the confusion, the strange pull of desire. He remembered what the psychiatrist had said–that subjects sharing brain matter could go mad hearing each other.

But there was no going back. No matter how messy things got.

The wind whipped Kaya's hair against his cheek, and she let her hands roam, leaving paint smudges on his arms, the back of his neck. The world was brighter through her eyes.

"Well, if that isn't just utterly predictable," a voice called over the rooftop.

Kaya broke the kiss. "Shove *off*, Samir."

"Nah. I'm happy for you. Really. But we need to break this up for some important business."

Ty reluctantly looked away from Kaya. The whole crew was slipping through the roof doors. One sleeve of Diego's jacket hung flat below the elbow, where he'd removed the cybernetics Ty had crushed, but he held Samir's hand in his left. Riven guided Asa through the door, a hand on the small of her back. Asa wrung water out of the ends of her dark hair, and Ty couldn't help but notice Riven's shirt was on backward, with the tag sticking out the front.

Behind them was Morphett, slurping noisily on a slushie cup, looking bored. "Hmph. Important business, and your info-guy shows up plastered."

"Not *plastered*. Reasonably inebriated." Diego's perfect articulation was off, and his smile came easier than usual. Ty hadn't thought it possible for Diego to get drunk. "Though I think I've earned the opportunity to be *your* problem for once. At least before I take some time away from this place."

"Don't tell me you're skipping town too," Riven said.

"Only for a few weeks," Samir said. "Our transit leaves Brightday-II. But yeah. Figured it was high time I introduce Dee to the family and tell them about the new arrangement that'll keep me busy for the foreseeable future." He squeezed Diego's hand.

"Have fun breaking that news to them," Diego said. "Running off to play operative for a queen among delinquents. They'll be thrilled."

"They don't need to know the details."

"So," Riven said. "You're sticking around after all?"

"For now." Samir grinned. "Looks like we're all here. Time to call our first meeting as Rio Oscuro."

"Rio Oscuro or no, we're still the Boomslang Faction. And this"—Riven approached the new ship like a skittish horse and set a hand on its nose—"is our new *Boomslang*. A Starslinger R5. They only made, what, fifty of these things? I don't even *want* to know how Rio Oscuro got their hands on one."

It was bigger than the Marauder model the old *Boomslang* had been. The ship Emmett had poured his heart into for Riven, for all of them, was gone. But maybe it was time to move on.

Samir cleared his throat. "A proper coronation, for our new matriarch. Something more exciting than the Duchess handing Asa a bunch of keycodes and launching her into the world, with the other syndicates' spies watching her every move." He tilted his head back. "That's right, you slick bastards. We know you're watching."

Unlike Diego, Samir was dead sober, but he was downright sunny today. Ty had missed this. It felt like a shadow was lifting off all of them.

Kaya scooped Zephyr up. "I hope they like spontaneous dog butt, when I find their cameras."

Morphett shoved a cigarette between her lips and tapped it with her smoldering cybernetic finger. "Look, this little party is cute, but I'm here for my data."

"Not looking to join? After all we've been through?" Kaya said. "Not even for the gaming tournaments?"

For a moment, Morphett looked grudgingly interested. Then she rolled her eyes. "Not a chance. But I'd consider being an associate, if you play your cards right."

"I'll get you the data as soon as I get the networks sorted," Asa said. "And still, we probably owe you a lot more."

"I might have to hold you to that." Morphett exhaled a cloud of foul smoke, which the wind snatched away.

"Want to make an acceptance speech, Matriarch Almeida?" Samir said.

"I, um." Asa blushed. "I might be appointing a co-matriarch, actually."

Riven gave her a secret smile, the one she'd given Emmett once. It was good to see her happy again.

"I know I can count on you all," Asa said. "As my advisors, and as my friends. We need to clean up my dad's influence and fix the damage he caused. It won't be easy or safe, but we'll get through this like we always do. And afterward . . . well, we've got a ship, and we've got a crew, and we've got two star-systems' worth of trouble to get into."

Samir handed Asa an expensive-looking green bottle. "Crack it over the hull. Make it official."

Riven gasped. "Wait—"

Glass shattered, and frothy champagne bubbled across the camo paint.

Samir cheered while Riven swore about denting the ship, until Asa silenced her with kisses, and they all ended up lounging in the new ship's cabin as the sun rose. People Ty would never stop fighting for, in a city they'd never stop trying to make right.

Kaya's shoulder brushed his as the streets woke up around them. A dawn he'd dreamed of for months. It was even better than he'd imagined.

ACKNOWLEDGMENTS

First off, I'm so, *so* grateful to the readers and fans who made this sequel happen. To everyone who posted about the first book, told a friend, left a review, or stayed up too late reading it. To everyone who's done fan art, aesthetic videos, cosplay, or even DMed me to tell me how much this story meant to you—it meant the world to me. There are too many of you to list here, but I've noticed and appreciated each and every one of you. You're the reason this book exists, and I hope you love it almost as much as I do.

Major thanks go to Drew (again). Thanks for carrying me through the lows, hyping my books to everyone within range, and masquerading as a normal human with me.

To my family. My parents, who tolerated my angsty creative tendencies growing up. To Rad, Kris, Carl, Chase, Aderan, and relatives who bought my book simply to support the weird kid in the family.

To my amazing agent Cortney Radocaj, for believing in my work from the slush pile. My editor Meg Gaertner, for picking up the reins on this series with so much enthusiasm and insight (and for your wicked attention to detail!). To Mari Kesselring and Kelsy Thompson for their tireless work in bringing these characters and their world to readers.

To the Bastards, my LARP guild. Thanks for all the 2AM hot-dog-roasting, pumpkin-smashing, pit-fighting, haunted-mansion-flipping shenanigans. You remind me how much the found-family hijinks are more exciting than the actual plot, even when the world is burning down. To my friends and hype squad—Kristina, Hannah,

Kristi, Dana, both Katies, Chelsea, and Kenny. For Dana, my Official Canine Consultant for matters concerning Zephyr. To faithful beta readers Krista, Kelsey, Michael, and Stacy.

To my critique partners and author friends: Ren Hutchings, Kate Murray, Nicole Brake, Kate Dylan, Meg Long, Rebecca Coffindaffer, Christine Daigle, Bill Adams, Travis Hightower, Briston Brooks, Keala Kendall, SJ Whitby, Stone Sanchez, Rohan Zhou-Lee, Jared Nelson, and Sasha McBrayer. It's incredible to see your stories making their way into the world, and to be on this journey alongside you. To Alechia Dow, Maria Ingrande Mora, Sheena Boekweg, Laura Rueckert, Rachel Menard, Andrea Tang, MJ Kuhn, and Lora Beth Johnson, for being there to answer questions, commiserate, and encourage. And to more authors who've provided support along the way: Susan Dennard, Marissa Meyer, Meg LaTorre, Jonathan Maberry, Emily Skrutskie, the 21ders, and many others.

To incredible booksellers who helped the first book connect with readers: Kel Russell, Mike Lasagna, Belle Ellrich, Alice Scott, Kayleigh Carpenter, the whole B&N Brighton team (including Tina, Taylor, and Sam!), Amanda Strong (and the Schuler Books team), and everyone else who hyped the book or welcomed me in to sign copies. We authors owe you so much! To Min Trindade and Melissa Shank (Bookasaur), for their immense support along the way. To Dri Gomez, Sanjay Charlton, and Ellie Lin (Kynerie) for bringing my characters to life through your amazing artwork, and to Sarah Beth Pfeifer for giving a voice to my characters (I will never get over Morphett's perfect cartoon snark). To the rest of the Flux team, including Taylor Kohn, Heather McDonough, Jake Slavik, Ben Coward, Karli Kruse, Emily Temple, and Sam Temple.

To everyone on this list, anyone I've left out, and those I have yet to meet: you all make this journey worth it.

ABOUT THE AUTHOR

Claire Winn spends her time immersed in other worlds—through LARP, video games, books, nerd conventions, and her own stories. Since graduating from Northwestern University, she's worked as a legal and technical writer. Aside from writing, she builds cosplay props and armor and battles with boffer swords.